Advance praise for Anna Bliss

"*Bonfire Night* is a remarkably impressive debut and a most tender work of art, providing a heartrending look at a couple in love while the world implodes and explodes around them. With the eye of a painter, Bliss uses the finest of brushes to vividly and crisply depict her characters while displaying an astonishing breadth of compassion for the situations in which they must struggle and persevere. *Bonfire Night* is a treasure of a novel, beautifully written with the unflinching style and subtle psychological insights of such masters as Ian McEwan and Graham Swift."
—Natalie Jenner, author of *Bloomsbury Girls*

"If you are a fan of Kate Quinn or Kristin Harmel, pull up a chair and settle down with Anna Bliss's propulsive debut *Bonfire Night*. Wonderfully written and exquisitely researched, the work is a rare look into the rise of fascism in London preceding World War II, while exploring the costs of both love, female ambition and the lengths we will go to in order to make our mark on the world."
—Jo Piazza, international bestselling author
of *We Are Not Like Them*

"This beautifully written, timely historical novel encompasses so much—difficult family ties, female ambition, and the sacrifices we make for love. With her meticulous research and heartrending descriptions of life in Brighton during the war, Anna Bliss had me turning the pages into the night."
—Janet Skeslien Charles, *New York Times* bestselling
author of *The Paris Library*

"*Bonfire Night* is a beautifully crafted book about love, war, hope, fear, betrayal, and forgiveness; about missed chances and impossible choices. And although this is Anna Bliss's first novel it's the work of a wise and warmhearted storyteller, someone who understands what's at stake when decent people find themselves caught in the surging currents of history."
—Stephen Harrigan, author of *The Gates of the Alamo*

Please turn the page for more advance praise!

The praise continues for Anna Bliss and *Bonfire Night*!

"Magnificently written, Anna Bliss's *Bonfire Night* is a captivating story of love and war. It's a beautifully crafted novel with a fresh view on the rise of fascism in World War II."
—Alan Hlad, international bestselling author
of *Churchill's Secret Messenger*

"*Bonfire Night* is the whole package: an immersive World War II read with a sweetly fraught love story and strong, unforgettable characters. I was mesmerized by it and read long into the night, unable to put it down."
—Martha Conway, author of *The Physician's Daughter*

"*Bonfire Night* is a powerful, poignant debut written with the skill of a master. Ms. Bliss's perfectly flawed characters and exceptional research led me on a rich, multilayered journey of love, betrayal, heartbreak, and most compelling of all, a burning search for freedom within the raging fires of war."
—Genevieve Graham, *USA Today* bestselling
author of *Letters Across the Sea*

BONFIRE NIGHT

ANNA BLISS

JOHN SCOGNAMIGLIO BOOKS
Kensington Publishing Corp.
www.kensingtonbooks.com

JOHN SCOGNAMIGLIO BOOKS are published by

Kensington Publishing Corp.
119 West 40th Street
New York, NY 10018

All Kensington titles, imprints, and distributed lines are available at special quantity discounts for bulk purchases for sales promotion, premiums, fund-raising, and educational or institutional use.

Special book excerpts or customized printings can also be created to fit specific needs. For details, write or phone the office of the Kensington Sales Manager: Kensington Publishing Corp., 119 West 40th Street, New York, NY 10018. Attn. Sales Department. Phone: 1-800-221-2647.

ISBN: 978-1-4967-4734-1

ISBN: 978-1-4967-4735-8 (ebook)

First Kensington Trade Paperback Edition: January 2024

10 9 8 7 6 5 4 3 2 1

Printed in the United States of America

For my husband, Michael

Part I

London

Chapter 1

Ambition bowed Kate Grifferty's head as she reviewed the shots she'd taken that morning: a fishwife and her daughter scrubbing barnacles off oysters in the basement of Billingsgate Market, a florist rejoicing over a crate of black tulips in Columbia Road, the queue outside the milk bar in Fleet Street. As her eye ranged from image to image, she used a white grease pencil to plan cuts on the contact prints. It was Sunday and the office was quiet except for a few stringers popping in and out, so she was startled to see her boss come through the door.

"I don't like the idea of you going down to the East End today," Mr. Scargill said, jiggling keys in the pocket of his cornflower-blue suit and leaning over her desk. In '28, he had taken an iconic photograph of Amelia Earhart standing on top of the Hyde Park Hotel, with London at her feet. Even before Kate met him, she had a postcard of the picture pinned to her bedroom wall.

"A riot is no place for a lady," he went on, puffing out his doughy cheeks, reminding Kate of a middle-aged cherub. "Oswald Mosley has some fruity ideas and I don't blame the Jews for resenting him. But they're getting a mob together. You won't want to be in the middle of that."

Kate nodded thoughtfully, as if weighing his concern. Inside, she prickled with impatience. She had no interest in being a lady. She'd already had her share of being jostled and pushed on the job, and felt quite powerful physically.

"You're kind to worry," she said. "But I was born and raised in the East End. I know those streets. I can look after myself."

"I wouldn't be so sure. Hackney is a far cry from Whitechapel." Mr. Scargill ran his hand down his tie and eyed her bare arms. "It's a cesspit of vice. And you're just a skinny little thing."

Kate slid on the angora cardigan she kept on the back of her swivel chair.

"I'm taller than my father," she said, straightening. "He was a boxer when he first came over from Ireland. Accidentally killed a man once, as the story goes. Still has great big hands like oven gloves."

"Well, I'm certainly not your father . . ."

"Mr. Scargill. I'm a photographer. I go where the story is. That's the job."

He shrugged. "Please yourself, Shutterbug. Just don't forget that the job I pay you for is in the darkroom, not the street."

It was difficult to eavesdrop in Whitechapel; every third voice was Russian or Yiddish and David Rabatkin was no longer fluent in either. He strained to hear what the marchers were saying, to discover why they were so keen on endangering themselves. Perhaps the last of the summer sun had lured them into the streets, made them forget who—no, *what*— was coming for them. Would they be ready when the Blackshirts arrived to declare them Yids, Paddies, parasites?

David glanced over his shoulder, back at London Hospital, and a cool line of perspiration traced his spine. If he got injured today, there would be trouble. A lanky, working-class

Jew couldn't do ward rounds with knocked-out front teeth, and the consultant David was assigned to that term already looked at him like he was covered in pox.

Head tucked down, David nudged through the gathering crowd, toward the old Bell Foundry, where he and Simon had arranged to meet. He clambered over a corrugated iron barricade and dropped down into the spectators shuffling up Fieldgate Street. The farther he got from the hospital, the less anxious he felt, and his arms began to swing along with a mangled brass band rendition of the "William Tell Overture."

Finally, he spotted his brother standing next to a tall woman with a press camera. Her auburn hair and delicate features were pretty in a stock Irish sort of way, but pretty girls were always speaking to Simon.

"Everyone knows Oswald Mosley hates Jews," Simon was saying to her, "but today the police commissioner and the home secretary are allowing him and his militia to parade through our patch. The Communist Party of Great Britain is here to say, oh no you're not. They shall not pass. You jotting this down, love?"

"Sorry, no," the woman said, rifling through the leather satchel slung over her long torso. Her voice was raspy but sweet. "I'm not a writer."

David clapped a hand on Simon's shoulder and introduced himself to her. She didn't exactly smile, but a dimple appeared in her left cheek. It felt like someone grabbed David's heart and squeezed.

"Kate Grifferty," she said. "Central Press."

Grifferty. Just as David suspected: Irish, Catholic, not for him. He knew he should throw his arm over his brother's shoulder and just walk away. Instead, he watched Kate Grifferty step onto the running board of a parked Austin Twelve-Six and prop her camera on its roof. Her paper-white skin suggested that she, like David, had spent the summer indoors. Lips pursed, she repositioned the camera and glared through its lens. The outline of her thigh was visible through the fabric of her wide-legged trousers, which buttoned all the way up the side of her hip.

David asked his brother how he knew her.

"I don't," Simon said. "She asked to take my picture and I thought I might make a name for myself, you know? In the papers. As a radical."

"This will be the follow-up to your becoming an intellectual?"

Simon grinned. "Yeah, well, exactly."

Meanwhile, Kate had wedged the toe of one brogue into the Austin's window ledge and was hoisting herself onto its domed roof. In seconds, she was standing on top of the car. She yanked a card out of the side of the camera, flipped it over, and slid it back in with the heel of one hand. Then she surveyed the crowd, her eyes narrowed like a vengeful Celtic goddess. Simon started to walk away.

"Hold your horses," David said, grabbing his brother by the elbow. "Shouldn't we wait and help her down?"

"She don't look like she needs helping, mate."

"Did you ever see a girl press photographer? God, she's bold."

"Yeah, I will give you that." Simon shifted back and forth on his feet, like a kid itching to jump into a pile of leaves. "I know going on demonstrations ain't your idea of fun . . . ," he said. He looked from David to Kate. "Why don't you hang round here for a bit. *Help her,* as you say."

"I dunno." David hesitated. "I'm meant to be looking after you, aren't I? I promised Mum."

Simon waved him off. "I'm good. Just meet me at Shoreditch Town Hall at four. Tom Mann is speaking. We'll walk home together from there."

Kate was still taking photos. David could not keep his eyes off her. She worked slowly and methodically, seemingly unfazed by the raucous crowd swirling at her feet. Watching her, he couldn't think; he was just a pulse.

"All right," David said, more reluctantly than he felt. "Just don't get yourself hurt, Simon. I mean it."

And before he could change his mind, his brother was gone.

Kate knelt and slid down the side of the Austin. With the slightest glance at David, she walked into the road.

"I'd love to see that bird's-eye shot in print," he called, jogging after her. "Do you work for one of the dailies?"

"No," she said. "A picture agency, in Fleet Street. Next door to the new *Daily Express* building. You won't know it." She tucked a shock of dark red hair behind her ear. "What about you? Are you a communist, like your friend?"

Of course, thought David, *she fancies Simon.*

"He's not my friend. He's my brother. I'm a medical student. I don't have time to be a communist."

"You've come today as a medic?"

"No. I've come as a Jew."

"Oh," Kate said with a small frown. She looked down at the pavement. "Right."

She doesn't like Jews.

So, David knelt to tighten his shoelace, giving her the opportunity to go on without him. But Kate waited, and then kept walking alongside him, her hand almost close enough to brush his.

"You live in Whitechapel?" she asked, skipping over a curb to keep up with him.

"Yeah. Born and bred."

"I'm in Hackney," she said, tilting her dark gold eyes toward him. "Just over the road from Vicky Park."

David noted that Kate had not seized her chance to lose him in the mob and—twice now—had volunteered information about where she might be on any given day. She was obviously Gentile, but that hadn't stopped him with Connie

Bell and they'd parted as friends. It just meant there was a limit to how far things could go.

The tightening crowd gave David an excuse to stand near enough to feel the heat from Kate's body, but he was careful not to touch her. He became acutely conscious of the borders of his own flesh.

As the mood around them grew more and more frantic, he sensed a lightness coming into his body, an optimism. Kate kept walking deeper into the fray and he went with her. It suddenly didn't matter that the world was in a hell of a mess, or that fascism was at this very moment bearing down on Whitechapel High Street like a deranged lorry driver. Danger was everywhere, but David felt fleet-footed, untouchable.

She ducked into the arch at Gunthorpe Street to reload her camera.

"It's a Speed Graphic," he said, reading the silver label above the lens and pretending to know why that might be special.

"Yes, there are three viewfinders on this one," Kate said devoutly. "Mind the flash apparatus, it will be hot to touch."

From where they stood in front of the White Hart Pub, the Blackshirts were now in view, gathering like crows at Gardiner's Corner. Some goose-stepped self-consciously, an embarrassingly English imitation of Hitler's endless columns of glassy-eyed goons. The Blackshirts—their uniforms a pastiche of tatty fencing jackets, black turtlenecks, and homemade British Union of Fascists badges—were being protected by a ring of police guards, four men thick and counting. People in the flats above the shops hurled dirty nappies down on them like grenades. After a direct hit on one of the policemen, a chorus of cackles erupted from the windows.

Standing next to David, Kate seemed to use her forearms as a brace, her elbows tucked tight into the narrowest part of her waist. She noticed David watching her, grinned, and looked back into the camera with a furrowed brow. From the west, Mosley's motorcade was approaching. Kate pointed to the silver Rolls-Royce nosing its way through the crowd, only about fifty meters in front of them. They could see Mosley's beady eyes and rummy little mustache through the windscreen, his sham military officer's hat and the gold buttons down his chest. According to the newspapers, women swooned over him.

Kate darted out ahead of David, shoving through until she was alarmingly near Mosley's car. David watched in shock as she raised her free hand and smacked the bonnet of the Rolls. Mosley looked directly at her, his face blank with surprise, and gave her a magisterial wave. Kate got her shot and then *stuck her tongue out at the leader of the BUF.* All David could do was block people from banging into her.

"Bloody hell," David said, shaking his head. "You're terrifying, Kate."

"I got him, didn't I?" She was already reloading her camera.

Mosley's car was swallowed back into the crowd and David's eyes went to three plainclothes men, throwing the Nazi salute under the impervious gaze of a mounted policeman.

"THE YIDS, THE YIDS, WE MUST GET RID OF THE YIDS!"

The chants were coming from every direction, punctuated by pops of shattering glass. One of the men, tongue coiled in a mouth full of mustard-yellow teeth, locked eyes with David. He spat: "What are you looking at, Yid?"

David's vision syncopated, like the pages of a Filoscope, and his fingers curled into fists. He wanted to say: *I bring people back from the dead, you fucking caveman. What do you do, dig ditches?* But the air had gone from his lungs, and then the man was gone.

Kate averted her eyes and put away her camera. "I've got to get back to process these negs," she said. "It was lovely to meet you."

"Wait!" David cried, not wanting that to be the last time they saw each other. He was ashamed the Blackshirt had shaken him, especially in front of Kate. "We could duck into the pub there, have a quick drink."

"I can't. I'll get scooped."

"Of course. Sorry if I slowed you . . ."

He broke off. Across the road, in front of Levenberg and Sons' chrome-and-black facade, there was a body on the ground. Without thinking, David ran toward it. Somewhere in the throng of people, a blunt flying object connected sharply with the bridge of his nose.

When he reached the fallen man, David knelt down and easily found the racing pulse beating through his neck. When David glanced up, Kate was there, taking their photograph. Although the man was conscious, his skin was gray and his face was as rigid as a mask. He wore a black dress shirt and tie—one of Mosley's tin soldiers.

"Don't try to sit up," David told him. "I'm David. I'm a medical student. What is your name, sir?"

The man groaned. His eyes rolled closed.

David looked around. There was almost no daylight between the marchers. They created their own atmosphere, hot and sticky and suffocating. The man needed a hospital, but nothing was getting through that crowd.

The freshly cracked plate glass window of Levenberg's pharmacy was just a few yards away. Inside, behind jars of senna pods, sulfur, and arsenic album, the chemist's wife surveyed the scene in the street, her eyes wide and her palm pressed to her forehead. One of the Levenberg sons, Marty, was a year younger than David and had gone to the local comprehensive with Simon.

"Help me get this guy off the street," David said to Kate. "In there."

She lifted the man's feet; David lifted his head and neck. The proprietress did not open the door.

"Mrs. Levenberg, this man is gravely injured," David called through the broken window. "Might he rest in your shop until an ambulance can come through?"

Mrs. Levenberg looked as if David had asked to bring in a rabid dog.

"It's all right, he can't hurt you, he's barely conscious. I'm Davy Rabatkin, remember? My brother, Simon Rabatkin, was at school with your Marty."

Recognition flashed in Mrs. Levenberg's eyes. "Davy! The doctor. Yes, of course. All right then, come in . . ."

She unlocked the door. With Kate's help, David lowered the man onto the scuffed wooden floor in front of a large glass cigarette case. The store was cool and dark and smelled of burnt herbs. David asked Mrs. Levenberg if she had any ice.

"*Oy vey iz mir,*" she said, scurrying behind the counter. "I don't like this. My husband will not be happy if he comes home to find a Blackshirt in his shop, Davy."

"Your husband is a professional," David said. "He would feel obligated to save a life, as do I. This bloke will be trampled to death if we leave him on the street."

"I don't know . . ."

"And if he dies," Kate said, "people will say the Jews of East London killed him. It won't matter that the Blackshirts came here intentionally to provoke such an outcome. 'Jewish Mob Kills Local Man' would sell loads of papers."

David looked at Kate with renewed awe. "That, too."

With a sigh of resignation, Mrs. Levenberg went to the back and returned with a cold, wet flannel for the man's forehead. David took his pulse. The heart rate was still galloping, well over a hundred and twenty beats per minute.

David stood up and wiped his hands on his trousers. In the mirror behind the counter, he saw that there was dried blood under his own nose.

Mrs. Levenberg's eyes darted from David to Kate and back again. "Your mum is called Hetty, isn't she?"

"Yes," David said, searching his pockets in vain for a handkerchief.

"I know her. She'll have fifty fits when she sees the state you're in."

"I'm all right."

"You'll have a cup of tea while we wait for an ambulance. And a plaster for that nose."

"It's not bleeding anymore." David glanced at Kate, who had not been offered a cup of tea and was buckling her kit, preparing to leave. "Hang on—"

"I really have to get back to the office," Kate said, one hand already on the door. "I've stayed too long. If I don't leave now, I won't be able to sell anything. But . . ." She hesitated.

"But what?"

"You could always tag along, if you wanted. We could go to the pub you mentioned after."

Mrs. Levenberg made a show of shuffling for something in the drawer under the till.

"I can't," David said, trying to telegraph with his eyes how much he wished he could. "I've got to look after this bloke."

Kate scoffed, like he'd said he was going to give the Blackshirt his wallet. "You're escorting him to the hospital yourself?"

"No, but I won't feel right until I know he's sorted out."

She pushed the door open with her back. "Right," she said. "Well, good luck with everything." The bell jingled above her head and she walked into the street.

The crowd had started to thin. Shopkeepers were sweeping up their shattered windows. Police officers dismounted from their horses to note damages in their little blue books, as if they'd just arrived to tidy up. In seconds, Kate disappeared.

The man had pushed himself up against the counter and was sitting with the wet flannel in his lap. He stared, dazed, at the red-, green-, and violet-colored bottles that lined one wall of the shop. A bulbous hematoma was blooming on his temple, but he no longer looked like a corpse.

"Can I have some water?" he croaked, scratching his side.

David would have loved to bolt after Kate. But he couldn't do that in front of Mrs. Levenberg without it getting back to his mother. More importantly, he wouldn't leave this Blackshirt alone with the chemist's wife.

David pressed his tongue hard into the roof of his mouth and closed his eyes for a moment. When he opened them, he noticed what looked like a silver bullet on the counter. He picked it up and turned it over in his fingers. It was a camera part with *GRAFLEX* etched on its side. He slipped it into his pocket just as Marty's fourteen-year-old sister came out from the back with a cup of tea.

"Who is your girlfriend, Davy?"

"You're a little spy, Sylvie."

"Mummy made me ask you," she whispered, and pursed her lips, restraining a giggle.

David looked into the hot teacup Sylvie placed in his hand. It was identical to the ones his mother used for guests— painted with red and brown roses, probably from the same stall in Petticoat Market.

"Beats me who she was," David said. "She was just helping me with this geezer. I don't know her."

Chapter 2

5th October, 1936

The Central Press was not a press at all. It was a photo agency, a collective of photojournalists who buzzed in and out of Fleet Street and chased stories around England. Kate had the furious occupation of processing, drying, trimming, and contact-printing their negatives. If Mr. Scargill could not immediately sell a picture to a newspaper or periodical, she delivered the negatives to the photographer.

There were no staff photographers at the Central Press, only a scrum of freelancers and stringers. Kate and her counterpart, Gordon Davies, got the overflow jobs and were allowed to submit photos they took in their spare time. Officially, though, they were darkroom boys.

On Monday, Kate sat at the photo desk, hunting through the morning editions for coverage of the previous day's demonstration. The *Times* was typically vague, writing the whole thing off as a public nuisance: *On one hand Communists seem to make a practice of creating disorder at Fascist meetings and on the other hand the proposal of the Fascists to march through largely Jewish districts does not suggest a desire to avoid provocation.* The *Mail* fumed that girls were among the injured, while the communist *Daily Worker* declared victory with a front-page headline: *MOSLEY DID*

NOT PASS: EAST LONDON ROUTS THE FASCISTS.
Kate sighed into her mug of tea. Not one of the papers had
her incredible photograph of Mosley. She had been too slow
returning from the march and missed the deadline.

Meanwhile, thirty-year-old Gordon captured the shot that
now graced the front page of the *Mail*—a photograph of a
young woman being carried away by the police. He knew
how to start developing his negatives on the Tube and, once
again, had beat Kate to the punch.

Next door, the *Daily Express* printing machines churned,
sending tremors down the walls and up through the soles of
Kate's shoes. She folded the papers and went back to trimming negs.

At ten, Gordon came in with a cocky grin. He was wearing
the same natty black suit and pressed white oxford shirt he
wore every day.

"Any fresh negs come in?" he asked, his intense gray eyes
scanning the numbered pigeonholes that lined the wall by
the door.

"I developed them already."

"Cheers. I've a blinding headache. Shot craps all night
with the copyboys at the *Express*. Won a tenner. Must be my
week."

"Not a problem."

"Don't be jealous," Gordon said, rubbing at some splat-
tered chemistry on the cutting board with his thumb. "One
of the weeklies may still buy something off you. Scargill
could call in a favor."

Kate shook her head. "I don't think so. I lost the flash sync
attachment off his Speed Graphic yesterday."

"Pah! Don't worry about that. You can do no wrong in his
eyes, *Shutterbug*."

"Don't call me that, Gordon."

Kate tied on a waxed-canvas apron and went into the darkroom to make a few prints. When she was in a bad mood,

the red-lit darkness was the only place for her: the percolating tanks, the swish of water in the sinks, the concentration required to smooth one grainy half millimeter. The room had a revolving cylindrical door, like a film canister, that divided the office from the lightproof laboratory.

She stood at the enlarger, put the negative in the carrier, and brought a handsome young man's face into focus—his straight nose, the cowlick at the front of his wavy hair, his full lips. David Rabatkin reminded her of the *Eagle Slayer* statue at the V&A in Bethnal Green, but with clothes on. She closed the lens to f/8 and placed a sheet of Ilford paper on the baseboard. First a test print: two seconds, four seconds, eight seconds, twelve seconds. Kate dipped the test print into the developer, the stop bath, the fix, and used her fingertips to push it around in a water bath for a minute.

She determined that the print needed about ten seconds of exposure. Another sheet of paper, and she switched on the projector lamp. This time, she dodged the edges to make them a bit lighter and to increase the drama of the face.

Just as the print went into its water bath, Mr. Scargill knocked on the darkroom door.

"Shutterbug!" he bellowed through the wall, jolting Kate from her reverie. "Please come speak with me immediately!"

The Central Press was a well-regarded agency and she knew she was lucky to work there. When she was first hired, Scargill had taken her out on his shoots and saw to it that she had all the film she wanted, even for her own personal projects. Out of all the staff and stringers and freelancers, she was the only woman, but everyone seemed nice and Kate had felt very fortunate indeed. But after two years working for Scargill, she'd learned his mentorship came at a cost.

Leaving the cool sanctity of the darkroom and stepping into the bright corridor, Kate wondered what toll he would exact today.

Scargill's office was stacked with boxes and smelled like

her father's dirty laundry. She had to shuffle sideways into the room. He smiled at her and crossed his legs, pressing one thick thigh over the other.

"Shutterbug," he said, after goggling at her for a few seconds. "I wanted us to have a little talk together, about your career."

"And the Speed Graphic," she said. "I'm so sorry, sir. I will replace the part."

Mr. Scargill shook his head, held his hand up—a pantomime of benevolence. "I can easily replace it myself," he said. "I cannot, however, replace your eye. If you were a man, DeMire at the *Times* would poach you, but fortunately for me the bloody fool doesn't like ladies in his newsroom." Scargill tutted. "Poor old girls. You're just as talented as the lads. But there it is."

"Thank you, Mr. Scargill. I'm grateful for the job."

"It's not camera parts I want to discuss. It's you. I have been thinking about you . . ."

Kate felt her shoulders drop.

"When I look at you," he went on, "I don't see a woman. I see creative intuition. Females have this incredible power. If only you knew how to use it."

Mr. Scargill studied the Zeiss Camera Company calendar on the wall next to the desk. He seemed to be trying to remember something. He uncrossed his legs, moved something around in his trouser pocket, and then crossed them again. Kate felt like she was looking down on them both from the ceiling. This was the routine and there would be no escape. If she wanted to keep her job, she would have to stand there and pretend, mostly to herself, not to notice.

"When I was at Oxford," he started again, "some of the female students were exceptionally clever. They made fools of the rest of us." He cleared his throat. "These girls did rather well by attaching themselves to the older dons. They got invited to all the important parties, met the right people. That sort of thing." He looked at her expectantly, like he had just made a joke and was waiting for her to laugh. His hand remained in his pocket.

Kate managed a smile, but she felt ill. "There were no important parties at Regent Street Polytechnic," she said weakly. "I suppose I was lucky."

"Regent Street Polytechnic!" Scargill burst out laughing and finally brought his hands above the desk. "Oh, I *do* like having you about. That reminds me! A chap from *Time* magazine will be over from New York in a few weeks. I want to give him an idea of what our shop could contribute to a new photography magazine they have cooking. They're pouring a fortune into this thing. I'd like you to meet him. Unfortunately, I can't bring Davies."

"Why not?"

"Because he's colored and I don't see our transatlantic friends appreciating it. You know I don't pay any attention to such things . . ."

Yes, you do, Kate thought. Gordon's mum was Indian. Scargill often commented on it, but Kate didn't remind him of this because she was desperate to finally be brought in on a pitch.

He went on: "I'd like you to tell the Americans what will make a girl spend her nylon money on a news magazine and maybe even read it."

"Girls read news every day," Kate said, light-headed with relief that Scargill's hands were now busy searching for something in a file box behind his desk. When he wasn't being disgusting, she didn't really mind their chats. "I read at least five newspapers this morning."

"Because you're in the trade. You're not a normal girl. From what I hear, Time Inc. want this photography magazine to have pride of place on coffee tables around the world. The photographs we present to them must be impeccable. And you, Shutterbug, shall need a finer class of instrument."

From the file box, he pulled a brand-new 35mm Leica, still in its box, and put it on the desk in front of Kate. "It's a miniature," he went on, opening the box and handing Kate the camera. "I insist you start using it immediately. Get a feel for it."

Leicas cost more than thirty pounds and Kate was lucky if she earned six pounds a month.

"Gosh. Thank you, Mr. Scargill."

"Cartier-Bresson uses one," he pressed. "Do you like it?"

"Of course," she said, noticing that the Leica fit perfectly into her hand like a hammer, heavy and precise. She clutched it to her chest. "But I will return it to you after the meeting."

Scargill smiled. "Whatever you say, Shutterbug."

Kate hid the Leica under her desk and tried to put Scargill out of her mind for the rest of the day. She returned to the synthetic, hermetic safety of the darkroom. She felt cocooned by the constant whir of the fan, the scent of dust and chemicals, the cracked cement floor with a drain by the sink. From upstairs, she heard muffled thuds, heavy footsteps, doors slamming, but nothing could bother her in the darkroom.

"Okay!" Gordon announced, appearing in the revolving door with a magician-like flourish. "We've got fresh negs! And there's a chap at reception for you. Says he's returning something of yours."

"What does he look like?"

"A gangly kid in a cheap suit." Gordon switched on the red light. "A Cockney with aspirations."

Kate grinned. She knew who her visitor was. "Thanks, Gordy."

"Now I'm Gordy again, eh?"

As she bounded up the stairs, she dug her teeth into her lips to make them redder.

Just as she'd hoped, David Rabatkin was by the front windows, his hands clasped behind his back, looking out at Fleet

Street. His coal-colored hair was thick and wavy above his ears, but shaved close to his neck. There was a large book on the unmanned reception desk, its jacket wrapped neatly in brown paper and white tape, with a cutout around the title. Kate examined it—*A Textbook of Clinical Neurology.* Before David noticed her standing behind him, she flipped through the pages.

"Is this for me?" she asked.

David startled. "No, that's mine. Sorry, I'm a bit jittery. I've been studying in the café over the road and had about four coffees. How've you been?"

"Since yesterday? Fine."

"I have something of yours. You left it at the chemist's."

He pulled the flash sync attachment from his suit pocket and handed it to her. Something in his expression was too vulnerable and suddenly Kate felt uncomfortable. He looked like he needed something from her, and she wasn't sure she liked that.

"Thank you," she said briskly.

"I thought you might be finishing work soon. Perhaps we could get a drink?"

"I can't," she said, wanting to be back in the solitude of the darkroom. "I have heaps of work to do."

David's face fell. "Oh, okay." He picked up his book. "I hope the, uh, lens thingy helps. It was lovely to meet you anyway."

He turned and walked out into the street. The way he moved, his long arms in motion, provoked a frantic feeling in Kate. Without thinking about what it was, she came out from behind the desk and followed him outside.

She called after him: "You drank burnt coffee all afternoon just to give up so easily?"

David, already walking up Fleet Street toward St. Paul's, froze.

"I'd have thought you were going to ask for a date," she said. "A proper one."

He turned around. "Do you fancy it?"

"Sure. Why not?"

"All right," he said, striding back to her with a big grin on his face. "Do you like music? My brother and I are going to see the Ivor Kirchin Band tomorrow night. He's bringing a girl, my brother is, I mean, so you wouldn't be the only one."

"I'm quite accustomed to being the only girl."

"Join us then," David said, reassuringly nonchalant. "If you like. Eight o'clock. The Tottenham Royal."

Kate nodded. "Yes. I'll be there."

Chapter 3

6th October, 1936

The Tottenham Royal resembled a small white castle with a central rotunda. Pink light from the marquee glittered on the water-slicked pavement and gulls swirled like paper airplanes under the starless, bruise-colored sky. As Kate emerged from the bus, the burnt-wood air set her heart racing. She loved autumn, its anticipation of change. She'd worn her most bodice-hugging frock—a chocolate satin tea dress that belted tight at the waist and swished around her calves. She knew she was looking lovely, which made her fond of everyone around her. On the bus, she had noticed the admiration in the other passengers' eyes, an unusual eagerness to shove over.

David was waiting for her under the marquee with his brother. They did not see her at first. Glancing at his watch, Simon leaned his right shoulder against David's left for a moment. Kate could still hear his voice in her ear at the demonstration: *Hey, lady, take my picture, put it in the paper.* She saw how handsome Simon was, like Errol Flynn with black hair and no mustache, but she felt blank looking at him. He was pretty, while David was sexy. It was the shape of David's long body that seized her own, his broad shoulders, and his eyes—warm and deep. The confident way he stood, leaning back on his heels with his hands in his pockets, seemed to draw her toward him.

When David spotted her, joy broke across his face. His dark, arched eyebrows nearly grew together at the middle, which somehow added to his attractiveness. Kate lifted her hand to wave and he made the same small motion with his.

As she approached David, a willowy woman emerged from the Royal and attached herself to Simon. She wore a man's black suit jacket over a yellow-and-silver–beaded flapper dress that barely grazed her knees. No one dressed like that anymore, but she looked sensational, with blond hair slicked back into a severe bun. The woman had a face like a garden spade: sharp and simple and flawless, neither pretty nor ugly.

"Hullo, hullo," Simon chirped, extending a hand to Kate.

"Mim, this is Kate," David said, addressing the elegant woman, the smile lines deepening around his mouth. "Kate, this is Mim. Myriam. And you remember my little brother, Simon."

"Hello, darling." Myriam, her voice deep and accented, kissed each side of Kate's face. "You're late."

David offered Kate his arm. He was very close; she felt his hip against hers. The skin around her throat seemed to tighten and she ran her fingers over it, reminding herself that she was not a skittish person. He was just a man; she spent her life surrounded by them. But she'd had very little physical contact with male bodies, a few kisses at art school, that was it. For the most part, the risk of sex had always outweighed its appeal to Kate.

The Royal's outer doors opened to an alcove where David paid their half crowns. The inner doors opened to a smoky ballroom with lamps like upside-down lilies hanging from the ceiling and a large stage at the far end of the room. Simon and Myriam made a beeline for the zinc bar. David led Kate to a table near the stage, where the band was tuning their instruments in the semidarkness. In the middle of a dozen or so musicians, the band leader, Ivor Kirchin, sat at a grand piano. Bald with thick black spectacles, he looked more like a dentist than a musician, but David told Kate he was one of the best in London.

There was a moment before David pulled out her chair—a pause, like he was steadying himself—which excited her. It felt like the whole room stopped, like something important was about to happen. Sitting, Kate studied Kirchin, the band, the fluted ceiling lights—everything but David. She didn't want to appear overeager.

"Your brother and his girlfriend look like film stars," Kate said. "I got a great shot of him at the rally. I can make you a print if you like."

David ran his hand along his chin. "Sure, okay," he said.

For some reason, it was that disinterested "sure" that sent her over the edge.

Kate wondered what it felt like to walk through the world in his body. She wanted to steer a bicycle with his strong arms, to swim in London Fields Lido with the feet that filled those long, wingtip shoes.

"Have they been going together long?" she asked, clearing her throat. "Simon and Myriam, I mean."

"A few months. They're both political sorts. She's a communist and got him involved."

"Really? Does your father mind?"

"My father? No. He'd be all right with Simon bringing home a goat if it was Jewish."

"I'm not Jewish."

David's mouth twisted into an expression Kate could not decipher. "I know," he said, his eyes shifting to one side.

"Fascinating. How do you know?"

"I just do. Your name, to start."

"I guess you had better not bring me home to Father, then."

David looked at her incredulously, then laughed.

"I'm a Catholic," Kate said. "But I guess you knew that, too."

"Ah, well. No one will begrudge us a few spins around the dance floor anyway. Let's have a drink first?"

Kate watched David stride across the plank floor and lean against the bar next to Myriam. He returned with two G&Ts just as the band started playing an old-fashioned waltz. When she took a sip, the bitter perfume of the gin puckered her lips and soon her lower back felt soft and warm.

"Did you get the shot of Mosley you wanted on Sunday?" David asked, fixing her in a long gaze. "I checked all the papers, but couldn't find it."

"It might be in the *London Illustrated* at the weekend. Do you normally read all the papers?"

"No."

Simon appeared and took the chair on the other side of Kate. "So, you're mad for the Kirchin Band?" he asked. His accent was slightly different from David's: sharper, less trained. Simon sounded like an East London boy; David's voice betrayed no particular background.

"I've never heard of them," Kate said.

"That's funny. Davy was desperate to get you here."

Kate glanced at David and found his face had closed. Simon rested one elbow on the table and yawned, not bothering to place his palm over his mouth.

"Simon enjoys stirring things up," David said. "He's a hooligan."

"I'm not a hooligan." Simon shifted his shoulders and shook his head. "I'm very respectable. But I'm not here to get whacked about. If someone wants to do that, I will respond. I'm up for it."

David raised an eyebrow as if to say: *See what I put up with?* Next to Simon's constant movement, he appeared very still.

Myriam came over with a glass of something dark red and Simon leaned back in his chair, away from Kate.

"Are the boys quarreling?" she asked.

"Not quarrelling," David said. "Simon just can't be bothered to act civilized."

"I rather like that about him," Myriam said.

"Tell my brother, Mim," Simon said, "how civilized they are in Berlin. Myriam was there last year with the ballet. The civilized Germans aren't bothered when Jews are attacked in cinemas or arrested right out of shops and disappear."

Kate nodded. "I've read about these things happening."

"I have *seen* them happen." Myriam angrily flicked the handle of her purse, a small rectangular box covered in tiny square mirrors, from one side to the other. Her nails were painted the same red as her drink. Kate tucked her own hypo-ravaged, unmanicured hands under the table.

"Have you been abroad, Simon?" Kate asked.

"No," he said. "But I'd go to Spain at the drop of a hat. I've volunteered to go, but Aid Spain say I'm more useful organizing at the moment. Particularly in bringing in funds . . ." He glanced at David and narrowed his eyes. "There's that face."

"You don't know a word of Spanish," David said.

"I'd pick it up quick."

"You can't read Hebrew even though Dad spent years trying to teach you. And you're skint, not a halfpenny to your name. How would you even get there?"

"They might send me. I'm prepared to take a risk in the interest of liberty and the Republic of Spain." Simon set his eyes on Kate again. "What do you reckon, love?"

"About the Spanish War?"

"About Franco, Hitler, Mosley, the lot."

Now Simon, David, and Myriam were all staring at Kate. She felt like she was being charged with a crime.

"If you mean fascism, I despise it," she said. "Of course."

"Is that why you went to the protest?" Myriam asked.

"No. I went to take pictures. I was caught up in the protest, but . . ."

"But what?"

"I was more caught up in the photography, if I'm honest. It's great shooting. People are comfortable being photographed during demonstrations because they feel they're making a historical statement."

"We *are* making a historical statement," Myriam and Simon said in unison.

"I know that," Kate said, flustered. "I think it's brilliant."

"Don't mind these two," David said. "Whenever they start talking about Spain, they get all belligerent and horrible."

"We're just keen to know where your girl stands," Simon said.

"I'm not his girl."

"And she's plinking well told you where she stands. Now leave it." David shook a cigarette out of Simon's pack. "Do you want one, Kate?"

"No, thank you. I don't smoke."

Sitting between these two brothers was dizzying. Emotions seemed to be constantly volleying between them; Kate couldn't work out if they were best mates or worst enemies. Feeling out of place, she turned to watch the band and let her face cool down. Clearly, Simon and Myriam were trying to scare her off. David had known that Kate was not Jewish; perhaps they knew, too, and did not approve. Well, she was used to being disapproved of and wasn't going to let them spoil her evening.

When the violin section started to play the opening notes of "Why Stars Come Out at Night," Kate's foot swayed to the tune. David stubbed out his cigarette and tilted his head toward the dance floor, which had filled up.

"Do you want to?" he asked, an apology in his eyes.

"All right."

On the stage, a male singer crooned: *"When I set eyes*

upon you, I was set a'fire wiiiiith happiness . . . which ne'er before had come my waaaaay . . ."

Kate and David were absorbed into the sea of dancers whirling around a tuxedoed master of ceremonies, who stood in the middle of the floor, waving his arms in time with the music. Before long, Kate had caught the rhythm. She tried to stop herself leading. She'd always had trouble with this.

David lost his footing and paused. "Are you leading?" he asked.

"Sorry. I'm trying not to."

He laughed. "You're all right. I'll do whatever you want me to."

"No, no." Kate loosened her shoulders and gave her weight over to him. "I've got it now."

As they turned and turned, the garland molding at the top of the ballroom blurred into a thick gold band.

"Tell me . . . ," she said in his ear, "why don't your brother and Myriam like me?"

"Simon and Mim? They like you."

"I think they just accused me of being a fascist."

"They just want to know you," David said. She stepped back and he stepped forward, the top of his thigh pressing into hers. "That's why they're asking all those questions. I like you and they want to like you, too. Unfortunately, they can be really annoying going about it. Sorry."

"They sound like journalists."

David laughed. He moved his fingers to alternate with hers.

"You dance well," she said.

"Thanks. So do you."

A rendition of Billie Holiday's "Summertime" started. The trumpet dipped, the clarinet rose, and David and Kate looked at each other and smiled. It seemed to her they were feeling the same thing, the same fullness, in that moment.

She had always preferred dancing alone in her room to dancing with men. Dancing was a way to diffuse the exuber-

ance inside her, to clear work out of her head. Couples twirling in a ballroom seemed like a performance of manners.
Kate had never really known what the fuss was about.

But when her lips grazed David's neck, she swore she felt
the sensation in his body as clearly as her own.

Later, the bus driver drove along the Tottenham High
Road, discussing an impending transport strike with Simon,
who stood holding the pole by the front door. Myriam had
taken a cab to another party. Kate and David sat side by
side in the last row of the mostly empty bus. David, with his
warm hands, ran a finger around the back of Kate's neck to
adjust the collar of his suit jacket, which she was now wearing. Simon swayed tipsily as the bus turned east into Mare
Street. They had all had too much to drink at the Royal and
the night had passed too quickly.

David looked at his watch. "Quarter past ten. Time goes
fast with you," he said just as Kate thought it.

"I'm so glad we did this," she said happily.

"Me too," David said. "Will your mother be waiting up?"

"That's a whole story. You don't want to hear that."

"Yeah, I do."

"She died when I was born. I live with my father. It's just
been him and me for a long time."

"I'm sorry. Are you and your dad close?"

"No. He . . ." Kate hesitated. "He doesn't like me very
much. Never has. I don't much care for him, either. See, I
told you it's not nice. Don't feel sorry for me though. My
father looked after me. He's given me loads more than most
people get."

"I am sorry. A dad is someone you should know loves
you." David was quiet for a moment. "Maybe as you both
get older, you'll get closer. You'll understand each other better. I read a psychiatry paper recently—"

"Psychiatry won't work on my father. He's Irish."

David laughed. "The claim is that children tend to interpret their parents' fear as anger. Maybe your dad was just really, really worried about you, raising you without a mum. It can't have been easy." He cringed. "Sorry, I dunno if that's helpful or patronizing . . ."

Kate shrugged as if she didn't give this theory much weight, but actually she loved what David had said. He'd wanted to comfort her and offered more than just a platitude.

She laid her head on David's shoulder, feeling weirdly close to him and drowsy from the gin. "Pa must have been pretty damn worried about me then," she mused and David intertwined his hand with hers.

"Davy!" Simon hollered. "We change at the next stop!"

David did not let go of her hand. "I don't think you should walk home alone," he said, frowning.

"Don't worry. I'm on a main road. The bus stops at the corner. I do it all the time."

Simon was jumping up and down at the front, waving for David to hurry. David told him to go on and waved as his brother alighted from the bus.

"I'm gonna ride with you," David said to Kate, "then double back."

"It will take you forever. It's late. What if you miss the next—"

"Nope," David said resolutely. "It's no trouble. I won't feel right if I don't get you home safe."

Kate nuzzled into his shoulder and closed her eyes.

When Kate returned from work the following evening and shut the door behind her, the echo revealed someone else in the house. The stomping overhead confirmed it was her father. Although he was not a large man, Frank Grifferty walked heavily, like the dockworker he once was.

She went to the kitchen, put the kettle on, and made a cup of tea. Then she carried it to her father's lair, one flight up from the kitchen, past the library and the pink-and-lace parlor no one used.

Her father was at his big accordion desk, in front of windows overlooking Victoria Park. His horn-rimmed tortoise shell spectacles were perched on the tip of his nose and he was working his way through a large green accounting ledger. Kate leaned in the doorframe, blowing on the tea and waiting for him to acknowledge her. As usual, he was dressed impeccably: today in a pigeon-gray suit with a dark red tie. His face and half-bald head were seared by the sun, even though he'd not worked on a ship for years. In a nickel frame on his desk was a photograph of himself as a dashing young man, grinning in front of the original Grifferty Timber Importers sign. The atlas on the stand next to his desk was turned to Norway.

Kate's father was the only thing in life that frightened her. She was not sure why he had this effect, because he had never laid a hand her. But he had also never hugged her, nor said a tender word. Kate suspected that her father secretly blamed her for killing her mother, his wife, in childbirth. There was always this tension. She could feel it even now, as a grown woman, watching him work quietly at his desk.

Her father shifted around in his pivot chair and pushed his glasses to the top of his head. He looked at her, his ice-blue eyes impatient.

"I brought you a cup of tea," Kate said, placing his cup on the ink-stained leather desktop.

He looked at her askance. "What for?"

"No reason. Just thought you might fancy one."

"Aye. Thank you, Kathleen." Her father sipped the tea and smiled tersely at Kate, then knocked his glasses back down on his nose. "Was there something else?"

"I went out for a date last night," she said, hoping to engage him. "The boy didn't pick me up. I met him and his brother at a dance hall."

"Sounds like a real gent." He turned back to his ledger.

"He's a university student." And when that garnered no comment: "A Jewish boy."

Jewish, in Frank Grifferty's lexicon, was synonymous with odd. He referred to the Henschels—the Jehovah's Witnesses who lived next door—as Jews. But her father was miles away already, counting his timber and the money it would fetch him. Disappointed, Kate turned to leave. He called after her.

"I'll tell you about Jews," he said. "They only care about three things. Food, sex, and sterling." Her father screwed up his face. "And I'm not eating any Jew food. I like a nice corned beef. A nice stewed cabbage."

"Fine," Kate said, pleased she'd hooked her father's interest. "We shan't ask him to cook for you, then."

"Jews are good at making money, but everyone hates them."

"Are you trying to tell me you're Jewish, Pa?"

"Ha! If only. The Irish have it much worse. I've not seen a sign that says 'No Jews Need Apply.' You're already Irish. Are you specifically after making your life more difficult?"

"I didn't say I was marrying him."

He waved her off. They had already passed the limit of his interest. "Ah, well," he said, scribbling something in the margin of his book. "You'll go your own way. You always do."

He said it like Kate had ever had a choice.

Her sister, Orla, was twelve years older and ran her late husband's boardinghouse in Brighton. She never visited London. Although Kate did not remember much from when Orla lived in the house, she could still feel the aching loneliness of when Orla left to marry Edward Sherwood.

Unfortunately, Orla's room had soon been filled by Mrs. O'Malley, a war widow who styled herself as Kate's governess but was actually the housekeeper. All she taught Kate was how to polish fire irons with stale beer and blacklead, and glass with vinegar and newspaper. But Kate's father loved the way Mrs. O'Malley ironed his shirts, so Kate had to suffer ignorance until she was old enough to be sent away to school.

At first, Orla would send Kate postcards at St. Eunice's, with a line or two about the sea or a pantomime she'd seen. Then, when Edward died of a fever five years into the marriage, her postcards dwindled. Kate wondered if she had done something wrong, perhaps by not demanding that her father bring her to Edward's funeral, but never knew how to ask until it felt too late and the bond between her and her sister was broken.

Kate's bedroom was at the top of the house. She kicked her court shoes into the corner with two thuds, plucked off her garters and stockings, and tiptoed to the gramophone on bare feet, knowing exactly what she wanted to hear. She pulled Billie Holiday from a small stack of records in paper sheaths and cranked the gramophone a dozen times so it would play through.

As music filled the room, it seemed to pour down the walls, over Kate's photographs and around the oval-framed watercolor of her sad-eyed mother, Margaret. She'd married Frank Grifferty, suffered his moods for over a decade, and died of eclampsia giving birth to Kate, their second child. That gloomy portrait above the grate was the only picture of her.

"Summertime" crackled and Kate reclined on the floor on her back, massaging her spine on the nubby carpet. She rubbed at the red marks the elastic garters had bit into her thighs, then propped her feet on the bed. She wondered about David, especially what he was feeling about her. She knew what she was feeling about him, and exactly what she wanted. Kate was twenty-one, not young, with no ideological reasons for maintaining her virginity. Lots of the bohemian types in art college had had sex, or at least claimed to. Why shouldn't she experience it?

Sex was cloaked in mystery, but she'd seen Hollywood films, she'd read books. There was a weird old sex manual called *Aristotle's Masterpiece* high on a shelf in her father's library; she'd read it cover to cover by the time she was fourteen. It said nothing about how to prevent conception, but a medical student like David would certainly have that knowledge.

Kate zipped the pendant on her necklace back and forth over her collarbone. It had belonged to her mother: a small gold heart with a ruby set in it and a tiny cross hanging off the bottom point. Orla used to wear it; she called it the Rosicrucian. For some reason, she'd left it behind when she went to Brighton and Kate's father gave it to her at her First Communion. It was, by far, the tenderest gift he'd ever given her and Kate treasured it like a holy relic.

She thought about how David had implied he would only marry a Jewess. It was actually sort of perfect. A husband was the last thing Kate desired. She wanted to be a photographer, not a domestic drudge, wasting her life looking after a man and his children and then probably dying of it, like her mother before her.

"No need to make a fuss," Kate's father said when she arrived at the wharf with the Leica the next day. "Just at my desk will be fine. It's for my club. They've pinned me as their next president."

"It's a bit dark in your office," she said. She had never done his portrait before and felt more nervous than she had at the BUF march. "Would you be up to trying a few outside? There's nice light for it."

"Fine." He made a shooing motion at her. "It's not important."

Kate knew this was a lie because her father had tarted himself up in a full suit of heathered tweeds, including a matching vest and cap, and translucent pince-nez instead of his usual horn-rimmed glasses.

In the basin, the barges docked under a frothy blue, Turneresque sky. A sudden rush of water from a spigot in the railway arch sent a barge horse—a huge bay with silky white socks and doleful eyes—stumbling into the water. Her father's workers coaxed the horse up one of the moss-submerged brick ramps that were built for such occurrences.

As Kate set up, her father leapt from the pathway to the roof of a barge. One of his yard workers was sitting on the deck, smoking and laughing with the bargemen.

"I'm getting a tattoo tonight," one of the men was saying.
"Of what?"
"I dunno, but it's gonna be big . . ."
Her father grabbed his worker by the arm, hauled him up to standing. There was always a roughness to the way he moved, a resentful impatience. His staccato voice bounced off the warehouses on the other side of the canal.

"I'll tell you what I want you to do," he barked at the man, "and I want you to do it today . . ."

The Commercial Road Lock opened and a parade of boats floated under the footbridge where Kate stood, toward the meadowsweet-bordered basin and her father's life's work— Grifferty Timber Importers, a great plot of ground where timber was stacked before transport to buyers or the warehouse. Mature stumps of aspen trees, imported raw from Russia especially for the Bryant & May Match Company. Walnut from Italy for choir stalls and furniture. Scandinavian birch, destined to become brooms and brushes and cotton wheels. Hornbeam—French only, British was too expensive—for piano keys and hammers. And slab upon slab of golden-brown English elm, for the keel pieces of ships, wheels, and coffins.

"Kathleen!" her father shouted, making her jump. "I'm ready now. Take the bleeding photograph!" He had framed himself in the railway arch and was adjusting his pince-nez and tweed cap. "My train for Liverpool leaves King's Cross at half past."

Kate snapped a photo of him—straight on, shoulders level, proud. "Where are you off to this time?"

"*Eire*," he said, with a *God help me* roll of his eyes, like

Ireland was a relative who always asked for money. "County Offaly. There's an entire forest of Irish yew for the taking and cheap. Hearty specimens, around five hundred years old, my seller says. And I've a customer who has it in his head to produce premade outhouses. The smell of yew wood repulses flies."

"Cruel end for an ancient tree," Kate mused, winding her camera.

"A very formidable species. Very difficult to destroy."

"And how long shall you be gone?"

"A month. Six weeks. I've some business to attend to in Dublin as well."

Kate's father had traveled often throughout her childhood, leaving her with Orla and then Mrs. O'Malley. Later, at term breaks, Kate was frequently left at convent school with the few other girls whose parents did not care to spend the holidays with them. Her father never invited her to join him on his journeys, even in summertime. When she was old enough to light the stove, feed herself, and lock the doors, her father would leave her pocket money and she would occupy herself by walking for miles through London with Orla's abandoned Brownie camera.

After her father departed for King's Cross and Ireland, Kate wandered along the basin, toward Narrow Street and the Thames. The river was dark amber in the evening light. She set her camera on the embankment and took a photograph of a tugboat, rung with rubber tires, pulling a barge stacked with shipping containers out to sea. A gritty eastward breeze cooled her neck. She imagined climbing over the wall and swimming across the water to hitch a ride to Copenhagen or The Hague.

Every few minutes, a sailboat mast or a little black-and-red steamer chugged past on the river, bound for places she promised herself she would one day photograph.

Chapter 4

9th October, 1936

On Friday evening, Kate Grifferty was a tune caught in David's head as he walked up Brick Lane. The way he felt about her was his first genuine secret. When her lips grazed his neck on the dance floor, his soul had buckled at the knees.

As David approached Prince's Street Synagogue, the congregants milling outside nodded to him in gentle recognition. His father, Max, leaned in the doorway, so absorbed in conversation with Reg Zolowitz that he jumped when he saw David standing in front of him.

"Davy! What a treat. I thought you were studying."

"I finished early."

"Reg, my son has come to *daven* with me!" His father proudly put his arm around him and led him into the synagogue. Then, under his breath: "Why didn't you bring your baby brother with you?"

"I tried, but he's completely infatuated with communism at the moment. He's renounced religion."

"Hah. He'll come round. So will you."

Before stepping down into the small chapel, David and his father donned prayer shawls and *kippot*—the round skull caps that symbolized God's authority and perfectly covered Max's bald spot. In the gallery, in front of the ark, a few dozen men were already bowing and bending in prayer. The setting sun filtered through the synagogue's cracked skylights and curlicue iron chandeliers.

David's uncle Sol was in a pew near the back. For several months, he and David's father had not been on speaking terms. There had been an argument when the driving business they co-owned collapsed—something about debts—and David suspected that his father was the offending party. As he took his seat, David returned Uncle Sol's nod with a smile that he hoped was not disloyal to his father. It felt wrong to ignore his uncle, whose towering height, wiry hair, and pond-green eyes matched his father's and his own.

"I haven't a clue why my brother insists on coming here," David's father muttered. "There's gotta be a hundred *shuls* in the East End."

As the rabbi made his way through the prayer book, David, as always, struggled to engage. He did not believe in a Supreme Being and, when he was not with his parents, performed none of his religion's rituals. It wasn't entirely his fault—he had inherited his earthbound mother's inability to think in hypotheticals. Something was either real or it wasn't, it mattered or it didn't. The sunset was good enough; a Sabbath Bride seemed superfluous.

"Boi v'shalom ateret ba'alah, Gam b'simḥah uvetzahalah, Tokh emune 'am segulah, Boi khalah . . ."

To stop himself drifting, David scanned the list of names on the new benefactor wall—Hart, Bloom, Shafter, Spiegelstein, Chapter, Levy. They were families he knew, and he glanced around in vain for younger faces he might recognize. It was just the old fellows tonight.

David rose and sat as called upon, but soon fell into his own thoughts. He was not a spiritual man. He did not have that gift. Yet, among his own people like this, he felt a deep peace that he could not explain. It might, he rationalized, have been a primal sense of safety.

When David was eleven, he won a free place at a prestigious school in North London. Before he went to that school, he had assumed everyone was Jewish. He thought the world would love him because, thus far, they had. But his new classmates, almost all Gentile, had started a cruel and lasting rumor that he had horns. They knew David was a normal kid who supported Tottenham and had a mother waiting for him at the school gates. But the fact that he was different, both Jewish and poor, made him monstrous. The only way David made it through was by being better than them. His marks, the shine on his shoes, even his hair—it all had to be perfect. Every day, he had to prove he deserved to be there. It was exhausting and, until David hit his growth spurt at fourteen, physically terrifying.

As a Catholic in England, Kate was different, too. David wondered what it meant to her: was Catholicism a hereditary thing, a family tradition, or a belief system that spoke to her soul? There was so much he wanted to ask her. When she was frightened, did she ask God for help, or, like David, assume no one was listening?

It would probably be best for him if she turned out to be a devout, regular churchgoer. Then they would have one less thing in common and it would be easier for him to disregard his feelings for her. Which he would eventually have to do anyway.

In his family and in every Jewish family he knew, romantic relationships with non-Jews were forbidden. Sometimes affairs were conducted in secret—he'd had a brief, sexual one of his own, with a voluptuous nurse from the hospital named Connie. But a public relationship with a Gentile would be knowingly subjecting his family to gossip and shame. In spite of how hard David had already fallen for Kate, there was only so far he could follow his feelings. Because, more than anything, he loved his family.

At the end of the service, when the rabbi called for them to stand for the *Kaddish*—the mourner's prayer—David knew that both he and his father were thinking of Rachel, David's baby sister who'd died as a toddler. He put his hand on his father's shoulder and squeezed, and his father closed his eyes.

"*Yitgadal ve-yitkadash shemei rabbah . . .*"

The Rabatkin flat usually smelled of the bleach David's mother used to clean everything, even the wood floors. But it was Friday night and roast chicken mellowed the air. Before dinner, his father went to lie down. Simon sat at the kitchen table, languidly polishing spoons with a flannel. David could see into the narrow dining room, where the table had been set with the chipped rose china and a bowl of green apples. Two tallow candles had already been lit for the Sabbath.

David wanted to consult privately with Simon, but before he could, their mother swept into the kitchen from the bedroom.

"Hullo, my boy."

"Hullo, Mum."

When he hugged her, she squeezed him hard and didn't let go until he did. David noticed she was wearing her posh dress. Then he remembered who was coming to dinner.

"I've hardly seen you all week," his mother said, searching his face. "Where've you been?"

"Working. Studying."

"You're looking forward to seeing Minnie again." This was a statement, not a question. "The Schwartzes will be here soon."

David leaned over the sink to look out the kitchen window. There was nothing about Minnie he disliked; in fact, she was comfortingly familiar. But he resented his mother's assumption that just because they were both Jewish, intelligent, and born in 1914 that that would be enough for David to yoke his life to this young woman. It wasn't modern and it bored him.

His mother pressed on, her voice betraying a hint of anxiety: "Her mother, Leah, and I were great friends at school. A wonderful family. It's *beshert* that you two met."

"Not really. I took her out as a favor to you."

She turned her back to him, dipped a wooden spoon into the soup she was preparing. Although her own parents were long dead, David's mother was still gifted with an only child's confidence that people were who they should be: her husband was a shrewd entrepreneur, her sons could not wait to settle down with nice girls, and all Jewish people—especially the well-off ones—were wonderful.

"Simon, hand me the salt," she said. "Minnie is a beautiful girl. Absolutely stunning. The kind of girl David could get serious with. Her father is a brilliant businessman. They just bought a mansion in Stamford Hill. You've never seen anything like it in the world."

"Bloody hell," Simon said, picking at the fried onions on the hob. "A mansion!"

"Don't curse," their mother said. "The Schwartzes will think you're common."

"I am common."

She ignored him. "*Neither* of you will have any trouble finding wives, once you put your minds to it. But David needs a serious girl. Minnie went to secretarial college. She'll want a husband with direction . . ."

David sighed. He'd known since time immemorial that he would marry a Good Jewish Girl and that singular act, more than any other decision he would make in his life, would signify that he respected his parents and ancestors. A Jew who "married out"—not that David personally knew anyone who had—would be cast out of his or her home in a hyperbolic scene, mourned for dead, and only spoken of in whispers. They would be an embarrassment, a tragedy, a *shandah*.

And yet, David could not get Kate out of his head. David had never met a woman like her. She was interested in real-world things that were interesting to him, too. In conversation, she was quick. It impressed David beyond measure that this beautiful, refined-looking woman was hustling on Fleet Street, bounding into riots, creating a new kind of art. Here, finally, was someone who would never bore him.

The Schwartzes arrived at eight. They were not observant and had driven over from Stamford Hill. Minnie was as David remembered her: large breasts, curly hair, clear skin, shy smile.

They said hello and everyone settled in the front room for wine and olives and carrots before the meal. David and Simon resumed their lifelong conversation about football. Like a shopkeeper, their mother proudly pointed out each piece of furniture to Mrs. Schwartz: the real silk fern, (imitation) Persian carpet, two velveteen side chairs, blue tweed couch (with stains hidden under throw pillows), torch lamp with a fringed shade, and, finally, the (secondhand) radio cabinet that doubled as a side table. It was set with a tin-framed photograph of a chubby infant Simon, four siddur books, and a small desk calendar.

Mrs. Schwartz obligingly complimented the Rabatkins' furniture. Meanwhile, her rich husband pretended to share David's father's dread about the rising price of petrol as they settled onto the couch.

"My wife tells me you're in the *schmatta* business," David's father was saying.

"Yes." Mr. Schwartz nodded. "But who isn't?"

The older people chuckled. Simon shot David a look.

"Right you are," David's father said. "Actually, I wonder if you might be interested in a deal I'm consulting on. Mate of mine recently found himself in possession of a hundred fox collars, for ladies' jackets and frocks. Finished beautifully, you just have to stitch them on. Problem is he's got no place to store them whilst he secures a buyer. He might even have to give them away. I could make an introduction if you'd like."

"That *is* interesting," Mr. Schwartz said, smiling tightly. "What a windfall for your friend."

"Ain't it though? Fancy an introduction? It's nothing to me. I enjoy being helpful."

"Let's see, shall we?" Mr. Schwartz looked at his wife and something passed between them, little more than a blink.

Minnie perched at her mother's side, gawping at Simon as he mindlessly ran his hand back and forth across the edge of the plaster mantel. Women always watched Simon like that. It made David both jealous and proud.

Feeling petulant—*he didn't want Minnie anyway*—David flopped down on the couch and tucked into a bowl of black olives on the coffee table. He considered the Schwartzes. They were the sort of people his parents favored—similar to themselves but with a little money. Minnie's father was massive and gray-haired with a gold signet pinkie ring and an air of paternal authority. A big *macher*, the type David's father had spent his life trying and failing to be.

Mr. Schwartz, apparently less interested in Simon than his daughter was, turned to David.

"How are your studies coming along, David?" he asked.

"Very well. I enjoy it."

"My wife tells me you're top of your class."

"It depends on how you—"

"Tell them about the conference," David's mother piped in. "He was invited to an infectious diseases conference in America next summer."

"New York City, Adam," Mrs. Schwartz said. Apparently, she had been briefed. "Columbia University."

"All sorts of strange afflictions on those cross-Atlantic ships," Mr. Schwartz mused. "My great-uncle died on one of them. I don't believe in travel . . ."

Minnie sat mostly silent, a mild smile on her lips. David wondered if she was intimidated by her parents or just feeling the effects of the Palwin No. 3 white wine she was sipping.

"It's dangerous everywhere these days," Mr. Schwartz went on. "That is why we left the East End. That riot last Sunday was a disgrace. No self-respecting Jew had any business there. Those so-called *protestors* were out of control. It was not a safe situation."

"Dave and I were there," Simon said and their mother winced.

"Our Simon is political," David's father said, unable to hide the pride in his voice. "Davy was only there to look after him."

"What your sons need to do is to set an example of hard work and respect," Mr. Schwartz retorted. "If the Gentiles are made to acknowledge our decency, antisemitism could be wiped out in a generation."

"I hear you, Schwartz, but we've already been thrown out of every country you can think of. It will keep happening. Our family lived in Russia and Poland for centuries . . ."

"As did ours."

"But I don't feel Russian or Polish, do you?" David's father asked. "I'm English, but perhaps that's temporary, as well."

"Yes, we are a people without a nation," Mr. Schwartz conceded. "Doomed to be guests. I've even taken the *mezuzah* off our front door. It's too dangerous. I don't want our family to be targeted."

David's mother looked alarmed. "Do you really think it's gotten so bad? I hadn't thought of someone coming into the building . . ."

"No, Het," said David's father. "We're safe here."

"It's only because we have a house, Hetty," Mrs. Schwartz said smugly. "Our doorway is in full view of the street. You're in a third-floor walkup. No one can see what your door looks like . . ."

This same debate was taking place in every front room in East London, about whether to dodge abuse by assimilation or excellence. It was a waste of time, an intellectual exercise, as far as David was concerned. Jews would always be looked down upon, no matter how great or small they made themselves. He knew that as well as anyone.

The green-and-white corridors of the London Hospital Medical College teemed with students, lab coats over their suits and ties. Most of them were middle-class sons and grandsons of physicians, lawyers, and bankers. They played rugby and went home to Berkshire and Surrey at the weekends. They slept through lectures yet expected to one day join the ranks of the Great Men of Medicine whose portraits hung around the central stairway.

The ease with which these men moved through the world, their certainty that all of it was created for them, astonished David. Whilst they dozed and read newspapers in the Milton Lecture Theatre on Wednesday morning, he furiously transcribed every word of Dr. Montague's lecture on diagnosing and treating hypoglycemia. But he was somewhere else, too.

A film was running through his head, featuring Kate in various incarnations. Remembering her face change as she spoke, the light that came into it when she was talking about something interesting, he could not decide if she was just ordinarily pretty or the most beautiful woman he had ever seen.

Since the Kirchin show last week, David felt as if he had been living two different lives: his real life—eating dinner with his parents, riding the bus, filling out paperwork at the nurses' station—and a fantasy about making love to Kate. At night, the fantasy took over completely and in the mornings he nearly wept with frustration. In his waking life, his daydreams about her were so vivid that when people spoke to him it felt startlingly rude.

Dr. Montague droned from the front of the half-cone-shaped theatre: "They'll be sweaty, palpitations, they'll be ferociously hungry . . ."

David had seen hypoglycemia on the ward, but he wrote

it all down anyway, the right side of his hand determinedly wiping Kate out of his mind as it pushed across the paper. No matter how preoccupied he was, he would not miss a word.

Now that he was in his fourth year, David knew enough to be trusted with a human life. That fact, agreed upon by powerful people, made him sit up taller in the creaky wooden stadium chair. He knew things—important things, the mysteries of the body—that most people would never understand. No one could take that knowledge from him, no matter what they thought of him.

Lunch that day was in the faculty dining room: treacle-marinated pork chops served over stewed apples and parsnips. Dr. Montague had invited David and another fourth-year, George Clearing, to join him.

"Delicious," Montague said through a gray mouthful of pork chop. Then his eyes rested on David's full plate and he looked stricken. "I didn't think. You probably don't eat pork, do you, Mr. Rabatkin?"

"It's fine," David said. It infuriated him that an overcooked piece of meat required him to publicly declare his stance on Jewish dietary law.

"One wants to be conscientious," Dr. Montague said. "But at my age, one can't keep up. In my day, one ate what one was given."

"At Gordonstoun we were served the most dreadful slop," Clearing said. "We loved it."

"Ah, you're an Old Gordonstounian. I'm an Eton man, myself. We ate quite well."

"I'm sure you did."

They both spoke like their molars were glued together, almost shouting, like they wanted other tables to hear them. Clearing eyed David, probably waiting for him to announce the name of his ludicrously inferior school, but David would not give him the satisfaction.

He picked at his parsnips and apples, ignoring the musky taste of the pork they were steeped in. If Clearing wanted to make everything a competitive event, that was fine. The bugger didn't know who he was up against. David sliced into the pork chop and put a rubbery piece into his mouth.

Montague cleared his throat and dabbed at his mouth with a serviette. "I invited you two gentlemen for luncheon today because you have the two highest marks in your cohort. If you qualify, as I expect you both will, I shall put one of your names forward for a house post here at the London. Before I do, I would like assurance that given the opportunity, you will accept."

"Absolutely, sir," Clearing said. "Thank you, sir." He didn't even need the job. His father was a physician with a practice in Harley Street.

"Yes, sir," David said. "I'd be honored."

A house post would be like finishing school. It was the only direct path to being hired on staff and later becoming a specialist.

"As you will both be aware, these are very demanding posts and you won't be paid. You'll get your food, but your parents will have to pay for your laundry, et cetera, and so on and so forth . . . Rabatkin, will that be a problem?"

"Not at all."

Clearing smirked.

"I know there were some complications with your tuition last term . . . ," the old doctor went on, scrutinizing David's face. "Was your father able to sort the matter out?"

"Yes," David said briskly. "Absolutely sorted. Clerical error at the bank."

Montague nodded and made a brushing motion over the table with his hands. "Good. These things do happen. But I should tell you that I have heard some questions from Surgery about your availability on Fridays and Saturdays . . . ?"

"I assume you are referring to my requesting days off on

two Fridays, Yom Kippur and the anniversary of my sister's death?"

"I don't know the particulars," Montague said. "But I prefer to be aboveboard on these matters, don't you? Just so we all know where we stand."

After his last lecture of the day, David crossed the road to the student pub, the Good Samaritan, and settled into a booth by the stained-glass round window. Then he got up and switched seats so he wouldn't have his back to the door. A piece of coal rolled out of the fireplace and he kicked it back in with the side of his foot and waited for someone to take his order.

When Simon arrived at the pub, so did the prettiest waitress. She placed a bag of crisps on the table in front of him.

"On the house," she said, smoothing her pinafore against her slim hips. "What'll you have, duckie?"

"Four lagers," Simon said. When the waitress sauntered away, he slid the crisps over to David.

"I'm not hungry," David said, pushing them back.

"Me neither. Hell of a week."

"Yeah."

"I really thought we were getting somewhere, stopping the Blackshirt march and all." Simon sighed.

Three days earlier, there had been another raid on Jewish-owned shops, this time in Mile End. Hundreds of fascist teenagers ran unimpeded down Clinton Road, smashing windows and stealing sweets and tobacco. In an effort to avenge Mosley's recent humiliation by Jewish East Enders, the teenagers beat resisting shopkeepers with planks and threw them out of windows. If you were Jewish, it seemed you weren't safe anywhere.

Simon opened the bag of crisps and stared into it, listless. "You start to wonder if there's more of them than us. Hiding in plain sight . . ."

"Who's hiding? Of course there's more of them."

"And just fucking despising us."

"I know, mate. Believe me."

The pretty waitress delivered the lagers, two for each of them.

"Actually," David said, sipping his lager, "the whole thing has got me reconsidering Kate."

"I knew she was a fascist!"

"I hate you."

Simon sniggered.

"But with everything that's happened recently . . . ," David said, "and her not being Jewish . . ." He waited, hoping his brother would quote Marx on religion's futility and joke about their mother's bourgeois notions of propriety. "It all feels a bit wrong. I'm not sure I should see her again."

Simon appeared to consider this, scratched his jaw. "How many brothers has she got?" he asked. "Do you reckon they'll come for us when they find out their sister's got a Yid boyfriend?"

"Kate's not like that. I've told you. And she doesn't have any brothers."

"Let's hope not." Simon took a drag off his cigarette and held it in his lungs, squinting at the lit end before exhaling it.

The pub was filling up. When someone switched the radio on, David relaxed a little. If only he could go through life to the music of Benny Goodman, at the start of his second lager.

"You couldn't have picked a worse time to get mixed up with a goy," Simon said. "I will give you that. What about Mum and Dad? They'll disown you."

"Don't tell me you're becoming all conventional now. I don't see you getting down on one knee for Myriam. She's a good Jewish girl. She must be gunning for it."

Simon shrugged. "Not really."

"Yes, she is," David teased. "She's a good Jewish girl, from the *shtetl*. Soon enough you'll take her up the aisle, become domesticated, have loads of little children. No more marches. No more Spain."

"Warsaw's not the shtetl. And you don't know Myriam. She ain't as good as she might seem. I'm telling you, Davy." Simon hesitated. "She's already married, to some Polish guy."

"What?" David was stunned. Even for Simon, courting a married woman was unimaginable. "You're joking."

"No, I'm not joking. See, I'm not bound by convention. But *you* are." Simon thought for a moment. "It's just a craving, you know. Cravings wear off. Don't see this Kate again, that's the trick. Find someone new. There's more than one hare at the track."

"There's only one hare at the track. That's the point, isn't it?"

"Nope. There's always another hare. They've got loads more in cages, round the back."

Chapter 5

18th October, 1936

At midnight on Saturday, six hours into his shift, David was sent into the neighborhood with the obstetrics consultant, Dr. Warren. The mothers looked at David like he was a visiting angel who could relieve their suffering. He could not. He feared, in fact, that he was making it worse, administering castor oil and enemas—nurses' tasks at the hospital—per Dr. Warren's instruction.

David had never been out with obstetrics before. In university lectures, the emphasis was on grasping the scientific method rather than a knowledge of its detailed application. In the field now, with these experienced mums whose bodies did all the work, David understood that he was about as useful as a hat rack. He found himself refolding flannels, giving updates to the husbands and older children, anything to show he deserved to be there.

They successfully delivered three babies that night—two girls and a boy—and each time, just before the birth, Dr. Warren shoved David in to catch the baby and clamp the cord. David did not feel worthy of the honor. But handing the babies, wet and mewling, to their mothers was transcendent. David left each flat certain he had glimpsed the primordial depths of parental love and, at dawn at the end of his shift, he crossed Stepney Green high on adrenaline, springs in his blood-splattered shoes.

Reaching home, he collapsed on the couch. He slept for a few hours and was lying there with a back issue of the *Lancet* tented on his face and a cold mug of tea balanced on his stomach, when his father tiptoed into the front room.

"A little word, my son," he said, settling into the armchair next to David's head. "I ran into Arnold Birch today . . ."

David groaned from under his magazine. "You've been to the track?"

"No, Petticoat Lane, but funny you should say that! That's a good sign, I reckon. Birch has got a deal going. I wanted to get your view on it."

"Whatever it is, don't do it," David said, his headache tightening like a key turning between his eyes. "That's my view." He closed the magazine and put it on the coffee table.

"Do you know the food stalls," his father asked, "at Walthamstow, that posh new stadium?" There was a glow in his eyes that filled David with a special kind of foreboding— familiar, sickening, like grief.

"Not really," David said, trying to sound disinterested, as if he could stop his father from jumping off a skyscraper by pretending not to be afraid of heights.

"They've got snack bars, selling refreshments, sweets, cocktails, ice creams. Birch has a mate who's trying to break into that business. *Has* broken into it. Incredibly lucrative, apparently. Very clever bloke. You'll love this—he sends his household staff in to bet on the dogs or the fillies or what-have-you, and when they can't pay, he swoops in and offers to pay the track owners off with ice creams from his dairy business!"

"Is that before or after they break his legs?"

"He's already pulled it off at Ascot. Now the clientele will never stand for anything less than his ice creams, so the track is locked in."

David had a visceral memory of the first time he'd noticed his father in an exuberant mood like this—eyes twinkling, dancing in the kitchen, inviting strangers to dinner. That time, his father claimed to have gotten a big new client at his catering business. It was 1929, which turned out to be a great year for birthdays: in March, for his fifteenth birthday, David was given a bike; in June, Simon got a Zenith shortwave radio; and in July, their father motored into the courtyard in a shiny black Crossley 15-7. It caused a huge sensation in Spelman Street and he took every kid in the building for a spin.

Then there was the holiday in Whitstable that August. David's father had spent the whole time bouncing back and forth between two seafront jewelry shops, trying to find the perfect hexagon-shaped brooch for his wife. Every moment was infused with a freewheeling prosperity that David found unsettling, although he did not know why at the time.

By that autumn, the true source of his father's optimism was revealed: he had invested all they had and more with a "high-end" stockjobber. When the London Stock Exchange collapsed in October, the Rabatkins lost not only the car and the gifts, but the catering business, all their savings, and Hetty's small but precious jewelry collection. She hadn't known about the stocks—she would have forbidden it. In their circle, jobbers were notorious wretches and not to be trusted.

So, the market crashed in '29 and David's father went into a deep depression, began auguring his own death, and did not stir from the flat for months. In an effort to minimize their debt and ensure David's future education, Hetty went to work at the Italian bakery and rented David and Simon's beds out to night-shift workers who needed sleep during the day.

That was exactly seven years ago. Just time enough for David's mother to pay off the debt and David's father to get back on his feet, build something new, and now, apparently, destroy their lives again.

"Dad," David pleaded, "don't tell me you're going to be one of Arnie Birch's shills with this dairy business."

" 'Course not. I'll be a full partner. It's quite respectable. He's ready to expand and looking for investors. Couldn't be better timing. Your uncle Sol and I have just divided things up. I've finally got that chauffeuring business off my shoulders."

"Going into debt at the track is not a business."

David's father chuckled, undeterred. His eyes were glassy. "Not that bit," he said. "The *dairy* bit. It's a completely legitimate business. That's what I'd be investing in. There'd be a chance to really get my hands in the business as it grows."

"Why don't you just get a job in a shop or something?"

"They won't hire an old fellow like me."

"You're only fifty!"

"Precisely. I can still make something of myself. Like you."

Keys rattled in the front door and David's mother came in, carrying a large paper bag of day-old bread from the bakery. When she went to put it down in the kitchen, his father leaned over to him.

"Don't mention it to your mum," he whispered. "Just wait till I sort the details."

She reappeared holding a tray with tea and broken amaretti snaps. "Do you have anything on this afternoon, Davy?"

"Not really."

"Perfect. Leah Schwartz came round yesterday. She said Minnie hasn't heard from you. After you sulked through my lovely dinner, you're lucky she'll still grant you the time of day. Why don't you ring her?"

"I've been up all night. I'm shattered."

"You're fresh as a daisy. Minnie won't be in if you don't ring her now. I told Leah you would ring her by three today. The girl is expecting to hear from you! Don't be a brute."

* * *

Kate was having a melancholy bath in the little room off the side of the kitchen. She was flicking water into the gas stove on the wall, making the flames rise and hiss, when the telephone rang. She whipped a towel around her body and ran to the little wooden telephone nook in the front hall. Her eyes were still adjusting to the darkness when she heard David's voice—casual, warm, as if it hadn't been twelve days—on the other end of the line asking her to come to the pictures with him.

"*The Florida Special* is on at the Troxy at five," he said. "Please come."

"Hmm." She pressed her thumb into her thigh, pink from the bath, and made a small white oval on her skin.

"There's a nice fish and chip shop next door to the theatre," he pushed. "It's nearly tea time, you must be hungry."

"You could have given me more notice . . ." Kate said, but she could not help smiling and wondered if David could hear it in her voice.

At quarter till five, he was waiting for her outside the Troxy, clutching two newspaper-wrapped parcels of fish and chips. With rumpled tan trousers and a gray blazer over a collared jumper, he looked younger than Kate remembered him. In fact, he looked like he had just rolled out of bed. He awkwardly raised a packet of fish when he saw that she had seen him.

It was quiet and cool inside the theatre, a change from the sooty, crowded streets of Whitechapel. The walls of the grand staircase were swathed with confectionery pink and mint-green fabric and the mezzanine level was all purple and gold velveteen. The whole place stunk of grease and vinegar and fried fish from the shop next door.

As they sat down, a powder compact fell out of Kate's purse. David reached under her legs, picked it up off the floor, and presented it to her with a shy smile. It touched her, the way he handled the cheap plastic compact like it was a precious object because it was hers.

The film was about an American newspaper reporter chasing jewel thieves on a train. Kate wondered if David would reach for her hand at the suspenseful parts, but he didn't. The glow of the screen etched his profile in light and she recognized her attraction to him, taut as a shoreline cord.

It was dark and cold when the film ended and the audience spilled back into the street. Kate wrapped her tartan scarf around her neck twice and tucked the edges into her coat. She adored the smell of London, her hometown: the thick layers of it, bracingly fresh and filthy at once. Burnt garlic mingled with river water and open drains and fallen leaves. David offered her his arm and she took it and they began to walk east on Commercial Road. The noisy pin-table saloons, sweet shops, and gangs of braying adolescents fell off and were replaced by dim cafés, chop suey houses, and dockers out seeking mischief.

He led her through the narrow lanes to a pub called The Grapes. Kate asked for a sherry and David ordered himself a pint of lager.

Kate walked away from the bar before he got their drinks. She was going to pick where they would sit. David would have to follow her. It was like a play, she decided, casting him as the pursuer. Kate chose a tiny round table in the corner by the French doors, under an oil painting of Charles Dickens, and waited.

In a few moments, David was sitting facing her, his legs spread wide under the table with her knees between his. Kate wondered if he had intended to sit so suggestively, but he did not correct it and neither did she. At first, they talked about the film.

David wondered how they shot it. "Was it on a real train or a built set?"

"Probably a built set in a warehouse," Kate said. "Much easier to light."

"Oh, right. Did you ever want to do that sort of camera work?"

"Motion pictures? No, I don't really fancy shooting in the studio. It's not spontaneous. Sort of takes the magic out of it for me."

"How did you learn photography?"

"I taught myself with my sister's camera. She's twelve years older and left to get married when she was sixteen. I was alone most of the time and had to find ways to keep myself busy."

He smiled. "You became an artist out of boredom."

Not boredom, she thought. *Loneliness.*

She shrugged. "I'm just a curious person. I'm interested how people manage to be happy when conditions are rather terrible. I'm far too practical to be an artist. I always wanted to have a proper job. That's why I set my sights on Fleet Street, and the Central Press hired me straight out of college."

David was making little tears in a round beer mat someone had left on the table: *HOBSON'S BLACK BEER HOT AT BEDTIME FOR COLDS.* Kate could not tell if he was nervous or excited or both, but she liked that she was having a bodily effect on him. Under the table, the length of one calf pressed against hers. When he turned to look back at the door, she could feel the muscles in his leg move.

"Kate, do you ever think of dashing off somewhere?" he asked suddenly.

"What, now?"

"No, I mean someday. Leaving London forever. Leaving everything and everyone behind."

She nodded enthusiastically. "I want to go everywhere. Cairo. Paris. New York."

"Yes!"

"Whenever I see the river, even smell it, I think about how

big the world is. I imagine leaping on a boat with my camera and a little suitcase and having a great adventure."

They both turned to look through the French doors at the Thames, where the spectral boat-shaped shadows were darker than the night sky. In the distance, ship horns groaned from the West India docks.

David cleared his throat. Another tear of the beer mat; he was making ribbons of it. "I should probably tell you," he said, "that I can't get mixed up serious with anyone, not at the moment."

Kate took a large drink of her sherry. She wanted to make him feel understood, to blow on the little ember of understanding between them.

"Neither can I," she said. "I want to do what I want, when I want. Don't you?"

David nodded, visibly relieved. "I can certainly see the appeal of it. I very rarely do what I want." He sipped his lager. "What's your plan?" he asked.

"For what?"

"For going everywhere, for doing what you want."

"I'm keen to work my way up to editor at one of the broadsheets," she said. "I want people to work for me. It's a bit tricky because there aren't many women in my job. At least I don't know of any. But I'll get there." She cringed. "Do I sound pretentious?"

"No. That's why I asked."

"How about you? Have you always wanted to be a doctor?"

"Yeah, since I was a kid. At school I took physiology and anatomy courses and got good marks. When one of my instructors suggested to my mother that I might consider medicine, that was it."

"Do you always do as your mother tells you?"

"Not as much as she'd like."

"Well, I think it's nice you were encouraged. At convent school, the nuns preferred we maintained a perfect ignorance

of physiology and anatomy. To stop us from becoming har-
lots, of course."

"And were they successful?"

"Very much so. But art college caught me up on all that . . ."
Kate paused to sip her drink, aware that David was hanging
on her every word. "Life drawing class. Imagine my surprise
when I walked into drawing class to find a chap naked as the
day he was born, sitting on a folding chair on a platform in
the middle of the room! But after a while, you get used to it
and it becomes quite ordinary."

She was trying to fluster him, but he calmly met her gaze.

"It's the same, seeing people without their clothes in
clinic," he agreed. "One becomes desensitized. Not like in
normal life."

Was there a dare in that last look? A confession? Kate
wondered what David knew of women, outside the hospital.
He was tall and good-looking; she guessed he'd had his op-
portunities. She hoped he didn't sense her own inexperience.
It might make him too precious about her. As it was, he still
hadn't kissed her.

Chapter 6

24th October, 1936

On Saturday afternoon, ramblers and schoolchildren and grazing sheep crisscrossed Hampstead Heath, just north of London. The air was muffled by a low, drifting fog and threaded with birdsong. In autumn, the heath was always beautiful and every shade of orange and brown and green, but that was not why David had brought Kate there. He'd brought her there because no one he knew lived nearby.

At the top of Parliament Hill, the few benches overlooking the city were occupied. There was a small opening in the gray sky above London; sun streamed through the crack in the clouds, making it look like God's special favorite. Kate busily churned through film, exclaiming that she felt like she was in the countryside. David trailed after her, holding her umbrella under his arm.

"You never stop," he said.

She grinned at him over her shoulder. "Perhaps you're my muse."

"If I'm your muse, why aren't you taking my picture?"

She snapped a photo of the horizon—blurred smokestacks on the eastern outskirts of London. "I have. I do."

David eyed the trails carved into the base of the hill; they were quiet, close, private.

"Let's walk down there," he said.

Kate followed him along a narrow trail, almost covered by brush. At the first clearing, just as he was about to take her free hand, she was possessed by a wide, weird, gnarled tree with branches that swirled like a whirlpool. She circled it, peering up into its branches, and put a different lens on her camera.

"What will you do with tree photos?" David asked, watching her. "They can't be for the news agency."

"It's a Surrealist tree. I'll put it in my portfolio."

"You should take your portfolio round the London galleries. See if they'll give you a show."

"No. My heart's in Fleet Street," she said. "It's where I want to be, even though my boss makes my skin crawl."

"Can't you go to another agency?"

"Mr. Scargill is one of the only editors who hires women. And if I ever leave, he'll say nasty things about me, I know it."

"If you need to get out, tell him he's too clever for you," David said. "He's not, but that's how you cope with people like that. You have to praise them away from you. You can't just tell them you don't want to work for them anymore. One hint of criticism and . . ." David mimed holding a stick of dynamite, throwing it to the ground. "Boom. They have no choice but to ruin your life."

"Has it happened to you?"

"I have had instructors punish me if I don't grovel at their feet. Because I'm Jewish, they want to make sure I know that they're better than me."

"Oh, David. How do you bear it?"

He shrugged. "The world is full of bastards, Kate. We have to work round them, don't we?"

"I'm trying," she said, with a wry smile. "Say, my perspective on this tree is too low. I want it to feel like I'm inside it. Could you give me a boost?"

"Lift you?" David placed the umbrella on the grass.

"Yeah." Standing behind Kate, he wrapped his arms around her hips, and hoisted her up so her backside was pressed against his stomach. He thought: *I'd give ten years of my life to sleep with you once.* He said: "This high enough?"

"No. Put me down and lift me facing you. I'll take the picture over your head."

He lifted her to where her rib cage could rest on his shoulder. The fog turned to a light rain. The fabric of her skirt was slippery, so he had to keep readjusting his forearms. His heart beat with the effort and the excitement of having her so close. His composure had gone.

As Kate slid back down the length of David's torso, his need to finally kiss her felt like drowning. When he did, the electricity between them made everything else, even the sky, dim. He breathed in her breath, her soft lips, the tilt of her hips into his.

With that kiss, he stopped caring about whom he might hurt with this affair: his parents, himself, even Kate. He'd been holding off things getting physical, trying to pace things out between them, but he just couldn't anymore. He wouldn't.

When Kate drew back for a moment, the grin on her face was victorious. David wondered what exactly she thought she was pulling over on him.

It was fully raining now, but he pretended it was still mist so he didn't have to do the polite thing and insist on immediately escorting her home. The umbrella remained folded on the trail.

On the pediatric ward on Monday, David's first patient was a seven-year-old German boy, escorted by a woman named Mrs. Levy from the Jewish Board of Deputies. The child looked up when David came behind the curtain, then went back to staring at his knees and loudly kicking his heels into the side of the exam table.

"He's been in my charge since he arrived in England three

days ago," Mrs. Levy said, frowning, "and I'm afraid I'm not doing a very good job of it. I'm rather out of practice. My own sons are all grown up."

"Do you speak German?" David asked her. "I'd like to ask him a few questions."

"I don't, but it's not necessary. Alexander does not speak at all. That's why I've brought him in. He understands English, I'm told. He's very well brought up and went to an American school in Germany. His parents are lawyers in Munich and paid a great deal to get him out. He came to us through a children's aid group there."

David looked at the child's chart. *Alexander Verb. Selective mutism.* He smiled at the boy, who was regarding him from the corner of his eye.

"Good morning, Alexander. I'm David. Do you understand me?"

A minuscule nod.

"Good lad. You're safe here. I'm not going to give you any jabs or anything like that."

David pointed to his own ears and then the boy's, then handed him his otoscope to look at it.

"His parents are still in Germany?"

"Yes," Mrs. Levy said carefully, "but apparently, just before he left Munich, his father was taken to some sort of work camp. I believe Alexander was there when they took him. I'm not sure if there was a formal arrest or . . ." She shook her head.

"Does the boy eat his food?"

"Hah! No, he'll never eat my cooking."

"Does he sleep well?"

"Not really," Mrs. Levy said. "He has night terrors. I let him keep a light on."

David turned back to the boy. "All right, Alexander, now that you've had a good look at my scope, could I peek in your ears?"

Alexander nodded and David examined his ears. "Ear canal and ear drum look perfect. And I don't get the sense that there's a cognitive impairment, although we could run some tests . . . Alexander, you've been missing your mama and papa?"

The boy nodded. Tears filled his eyes and David handed him a fresh handkerchief.

" 'Course you have. Mrs. Levy here, she seems like a good sort. Has she been kind to you?"

Small shrug.

David checked Alexander's reflexes and his eyes and his tonsils—all perfect. The boy was physically fine, but there was terror in his large brown eyes. David suddenly felt very uneasy, like he was being chased.

"We might assume this child is having a response to the acute trauma of being separated from his family," David said, trying to shake the cold hand of panic off his shoulder. "I'm going to refer you to neurology so that they can evaluate him, just in case. One of the neuro consultants, Dr. Spar, is a German Jew. He will be helpful. Did Alexander make the journey to England with any other children?"

"Six of them. They're all having a bad time of it, poor lambs."

"Well. Let's see what we can do."

"What the Jewish Board of Deputies is attempting is very important," Dr. Spar said, the following afternoon. He had grown up in Germany and still had an accent, but had been in England since attending medical school at Guy's. David did a rotation with him in his third year and the Jewish neurologist had become a sort of mentor to him. "But they have no idea what they are up against. The children who are fortunate enough to escape Germany will have seen their families beaten, arrested, even killed. My brother writes that friends are disappearing every week."

David nodded. He had heard these disappearance stories before, but he had not felt the truth of them until he looked into Alexander Verb's eyes. "Are your brother's friends accused of crimes?"

"Only the crime of being Jewish," Dr. Spar said. He took off his glasses and blew his nose into a white linen handkerchief, then put them both into his breast pocket. The resigned look on his face made David uneasy. "These are pillars of the community. Teachers, bankers, physicians—that sort of thing. Not criminals."

"The lady from the Board of Deputies said something about Alexander's father being sent to a work camp . . ."

Dr. Spar scowled. "An *arbeitslager*. This is a German euphemism. It is a prison. A death camp."

Another icy wave of fear washed over David and he scolded himself. It was counterproductive and selfish. He tried to focus on the question Dr. Montague said should always be top of mind when confronted with a patient's suffering: *What is my role here?* The victims of illness, Montague taught, did not need a physician's grief or pity. They needed remedies: flesh mended, X-rays interpreted, and tablets prescribed with respectful detachment. It was crucial that the physician did not absorb the pain. But, like many senior consultants, Dr. Montague appeared disinterested in the emotional aspect of disease. He seemed to take comfort in speaking about his patients like they were motor cars.

Dr. Spar had examined Alexander that morning and agreed with David's assessment that the child was physically well. He would speak when he felt safe again.

"But I want to help ensure that refugee children who make it to our hospital are looked after properly," David said. "Their injuries may not be visible, but, surely, they will be profound. Might you refer Alexander to psychiatry?"

Dr. Spar gave David a look that reminded him of his status. Lowly students did not tell consultants what to do.

"Psychiatry? David, the child is sound. He will speak to his guardian when he is ready. There may not be anything more we can do for him, at least not under the hospital's remit. In the coming months, there may be hundreds of Alexander Verbs. And they shall be the lucky ones. Scores of Jewish children will die in Germany, if Herr Hitler continues to have his way."

"I can't just accept that. We need to at least try to help them."

Dr. Spar smiled. "*Gut,*" he said. "I always suspected you were a *mensch*. But we may need to work outside the hospital. There is a woman in Essex named Anna Singer. My family knew her in Ulm, she's a childhood friend of my brother's. She founded a school for Jewish children in Germany and has moved it here. I assist in the infirmary occasionally. You might make a start there."

Chapter 7

28th October, 1936

Through an Oxford friend, Scargill had scheduled a pitch meeting with Ralph Cohn, a managing editor at *Time* who was visiting London to take meetings with the Fleet Street photo agencies.

"Henry Luce is preparing to launch what he calls a show-book of the world," Mr. Cohn explained, the light above the Central Press conference table glinting off his bald head. The rest of his body was hirsute—hairy hands, stubble on his cheeks, black caterpillar eyebrows over kind blue eyes. Kate liked his voice—chewy and direct, seemingly on the precipice of laughter. As he spoke about his work with *Time* magazine, he kept breaking into a proud grin.

For the meeting, Kate had her hair cropped just above her jawline, so she could pin the waves back like Norma Shearer's in *A Free Soul*. Her black blazer was from John Lewis and the most expensive piece of clothing she had ever purchased. Under it, a black-and-white cravat and a white blouse, tucked into balloon-pleated gray trousers. Planning this ensemble, Kate had wanted to appear older, but now feared she looked like an effeminate solicitor. Her blouse fastened so tightly around her neck that she had a sore throat. The windowless room and the men's cigarettes made it worse. She sipped her water compulsively, waiting for Scargill's cue.

Across the table, he nodded calmly, but Kate knew he was desperate to close the deal. A relationship with Time Inc. would officially put the Central Press on the world stage, Scargill's greatest ambition.

"This new publication will be a sister publication to *Time*," Mr. Cohn said excitedly, "christened *Life*, and will revolutionize journalism. *Life* will tell the news visually. As it stands today, none of the major American periodicals give the news principally and coherently in photographs. Those that have tried, have failed. We're going to change that. Time Inc. is putting the full heft of its considerable resources into ensuring this one can't fail . . ."

As he spoke, little thrills ran down Kate's spine. Mr. Cohn was describing what she had always wanted to do: to tell stories with her pictures, with the time and space to say something true.

When it was time for the Central Press pitch, Scargill started with his news photography presentation. Then it was Kate's turn, for the "lady's perspective" bit. The next three minutes would determine if she was ever given the opportunity to pitch a client again.

"Go ahead, Miss Grifferty," Mr. Cohn said with another mustache pinch and a smile. Kate stood.

"As you say, Mr. Cohn, *Life* shall tell its stories visually . . . ," she started, leaning onto her fingertips on the table. Then the speech she had practiced came to her: "In addition to the news, people are drawn to stories that make them feel connected to one another, that lift them out of their suffering. Not just actors and aristocrats, but ordinary men and women, making their way in the modern world. We can hold up a mirror for them. There's no going back to the way things were before the war, before the Depression. Once again, war threatens. Along with it, the suppression of culture by authoritarian forces . . ."

Kate glanced at Mr. Scargill. Almost imperceptibly, he shook his head. He wanted her to change tack. *Be pretty and SELL* was what he had said to her that morning. Kate cleared her throat, smiled brightly at Mr. Cohn, and walked along the conference table to turn over the large matte boards on four easels that stood along the length of the room.

"In this essay the Great Slump is envisioned as the first step toward a brighter future, a future where women can have careers and dream of a different station in life than their Victorian mothers and grandmothers . . ."

After her presentation, she stood back to give him a moment to look at the photographs.

"We think your women readers will be drawn to stories like this," she said, "and want their husbands to see them as well."

Mr. Cohn grinned. "You sure you're not American, Miss Grifferty?"

"I told you she was forward-thinking," said Mr. Scargill, a gleam in his eye.

"I think . . . ," Kate said, and Scargill cleared his throat. "*Central Press* think that women in Britain and America might have more in common with each other than not." She paused, as Scargill had instructed, to let that land. "We're curious about the world, we're eager for connection. What if there was a way to illustrate those similarities and make readers feel more connected in this new world? Take this young lady . . ." Kate, her nerves quiet now, pointed to one of the photo boards. "An ordinary shopgirl, living her life independently, with all the excitement and heartache that entails, presented in a sort of newsreel format." She pointed to another. "Helping a customer select a lipstick color, dressing for a date with a beau she hopes might turn into a husband, doing the weekly shop with a girlfriend. There is quiet desperation here, but also hope. These are really interesting moments, visually and emotionally. You can see beauty in the ordinary."

"Indeed," Mr. Cohn said. "Who took these photos?"

Kate looked at Mr. Scargill and he nodded. "I did," she said.

"They're great. And what do you propose in terms of Time's potential partnership with the Central Press?"

"If I could just step in here," Mr. Scargill said, standing up. "Thank you, Miss Grifferty, you may take your seat. In addition to providing our usual services, including right of first refusal on any of our photos, I propose a regular photo essay between your office and ours with a special eye to the things young people in Britain and America have in common. Sort of *Our American Cousin*, yet reversed."

"I like the concept," Mr. Cohn said. "As you can imagine, I'm swamped with photographs. Problem is, they never have any narrative thrust. Every week in New York, five thousand photos are offered up for sale. Fluff and murder scenes, just floating out there like . . ."

"Exclamation marks with no words," Kate said.

Mr. Cohn laughed. "Bingo! Meaningless garbage. My boss, Mr. Luce, is keen on groups of related pictures that talk to each other. Pictures that tell stories with an international reach. As you say, Miss Grifferty. There's a woman we're working with, Miss Bourke-White. She's a photojournalist, the first staff photographer Mr. Luce hired at *Fortune*. Confidentially, we're giving her the cover of *Life*'s inaugural issue. It's all about people, their capacity for finding joy and community in hard times. That's all I can say, for now. I'll send you a copy when the magazine comes out next month. In the meantime, let me run this whole English Cousins concept up the flagpole and see if anyone salutes. This study you have here, Miss Grifferty, I like where you're going. Keep it up and I'll be in touch, Mr. Scargill."

After the meeting, Scargill and Kate walked downstairs together. They were both exhilarated—him at the potential sale, her at the idea of a woman photographer's work on the cover of an international publication.

"You were brilliant," Scargill said. "Well done, my dear, well done . . ."

"You think he wants to partner with us?"

"I think he's considering it. We should endeavor to see him again before he returns to America." He made an *I'm looking at you* motion with two fingers. "Well done."

"How might I help?"

Mr. Scargill's eyes lit up. "There's a photo exhibition this evening," he said, "at the New Burlington Galleries in Mayfair. Cecil Beaton. All the photography people in London will be there. Cohn, too, I'd wager."

If Kate was overdressed for the pitch meeting, she was underdressed for a gala, but there was no time after work to go home and change. All she could do was take the pins out of her hair, loosen her waves with her fingers, and stash her blazer in a desk drawer. She also ducked into Boots and bought a tube of brown-red lipstick.

The Cecil Beaton opening—the vernissage, according to the pamphlet a gallery attendant handed Kate—was packed with scores of people, mostly in evening dress, dripping with jewels. The attendant was a woman about her age, early twenties, with a peroxide-blond permanent, an ankle-length silver sheath, and starlike diamonds in her ears. She leaned into Kate and lowered her chin, as if she was going to ask her for a sanitary napkin.

Instead, she said: "Are *you* Lindsay Scargill's new girlfriend?"

Kate laughed. "No. Of course not."

"I think you are," the girl said, smirking. "I think I've heard of you."

"Nope. I just work for him."

Kate brushed the woman off and looked around the packed room. At art college, the student exhibition openings were sparsely attended detours on the way to other parties.

It had always irritated Kate that no one took them seriously, but now she wished she was back in one of those classrooms, drinking whisky and water from a varnish-stained coffee mug.

Scargill was already at the party, shaking hands with some City types across the room. He waved to Kate and said something to the men, and they all turned to look at her. Kate pretended not to have seen them and headed for the champagne bar. She looked at Beaton's photographs on the way. The work was beautiful and remote—well-executed, semi-intellectual portraits of famous people in white rooms. Probably printed by a cadre of long-suffering assistants.

In the crush at the bar, a woman stepped backward into Kate and something hot bit into her belly—a cigarette, which burned a tiny round puncture into her rayon blouse. Kate cried out and the woman turned, looked her up and down, and huffed away.

"For God's sake . . . ," Kate muttered, rubbing at the burn on her belly. It wasn't deep or bleeding, but it stung. She wrapped her arm around her waist to cover the hole and looked about the room—its modern, asbestos ceiling tiles and expensively dressed, ugly people. These weren't the people who made art, they were the people who bought it.

The room was thick with the smell of freshly bathed bodies: soap, face powder, clouds of fine perfume. Kate gulped down a glass of champagne, then drifted like a jellyfish, watching it all, quietly taking pictures with the Leica. No one noticed her; she was an unthreatening set piece. Kate had always been that kind of pretty—a pleasant face in the background but not conspicuously beautiful. Just enough to get her foot in the door and move unobstructed through any crowd, any class.

As she was studying an interesting portrait of the artist Jean Cocteau, in front of a curtain of his own drawings, a voice came from behind: "Shutterbug, there you are."

Kate pasted on a smile as she turned. "Good evening, Mr. Scargill."

"What a bore this party turned out to be! Let's go and have a marvelous dinner."

"What about Mr. Cohn? Isn't he here?"

"He left," he said. "No bother, we've got him. Hang on, there's Roland Penrose by the door. Let's go and say hello and then I'm bundling you into a cab and taking you straight to the Ritz. No excuses, Shutterbug. Do you like oysters?"

"I think they're repulsive." Kate pretended to wave at someone in the crowd, to buy time to decide what to do. "I'd like to spend a bit more time here, if you don't mind. Wouldn't you like to stay? Let's look at some more pictures."

Mr. Scargill frowned. "No," he said. "I wouldn't like to stay. It's fantasy. It's all touched up. The people who sit for Cecil own *him*. Not remotely the sort of thing I'm interested in." He put his hand on Kate's shoulder and squeezed. "Look. Penrose is a painter, and he has impeccable connections. Exactly the sort of person you should know, Kate. We'll ask him to join us."

Scargill had never called her by her first name before, only Miss Grifferty or Shutterbug. Her mind was racing. She remembered David's face when, walking from the Troxy to the pub, she had mentioned that her boss had given her a Leica. *Keep an eye on him,* David had said. Kate felt her jaw set. Nothing would induce her to leave with Scargill now, not even the possibility of losing her job.

"You go," she said in her most reverential tone, but inching away from him. "I'll catch up with you in a few minutes."

Scargill gave her a wounded, pop-eyed look. "Promise?"

Kate nodded. "Mmm-hmm."

But as soon as he was across the room, safely engrossed in conversation with Roland Penrose, she slipped out the side door. She stepped straight into a deep puddle on the pavement and dirty water filled her shoes. Her stockings would be ruined, but she couldn't go back to that party and rinse them out in the lavatory sink. She felt like she was fleeing for her life. If she got into a cab with Mr. Scargill, if she dined with him at the Ritz, she would be a mistress-in-waiting, like the bottle blonde said. Not a serious person. Not herself.

Kate wished she could ring David and tell him about it, but she had no way of getting in touch with him. She just had to wait until he rang her. It was not the dynamic she'd hoped for. She hugged herself against the wind and sighed, hungry and alone. It would have been nice to just have someone to talk to.

Mayfair was not a part of London Kate knew well. Once she was at a safe distance from the gallery, Kate ducked into a café and sat at the counter and ordered a cheese sandwich and a cup of tea. Surreptitiously, she slipped off her shoes so they would dry a bit before the journey back to Hackney.

The café was clean but not the sort of place in which men bothered removing their hats. Kate was the only woman there. The fellow next to her perused the want ads and inhaled a bowl of dry-looking fruit crumble. He finished in a few bites, closed his paper, and left. Another man immediately slid into his seat. He ordered a slice of bread and HP Sauce, hot water, and a slice of lemon. A poor man, dejected and downtrodden. And yet he had the cheek to pointedly rub his arm against Kate's side as he poured free sugar into his water and squeezed his lemon.

The hell with them all, Kate thought, scooching away from the man. *The hell with Lindsay Scargill. I'll quit. . . .*

Then she reminded herself that there were about a dozen women in all of Fleet Street, and every one she knew was a typist or a cleaner.

Chapter 8

31st October, 1936

When David rang Kate from the hospital, he was surprised when she asked him to come to her house after work. He had not planned on ever meeting her father, but could not resist the opportunity to see her that very night. He promised to reach her by eight o'clock, but didn't make it out of the hospital until half past and arrived at the Griffertys' stately, terraced house sweaty and apologetic after a bolt through the Halloween festivities in Bethnal Green.

Kate opened the door wearing dungarees and an untucked silk blouse. She'd cut her hair short and it suited her. To David's surprise, she did not seem annoyed that he'd arrived almost an hour late. He tried to reflect her serenity, but found himself nervous as a rabbit.

She quickly kissed him hello, took his hand and led him down a corridor, deep into the house, until they reached the kitchen. Her father was nowhere to be seen. Other than a round wooden table and a few dust-covered copper cooking pots hanging from one wall, the kitchen looked unused. The table was spread with photo negatives in wax-paper sleeves. An empty brown cardboard suitcase sat open on the parquet floor. The room felt more like an office than a family kitchen. There was no bicycle leaning in the alcove by the garden door, no cooking smells, no baskets of apples or bread, no *tchotchkes* on the countertops.

David cleared his throat. "How was your day?" he asked, intentionally loud. If her father was somewhere listening, he didn't want to appear secretive.

"Fine, thanks." Kate opened a cupboard and pulled out a tin of McVitie's biscuits. There was only one left and she ate it herself. "Sorry, I really wanted that. Would you like a whisky?"

"That's all right. What are you working on?"

"Nothing important. Just doing a bit of archiving." Kate frowned at the pile of negatives on the table. In the electric yellow light, her hair was darker. It fell forward over her face as she nibbled the edge of her thumbnail. She looked distracted. "I sort of forgot you were coming."

David's stomach turned over with embarrassment. "I came too late. I'm sorry, I won't stay long. I'd hate to wake your father."

"My father's not in. He went to Ireland."

He grinned involuntarily. "I'm sorry to hear that. I was really looking forward to meeting him."

"Really? Why?"

"Just thought it would be nice," he said stupidly.

"It wouldn't be."

"Right, okay."

David wondered if Kate had changed her mind about him. He wondered if he should leave.

But then she smiled brightly and asked: "Would you like to see the rest of the house?"

"Yes! Yes, please."

"I'll give you the tour." Kate waved for him to follow her back to the hall and then into a dark drawing room. "We never use this front room. I think it's just how my mother left it . . ."

The room smelled dusty and stale. There was a sheet over

the couch and Kate made no motion to sit down. David stole a glance at himself in the oblong mirror over the fireplace, just to see if he looked as crazed as he felt. He didn't. He looked like a prospective estate agent, with his hands clasped behind his back and a vague smile.

Next Kate took him up the stairs. David did not allow himself to hope that she was taking him to her bedroom. It seemed outrageous to even think it.

She showed him a parlor, a library, and her father's rooms on the first floor, then led him up another flight of stairs to the top of the house, where there was a landing, a washroom, and two bedrooms. One of them was Kate's.

Through the open door, David observed her four-poster bed, piled with clothes and coats. The bedspread had an Asian-style pattern of white birds landing on water. His eager heart began to beat very fast. There was an empty chair by the door and an upholstered bench between the windows, but he didn't dare enter her room without being expressly invited. So, he stopped in the doorway and watched Kate hang all her weight on one of the windows to close it, and resisted the urge to reach for her narrow waist.

This room smelled like her, like metal and spring flowers. A framed postcard hung over her dresser—a picture of a woman who looked like she was about to leap off a skyscraper. There were unframed photographs pinned all over the walls and a painting of a redheaded young woman, maybe Kate or her mother, above the coal grate. A stack of books teetered on the bedside table. Hoping for something he could comment intelligently on, David leaned down to read their spines: *Rebecca* by Daphne du Maurier, a Mills & Boon romance called *How Could You, Jennifer!*, and several technical photography books.

David's parents didn't own books, other than a few prayer books, issued by the synagogue. They couldn't afford them and didn't care enough to go to the library. They did appreciate stories, they loved the Yiddish theatre, but there were only so many hours in the day. He'd seen his mother read the newspaper, but never a novel, nothing for pleasure.

Kate, pushing her clothes to the side and sitting on her bed, noticed him noticing her books. "Do you enjoy reading?" she asked, smiling sweetly. She gestured to the chair with her socked toe. "Do you want to sit?"

"I just finished *The Case-Book of Sherlock Holmes*. It's twelve really clever stories. I loved it." David paused. He was speaking too quickly, he wasn't thinking. He sat down. "Actually, I don't know why I lied about that. I read Sherlock Holmes the summer before medical school. I haven't read for pleasure in years."

There was a gramophone on Kate's dresser—he was on firmer ground there. But where were her records? Was she the sort of person who kept records in a tidy box, organized by date? David looked around the room for where she kept them. His fingers twitched. He wanted to touch all of her things, pull the postcards off her vanity mirror to see who sent them, read the first sentences of her books. All of his synapses seemed to be firing at once, making him forget how to sit like a normal person, how to lean his elbow casually on the back of a chair.

"What *do* you do for pleasure?" Kate asked, pinching her lower lip between her thumb and index finger. He felt her studying him. He wondered why she was so composed, and if she'd had men in her room before.

David cleared his throat. "I dunno. Music. The odd film . . ."

Still touching her mouth Kate narrowed her eyes. The light-gold flecks in them turned every switch in his body on. He just looked at her, enjoying the luxury of it.

"David . . ."

"Yes?"

"Have you been with a woman before?" Kate asked in a different, quieter tone. "For pleasure?"

This he was not expecting. His reflexive instinct was to say *no*. He didn't want to upset her or, worse, scare her off from whatever might be about to happen between them. But he would not lie to her.

"Yes," he said, embarrassed. "Not, like, loads of women. Just one."

To David's surprise, Kate's eyes lit up. "Really? Who is she?"

"A nurse at the hospital. I don't see her anymore. It wasn't serious."

"Not serious? You mean, like us?"

He hesitated. "No. Nothing like us. The way I feel about you is . . ." He wanted to say *terrifyingly serious*. "Very different."

Kate moved to stand in front of him. She lifted his face and brought her nose down to his. Then she kissed him, open-mouthed, expertly, and a current ran from her body into his. Something, maybe even everything, would happen tonight. The only thing that could stop it was this distant-but-persistent, guilt-ridden voice inside him. He did not want to take something from Kate she did not know she was giving.

"Have you, ah, been with a man before?" he asked gently.

"Not yet," she said.

Kate lovingly smoothed her thumbs across his cheekbones. They had a light chemical scent. David stood and slid his hands under the back of her jumper and her spine curved miraculously under his palms. He kissed her again and she dug her nails into his neck. The feeling of her body against his was like the piano section of *Rhapsody in Blue,* softness falling through softness.

At some point, she slipped off her blouse. Her brassiere was a sand-colored system of straps and pulleys that seemed superfluous for her small breasts. She wore a necklace, a small gold heart with a red stone. A tiny gold crucifix dangled from the bottom of the heart. If David wasn't already out of his head with desire, it would have alarmed him.

He told himself to calm down, that he saw women without clothes frequently. But those bodies were in various states of disrepair, they were ill, torn and trod upon, worked to death. The women in the Whitechapel clinic had fed battalions with their impressive, pendulous breasts. Kate's were small and factory new. They seemed to have their own gravity; how soft they were, like butterflies' wings, suspended by invisible silken threads. The pink of her nipples on her creamy skin was excruciatingly pretty. Exploring her, David's hands stopped at a small lesion on her belly.

"What's this?"

"A Bright Old Thing burnt me with a cigarette at a dreadful party in Mayfair."

"Mayfair? What posh circles you run in."

"I don't have circles. I'm happier here with you now."

Now Kate was unbuttoning David's shirt. When he lifted her around her waist to carry her to the bed, she started to laugh and he asked her why.

"I don't know," she said, weaving her fingers through his hair, a blush spreading across her collarbones and up her neck. "I'm just happy, I can't contain it. Don't be angry."

"Angry? I am the least angry I have ever been," he said, still holding her off the ground.

She said that was good and kissed his neck. They shifted onto the bed. Kate undid his belt, seized his hips. Heaven was her thighs around his waist, her fingers tracing the lines of his back, her voice breathing his name. David had a sense of falling right through Kate's body, through the bed and the library and the kitchen, deep into the earth. Then just as suddenly, she was with him again, part of him, as if she always had been and would be.

*   *   *

At half past one, David was asleep, his arm slung over Kate. When he began to breathe steadily and then twitched in the way only sleepers can, like he'd almost fallen out of a tree, Kate slipped out from under him. She paused and breathlessly studied him, admiring his dark eyelashes and broad, moonlit back, then crept downstairs for a wash and a cup of tea. She needed to be completely alone for a while, to collect herself.

Wrapped in nothing but her satin dressing gown, Kate felt ethereal, like a candle gliding down the stairs on the palm of a ghost. She put the kettle on in the kitchen and went to the bathroom and washed herself with a warm, wet towel and glycerin soap. Then she shook some violet talcum powder into the air above her and spun through it.

When the tea was brewed, Kate poured cream into her cup, not milk. She grilled herself a piece of toast, slathered it with butter and a teaspoon of sugar. She felt compelled to celebrate. She was a woman now, in full possession of herself, no slave to convention or doctrine. There was a gorgeous man upstairs, waiting for her. She grinned with pride as she pressed the tea bag into the side of the cup to squeeze out the last dark dregs. She knew she was meant to feel guilty about having sex without being married, but she didn't. It was sore between her legs and the moment itself had hurt but, somehow, she couldn't wait to do it again.

The only thing Kate had to fear was pregnancy, but clearly David knew what he was doing. He had told her when they needed to stop things, when it wasn't safe anymore. As he'd said, he wasn't a virgin but he didn't have any kids running around. They'd obviously taught him in medical school how and when to stop sex in order to prevent pregnancy. And what was medicine for if not to prevent that sort of tragedy befalling a woman? Next time, he promised, he'd have French letters.

Kate's father always kept a pipe and tobacco in a brass bowl in a kitchen cupboard. She had never smoked it before, but loved the way it smelled, like cherries dipped in chocolate. She pulled a chair up to the window, stretched out her long, smooth legs, and rested her heels on the sill. She had a bright view of the garden; the moon looked full. She packed the pipe with a thumb's-length of tobacco and lit it like her father did, shook her hair out luxuriantly, and puffed at the pipe. The pipe didn't taste as good as it smelled, so she propped it on its bowl and ate her toast while watching the smoke drift to the ceiling like incense.

Sitting there in the half-darkness, Kate could feel her life moving past, swift as water. She had always dreamt of being this sort of woman—a free, wanton woman. Now it had happened and she felt triumphant. She slowly sipped her creamy tea in the moonlight, savoring it, feeling everything: her changed body, the quiet house and cold midnight air, the soft violet scent on her skin mixed with rich pipe smoke, her father's absence, David's presence, and her own dreams.

In the morning when David woke, Kate was spread out under the sheet like a starfish, leaving just a sliver of space for him on the edge. He watched the light on the wall change from gray to blue to yellow and incredulously reminded himself of last night's events.

When he lifted himself up and turned to her, she folded her arms under her head. David could tell she was awake now, even though her eyes were closed. She smiled and sighed. He took her cross-heart pendant between his fingers and ran it back and forth along its chain, studying Kate's profile and the constellation of freckles connecting her eyelid to her cheekbone to the corner of her mouth. He searched her face for a mark, a scar, a memory—something that would be just his, something no other man would ever notice. How sweet and vulnerable she looked, pretending to be asleep. David felt like a cad.

"Kate?"

"Good morning."

"I feel really bad about something."

She opened her eyes then, looking alarmed, as if she had not invited him into her bed. "What?"

"You know I have to marry a Jewish person?"

She groaned and rolled away, snatching the blankets off him and taking them with her. "I didn't expect you to propose this morning," she said, "if that's what you were thinking. I can look after myself."

"I know you can," he said to the back of her head, feeling foolish. "I didn't mean to imply you're desperate to marry me or something."

"Why'd you have to bring it up then?"

"Because I feel guilty for misleading you. I don't want you to have . . ." *Hope? Principles?* "Expectations."

"Do you have another girl or something?"

"No. There's no one else. I don't want anybody else."

"Then you've not misled me," Kate said, sitting up. She pressed her middle finger into the hollow of her clavicle and rubbed at it, perhaps nervously. "I told you, I'm not interested in being a wife. Don't be a stick. Now, do you think you could manage me a cuppa, downstairs, while I get dressed?"

Delighted at an opportunity to redeem himself, David pulled on his trousers and dashed down to the kitchen. When he returned with tea for both of them, Kate had made the bed with fresh sheets and was wearing a satin robe with purple pinstripes. She'd combed her hair back with a thin plastic headband and sat on the bench between the windows, one bare foot massaging the other, watching him.

"Careful," he said. "The cup is quite hot."

"Cheers." She smiled and he felt forgiven. But then: "Who

was that girl you were with? The one you mentioned last night."

He looked sideways at her, worried he had set a trap for himself and walked into it. "Why?"

"I'm just curious. I love a bit of gossip. What was she like?"

"Do you really want to know?"

"Please." She leaned against the wall and blew on her tea. "Paint me a picture."

"Okay. Her name was Connie. Connie Bell."

"What did she look like? Was she beautiful?"

"No."

"Good."

"But she had a pinup figure and this great, sandpaper laugh."

"Did you love her?"

"I liked her. Most important to me, at the time, was she liked me. She pursued me. I think it a bit of an annual tradition for her, to choose a medical student."

"Golly. A vixen. I like her. Was *she* Jewish?"

David felt his face redden. "No. But it didn't matter. The whole thing was a big nothing."

"You broke her heart?"

"No. It just petered out after a few months. A new class came in. Connie moved on, eventually got a job somewhere else. I think she's at Thomas's now." He longed to change the subject. "What about you?"

He wanted to ask her if she'd ever been in love, but the question stuck in his throat. Instead, he asked: "Have you had many boyfriends? I bet you're fighting them off with a stick."

Kate laughed. "No. A few kisses here and there. Nothing remotely exciting. And I want excitement. Passion. Torrid love affairs. Like Connie. I wish I had her courage."

"Be yourself," he said. "You're perfect." He drank some of his tea and felt more awake. He wanted Kate again. "I was looking at your pictures this morning, while you were asleep." He pointed to a photo taped on the wall behind her bed—a close-in shot of two children playing on the beach under Tower Bridge. "I like that one. They're cute. Are they your cousins or something?"

"No, they're strangers. I've never met any of my cousins. I'm sure Ireland is crawling with them though."

David considered this. He knew his first and second cousins. The Rabatkins and the Bakers, his mother's family, kept track of each other. He sat on the floor in front of Kate and leaned against the bottom of the bed. "How do you decide who or what to photograph?"

"I don't know," she said, turning away from him, gazing out the window over Victoria Park. "What happens is . . . I become very curious about something. I have these obsessions, people or places or feelings I want so badly it hurts. It feels like missing someone really important. It used to make me miserable."

"And now?"

"Now my camera lets me possess things, so I don't long for them anymore. They feel like they're mine."

David liked listening to her speak. It was fun watching her face vacillate between pleasant and goddesslike. He waited for her to ask him something about himself but she did not. She ducked under the bed and pulled out a box full of camera parts and film. Maybe she wanted to take his portrait, to possess *him*. David liked the idea of this.

"How long did you say your father would be away?" he asked, watching Kate's long, bare legs fold under her as she loaded a small camera with film.

She shrugged. "A couple of weeks. Look up at the window, would you? The light's good. Don't look at me."

He obeyed and she took several photos of him, near to his face. The wind rattled the windows and whistled through the cracks in the frames. Winter was creeping in. The trees were shedding their leaves, like yellow confetti drifting through the bare branches.

"So," he asked, "your father won't be home until the middle of November?"

"Maybe. He never tells me exactly when he's coming back. Why are you so keen to know?"

He decided not to tell her that he planned to clear his schedule as much as possible, on the chance he might make it back into her bed. "No reason," he said, shrugging. "I'd just like to see you again."

"Why can't you see me when my father is in town?"

"I'll see you whenever you'll see me," he said, tugging the cord on her dressing gown, and she put down her camera.

As David left through Kate's garden gate that afternoon, he looked up at what he now knew was her bedroom window. She was standing there, watching him. She kissed both of her hands and reached out to him and he understood why people—in spite of all their obligations and tragedies—smiled to themselves on the Tube.

Chapter 9

5th November, 1936

Victoria Park glowed orange on Bonfire Night. Men in red scarves and black-and-white striped shirts performed a pantomime show with little boxes of gunpowder that shot out stars and flashes of light in every color. They brandished torches, pretending to be vigilantes of a bygone age.

A thirty-foot bonfire of wood pallets and branches blazed in the middle of the park. Excited by the light and heat, the crowd whooped and shouted like wild beasts around a kill. Children kicked Guy Fawkes dummies and hoisted banging Catherine wheels and skittered around the smaller bonfires burning along the perimeter of the park. The smell of sulfuric acid and charred wood filled the air and clouds of smoke rolled down the paths like fog.

Kate and David stood together by the Gothic fountain, their hands in each other's pockets. His heart beat against her cheek and the fireworks dazzled her eyes. It had been only a month since they'd met, five days since they'd made love, but she felt as changed as water into ice, oil into fire.

Because Kate had spent her entire life being unwanted, it felt intrinsic to her. It wasn't that her father didn't want another daughter; it was that Kate herself was objectionable. Her sister, Orla, had seemed to love her but then abandoned her with barely a backward glance. The nuns at school had regarded Kate as a headstrong, unfocused student and spiritual lost cause. They were happy to see the back of her at sixteen. She supposed Scargill wanted her at the Central Press, but it was increasingly obvious that any young woman would do.

The idea that someone could adore Kate, could want her as close to him as possible, was revelatory. She had never realized how much she needed it, or how much pleasure it would give her. In David's arms, she felt like a cat on a sunny patch of grass.

Kate had brought her Leica to the bonfire, but only took a few pictures. She was afraid of missing something in the seconds it took to set up a shot. For once, she didn't want the distance the camera afforded her.

David had given her access to a feeling she had not known existed, a new sense that made the mundane magic. She didn't know what the feeling was, but it was marvelous. She didn't even mind when a costumed pirate walked by her and David, belched, and flicked his cigarette toward their shoes. They just laughed. A police siren wailed and a tram squealed in the distance, full of unlucky people who were not them.

It was bitterly cold. Kate and David walked closer to the fire and she held her mittened hands up toward it, opened and closed her fists, caressed the hot air. The collar of David's black winter coat was turned up, making him look cozy, a safe harbor she wanted to dive into. She noticed that his eyes were very tired. He seemed weary, older than his years, and Kate wanted to look after him. She wanted to give him pleasure and ask nothing of him. She wanted to give him everything. David could ask her to strip naked and jump into the bonfire with him, and she would do it.

In her room that night, his fingers went to her hair, tilting her head to the angle where he could kiss her most deeply.

She felt a loosening between her hips like a bow being untied. David tore at her garters and, keeping one hand on his neck, she stepped out of her stockings. The tendons above his collar bone were thick and she lightly squeezed his neck as she kissed a line up from the top of his skivvies, up his firm belly to the patch of dark hair between his nipples. She tongued the rough skin of his neck. He tasted like he'd been swimming in the ocean, both salty and clean. His torso straightened, and he made a sound that was more vibration than noise. Kate stepped away from him and shrugged off her blouse, then her bra. David seemed mesmerized as he watched her unzip the back of her skirt and shimmy first out of it and then her bloomers. His chest was rigid; he was holding his breath.

Kate stood in front of him, naked, and waited. She wanted him to know she was a gift—just for him, just to give him joy. That she was someone who could do that.

The next morning, she woke in the blue-black darkness. Before Kate remembered David was beside her, she felt him in her chest—her heart as heavy and thick as a sponge plucked from a bucket of water. She reached for him, needing his body closer, brought his face to hers, but it was not enough.

Neither of them fully awake, he slid on top of her, where their bodies could continue the conversation they needed to have with one other—long-lost friends, sharing secrets that had been burning holes in their hearts for years.

The sun came up eventually, breaking the spell. Work waited for them both. As they left the house, David asked when he could see Kate again, and his face clearly fell when she told him her father would be returning to London that evening.

"I thought you said he'd be away longer," he said glumly.

"Well, we could go to the pictures?" Kate offered. "Tonight?"

"I can't see you tonight," David said, shaking his head. "I'm at the hospital." He took a step back and cold air filled the space between them. "And every night until Tuesday."

"I understand," Kate said, fighting a pathetic feeling of anguish. "You only want to see me when there's an empty house at our disposal."

"Not at all." The hurt expression on his face jarred her. "That's not fair."

"It's all right," she said, trying to smile. "You warned me. No getting *mixed up serious*." She rebelted her trench coat and looked toward the bus, which was sidling up to the stop at the corner. "I have to go now."

"Wait!" David grabbed her hand. "What's your favorite place in London?"

"The National Portrait Gallery."

"Good," he said. "Take me there. How's Tuesday, half past four?"

The relief that washed over Kate was alarming. "Fine," she said, as breezily as she could muster. "Now let me go." She squeezed his hand and ran toward the bus.

After she finished her work at the Central Press that afternoon, Kate printed her father's portraits for his club. She was in a wonderful mood. She'd chosen three pictures to present to him: one of him standing on the barge, one close-up in profile, and one leaning against the railway bridge. On the barge photo, she added a filter to bring up the contrast for dramatic effect.

In the darkroom, Gordon came up behind her and watched the final image appear in the developer. Even she had to admit that her father was ruggedly handsome. Those fussy co-ordinated tweeds actually looked elegant—Frank Grifferty was a gentleman on the Thames, just as he had always aspired to be.

Gordon whistled. "Nifty shot," he said. "Who's the man?"

"My father," she said proudly.

"I explained what I wanted," her father complained that night in their kitchen. He had just arrived from Kings Cross and she could not wait to show him the photos. As soon as he looked at them, he pushed them away. "Just a straight portrait, I told you."

"But these *are* portraits. I think they're rather good. My colleague thought so, too."

He rolled his eyes. "You were meant to have been doing a bookkeeping course at that college, you know. I'd never have paid for it if I'd known you'd switched to painting and all that. We're not that sort of people."

Kate gritted her teeth. In that moment, she really hated her father. She could not remember him once praising her work. Sometimes he seemed intent on making her feel worthless, but she wouldn't let him.

"Photography is a trade," she snapped. "And these portraits are better than you asked for. You looked like Bob Cratchit, huddled over your desk. I've managed to make you appear noble."

He looked at the pictures again. "This is noble? It doesn't even look like me."

"Why did you even ask me to do it? Why do you hate me so much?"

Wild with hurt, Kate wanted her father to finally admit it, to say the thing that had always floated between them: he resented her for existing in place of her mother. She'd been sure of it since she was five years old and overheard him trying to convince Orla's new husband, Edward, to take Kate with them to Brighton, to raise her as their daughter so that Frank *could wash his hands of the whole tragic business.* That was just how he'd said it, as if Kate was an unfortunate kitten he longed to drown in the river but couldn't quite bring himself to tie the top of the bag.

Her eyes stung thinking about it, but he had already turned his back on her.

"Don't fuss," her father said flatly, putting the ham sandwich he'd made for himself onto a plate, balancing it on a mug of tea, and mounting the stairs toward his rooms. "I won't row with you, Kathleen. I'm knackered."

Foolishly, she'd allow herself to hope they could connect over work, the one thing that mattered to him. She was wrong. This was how her father was, how he would always be. He would leave food out for Kate, refrain from kicking her, allow her to shelter under his roof. Nothing more.

"I usually get paid for my photography, you know," she said, trying to sound strong. She was weary at the realization that she still hoped he'd stop and turn and say: *Well done, my Kathleen.*

"Take a pound out of the drawer then," he called over his shoulder. "Good night."

Chapter 10

10th November, 1936

There was a short queue in the lobby of the NPG. Kate stood next to David, his body distant under his clothes. She was relieved to see him, to feel his happiness at being with her. A sudden flash of memory—him beneath her, on her bedroom floor—made it difficult for her to make eye contact with the friendly clerk who welcomed them at the front desk.

"It is recommended to proceed at once upstairs," said the clerk, "and commence with Room One at the far end of the top floor."

Kate waved off the man's instructions. "The royals and their mistresses can wait," she said to David, taking his hand. "I'm going to show you *my* heroes."

She led him up the marble stairs to the first floor, to Room Seventeen, the great British artists—Morland, Opie, Flaxman, Turner, Rossetti, Ford Madox Brown. In many cases, the portraits were by the artists themselves. In the Screen Room were kept the female portraits—Romney's Lady Hamilton, Harriet Martineau, George Eliot. Kate paused to say a silent hello to the painting of Ann Mary Newton clutching her portfolio, daring someone to take it from her.

She was excited to hear what David thought about the paintings. His intelligence made her feel safe, like there was no place her mind could go where he could not join her. She could tell that he wanted to learn—not just about Kate, but about everything—and curiosity was something she respected.

Kate visited every painting, her old friends. To her surprise, David hung back, following her at a slight distance. There were only a few other people in the galleries, making the usual museum sounds: footsteps, whispers, walking sticks, bashful sneezes.

"You're quiet today," Kate said to David, wondering if he was self-conscious around her, too. The thought made her feel powerful.

"I don't want to say something daft," he said, "and have you think I'm thick. Art isn't my area."

"Don't be silly!" She pulled him over to George Frederic Watts's portrait of Cameron. "Come . . . just *look*. You don't even have to say anything, if you don't want to. This is Julia Margaret Cameron, one of the most famous Victorian photographers. Her portraits are beautiful. Biblical, like the Garden of Eden. Women and children, many of them hers. She's lovely, isn't she?"

David stood in front of the painting, his hands behind his back. The lithe ease with which he moved filled Kate with pride, almost like he belonged to her. She wondered if he recognized Watts's skill, the way he depicted the genius behind Cameron's huge golden-brown eyes, the way they seemed to be taking everything in.

"It's interesting," he said carefully. "How she's seeing something we can't . . ." His voice trailed off. "At first glance, I thought it was morose, but it's not that, is it? It's like her body is there, but she's miles away, in a better world."

"Exactly," she said. "There's melancholy there, but it's not something to be pitied. Watts is a wizard. There's a fine series by him in the East Wing. I love his portrait of Tennyson. He imbues the eyes with so much feeling. A complete genius. I would kill for that sort of talent. I couldn't paint my way out of a paper bag."

"Hmm . . . I don't believe that."

"It's true." Kate shook her head. "I'm not that sort of artist. I'm a darkroom gnome."

"Why do you run yourself down like that? I've seen your photographs. You're incredibly talented. Julia Cameron was an artist, wasn't she? She didn't paint."

"Ah, but I'm no Julia Margaret Cameron."

"How do you know?"

"I just do. Come along, there's more to see . . ."

In the next gallery, David selected as his favorite Brooks's painting of the Old Masters Exhibition in 1888.

"There's got to be at least sixty tiny little portraits in here," he said, examining each face. "Fascinating."

Kate stood next to David, considering him, not the Brooks. "What do you think?"

"I think it's incredible. But I don't know anything about how art works."

"That's like saying you can't fall in love because you don't know how love works. The feeling's the thing, not necessarily knowing the mechanics of something."

She was in the next gallery before she realized David was still standing in front of the Brooks, staring after her.

"Something else you wanted to see before moving on?"

He shook his head. "You just have a way of saying things, Kate. It knocks me out."

Fleet Street was built above a former sewer—fitting for the journalistic center of London, Kate thought. It was home to all the great newspapers and hordes of ambitious toilers like herself. The steam through the grates beneath their feet mixed with light rain, and her path to the office was blocked by people studying the map of Spain in the window of the *Express* building. Germany had just announced that it would no lon-

ger observe the Treaty of Versailles, and shown they meant it
by bombing Spain. A board in front of the empty newsstand
quoted First Lord of the Admiralty Winston Churchill's recent address to Parliament: *"The era of procrastination, of
half measures, of soothing and baffling expedients, of delays,
is coming to a close. In its place, we are entering a period of
consequences."*

A newsboy, emerging from the *Express* with fresh papers,
was mobbed. Kate gave him a farthing and with a twisting
stomach read about the new-forged alliance between Hitler
and Mussolini. Thinking of David and how this would land
on him, her eyes darted from paragraph to paragraph looking for but not finding some hopeful news. Knowing a Jewish person, adoring him, made the ever-worsening headlines
from the Continent even more disturbing than they were before. Before David, she had been able to keep a distance, to
read the news from the corner of her eye.

Gordon came up the street and stood next to her while she
read, holding his umbrella over both of their heads.

"What is the matter with you lately?" he asked, nudging
Kate in her side. "You're so distracted."

"Yeah. The world is falling apart."

"It's not that. You're *happy.* You've been going about like
Donald Duck when he sees a girl duck and hearts fly out of
his eyes. It's not because of . . ." Gordon cringed.

"What?"

"Scargill? Please, say it isn't."

"Hell, Gordy. No. Why would you think that?"

"Only you two seem proper cozy lately."

"I am not *cozy* with Lindsay Scargill," Kate said, turning
on her heels and going into the office.

"Just be careful!" Gordon followed her. "He has his eye on
you. You shoot better in low light than any cameraman out
there, Grifferty, you don't need him to . . ."

She spun around. "I have a boyfriend, if you must know. If

I'm happy, it's because of him, not Scargill. You've met him actually. The man who returned the camera part."

"The Jewish chappie?"

"How on earth can you know he's Jewish?"

"I can spot a Jew from a mile away," Gordon said, following Kate down the stairs toward the darkrooms. "Same with public school boys, Americans, actors, alcoholics, queers . . . I'm very intuitive. So, tell me all about him."

"I'm not sure I want to now." Kate opened the cupboard under the darkroom sink and straightened the bottles of developer. "You're in a revolting little mood this morning, Gordy."

"Go on! I love a bit of romance."

"He's a medical student."

"Oooh la la. I had a Jewish chum at school. Lovely boy. But, you know, eventually they do close ranks . . . Have you met the family and all?"

"I've met his brother."

"That's a good sign. What about the mother?"

"Not yet." Kate tossed an empty bottle of hypo into the bin.

"She won't be keen on you," he said. "They only marry their own kind. Mum's parents were the same way. They disowned her for not marrying a Hindu. Dad's staunch C of E parents weren't keen on her, either."

"Lucky I don't want to get married."

"How modern! Neither do I."

She went to the galley kitchen, to shake off Gordon and make a cup of tea on the stove the photo engravers used to heat their chemicals. Unfortunately, Mr. Scargill was already there, like a spider king on his web. His eyes lit up when he spotted Kate.

"Good morning, Shutterbug," he said. "There's no more sugar or milk."

"That's all right. I'll drink it black."

"My sort of girl," he said, nodding approvingly. "No frills."

"Actually, I prefer milk," Kate said. She filled the kettle. The way he was looking at her made her feel undressed and somehow ashamed. She reached up and touched her hat—black felt, saucer shaped, with a small grosgrain bow. Her favorite, but with Scargill gawping at her she wondered if it was overly girlish, even flirtatious. She tried to ignore him, tapping her fingernails on the iron rim of the gas range, waiting for the water to boil.

"Did I mention I've gone vegetarian?" Scargill asked, leaning against the counter beside her. "Perhaps you've noticed, I've lost a stone over the last month." She glanced at him and he sucked in his belly and smoothed the front of his button-down shirt against it. "See? I'm not such a porker anymore."

Kate shifted to put the boiling water between her and him and dropped a bag of PG Tips in a cup. Gordon popped his head around the kitchen door.

"Good morning, Mr. Scargill," he chirped, winking at Kate. "Are you making us a tea, Grifferty?"

She resented them both—Scargill for trying to entice her and Gordon for thinking it possible.

"The best thing," Mr. Scargill went on, ignoring Gordon's entrance, "to come out of this economic slump are these wonderful new ways of eating. It's a bit of a headache, me being vegetarian now, but well worth it. I went through so much trouble convincing my cook to serve more veg, you cannot fathom it. She loves to spoil me."

Why won't Scargill just acknowledge Gordon and stop staring? He was making it seem as if Gordon was right, like Scargill and Kate had some sort of special friendship.

"Last night, she made me an asparagus omelet and it was really delicious. You would be surprised, Shutterbug."

"I cook for my father sometimes," Kate said. "Have I told you he used to work on the docks? He's a big fella. Quite an appetite." She poured the steaming water over her tea and hastened from the room. "The darkroom's calling me. I'll see you gentlemen later."

Chapter 11

30th November, 1936

The train journey from Liverpool Station to Essex was only half an hour. The morning rush had just ended and the commuters had left behind their crumbs and their sleepy, early morning smells. The tea trolley rattled by, pushed by a bedraggled waitress.

David looked elegant, his dark hair neatly combed, his black suit pressed. Kate's affection for him felt like an extra person in their compartment. He stood over her, studied the train schedule, took his jacket off, and folded it over an empty seat. When he caught her looking at him, she busied herself loading her camera.

"I'm so pleased you're coming to see Grant Court," David said. "I've cleared it with the headmistress. It's not a normal school, more of an emergency association. And the more people that know about the work they're doing, the better. They're desperate for funds."

When David told her about the refugee children last week, Kate knew it was a story. This was her chance to actually shoot the human effects of the German anti-Jewish laws, which were increasingly targeting children—banning them from schools, swimming pools, and recreational activities.

British papers were able to write about the mistreatment of Jews, but photographs were scarce.

Kate checked her lipstick and smoothed her hair in the window. She wanted to look professional for the children and their teachers. Infinite rows of houses ran behind her reflection: council estates, a woman hanging the wash in her garden, a man in a vest picking his feet on his windowsill. As the train progressed east, the condition of the buildings became worse and then better. They went across a river and into open plains, past woodlands and marshes. Then there were newer council estates, commuter towns, and little whitewashed clusters in clearings, all the way to Braintree Station.

The school, Grant Court, was housed in a sprawling seventeenth-century estate with timber gables. The grounds were wild, with long yellow grasses and overgrown privet hedges and trees. There was a chicken coop and a rabbit hut, half covered by a canvas tarpaulin. An enormous fir tree in the middle of the yard functioned as a house for a group of children playing Mummies and Daddies.

The students ranged from about six to fourteen years old. They huddled together in groups, warmly dressed in winter coats and tam o'shanters. A girl with Shirley Temple curls cradled a baby doll, mindlessly pressing her lips to its bald plastic head. When she noticed Kate taking her picture, the girl smiled, showing off two missing front teeth. Kate grinned back.

As David and Kate walked up the drive, an older man appeared in the doorway to welcome them. David seemed surprised to see him. The man walked energetically toward them but, up close, Kate saw he was quite elderly. His eyes were intelligent and sad, with violet circles beneath them.

David introduced the man as his mentor, Dr. Albert Spar, and Kate extended her hand.

"It's a pleasure, Dr. Spar."

"This is Miss Grifferty," David explained, plucking at his

own shirt collar. "She is a journalist I invited to come have a look at the good work you're doing here. I hope that's all right. She's with a news agency, the Central Press. Could she take some pictures of the school?"

"Certainly!" Dr. Spar said. "Thank you for being interested in our work, Miss Grifferty."

Inside the lobby, two teenage girls shared a wooden bench, reading from the same paperback. They looked up and smiled shyly at Kate, and spoke to each other in German. They pointed to her wide-legged trousers and smiled approvingly. She wished she spoke their language so she could tell them she liked their frocks, too.

The headmistress, Miss Singer, came down the main stairs to greet David and Kate. She said hello in a thicker version of Dr. Spar's accent.

"*Sehr aufmerksam,*" she said, taking Kate's hand and smiling warmly. "How kind of you to come. How marvelous that you are here to take pictures for the newspaper."

Dr. Spar excused himself, he was wanted in the infirmary, and Miss Singer took David and Kate for a tour. The smell of the halls—chalk dust and dinner rolls and floor cleaner—took Kate back to convent school. That scent was part of her—the part that was still a stick-legged, bewildered, motherless child. Climbing the grand staircase in gentle Miss Singer's school, so many years later, Kate half expected a nun to sweep around the corner and smack her for dawdling.

"Since Hitler came to power in 1933," Miss Singer was explaining, "life has become impossible for Jews in Germany. They are no longer citizens. They cannot go to school or leave their houses without fear of attack. Most of our students are here because they have been expelled from school for being Jewish and their parents understand that they are not safe."

They paused outside the open door of a classroom and Miss Singer put a finger to her lips.

"We have classroom lessons and kinesthetics outdoors,"

she whispered. "The newer students have had a bit of trouble joining in. The situation in Germany is getting worse. They are distracted by worries about their families."

Kate shuddered at the thought of having a loving family and then having it ripped away. She let David and Miss Singer walk ahead and stood to the side of the classroom door, her back to the wall, listening. In melodious, accented English, a teacher instructed her students how to germinate a sprout for a potato plant in a paper cup. Kate peeked into the classroom. Twenty-five children, missed by fifty parents and countless siblings and grandparents. Their open faces, their eagerness to learn about a world that had betrayed them, made her want to weep.

Kate's gaze rested on a little boy with curious hazel eyes and a cap of unruly auburn hair the same shade as her own. She felt a spark of recognition, mixed up with the tenderness she'd been carrying around in her chest for the past several weeks. She realized that the yearning she had been feeling was not just for David; it was for the hope he had stirred in her that there were good people in the world.

After a few minutes, she rejoined David and Miss Singer in the girls' dormitory. It was spacious, with eight large windows all along one wall and twenty beds. A timetable hung on the wall: three hours a day spent learning English, then French, gymnastics, and geography. Every afternoon, an hour was set aside for games.

David and Miss Singer were speaking with a plump little girl, about ten years old, sitting on her bed. The girl's starched white blouse was embroidered with a rainbow of flowers. It had a Peter Pan collar and pearly buttons down the front. Peeking out from beneath her bed were two pairs of shoes in red and gray shoe covers. A handmade black, yellow, and red scarf was draped over the metal bed frame.

Miss Singer was talking between the girl and David, switching from German to English. The child looked so bewildered, so alone, that it hurt to look at her. Kate smiled gently at her.

"Freya is from Breslau," Miss Singer explained to Kate. "A Nazi Party stronghold. This spring, her teacher called to say she was no longer welcome in school. She finished out the term at a Jewish day school, but her parents realized it was best to leave Germany. Unfortunately, because her father was part of the Polish quota, it would have taken a very long time for him to be granted permission to leave Germany. So, they've had to split up their family. Her father manages . . . managed a glass factory. Her parents sent her here after her older brother was attacked by a neighbor, who kicked down the door and beat him when the parents were not at home. And . . ." She sighed deeply and lowered her voice: "I had a call last week. It seems Freya's father was arrested out of his bed by the Gestapo and shot in the head . . ."

Kate gasped. "What!"

"The family found him in the morning, in a yard behind the house. The police didn't even bother to hide his body." Miss Singer cast a fretful glance at Freya, who was innocently watching the adults' faces, trying to guess what they were saying. "Her mother does not want her to know. Poor child has been waiting for a letter from her papa . . ."

"Papa?" Freya asked, her eyes brightening, and Miss Singer replied to her in German: "*Ein anderer papa.*"

David was taking all this in with stoic nods of his head; none of it seemed to surprise him. Kate felt sick; she burned with a kind of shame she'd never felt before. Why did she deserve to have a happy, peaceful life, if Freya did not?

She made herself reload her camera and take some photos of the dormitory. Two portraits were taped on the wall behind Freya: a curly haired baby pulling up on a chair and a middle-aged couple with glasses. On her bedside table: a box of *Hansaplast elastisch*, a gold chain with a six-pointed Jewish star pendant, a German-English dictionary, a children's card game with photos of German sights, and a two-volume copy of *Middlemarch*. Freya's parents' love for her was palpable; the child was so obviously cared for, sent to England with everything they could guess she might need.

"Poor *liebling* is wracked with homesickness." Miss Singer sighed. "She misses her parents, her brothers and sisters left behind. I cannot give her any hope, nor can I take it from her."

Kate had thought she understood the terrible injustices the Germans were committing: passing laws that made it difficult for Jews to work and attend school, making frivolous arrests, seizing property. But this was more than injustice; Freya's father had been executed.

Kate had expected to see lonely children. That was the point of her visit: to not close her eyes to them, to help tell their stories. Yet she hadn't realized how afraid it would make her feel for David, and for the world.

She remembered Mosley's Blackshirts that day in Whitechapel—the cool, self-assured hatred in their eyes. Why had she assumed that there were so many miles between that hatred and murder?

A seed of what was happening to these German Jewish children and their families was already germinating in English soil.

Kate could set Freya's tragedy aside and scurry back to Fleet Street and the comfortable distance of the darkroom. There were different dangers to walking through David's world, and she was only now beginning to understand how little she knew of it.

"There's a fascinating story here," Kate said later in Grant Court's school canteen, feeling buzzy and purposeful. "An international story people need to know about. Child refugees in Britain, fleeing Nazi tyranny. I'm going to ask Mr. Scargill if we can pitch this to Time Inc. Their new photo magazine seems to have a humanitarian bent. Mr. Cohn, the editor I met with, sent me the first issue. The cover story is about life in a small American town, changed by the construction of a massive dam."

David nodded, sipped his tea, loosened his tie. He was hardly listening. All morning, he had seemed undaunted, but now he was visibly fatigued. She wondered if the weight of Freya and her classmates' story had just hit him, or if he'd been hiding his emotions for the children's sake.

"Do you think people will mind about a few dozen Jewish children?" he asked, skeptical. "I mean . . . I've never seen a story like that, outside the *Jewish Chronicle.*"

"That is because Germany will censor anything that brings attention to the atrocities they are committing," Dr. Spar said, appearing in the doorway to the canteen. "And the British press are encouraged to turn a blind eye. All while Hitler is conscripting German soldiers, building an air force, passing anti-Jewish legislation. There's going to be another war. And where will that leave these children? They may never go home again."

"A photo essay in a popular magazine could increase diplomatic pressure on Britain," Kate said, hoping she was not overpromising. The truth was she had no idea if Scargill, let alone *Life,* would agree to her idea. "I think photographs hit people differently, especially when children are involved. I can use the shots I took today as a study . . ."

While explaining her idea to Dr. Spar, Kate made a flourish with her hand which came close to David's arm. He visibly flinched, covered the spot she had almost touched and rubbed it, as if she'd been holding a lit match. He obviously did not want her to touch him in front of his mentor. It was understandable, but Kate felt a prickle of insecurity.

The men started to talk about a case at the hospital and Kate excused herself to go thank Miss Singer. When she returned to the kitchen, Dr. Spar had gone.

*   *   *

A few days later, Simon gave David and Kate tickets to see Myriam in the ballet at Clerkenwell.

The curtains opened on a line of guards holding ten-foot torches with red and orange paper flames fluttering at the tops. A dozen ballerinas streamed onto the stage, six from each direction, and Kate felt her own spine lengthen. It was hypnotic, the most direct art she had ever experienced. There was no camera, no canvas, no mechanical process for the dancers to hide behind. The thought of expressing oneself like that made Kate light-headed.

"Stravinsky," David said, his eyes fixed on the exquisitely beautiful ballerinas, curtsying on stage. They wore white silk leotards, white silk ballet shoes, white silk tights. Kate could not stop looking at them, either.

When a group of dancers swayed as one, she felt her neck sway with them. When their feet pattered across the stage planks, her own toes tingled. Their movements had no rough edges, no awkward angles, no ugliness. This was how Kate had always wanted to look, to move, but never had. Whenever the music and the steps paused for a moment, she stopped breathing.

Myriam performed in the third dance. A male ballet dancer stood behind her, intermittently lifting her by her rib cage, his fingers pressing into her small breasts. He carried Myriam across the stage with one of her long legs fanning behind her. It looked effortless, but when he finally stood still, his chest heaved. Myriam kept on jumping and fluttering and he spread out his own arms in a sort of *Ta-da!* gesture. *Taking credit for her strength,* Kate thought. *Unsurprising.*

At the intermission, Kate and David went to the bar, which was in a carpeted lounge off the lobby. The pumped-in hot air was thick with chatter about how wonderful the performance was. Women in silk and ermine slid past them, closer to David than they needed to be. They cast glances at him out of the corners of their eyes.

"What do you think?" he asked, unbuttoning his waistcoat.

"I think it's the most gorgeous thing I've ever seen," she gushed. "I feel like I've just been to Midnight Mass, but miles better. Did you enjoy it?"

"Yeah," he said, distractedly watching the clock above the bar. "I liked it."

They shared a G&T and went backstage to say a quick hello to Myriam and Simon. Myriam was sitting on a folding chair, now cosseted in a bright red corset and fuchsia nylons. Kate found herself tongue-tied at the sight of her—it was like seeing Bette Davis in the flesh. Simon leaned against one of the stage sets, chatting with one of the other ballerinas. A muscular man in workman's clothes knelt at Myriam's feet, wrapping fresh bandages tight around her bloody toes. Although it must have been excruciating, her face, smooth and powdered, registered no pain; she laughed lightly at something the man said and wriggled a long pin into the bun at the back of her head. She was exquisite, graceful and battered and brave. And Simon was so at ease with these beautiful girls bustling around him. In their presence, Kate felt awkward and plain.

Myriam noticed her and David waiting. She received them like a queen, and batted her long false eyelashes at David.

"You were marvelous, Myriam," Kate said. "I've never seen anything like it."

"You've never seen anything like what?" Myriam said, dabbing powder on her upper lip.

"The ballet. It's gorgeous. You are gorgeous."

"You've never been to the ballet?" Myriam's laughter was a string of tinkling bells. "Kate, you are so English. So provincial. Sometimes, I cannot believe it."

"Neither can I," Kate said, slipping the Leica out of her purse. "Do you mind if I take a few photographs of you?"

"Fine."

Myriam struck a pose, pressing the bend of her wrist against her forehead. Then she drew Kate into a shared dressing room.

Settling at a dressing table, Myriam gazed directly into Kate's camera and her face softened. "You look lovely," she said. "I like your dress."

"Thank you," Kate said, surprised by praise from Myriam.

"I'm not sure David deserves you."

"Why is that?"

Myriam hesitated, an expression of pity on her face. "Do you really want to know?"

Kate realized with a jolt that she did not. She didn't want to know anything that could diminish the elation she felt with David. But she couldn't say that; it was too pathetic. So, she kept shooting.

"This should come from a friend," Myriam went on, now gracing the camera with her long profile, perfectly framed by the lit vanity mirror. "Rather than from me. But I feel I must tell you. David has done this before. A couple of years ago, he fell in love with a pretty little *shiksa* nurse. Simon told me. Of course, he tired of her. These boys always do."

"What does *shiksa* mean?"

"A woman who is not Jewish. A detestable woman."

Kate flinched. "David would never use that word," she said, and screwed the lid back onto her lens. "I'll leave you now."

"Sorry, you misunderstand me. He wouldn't *say* it," Myriam said. "But he thinks it."

After the ballet, Kate sped up to walk in front of David. She was unsettled by what Myriam had said and didn't want David to see it in her face.

"My parents are in Bournemouth," he said. "Let's go to my flat."

Kate already knew she would do whatever David wanted. They had not been really alone together for weeks, since her father returned.

"What about your neighbors?" she asked.

"We'll run right in. They'll never see us. Don't fret."

The Rabatkins' flat was in a shabby courtyard off a narrow lane near Spitalfields. The entire side of their building was painted with an advert for Colman's Mustard. In the courtyard, a street vendor stirred chestnuts on a hot metal pan. David unlocked the front door and ushered Kate into a dark, dank front hall. She had not realized how poor the Rabatkins were. As they quickly ascended the stairs, David said nothing. Neither did Kate. She wondered if he was afraid of his neighbors seeing them or just eager to get her alone.

Another door unlocked and she followed David into his flat. He led her to a sitting room and began to kiss her like he never would again, then pulled her down on the carpet.

"David! Slow down."

"We don't have a lot of time," he said, his voice rough. One hand was wrapped in her hair, the other deftly undid her garters. "Do you ever think of me, Kate? When you're alone?"

She hesitated. "Yes."

David was pleased—Kate could feel his smile on her ear. He smelled edible, like fresh bread.

"What do you think about?"

"I think about . . ." The words she wanted to say dried up in her mouth and she squeezed her eyes shut. Maybe Myriam had been right: David *was* using Kate. But in this moment, she liked the idea of him drawing something out of her that she should not give. Extorting her. There was a progression, an escalation toward a place they hadn't been before.

Kate took his hand, put it between her legs. His touch was

light at first; he was afraid of offending her. She turned to kiss him and he ran his hands over her stomach and breasts, then back between her legs.

He asked: "Do you want more?"

"Yes," she said, tucking herself under him.

Afterward, Kate turned onto her side and took in the room. This was David's home. He had grown up looking out those windows. She scooted her back against his body, which was warm and long and solid. It stabilized her, like an extra spine. Now they were friends again, companions. David rested his palm on her lower back, his fingers grazing her hip. He was breathing softly and rhythmically, half asleep.

"I thought we were stealing time," she said. "Should I go?"

He yawned drowsily. "You're all right for a bit."

It was a pleasant flat. Every object seemed to be meticulously placed. There was an old blue sofa, a carved wood screen, cozy armchairs. A fern and a plant with rubbery leaves. Each wall and surface displayed framed family photographs.

Kate stood up so she could see the pictures on the mantel. There was a snapshot of teenage David and Simon in the street with a middle-aged couple. The woman was wearing a coat with a fur lapel, strings of mismatched beads, and a tilted hat with a fake bird fastened on the brim. David's mother. She looked proud and sad and gripped Simon's arm like she needed him to stand. The man, obviously David's father, squinting into the sun, his necktie askance. Then there was a seaside holiday portrait—young Mr. and Mrs. Rabatkin in bathing costumes, hinting at smiles. David, unmistakable, around four years old, posed on a mounting block between his parents. His arms folded across his chest, bare feet crossed at the ankles, and an imperious scowl on his face. Mrs. Rabatkin held a swaddled baby. On the step below David, an angelic three-year-old Simon beamed.

"You were quite the little emperor, eh?" Kate said. "This

portrait of your family on the seaside. How bossy you look."
She laughed. "Who is the baby your mother is holding?"

David paused. "I had a sister. Her name was Rachel. She
died as an infant. I don't really remember her."

Kate's heart sank. Another burden she did not know he
carried. "You never told me. I'm so sorry."

"Typhoid. All of us had it. She was unlucky."

"Your poor parents."

"Yes."

"Do you remember Rachel at all?"

David thought for a moment, frowning. "I remember her
being born," he said, "my mum standing at the top of the
stairs in her nightgown singing, '*The baby's coming.*' I sort
of thought Rachel was a present for me. Her perfect little
seashell ears . . . I remember them. Then she just vanished. I
think I remember my mother crying when she died. But people always seemed to be dying, it could have been someone
else. That may be why I wanted to become a doctor. I wanted
to make all the dying stop."

"Your parents must be incredibly proud of you."

"Yeah." David hesitated. "They've sacrificed a lot for me."
Kate realized that he was uncomfortable talking about them
with her.

Then there was an eight-by-ten in a gold-plated frame—
young David in a suit at least two sizes too big, sharp pleats
in his trouser legs. Next to it, a letterpress invitation in a
matching frame: "*Mr. and Mrs. Max Rabatkin request the
honor of your presence to the confirmation Bar-Mitzvah of
their son . . .*" and a translation in an alphabet Kate did not
recognize.

"What language is this?"

"Hebrew."

On the side table next to the sofa, another portrait: a bride
whose veil sprouted out of a colossal white bow on top of her
dark curls. She wore too-dark lipstick and held a bouquet of

lily of the valley and white roses. Kate placed the frame back on the table. Every one of these pictures dripped with affection. No family photographs hung in her own house.

"You have a lovely family," she said softly.

Kate ran her fingers along the plaster mantel. There was not a speck of dust. She walked into the kitchen, where a bare bulb hung on a chain from the ceiling over the round table. There was no icebox, no larder, just a cupboard. The flat did not have a lavatory, either. The dented kitchen linoleum was printed with a picture of a woven rug. An ironing board stacked with blankets took up the side wall; behind it, there was a small archway leading to another small room. Kate wondered what kind of mother ironed blankets.

David called after her: "What are you doing in the kitchen? Are you hungry?"

"Just having a look around."

"Come back to me."

With her toe, Kate pushed open a door in the other wall. It led to a bedroom, slightly larger than the kitchen, with a double bed and house dresses hanging from nails on the wall. There were more family photos on the dresser. Beaded necklaces were draped over the top corners of the mirror. Medicine bottles lined the windowsill. On the bedside table, a mint-green vase of artificial roses, two pairs of reading glasses, a leather-bound book. David's parents' bedroom. There was nothing special about it, nothing Kate wanted for herself. But she found herself overcome by a deeply unpleasant feeling—a bitterness so sharp that it took her a moment to identify as plain jealousy.

David had a real family, a full life, and parents who loved him. One day he would have a wife and children of his own. Even though she did not want marriage and children, it hurt. He would leave her, just as Myriam said. Kate would be alone and David would be surrounded by people who worshipped him. It wasn't fair.

When she returned to the front room, David was sitting on the blue sofa, tying his shoes.

"Where is your bedroom?" she asked.

"In there," he said, pointing to closed double doors on the other side of the room, but he did not move to show her.

Kate stood in the kitchen doorway, glumly watching him dress, noting the order in which he put on each piece of clothing: his belt before his vest and dress shirt. These were habits formed over years of being David. He had done these things before her and would do them after her.

He noticed her watching him and his face became somber.

"I love you, Kate," he said suddenly. "Did you know that already?"

I love you: fairy-tale words. His life, here in this flat, was real. The word *love* came too easily to him, with a family like the Rabatkins. Kate would not be fooled; she was just an interlude for him.

"No," she said, turning away, scanning the room for her purse and finding it on the desk by the door. "I guess I didn't."

"Kate . . ."

"What?"

Under her purse was a stack of colored envelopes. She shuffled through them as she stepped into her shoes: three from the Gas Light & Coke Company, two from the London School of Medicine and Dentistry, all addressed to Mr. Max Rabatkin, David's father who did not even know she existed.

David shot up and snatched the letters out of her hands. He opened the desk drawer, shoved them inside, slammed it shut. He looked almost frightened. Why had Kate not seen the truth before? Why hadn't she felt it? David had this loving family, this loving home, and she had no one.

Even though Kate knew exactly how the Jewish refugee story pitch should be laid out for *Life* and Scargill did not, he stood in the doorway of the conference room before their preparatory meeting Monday morning, shuffling through her photos. His body almost spanned the width of the doorframe, so she could not come through.

"We need to pick three to five or five to seven. Though that's probably too much. *I'm* interested in narrative thrust. *I'm* interested in historical backing. But photography is a visual medium and at the end of the day, after all my years of experience, the images that sell are those that tickle the eyeballs . . ."

Men did this. They stood in Kate's way: blocking, theorizing, wool-gathering.

She tapped her toe rapidly as anger gathered inside her. It was a useful distraction from David, whom she was trying not to think about so much. Irritation with Scargill was relatively comfortable.

A minute passed and Scargill still stood there, wondering out loud what he was going to do with Kate's idea. His instincts were wrong—they were always wrong—but because he had power and she did not, he was allowed to test out his ideas, muck everything up, and expect her to sort it.

Unable to take any more, she pushed past him into the conference room, laughing a little, as if she had tripped. He followed her to the empty conference table and sat down in the chair right next to her, his legs splayed to take up the most room possible. Kate clamped her knees together and tucked her feet under her.

There were two large milk-glass ashtrays on the conference table; she wondered what it would feel like to strike him over the head with one of them.

Scargill spread her prints on the table and reached across her chest while he explained her work to her. His dirty-sock smell crept into her nostrils.

"You've just about got something here," he said, tapping on the photo of David speaking with Freya and Miss Singer.

"Jews, looking after their own. They're not draining Britain, not taking advantage, no, they're contributing. A nice little story."

Kate stared at the ashtray and felt her upper lip twitch. Scargill plucked another photo off the table and waved it in front of her.

"This is the strongest image you got," he said, "this charming little Jewess with her son . . ."

Of course, he liked the least interesting picture—Miss Singer patting the head of a grinning six-year-old boy named Reuben. Kate *knew* Scargill was going to pick that photo. She should have thrown the negative out. She wanted the picture of Freya alone on her bed, with the portrait of her parents on the wall behind her.

"That's not her son," Kate said. "She's his teacher. That boy's mother sent him to England after his father and uncle were kidnapped by the German government. *That* is the point of this story. Jewish children are now safer with strangers in Britain than with their own families in Germany. I think people should be forced to confront that bit of reality, don't you?"

"It's not for us to decide what people should confront, Shutterbug. Our job is to sell photographs, not policy. And this photograph is charming." He shook his head. "Take the compliment!"

"But we're journalists," she insisted. "And the *Times* just printed a piece on the appalling treatment of Jewish children in Germany. People want to read about this. The Nazis are implementing anti-Jewish policies and legislation as quickly as they can . . ."

"I do not contest that," he said, an edge coming into his voice. "But as a viewer, I'm not seeing anything particularly provocative in any of these photographs. That's not the angle you've chosen. But this one . . ." He shuffled through the photos and selected one of the children reading on the lawn. "*This* grabs me. German kiddies are here in England, enjoying a British education, and everyone is happy."

"Just because a child is smiling does not mean he is happy."

Scargill gave Kate a warning look—she was being impertinent—and regathered the photos in his hands like playing cards. "I shall write the captions," he said. "Yours might be . . . rather emotional."

"I met these refugees and their teachers and doctors, Mr. Scargill. I can sell their story to *Life*."

"I get the gist. Just stick with the photos, Miss Grifferty. Hone your craft. I'll deal with *Life*."

Chapter 12

10th December, 1936

On Thursday afternoon, Mr. Scargill appeared at quarter to five, just as Kate was considering the clock. She had been in a fog all day and couldn't stop thinking about cheese and crackers and her bed. She had not heard from David since the day of the ballet.

"Hello, Shutterbug," Mr. Scargill said to her, ignoring Gordon, who was at the typewriter, banging away at captions. "How *are* you? Not working too hard?"

"Gordon and I were just finishing up here," she said. "Unless you needed something?"

"Brace yourself, Shutterbug . . ."

She made herself smile. "What is it?"

"I have it on excellent authority," Mr. Scargill said in a hushed tone, "that the Duke of York, at this very moment, is rushing back to London from Windsor. His brother the king is abdicating."

Gordon gasped. A bolt of alertness went through Kate. Rumors had been swirling about the king for months, but it was still hard to believe. She was wide awake now. This was international news and a major opportunity for them all.

"A shot of the new king arriving at his London residence is *essential*," Scargill went on. "Of course, Piccadilly will be a complete disaster. Are you up for it, Shutterbug? You'll have to walk, they won't be letting taxis or buses through."

"Of course!" Kate cried, not before watching a thunder-cloud pass over Gordon's face. "I'll pack up straightaway."

"Good girl! Push right up to the front, do whatever you have to do. Catch his eye. He could be there within the hour. If you leave now, you might just make it. I'll be here when you get back." Scargill smoothed his belly. "I'm just going to nip out for a sandwich. Settle the old nerves. Abdication! A terrible shock, even for a seasoned pressman like me . . ."

"I had better look in on Mum, anyway," Gordon said. "She'll be out the window, ready to jump. King Edward has been her special favorite since he was a lad."

"Why would your mum care?" Scargill balked. "She's not really English, is she?"

Gordon flushed. "Mum is very loyal to the Crown. Her father served in Queen Victoria's household."

As soon as Scargill left, Gordon pulled the cover over his typewriter and started flinging things into his bag furiously.

"Don't mind Sir Sod," Kate said, gathering her equipment, hoping they could make a joke of Scargill's nastiness. "You'll get the next assignment."

"It's not about that. Bloody Scargill only hired me because he knew it would be hard for me to ever leave for another job. There aren't half-castes in Fleet Street, besides paperboys. He can shit all over me and I just have to take it. He enjoys look-ing down on people who work for him."

"He hired you because you're good. You're an ice-blooded technician. You know that."

Gordon laughed bitterly. He wouldn't look at her. "I work quick," he said. "It doesn't mean I'm good." He started to walk out of the room, but stopped at the doorway, his shoul-ders tensed halfway up his neck. "He's just trying to get off with you, you know. Why do you think he brought you in on that *Life* pitch?"

Kate flinched. "That's not nice, Gordy."

"One can't be nice and do photojournalism. You know that. Shutterbug."

"Do *you* want the assignment?" she cried. "Take it!"

"Nope," Gordon said coolly, disappearing into the corridor. "You heard Scargill. He wants you."

145 Piccadilly was a stone-fronted, five-story mansion. Every window was lit. Kate had shoved her way through the crowd, all the way up to the railings. Gone was the weariness she'd felt earlier, but she was still rattled by her conversation with Gordon. She made herself put him out of her mind. An abdication was a once-in-a-generation news event; the story had to be the only thing that mattered.

When the Duke of York finally arrived, he looked surprisingly plain in his black suit and bowler hat. But the scores of people chanting "We want Edward!"—while pushing in to catch a glimpse of his replacement—distinguished the rising king from any well-off London businessman.

Alighting from his car, the duke's bright white gloves caught the flash of her bulb. He squinted, temporarily blinded, averted his eyes, and then raised his hat to his public. He had a haughty curl to his lips and good, strong features that would hold the frame of her picture. Kate crouched down and shot him again from below to exaggerate his stature. People would like that.

If she did her job, this assignment would certainly mean one of her pictures above the fold in a national newspaper. She did not linger in Piccadilly. Adrenaline coursed through her veins as she bolted back across Green Park and caught a taxi in Trafalgar Square. Nobody would scoop her this time.

The office was empty when Kate returned to develop her film. While she worked, she thought about Gordon. He was angry about Scargill's bigotry and the way his talent was being squandered as a darkroom boy. Kate understood that.

They'd make friends again on Monday. Maybe they could team up against Scargill, quit together, go out as a free-lance team. Not right away, but things were changing. Miss Bourke-White was on the cover of *Life*. Someday . . .

She was hanging the negatives to squeegee them, when the revolving door began to turn.

"Hello, Shutterbug," Scargill said. "Any luck?"

"Think so," she said briskly, hoping he would leave.

Scargill immediately filled her cool, serene darkroom with the stench of his panting need. There was a sigh and the scuffling of his boots. It would be all right if she did not look at him. She would make the prints, file them, and leave. If she did not see anything, he could not damage her.

"I'm just going out to look at this contact sheet in the light," she said.

"Of course! Don't mind me. I'm mending this leaky tap on the sink. It's been doing my head in for weeks, but there's never any time during the day."

Heart pounding, Kate escaped into the bright light of the office.

There were several strong shots. It would be best if Scargill wired the editors himself, but after five minutes he had not emerged from the darkroom.

She didn't want to go back in there.

Kate tapped on the wall. He did not answer, but from inside switched off the caution light above the door. She tapped again.

"Mr. Scargill," she called. "Do you want to come out and look at these? I think they're ready to send."

"Bring them here to me," he called. "I'm under the sink."

Kate stepped cautiously back into the darkroom. Before her eyes adjusted to the synthetic red twilight, she felt Scargill's belly press into her back. He kissed her neck, leaving a sticky patch of saliva on her skin. She shivered with disgust, then tried to pull away subtly so she would not offend him.

It felt imperative, to her job and to her safety, that she not humiliate him. But he saw her wipe her neck with her hand.

"Give me the photos," he said, and snatched them from her. After a moment's squinting, he shook one in front of her. "I suppose this one is good enough to be published as a newspaper halftone."

"What's wrong with it?"

"This is an historic moment, Miss Grifferty." He sighed, exasperated. "Perhaps I should have sent Davies or one of the stringers. Your news pictures always end up looking like portraits. There's no *context*. I wanted context. A nice little story, to tickle eyeballs and hearts."

"But everyone knows who the Duke of York is! He's going to be king. That is the context."

"Don't be disagreeable, Miss Grifferty."

"I'm not disagreeing, sir."

Scargill took a step to the left, positioning himself between Kate and the door. "Don't apologize, either. It's quite all right. You're learning."

She wanted to snap back at him: *I didn't apologize.* But she found she could not speak. It was only then she realized how terrified she was.

Scargill was the same height as her, but broader. She wondered what he would do if she tried to dart around him. Before she could, an impish smile crossed his face and he slowly reached out and placed one hand on her breast.

The thought that she could physically harm him landed softly on her consciousness and then exploded. She reached out, grabbed a fistful of his thinning hair, and yanked as hard as she could. When he did not move, she reeled back and smacked his face. Her palm tingled painfully but Scargill just rubbed his jowl and smiled.

"Let me out of here or I will scream," she hissed. "And scream and scream until someone comes or you kill me. Either way, you'll be ruined, you pompous, ignorant toad."

Kate held her breath. Scargill seemed to size her up and decide that she meant it.

"You are the one who is ruined," he said, finally stepping aside with a decorous bow. "I shall see to it myself."

The next morning, Kate sat cross-legged on the pink parlor carpet, inside a square of white winter light streaming through the window. She traced the shadowed border on the carpet with one finger. She had neither slept nor eaten since the previous day. Her belly ached, but she was not hungry.

She could hear her father puttering around in the kitchen downstairs. He chomped an apple, opened and closed the icebox and the cupboards, put the kettle on. These familiar sounds, knowing her father was in the next room, comforted her. She did not want to be alone with her thoughts. The memory of Scargill's hand on her breast kept returning, frightening her each time.

Gordon was right: Scargill had only hired her so he could seduce her, not because she was a good photographer. There was something about her that made him think he could.

She stood up on shaky legs and tightened the belt of her dressing gown. She felt ashamed even of her footsteps. It was as if she was made of glass. She took careful steps, looking at her feet. The muscles in her legs and arms and back were sore.

"It's a Friday," her father said when she came into the kitchen. He was wearing a new navy wool suit and an ice-blue necktie, the same shade as his eyes. "You should be at the office by now. Big news day, I expect."

"I can't go back there."

"Aye? Why not?"

"Because . . . I don't feel well this morning." Kate rubbed her arms; they were very cold. "Can I sit with you?"

Her father scowled at her. "Don't tell me you're heartbroken about the abdication like the rest of those sops. My foreman was weeping all over the yard yesterday. I'll sack him if I see one more tear. You're not English, Kathleen. You're Irish and don't you forget it."

"It's not that. I quit my job last night."

"Have you got another?"

"No."

"Then you're an eejit. You don't leave a job before you've got a new one. This is not an almshouse. If you're too lazy to work, find yourself a husband."

Kate sank into the chair opposite her father. His barbs didn't even sting. She just needed to be near another human being who would not physically attack her. She could at least depend on her father there: he had never laid a hand on her, for comfort or for harm.

He shook open the *News Chronicle*. "Christ, these Brits and their inbred aristocrats . . . ." Chuckling, he poked his finger into the headline: *THE KING ABDICATES: WILL BROADCAST TO-NIGHT*. "Your one here might be his own grandfather. It's Irish ingenuity and sweat that paid for his palace."

And there it was, above the fold—the photograph Kate had taken of the Duke of York arriving at his London residence. It was the one Kate would have chosen—a close-up of his head and shoulders with a shadow framing his face. No context, indeed.

"Here, have a hear . . . ," her father said, delighted at the Brits' humiliation. " 'With the renunciation of the Throne,' " he read aloud, " 'the King relinquishes all his titles except that of Prince Edward, but it was rumored last night that he might prefer to be known as plain *Mr. Windsor.*' " He smirked and turned to the next page. Kate had never seen him in such a good mood. "Mr. Windsor! Sounds like a dry cleaner. Poor slob. God bless him. And have you seen the hussy he's giving it all up for? Queen Wally! She's a filthy article if I've ever seen one. It's *gas craic*, that is . . ."

Chapter 13

14th December, 1936

David *knew* he had gone too far, too quickly when he told Kate he loved her. When he said it, she seemed to freeze over. She wouldn't even look at him. And then she'd seen all his father's overdue bills. It was humiliating.

So, he had left her alone for a while, trying to convince himself that he did not need her.

He finally rang her at home early Friday morning, just as she would be leaving for work. No one answered. David pictured Kate standing in her hall, next to that little telephone cupboard, knowing it was him and cringing to herself. On Monday, he tried her at the Central Press.

"Miss Grifferty doesn't work here anymore," said the man who answered the phone and abruptly rang off.

Instead of going to the library as planned, he walked to Kate's house. Above her street, the tree branches spread out like spiderwebs. Dead leaves curled like wood shavings on the frostbitten pavement. Everything seemed dead. He rang the bell until a small, congested voice came through it:

"I can't see you just now, David. Please go away."

"Kate? Are you ill?"

"I'm fine," she said, inches away on the other side of the

door. "I just want to be left alone." She didn't sound angry, just weak. There were tears in her voice.

"First tell me why. Then I'll go."

When she opened the door, her eyes were red and her nose and eyes were puffy. She had been crying.

"Why have you been avoiding me? Why aren't you at work?"

She glared at him and he was relieved to see a flicker of her old fierceness. "*I've* been avoiding *you*?"

"Yeah, I rang your office and they said you don't work there anymore."

"Why would you do that? I just want to be alone, all right? Please go. You're not *helping*."

The way she said that last word, *helping*—mocking, bitter, like David was inventing a reason to be a hero. It almost pissed him off. But then he clocked how she was holding herself, with her arms hugged tightly around her waist. She *did* need help. Something terrible had happened, he could feel it.

"Okay. I won't come in, I'll stand right here," David said, hoping that the fear creeping up his neck was misplaced. "Are you hurt?"

Kate shook her head. "I had to leave my job." Then, looking at her feet, she said: "I don't want to tell you why. I don't want you to think badly of me."

"I could only ever think well of you," he said. "Please, tell me."

She turned around and went back into the house. But she didn't shut the door behind her, so David followed her into the kitchen. She sat down at the table and put her face in her hands, and he knelt down in front of her.

"You mustn't think I encouraged him," she cried. "I swear I didn't."

Everything went still. This was bad. David gathered his feelings, knowing he needed to be calm for her.

Focusing only on Kate's face, he asked: "Encouraged who?"

She took a little breath, and pressed her lips together.

"My boss," she said finally. "Mr. Scargill. He trapped me in the darkroom. He asked me to work late, I came back in and he was there, waiting for me." She began to sob, great shuddering sobs. "You mustn't do anything. I want to pretend it never happened."

David clenched his fists. "Did he hurt you?"

"He grabbed my chest. And he kissed me. Here." She pointed to her neck and shuddered.

"Right. Anything else?"

"Isn't that bad enough?"

"It's bloody awful. I'm just trying to understand how far things went."

"I've told you already! I'm humiliated! I'll never get another job. Scargill will ruin me. He knows *everyone*."

"I'm so sorry." David pulled Kate to him and held her and thought about how he could help. "There has to be some way . . . The Central Press isn't the only shop in town. A man like that will have loads of enemies."

She sniffed. "D'you think?"

"Yeah. You can't give up. Actually, there's a big rally for Spanish aid next Monday in Hyde Park. Simon's been jabbering about it for weeks. Come along and meet his friends from the *Daily Worker*. We grew up with those blokes. They won't give a jot about bloody Scargill. They might have something for you."

"I don't know," she said, pulling back from him. "I don't want to go out. I'm too ashamed."

"He's the one who should be ashamed of himself. You have to get back out there. You'll feel better."

"I worried you'd think I'd done something wrong, something that would make him do it."

"Don't be ridiculous. It's not your fault."

She closed her eyes. "You think I'm disgusting. You're ashamed of me."

"What are you talking about? I am not. I love you."

"You're lying," Kate said, her voice rising. "You are ashamed of me. You say you love me, but you don't. You're hiding me from your parents. I'm your dirty secret. Myriam told me. You think I'm disgusting."

"Stop saying that! This isn't like you."

She set her mouth in a hard line. David had known it would come to this. In spite of his guilt, all he could think was that he could not lose her.

"I'm ashamed of myself, not you," he said carefully. "My parents taught me love is something you choose to feel. It's not. It's stronger than us. If I had known, I wouldn't have pursued you, because it wasn't fair to you. But here we are and, you know what, I'm glad because you're the best thing that has ever happened to me. The love I feel for you means more to me than anything in my life. And I'm going to tell them that, okay? I promise."

Kate's face softened. She let him wrap her in his arms, but she did not tell him she loved him back.

"When did you last eat something?" David asked after he'd held her for a while. He switched on the light above the table.

"I don't remember."

"I'm going to make you something."

Kate sat up in her chair and watched David put the kettle to the tap, fill it, and set it to boil. As wretched as she felt, she felt a hot spark flicker in her chest as she watched him. He opened the larder and stood in front of it, leaning back on his heels, rubbing the side of his jaw with his thumb.

"Right," he said, and took out a loaf of bread, an egg, some butter. He cut two slices off the bread and pulled one of the frying pans from the wall. He lit the oven and left its door open. Dry heat filled the room.

"Why don't you close the oven? It won't heat up like that."

"The room will. You're shivering."

"Oh."

As the egg started to sizzle on the hob, he put a cup of tea with milk in her hands.

"I didn't know you could cook," Kate said.

"Family recipe," he said. He assembled the sandwich, sliced it in half on the counter. "Here," he said, handing her a triangle. "Eat."

It was the most delicious sandwich she had ever tasted: crisp, butter-soaked bread, egg yolk that was hot and just a bit runny. She closed her eyes. When she opened them, David was smiling at her.

"Better?" he asked.

She licked a smear of butter off her thumb. "Did your mother make this for you when you were little?"

"All the time."

"My father once told me my mother made the most delicious toffee pudding. I don't know why I remember that, but I could almost taste it when he said it."

She sipped her tea, felt a little life come back into her body. When she finished her sandwich, Kate rested her chin on her hand and smiled at David.

"Your mum would be proud of you," he said. "You're incredibly brave."

Tears pricked at Kate's eyes again. She was very tired, so tired she could sleep for a hundred years.

"You are who you think you are, all right?" David said. He touched her shoulder. "Don't let that arsehole Scargill blow up your confidence."

"He said he would ruin me," she said.

"Sod that. You're not ruined if he gives up before you do."

I love you.

The words woke Kate in the dark. She switched on the

lamp and looked at the nickel alarm clock on her bedside table. It was only midnight, but she'd been asleep for nearly eight hours, since David left and she burrowed into her bed. He'd stayed with her all day, holding her until her father was set to return from work.

In all Kate's life, no one had ever said they loved her. Not that she remembered.

When Kate was born, had her mother whispered those words in her ear, just before she died? Had she known it would be the only time her baby daughter would hear them for over twenty years?

Turning over in bed, Kate began to cry for her mother and all the lonely years between them. She cried for her father, who could not bring himself to love her, and for the older sister who had left her behind. For the world that did not seem to want her.

Kate cried because a man like David had told her that he loved her, that he would defy his family for her, but the words were so alien that she had scarcely recognized them.

More than anything, she cried because she did not believe him.

Simon and David's friend, Danny Salter from the *Daily Worker,* had had a look at Kate's portfolio.

"Unfortunately, we can't pay anything," Danny said, at the CPGB rally in Hyde Park on the twenty-first. He wore a jaunty black beret and the fountain pen in his pocket had bled through the front of his shirt. "But, there is a darkroom you can use whenever you like, and any of your photos we don't use you're free to sell elsewhere . . ."

At the head of the crowd of about fifty spectators, a man climbed onto a wooden crate and waved his hands over his head. "One of our members would like to say a few words," he shouted. "Comrade Simon, are you out there?"

"Oi, Simon!"

"Oi, oi, oi!" Simon called back.

When he stepped up onto the box, everyone erupted in cheers. Kate smiled to herself and reloaded the camera—he would be the perfect cover model for the *Daily Worker*. In the crowd of tired-looking men, Simon glowed with youthful exuberance.

"Hullo, I'm from the East End and in the Communist Party," Simon shouted, his fine cheekbones flushed. "All the countries of Europe are capitulating to Hitler's operations and doing what he wants. But not the Spanish people. They're the first, I hope of many, to fight back. Their fight against fascism makes me want to go and help them. The British government and the French government have a plan of nonintervention and won't allow people to get into Spain, but we find ways, don't we? We've organized a food ship to go from Liverpool to Spain and I will be taking the journey myself. Aid Spain have collected I think two hundred parcels . . ."

Simon's body looked taut with feeling and he shifted forward and backward on his feet, sort of keeping time as he spoke. Kate thought he was a natural orator.

She glanced at David, who rolled his eyes. "He's not going anywhere," he muttered.

"I have been asked to be a political spokesman to enthuse the ranks, so to speak," Simon continued. "Above all, I'm concerned with making sure there is support for food supplies for stricken Republican Spain. We will be collecting donations of clothing and money to deliver to our brothers and sisters there. Everything you give will go to the Spanish Republican Armed Forces. Thank you all. I'll see you down the road."

Simon stepped down from his makeshift parapet and came straight over to David and Kate. He slapped David on the shoulder and enthusiastically kissed Kate's cheek.

"Are you really going, Simon?" she asked.

"'Course I am! You ought to come with us. Both of you. We need journos and doctors in this fight."

"Don't you reckon we Jews have enough problems in England?" David said, in the patronizing tone he sometimes put on when speaking to or about Simon. "That's the battle that needs you. I'm fighting it every day. Showing we have a right to our place in society."

"Here we go," Simon said. "You sound like Minnie Schwartz's daddy. '*We shall force the* goyim *to respect us . . .*'"

"I mean make something of yourself here, Simon. Don't flit off to a foreign war you don't understand."

Kate frowned at David. She did not like this pedantic side of him. Passion was not meant to be rational. She thought he knew that.

"I think Simon understands perfectly well," she said. For all his bravado, Simon clearly wanted David to look up to him. Some people weren't meant to be little brothers. "He's educated himself about the Spanish War, he obviously feels deeply for the people there. Simon, I think you're very brave. And maybe we *will* join you at some point. Who knows?"

"I do know," David said, his jaw set. "I can't leave school. I have a profession and parents who depend on me, *especially* if Simon buggers off to Spain."

Chapter 14

23rd December, 1936

There was no room at the counter inside Brick Lane Beigel Bake. It was freezing, but David and his father stood outside the restaurant, eating their salt beef sandwiches and discussing the wedding being hastily planned for David's second cousin, Lily Birnbaum. It was to be held at the Rembrandt Hotel in Kensington on New Year's Eve.

"Cousin Shirl is in a right state." David's father chuckled and wiped his mouth with a paper serviette. "Your mother is at the hotel with her now, working out the catering."

"You reckon Shirl and Sid will ever forgive Lily?"

" 'Course they will! The baby will be born a bit early and Shirl will have a grandchild to *kvell* about. What's to forgive?"

David knew he would not be extended the same clemency regarding Kate. Whatever Lily and her fiancé had gotten up to, Arthur was a Jew.

"Do you mind if we walk?" He started to walk so his father would have to follow him. It would be easier to tell him about Kate if he didn't have to look at him. "I've a meeting at the hospital at one."

"Shall we stop at the bakery on the way? Those macaroons . . ."

"Not today." David took a deep breath. His mind was racing, searching for a reason this conversation might go well.

Two days earlier, Simon had left for St. Pancras station, off to catch a ship from Liverpool. David reminded himself that his brother had not asked anyone's permission. He had just gone and done what he wanted, knowing the family would have to cope. When viewed in that light, David was doing his father a courtesy in warning him about Kate.

"I, ah, need to tell you something," he said. "I've met someone. A girl."

His father's eyes lit up. "Have you? Who is she?"

"You won't know her."

"Your mother will be disappointed. She had her heart set on that Schwartz girl."

David looked up at the winter sky, sickly gray like an old bruise. An airplane buzzed overhead; he wished he was on it. Bracing himself, he said it fast: "She's not Jewish."

His father stopped walking. "Don't tell me this. I don't want to know this."

"Will you at least meet her? Her name is Kate."

"Ach! Don't tell me her name. Is she in trouble or something?"

"No. It's nothing like that. Kate is a good girl. And I'm not stupid."

"You think only stupid people fall in love? I'm going to tell you a story. When I took your mother up the aisle, I was in love with another girl. Victoria Levy. I didn't even fancy your mum till we was on our honeymoon. We went to Whitstable for the night. I'd arranged for us to have all our meals at the kosher hotel, but your mum said it's our honeymoon and we're having a crab tea with champagne." David's father shook his head, his eyes soft, remembering. "We thought we were so wild. That's when I knew. I said to myself, 'Max, this is the girl for you.'"

"You never told me that."

"My parents knew me better than I knew myself. I trusted them. Now you're a university genius, you think you know better than your mother and me, but what you know could fit in my little finger here."

"I know I love Kate."

"Love is not two people. It is a family. You will not believe how much of your future happiness will be determined by your wife's family and hers by yours. Do you remember what happened when Shira Gold brought home that blond *shaygetz* taxi driver? It killed the grandmother!"

"Leave it, Dad. The grandmother was ninety if she was a day."

"Everyone knows what did her in."

Father and son walked for a while in silence. They turned into the wind howling up Whitechapel Road. David, undeterred himself, wondered what tactic his father would use next.

"You think this Kat's mother . . ."

"Kate."

"Whatever. You think her mother wants her to marry a Jew? No. No matter what the girl says. And you cannot burden a woman with raising a child away from her own family."

"Kate's mother is dead. And there is no child."

"Then what are we talking about?" David's father shook his head and ruffled David's hair. A gleam of pride came into his eyes. "Have your fun. Don't get her in trouble or make any promises. What your mother doesn't know won't hurt her."

"*I* don't lie to Mum," David said. "*I* don't conduct my life like that."

"Who said anything about lying?"

They were standing in front of London Hospital now, by the Jewish memorial drinking fountain. David's father sighed and rubbed his eyes. The skin under them was loose and it swished around under his fingers. The hospital was decked out with Christmas lights, like the rest of London. It always made David feel a bit lonesome.

"Dad, you should come in out of the cold," David said. "I've got to meet with Dr. Montague, but why don't you come have a nice cup of tea in the canteen?"

"Nah." His father shrugged him off. "Do me a favor," he said. "Trust me about that girl. Don't say anything to Mum. Not yet. At least wait until we get word Simon's safe. I've always found your mother to be more forgiving when she's not worried about something else."

On New Year's Eve, the morning of Lily's wedding, a Western Union cable arrived from Spain:

> 31 DEC 1936
> MRS. MAX RABATKIN 26 SPELMAN ST LONDON
> SAFELY ARRIVED IN BARCELONA LOVE TO ALL
> SIMON

David's mother read and reread it, frowning like it was a receipt from a shop that had overcharged her.

"He's safe," David said. "Thank God."

"Safe? It's nonsense," she said angrily. "Barcelona is a war zone. Your brother thinks I've never picked up a newspaper."

David pondered this: he had always assumed his mother wanted to be lied to. His parents' marital happiness seemed to depend on it.

It was just three of them in the flat now. David had not told his mother about Kate yet. To make extra money—he might need it if he was about to be thrown out of the house—he had taken on shifts washing dishes at the faculty club over Christmas.

"We mustn't worry," his father said, looking pointedly at David. "We have to get through this wedding, don't we? Your poor nerves, Hetty."

David's mother handed her husband the telegram.

"Put this in my jewelry box, would you, Max?"

She sat down at the kitchen table and set to slicing the line of carrots she had just peeled over the sink. Her shoulders looked both soft and brittle. David did not remember when he had last hugged her. He pressed his cheek against the back of his mother's head, rested his hands on her shoulders. Her hair was dry and she smelled sweet and comfortable, like his childhood. She patted his hand.

"Thank you, *boychik*," she said, although David was six-foot-two. She sighed heavily. "I'm going to wire Simon some money."

When she pulled down the salt box at the top of the cupboard, David's father rushed out of the bedroom and began opening and closing drawers like he was looking for something, too.

"What are you doing, Max?"

"Nothing!"

She shuffled two ten-pound notes and a handful of coins out of the box, and her frown deepened as she counted and recounted the money.

"Did one of you take twelve pounds out of this box?" she asked, looking back and forth between David and his father.

"Of course not," David said.

"Max?"

"I might've," his father said. "Not that much. But that would have been months ago. I don't know. It was for petrol, I think."

And, in the slump of his mother's narrow shoulders, David saw how much it taxed her to accommodate her husband's vices.

That night, they attended Lily's wedding. David was impressed by Cousin Shirl's quick work. She had transformed the old ballroom at the Rembrandt Hotel into a grand country manor. White satin drapes ballooned across the ceiling. Panels painted with French doors that opened on rolling hills, hedgerows, and latticed roses were mounted on the walls. Trays of delicious food kept appearing: cold salmon and mackerel, canapés of salted caviar, liver pâtés, deviled eggs, onion soup, chicken consommé, Persian melon, rack of lamb, filet mignon with artichoke marrow, sponge cakes, fruit glacés, and buckets of champagne on ice.

David's father was awestruck. "Who paid for this spectacular? Is Arthur a sultan or something?"

"His family is *very* well off," David's mother explained.

"I'll be sure to introduce myself."

The bride, David's cousin Lily, was radiant in a shining white satin dress. She and her new husband, Arthur, kept stealing proud looks at one another. No one would have guessed that they were marched to the altar at metaphorical gunpoint. Arthur came from a clan of more observant, monied, German-descended Jews. A few of his relatives were in full *frum* garb, with big black hats, and *tallit* strings hanging out from the bottom of their shirts.

Eyeing them, David's mother cringed self-consciously. "They'll be scandalized by us," she whispered. "Our family may as well be pagans, far as they're concerned."

Across the ballroom, David spotted his cousin Benjamin, Lily's brother, sitting at a table full of Arthur's friends. He went over to say hello. After a while, he noticed that his mother had found Uncle Sol and they seemed deeply engrossed in conversation. His father was distracted at the bar, *kibitzing* with his cousins. David decided to take the opportunity to say hello to his estranged uncle.

"Solly and I were just discussing your father's new business venture," David's mother said. Her voice was taut as a violin string.

"Yes!" Uncle Sol cried. "At the track."

Now David understood why his mother looked like that—

she had just been told that her husband was intentionally going into debt at racetracks across London, just so he could settle it with product from his mate's ice cream factory.

"I hear Max is trying to get the cousins in on it," said Uncle Sol said with a roll of his liquid-green eyes. "It's a bad deal, Hetty. But you know our Max, once he's set on something . . ."

David's mother's smile was pained. She could tolerate even the most egregious of his father's mistakes, so long as the family did not hear about it.

"Well," she said briskly. "Thank you for saying hello, Solly. Ever so nice to catch up."

"Nice to see you, Uncle Sol," David said.

Sol grinned. "Davy, come see me soon. We'll have a game of chess. I could tell you a few stories about what *I* got up to in my day. The French girls we met during the war, you would not believe. Not fit for ladies' ears, of course . . ."

"Goodbye, Sol," David's mother said. She waited until her brother-in-law was out of earshot and turned to David. "Get your father. We're leaving."

In the cab on the way home, David's father sulked at his own reflection in the window, vexed at being dragged out of the party.

"It's my family, ain't it?" he said. "I don't get dragged out of *her* family's weddings. Pfft. I should be so lucky . . ."

David put his hand on his mother's arm and she flinched away from him.

"Dad, I think you should tell Mum what's been going on," he said.

His father looked at him, incredulous. "*I* should tell her?"

"Yes. You owe it to Mum. It's her money, too."

"I haven't a clue why it falls on him to explain," his mother said, startling David. "What money? Don't you look at your father. He'll only agree with me."

"Sorry, what are we talking about?"

"I know what you've been up to, David, and I am humiliated. Humiliated."

"Me? I've nothing to do with that *farkakteh* scheme with the ice cream company! I told Dad not to do it!"

"Not the ice cream," she said through gritted teeth. "Your girlfriend. The little redheaded girl. Solly heard you've been parading her all over town. He saw you himself in Vicky Park a couple of weeks ago, kissing her face off."

David froze for a moment. He put his hand on the door handle. The cab wasn't driving very fast; if he jumped out, he thought he would probably survive. "Dad already knew about her," he blurted. "I told him and he said not to tell you."

"Thanks very much," his father said, screwing up his face. "Shows me for keeping your dirty secrets. Hetty, I told him to end it. I didn't want to upset you. You've been in such a state over Simon." He shook his head, but he did not look so devastated. He was probably relieved someone other than him was disappointing his wife.

"I wanted to tell you that I love her," David said to his mother. "What would you have me do?"

His mother gave him a cutting look. "I don't believe people follow my advice," she said. "I think you're going to keep chasing after her, no matter what I say."

"It's not real!" his father interjected. "It won't last, son. We don't have your schooling, but we've lived enough to know that."

"I've never felt like this before," David said. "I feel it in my guts."

"You've never been a twenty-two-year-old man before. Your guts aren't running the show. When the *schvantz* stands up . . ."

"Don't say it."

"The brain sits down."

David's mother was shaking her head weakly, like a drunk being forced to listen to the recipe for corned beef luncheon salad.

"I'm sorry I've disappointed you," David said, setting his jaw. He was going to be a man about this. He'd promised Kate. "But there it is."

"I'm not disappointed in you," his mother said. "I am disappointed in myself. I have failed to teach my son to respect his parents and his people. I've raised a bad son. That is my failure, not yours. I already lost one child. I can't believe you would make me go through this again."

"You've not lost Simon. He'll come home eventually."

"Not Simon. I lost your sister. I lost Rachel."

David had not anticipated this—his mother never, ever mentioned his baby sister.

"But I'm not dead," he said, desperation rising up inside him. "Please be reasonable." He looked to his father. "Dad, please?"

"I'm glad you brought up reason," his father said, his voice steely, and David knew he was finished. It was his parents versus him and together they were undefeated. "I am going to teach you about reason, Mr. University Genius. I'm going to show you just how in love you are." He banged on the window dividing them from the driver. "Where shall we drop you, son? Where does your *shiksa* live?"

"Stop it. I'm going home with you, so we can discuss this properly."

His father laughed. "It's not your home anymore. Look, there's the hospital. Brilliant. Perhaps they can scrounge a bed for you. Driver, please drop my son off at the traffic light."

The night porter at the hospital allowed David to spend the night on a bare mattress in a spare room in the resident dorm.

The radiators in the building were not connected, so he slept as far away from the window as possible, with his back against the wall shared with the corridor. All night long, doors slammed as new doctors came back and forth from the hospital. When David did drift off, he kept having the same dream: that he had found a way he could keep Kate and his family, he just had to find her so he could explain it to her. Startling awake to each crash of a door, he could never remember how.

In the morning, Kate was waiting for David by the canal, wearing an oversized fisherman's jumper. It was New Year's Day, 1937. When she spotted him walking along the wall, she put one fist to her hip and his heart sank. Was she angry with him, too?

"Happy New Year," she chirped, kissing him on the cheek. "I'm so glad you rang. I worried when I didn't hear from you yesterday."

"I told you, it was my cousin's wedding."

In that massive jumper, David thought Kate's auburn head appeared too small for her body. The illusion was a relief to him. Like a powerful painkiller that had saturated his neurons, her sexiness had begun to depress him. Since the day they met and he fell for her in one knockout blow, he had tried to note her imperfections: the way she went on about herself, her greediness, her furtive glances at Simon. They were meant to be exit routes for David, but only ended up endearing Kate to him.

"My father wants to meet you," she said. "You won't get on, of course, but then it's done. Perhaps you could come round for dinner next Sunday?"

David nodded. "Sure."

"What's the matter with you?" she said. "You look dreadful."

"Nothing." David rubbed his forehead, trying to push his headache away. "My parents have thrown me out. They're not speaking to me."

"You told them about me?"

"Yes."

"Oh my God! I hope you didn't tell them I'm a news photographer," she said excitedly. "They won't approve. They sound rather traditional . . ."

David did not have the heart to tell her that his parents had not asked anything about her. She was invisible—in a category that had no relevance to them whatsoever. Kate would not understand, and think badly of his parents, which David couldn't bear any more than them thinking badly of her.

Kate kissed his upper lip, then the bridge of his nose. "Where did you sleep last night?"

"A spare room in the hospital dormitory. My father lies to my mother every day and then has the nerve to throw *me* out of the house . . ."

Kate did not exactly smile, but a dimple punctuated her cheek—a reward for his disloyalty to his family. David wrapped his arms around her waist. He pushed his hips against hers and pulled her collar aside to kiss the base of her neck. She smoothed his back with downward strokes of her palms, making his inner ears buzz with pleasure.

"I wish you could stay with me," she said. "Like before. I'll try to find out when my father is leaving again."

David wished he could tell her everything he was feeling, but feared Kate would recoil from him. He wanted to tell her that whenever he felt happy with her, a voice in his head asked if it might all be an illusion. That it was possible that he did not love her, that he never had, that he was a bad person, and that his parents were right about her.

Instead, he said: "Don't think badly of my parents. They think they're helping me. A friend of one of my cousins married a Gentile, and his father was so outraged by it that he tore his clothes and sat *shiva*."

"What the heck's that?"

If David married Kate, there would always be questions like this. She would be lost in his world.

"It's like a wake," he said.

"I'm a Catholic and that seems a bit theatrical, even to me."

"He never spoke to his son again."

"Well, I feel sorry for that man," she said. "And I feel sorry for your parents. You're a brilliant son. I wish they could see that."

"They do see it. They . . ."

David turned away. Kate would hate what he said next. He could not be touching her when he said it.

He started again: "I only wonder . . ." He paused, afraid the tenderness between them could break with one misplaced word. "I only wonder what our future together might look like. My parents aren't wrong that it is going to be difficult for us."

Please, he thought, bracing for her response, *please show me you understand.*

She glared at him like he was a stranger trying to read over her shoulder on the bus.

"Are you chucking me?" she asked. "Is that what's happening now?"

"No. I need you. I love you."

Kate smiled. "In that case, we will be fine. Just the two of us."

David was surprised by how lonely that idea made him feel.

Chapter 15

4th January, 1937

On Monday, David tracked down Dr. Spar in his surgery and explained his situation: that he'd had the best intentions, but that he had fallen in love with Kate Grifferty and wanted to marry her. Unlike David's father, Dr. Spar was an educated man. There was a chance he would understand David's predicament and show him a way forward.

He loved Dr. Spar's rooms. The walls were lined with stuffed bookshelves; it felt like any question could be answered there.

The older man listened without commentary, nodding occasionally, until David finished the whole story.

"Might I ask, have you already asked this woman to marry you?"

"No. I haven't yet."

"Has she expressed that she wants to marry you?"

"She doesn't talk that way. But I know her. We are in love."

Dr. Spar made a little tent with his fingers and looked over them at David.

"These are matters of conscience," he said finally. "You must determine for yourself what makes a good man."

"But you are an expert on the brain," David pressed.

"You would like my professional opinion?" Dr. Spar

cracked a rare smile. This was a good sign. "David, your pi-
tuitary gland is being repeatedly flooded with oxytocin and
your cerebral cortex has rationalized those extreme fluctua-
tions by labeling them 'love.' "

"All love stories begin that way," David protested. "Love is
not meant to be rational."

"Does it not trouble you that your children will not be
Jewish? A friend of mine married a Gentile woman. A great
lady. I have dined at their home many times. They have four
sons." Dr. Spar held up four fingers. "Four sons." He shook
his head. "They would have grown up to have Jewish children, Jewish grandchildren, and so on and so forth."

"I don't believe in God," David said. "It won't matter who
my children's mother is. I won't teach them to believe in a
God who does not exist."

"Who said anything about God? *L'dor v'dor.* From generation to generation. Judaism is so much a part of you that you
can't even see it. I saw it when I first met you, I see it in you
now."

"Yes, but you and I are also men of science."

"And?"

"I want you to agree that being a physician is empirically
of more value than how observant a Jew I am. I can still be
a good man."

"No. You want me to agree it's a good idea for you to marry
out and I'm not going to do that. I don't agree. I think it is a
waste." Dr. Spar walked around his desk and opened the surgery door, dismissing David. "I'm a busy man. You asked for
my diagnosis. I gave it to you. I've told you. I've *shown* you,
at Grant Court. We are an endangered people, David. You are
aware of this. We face an existential crisis. Frankly, I find it
astonishing that you would want any part in that."

From a clinical perspective, David had left the butterflies-
in-stomach stage of love and entered the harpoon-in-chest

stage. The features of this stage, as he defined it, were: insomnia, arrhythmia, obsessions, and short-term memory loss about anything other than Kate.

David was sitting at a private desk in the medical library, massaging his forehead on his folded arms. He had been camping in the dorm for five days and had a terrible headache. He was meant to be studying neurology, Spar's subject, but couldn't seem to get any traction on his reading.

David flipped to the index of the neurology textbook and ran his finger down the page to *Sex*. Of the eight hundred and twenty-six pages in the book, there were three entries, five pages total, dealing with the subject—all of them in regard to self-gratification. *Unhelpful.*

At five o'clock sharp, he gave up on his work and dashed over the road to the Good Sam, where there was a telephone. He ducked into the smelly alcove behind the gents and rang Kate. No one was home.

Then he walked through Whitechapel for about half an hour, hoping the movement and the cold would flush the despair from his body. He walked into the wind, daring it to stop him. A sad song in the key of B minor ran through his head. It was a piece of piano music he could not place. What was wrong with him? He was exhausted. He was confused. His eyes felt like radishes dipped in saltwater. These were his streets, the streets he had walked on since he was a boy, but he felt self-conscious, like everyone who passed him saw him for who he really was: a double-talker, a *fonferer*, a bad son.

David resolved he would use his exile to prove he was not a complete disappointment. This was his final term of medical school. His qualifying exam was less than three months away and if he didn't pass, he would have nothing and be nothing. As he walked, he thought out a schedule for his days in which all time not spent at the hospital or in lecture would be spent at the library. He would pass his exams with brute force.

Then, as a test, he allowed himself to think of Kate again and felt flat—normal and fine. Not numb, but even-keeled.

Just as he was congratulating himself on achieving this homeostasis, David passed Levenberg's pharmacy and it all came flooding back. Kate standing in the doorway on the day they met, the clunky man's watch on her lovely wrist. One heartbeat tripped over the next. His passion for her surged back, shortly followed by the feeling of his head in a vise.

David was betting everything on Kate, trading almost everyone he loved for a dream.

All his life, he had condemned his father for making those kinds of bets.

Chapter 16

10th January, 1937

Sunday afternoon, Kate watched from the window until she saw David coming up the path through the park. She had asked him to arrive a little early for dinner, so they could talk before her father came down. His loping gait incited a feeling in Kate not unlike panic. When they met by the canal last week, he had been so consumed by guilt about his parents that he could hardly look at her. She knew she was in danger of losing him. As much as it terrified her, she had to tell him how she felt.

"*I love you,*" she mouthed to herself, practicing.

Before opening the door, she touched up her raspberry lipstick in the umbrella stand mirror, straightened her necklace, smoothed her cream satin blouse. She was out the door and on the front steps before he could knock. She had almost resigned herself to the idea that he would not come, but he had.

"How are you?" she asked. "You look better."

"I'm fine," he said, stopping still at the bottom of the garden steps. His skin and eyes were clear, he looked rested, and his hair had just been cut.

She guessed: "They've let you come back home."

David nodded. "Just for a night. I needed to get some rest. My January exams begin tomorrow."

It was as if he had flicked off the switch on the electrical current running between them, abandoning her in darkness with her arms outstretched.

"Mumma's boy," she said, stepping backward into the doorway. "I knew you'd go back."

"Kate, I can't do whatever I please," he said, still making no move toward her. "I'm not like you. My family need me."

"If they need you so much, why did they throw you out in the first place?"

David sighed and toed the ground. The blankness in his eyes was crippling her confidence. Confidence had been essential to her plan. She was going to praise him for being his own man and he would embrace her. Then she would tell him that she loved him, too.

"I might have been more honest about the pressure I'm under," he said finally. "I've been terribly unfair to you."

He spoke slowly and quietly, like the effort pained him. Just standing there making eye contact with her seemed difficult. But Kate could no more stop searching David's face for a sign of love than she could stop breathing the razor-sharp January air. At the thought of him walking away, her skin started to tingle.

"Aren't you coming in?" she pressed, feeling frantic. "Mrs. Hull is here. She's done a lovely roast."

"No. I don't think I should. I'm sorry."

His words wounded her, but she would not stagger. She was suddenly extremely angry. She wanted to hurt him the way he hurt her.

"Damn you, David! I've asked nothing of you, except to meet my father and you show up and stand there like the garden's quicksand. What is *wrong* with you? You're meant to be an adult, not a little boy clinging to his mother's apron strings."

"I'm miserable," he said simply. "And I'll make you miserable, too. There's too much stacked against us."

Rejection roiled in Kate's stomach like acid. Usually the

bulk of David would have drawn her toward him, but she was furious now. He was pathetic to her.

"You created this," Kate said, her voice trembling. She pressed on her throat with her fingers, as if she could smooth out the sound. "I didn't ask for any of this. You hunted me down, you tricked me, you made me believe I loved you."

At last, David looked like he'd been hit, cracked open. A hollow victory. Kate turned to open the door; he bounded up the steps and grabbed her tightly so she couldn't.

"Don't go yet," he pleaded.

"Get off of me," she hissed. "My father will come down here and beat you to death." She wriggled free of his arms.

Then she collapsed, pressed her face in his neck and inhaled the smell of him one last time, and everything came back to her—every touch that seemed guided by her own hand, everything she told him that no one else knew, every time she felt understood. He was taking all of that from her and she hated him for it.

When she pushed him away again, he let her and stood with his arms hanging limp at his sides.

"Goodbye, David," she said. For a moment she saw something in his face, the same startling vulnerability that had exposed his feelings for her on the day he returned the camera part. His eyes were pleading, open, full of what looked to Kate like love.

"David?"

He said nothing, just looked at his feet and shook his head.

Kate slammed the door as hard as she could and locked it behind her. She didn't know what love looked like; she was a fool. So was he. Silent sobs hammered to be let out of her chest and her life rolled out before her, cold and flat and interminable. David did not love her. No one ever would. She didn't even have her job in Fleet Street, the one thing she was good at, anymore.

She hid herself in the shadows of the foyer. David was still standing outside the door, facing the street. He could not see her but she could see him through the frosted glass. He seemed to hesitate, leaned his head back against the glass, and Kate went to the door, ready to forgive him, to take as much of him as he would give her. But then he jogged down the steps, crossed the road, and disappeared into the park.

A few nights later, Kate woke on her side, instantly alert in the darkness. She was calmer now, serene, even. She switched on the lamp next to her bed. The clock said quarter to four. The fire in the grate had gone out but she felt rather warm.

She sat up and padded to the lavatory on the landing. In the mirror, her nipples were visible through her thin cotton nightgown. Her breasts felt heavy, sort of feverish. When she lifted up her nightgown, she saw that they were larger than they had been in her bath before bed. They were jutting out from her ribs. Even her nipples had expanded, and darkened to a dusky red.

Something was happening to her. Something *had* happened.

And she just knew. She knew she was going to have a baby. And there was this sense of being very small and also part of everything that ever was. Of taking her place in it all.

Kate sank down to the frigid pink-and-lavender tile. It had happened: her birthright. She was another pregnant, miserable Irish girl, one in a long line of them. Would she abandon this baby to the nuns? Would she beg for help from David, who did not want her anymore? Or was she going to be strong and keep her head up, even at the expense of her own respectability?

Of course she was pregnant. It was always going to end like this.

It was humbling, like discovering she was just an ant carrying a crumb from the cutting board to the windowsill. She rested her forehead on her bare knees. At this moment, free will seemed like such an absurd concept. Maybe this was what all her swooning over David had been about—getting to this place, to the lavatory floor in the middle of the night with a brand-new life inside her. The baby was nothing to do with him anymore. It was part of *her*, making *her* body do queer and marvelous things. Her destiny, not his.

In the end, Kate had been too much for him. Well, he could go to hell.

Why had she assumed David was an expert on sex and babies and how to stop them coming, just because he was studying medicine? He was nearly as ignorant as she was and his withdrawing was apparently useless. He'd never brought any French letters.

Another useless man. God, she hoped this would be a girl.

If Kate didn't know anything about sex, she knew even less about children. There had never been any point in learning. Children had no place in the life she'd planned for herself. She closed her eyes and tried to imagine what this baby would be like: a small person Kate could be kind to and love and would love her back. If it was a boy, she would raise him to be a good man.

This prospect made her smile.

It felt like a new world opening up. Things had been dreadful and having a purpose seemed like deliverance. She could be a mother, a good one. Without her job and without David, she had been lost, but a good mother could not be lost. A good mother had a plan—making a safe and clean home, taking her baby to the park and the doctor's. Kate could do all that. The photojournalist's life she had wanted wasn't going to happen—that had already been made painfully clear to her. Her female body was an impediment in Fleet Street. It made her vulnerable, weak, despised. And she couldn't bear it anymore. Being diminutive did not suit her. It wasn't her nature. She was powerful, a creator. Raising this baby properly, with love, would prove it.

Kate felt fervently awake. She decided to make a record of her body, while she could still recognize it: an inventory as much as a self-portrait.

She went to get her Leica and stood in front of the long horizontal mirror above the troughlike porcelain washbasin. Then she took off her nightclothes and splashed water on her face and chest and rubbed herself dry with a towel. Her face was a little puffy but it looked fresh, like she'd been for a bracing walk in winter air.

Without thinking much, she started to take pictures of herself, in the mirror and behind her back and all around her naked body. She was shooting blind on most of them, knowing none might turn out, and that emboldened her. No one would ever see them anyway.

When she finished the roll, she wound it and put it back in its canister. She'd develop it when she had access to a darkroom again; she couldn't trust it to a lab. To mark it, she tied a thin red ribbon around the canister and put it in one of her negative storage kits. Then, suddenly spent, she wrapped herself in her dressing gown and fell into bed.

As she drifted off to sleep, Kate decided two things. First, her father would not be allowed to taint this baby in any way. It would not be raised in a home bereft of affection. This was her chance to have someone she could love and take care of and make a better life for. If she wasn't determined, her father would send her to a Catholic laundry in Ireland and force her to give it up. That was motivation enough to keep it.

Second, Kate would have to find a new place, a new life for her and her baby, because she was going nowhere fast in her father's lonely house in East London.

Chapter 17

15th January, 1937

David's mother patted his hand across the kitchen table. "He's come to his senses," she said. "Max, didn't I tell you he would?"

"You're a good boy, Davy," his father said. He was putzing around the washbasin.

David rubbed his eyes and studied the table.

"Some things are just not meant to be," his mother mused, a smile in her voice, and made a tutting sound. "Next time, you'll be careful. You won't scare us like that. Now, what would you like for your tea? What can I cook for you?"

"I'm not hungry."

"Beans on toast?"

"Fine."

She lit the range with a match and placed a tin pan over the flame. "You needn't worry about anything outside your exams now. Your father and I are going to wait on you hand and foot!"

"You don't need to wait on me," David said. "Actually, do you mind if I lie down?"

"Are you poorly? Do you have a temperature?"

"He's got a broken heart, Het," his father said. "Leave him be."

"I will, as soon as he's had his tea. Go to your room, *boy-chik*, and I'll bring you a plate."

David trudged to his room and sat on his bed in the dark. Doom sat heavy on his chest. He climbed under his freshly bleached eiderdown and switched on the lamp, picked up a textbook, and tried to read about the mortality factors in acute appendicitis. Then he forgot everything and read it over again. He looked around the room, at the shelf his father had built into one of the corners. It held all David's books, his memorization ribbons from Hebrew class, his collection of cast-iron toy cars. Simon had pasted a photograph of Lillian Roth in shorts, sitting on the bumper of an Oakland Eight, inside one of the shelves. His mother allowed it after David told her the actress's surname. Nothing had happened to him in this room. Everything had happened to him in this room. His ankles dangled off the end of the sagging cot he'd used for a mattress for the last twenty years; when he finally had money for his own flat, he would find a place with heating that worked and a proper bed for an adult male.

He listened to his father leave the flat, go down the stairs, and come back up. With a propulsive knock, his mother came into his room carrying a tray with baked beans on toast, an orange, and a large mug of tea with milk. There was a letter on the tray, too, in a red-and-white-bordered international envelope. The postmark said Barcelona.

"You've a letter from Simon," his mother said. "I'm jealous. You would think he would have addressed it to me."

She sat on Simon's bed and looked at David expectantly.

"Did you want me to read or eat first?" he asked.

"Read, of course!" she said. "Out loud."

David tore open the envelope and a photograph fell out: Simon, in shirtsleeves, kneeling next to a very small cannon. He was grinning for the camera like he was on holiday. Meanwhile, the British government had just announced that anyone volunteering to fight on either side in the Spanish

Civil War would be subject to prosecution. This was one of many recent concessions to Hitler and Mussolini, as the vast majority of British volunteers were anti-fascist.

"Dear God," his mother said, snatching the photo. "Your brother is trying to kill me. I've never been so sure. Why won't he come home?"

David scanned the letter to make sure it was fit for his mother's ears, but before he got through the first paragraph his mother pinched his arm.

"Out loud!"

"Fine, fine." David cleared his throat. "Dear Davy . . ."

"I can't imagine why he's only wrote to you. Don't I deserve to know my son is safe?"

"Would you please let me read, Mum?"

"Yes. Sorry. Go on."

" 'I am now stationed at the British hospital in Valdeganga,' " David read. " 'The second day I got here they gave me a lorry full of parcels and a map and told me to drive straight to Madrid and it was over very difficult country. When the people saw they were getting help they cheered and kissed me and tried to feed me. We aren't supposed to accept any food because they'll give you their last food and they have very little. So when I go out on a delivery, I always have a little bit of food. All the Spanish nurses want to learn English and have asked me to teach them . . .' "

"Well! I just bet they have," David's mother interrupted.

David ignored her. " 'I drive the lorry between Valdeganga and Madrid,' " he read on, " 'picking up supplies and people, delivering them. Every day I go to the village to collect bread and provisions. Sometimes I pick up wounded that the ambulances can't manage. We don't have enough medical people or ambulances . . .' "

Again, his mother interrupted: "Don't get any ideas."

" 'But I look after them. I give them water and make them

comfortable. Whatever is needed. Looking after the wounded has me thinking of you a fair bit. I did not realize how difficult it is to want to help someone in pain and not be able. If only . . .' "

David stopped reading and took a bite of his toast and a sip of his tea. The next paragraph had Kate's name in it, so he read it quickly to himself.

If only you were here. The hospital would put you to work straightaway. You would be far more useful in Spain than England. It's dangerous but I like it better than any place I've ever been. Bring your pretty Irish Kate. Be courageous, Davy. I know you have it in you. You're my brother, after all.

"Go on," his mother urged.

" 'Please tell Mum and Dad that I am safe,' " David continued out loud. " 'I am happy here, knowing that I am living out my ideals of liberty with people of the same mind. I will write them soon as I get a minute.

" 'Your loving brother,

" 'Simon.' "

The following afternoon, David lugged his bike into the vestibule. His mother was there on the stairs, waiting for him.

"Something has happened," she said. "I need to speak to you, away from your father. He's too distressed."

Her face looked calm, but she was choosing her words carefully. The ground under David lurched.

"It's Simon, isn't? He's been killed."

"No! Bite your tongue. It's the house. We have to give it up. With your brother gone, I've realized we don't need the space. It's not sensible."

"What are you talking about? Simon will be back. You love our flat. We've been here my entire life."

She sighed. "I know, but this is a place for a family. For grandchildren. And you'll be thirty, David."

"In eight years."

"Well, I've given up hope that you'll find someone suitable."

"We can't have this again," David groaned. "I've done what you wanted, haven't I?"

His mother held her hands up in a motion of surrender, then dropped them at her side.

"The truth is," she said, "we can't afford to stay here any longer. Your father, he was too trusting and got mixed up with some bad people. It isn't his fault. He thought this thing would never come to call, but well, it's a lot of money. And these people just keep coming. Vultures. I could wring that Arnie Birch's neck . . ."

David hated it when she spoke about his father like he was an innocent. He wanted to ask her: *Why do you let Dad do this to you? Why do you let him do this to us?* But he wasn't sure he wanted to know the answers.

"How much do you need?" David asked, rubbing his brow.

"A hundred pounds," she said.

An astronomical sum. David wouldn't make close to that for years. He sat down on the lowest step.

"This is why I didn't want to tell you," she said, her voice breaking. "I didn't want you worrying."

"Can you put them off for a few months? When I have a proper job, I can help."

"I thought you said the hospital post you want hardly pays a pittance."

"I might not get it."

His mother smiled sadly. "You will," she said. "That's you, *boychik*. You can't help it. You succeed."

"Even if I do, I don't have to take it."

"Don't be silly." She squeezed his arm. "You'll take it. I've already found us a cozy place in Bethnal Green, haven't I? Just up the road. Bit snug, but it will suit the three of us, and Simon on the settee when he comes home. Don't worry."

* * *

When Dr. Spar invited David to his office for a drink on Thursday afternoon, David was certain he was going to get another basting. He didn't want to talk about Kate. He didn't want to see the approval in Dr. Spar's face when he heard David had left her.

The door was closed and when Dr. Spar opened it, he looked surprised to see David standing there. The old man's eyes were red and he was ghostly pale.

"Is it a bad time?" David asked, his self-consciousness turning to concern. "Should I come back later?"

"No, it's good you're here. It's not healthy to mourn alone."

"Mourn? What's happened?"

The doctor pulled a bottle of Schwartzhog and two glasses from under the desk and handed them to David.

"If you could pour, please," Dr. Spar said, falling into the chair behind his desk. "I've just had some very bad news. My dear brother . . ."

Dr. Spar paused and traced the wood grain on his desk with his finger. His body was still, except for his hand, which had a gentle tremor as he moved it. He exhaled heavily and started again:

"We have been writing about friends he was helping leave Germany. Recently, the letters stopped coming. And today my daughter came to tell me the dreadful news. They killed him. The German police killed my brother," Dr. Spar said flatly. "Right in the street. He was trying to save a little girl the Gestapo took from her mother and hurled against a wall."

"My God." David covered his face with his palms for a moment. "I'm so sorry." He tried to breathe slowly. "Is your daughter still nearby? Can I get her for you?"

"She went to find a cup of tea for me." Dr. Spar reached for the glass of Schwartzhog and drained it.

"What about your brother's family?" David asked, pouring him another drink. His hands were shaking now, too. "Are they safe?"

"Of course not."

"Can we get them to England?"

"I don't know." Dr. Spar's lower jaw hung open as he seemed to consider this. "Probably not." For a while he just breathed, mandible twitching a little at the end of each exhalation. "Everything is compacted. The British Jewish establishment do not want Jewish refugees from Eastern Europe to come here. They are embarrassed by them. They want to send them to Palestine. But there is going to be a war soon. They are coming for us. Make no mistake. The Nazis are relentless and they are coming for *us*."

David knew he could not comfort Dr. Spar. All he could think to do was sit with the man until his daughter returned. It was raining outside the office window, and getting darker by the minute. The wind was blowing hard, telegraphing drops of water in horizontal lines and dots across the panes.

"My brother absolutely refused to leave Germany," Dr. Spar went on. "When the Nazis seized power, he drove to the border of Belgium in a panic but turned around at the last moment. He always argued that Germany is a civilized country. They are scientists, engineers, philosophers. He said it's not as if they'll kill everybody . . ."

He bowed his head and a young woman appeared at the door with a cup of tea.

"Here you are, *Vati*," she said to Dr. Spar. "Drink this."

Dr. Spar smiled weakly and took the tea from his daughter. "Rivka, meet David Rabatkin. He is a fourth-year at the medical college here. David, this is my daughter, Rivka. She has just commenced her studies at Cambridge. Maybe we can bring her over to medicine, like her old father."

"Call me Becky," the girl said. "And I'm reading English, not medicine. Thank you for sitting with my father." She settled into the club chair next to David's and took her father's hand across the desk.

"David," Dr. Spar said weakly, "would you mind if we met another day? I find I'm not fit for company after all."

"Of course not," David said, embarrassed to have intruded upon the Spars' grief. "I'll stop by in a few days. I am so sorry for your loss. If there's anything I can do, anything at all . . ."

"Thank you," Dr. Spar said. "Our family shall get through this together. This is the only way to face the inevitable despair of life. As one people."

Chapter 18

4th February, 1937

In spite of himself, David still found ways to be near Kate—strolling near her house, studying for his exam in Victoria Park. From the benches near St. Agnes Gate, he could see her front garden. Once, he saw the charwoman putting the bins out and once he saw a light switch on in Kate's bedroom. David had stood there, transfixed, staring up at the window with his heart trying to leap from his rib cage.

Even though he never saw Kate herself, just being on the street where she lived made him feel closer to her. Mostly her house seemed empty. In his first frenzy of feeling for her, David had not understood what a solitary life she led.

He was reading on the park bench one frosty morning, when the Griffertys' door opened. Kate and her father appeared. She was holding the two cardboard suitcases she used for her photography things. Mr. Grifferty was sliding a massive black Victorian trunk onto the pavement. From where David sat, about two hundred feet away, he could hear it scrape. He could see Mr. Grifferty's breath in the frozen air. Kate stood in the doorway, watching her father load the trunk into a black cab.

Something stronger than David yanked him to his feet. His ears felt like they were stuffed with cotton. He remembered

Simon's letter: *Be courageous, Davy.* He walked out of the park and then jogged across Gore Road, slipping on a patch of ice, ignoring the curse of a cyclist who clipped his arm.

"Wait," David shouted. "Kate, wait!"

Mr. Grifferty had bundled Kate and her cases into the back of the cab and was leaning in to tell the driver something.

David flung open the back door on the street side and climbed in. Kate gasped, pressed herself against the other side of the car, gripped her coat around her. She looked at him like he was a thug. David saw himself as Kate must and smoothed his hair.

"Please . . . ," he said. "Don't go. I love you."

Kate pulled farther back from him. She was guarding herself. "What does that mean?"

"Where are you going?"

Mr. Grifferty peered through the window. His large face was purple-red, like a thumb slammed in a door. "Who in bloody Christ's name are you?"

"Just a minute, Frank!" Kate shouted. Then said to David: "I'm going to Dublin." There was triumph in the tilt of her chin. "I've been offered a brilliant job with the *Irish Times*."

David was aware of an opportunity to be unselfish, which he did not take.

"Don't accept," he pleaded. "Stay here."

Kate chewed the inside of her lip. David reached out and touched her face with his hand and she leaned into it. She was warm against his bare skin and his spirit skyrocketed. There were so many reasons they should be together and only one they shouldn't.

"We could carry on just as we were . . . ," he said gently, resting his forehead against hers. If her father wasn't glowering at the window, he would have kissed her. "Unconventional," he went on, "like we talked about."

Then Kate's face closed, she swatted him away, and suddenly a separate force collided with David's back. It was Mr.

Grifferty, grabbing David out of the cab and flinging him into the street. For a short man, he was incredibly strong, like a pit bull. Mr. Grifferty closed the cab door, banged on the roof, and shouted: "Victoria Station!"

David was still scrambling to his feet.

"I don't know what you're after," Mr. Grifferty growled, "but you've got a massive pair on you, coming round here."

"I'm sorry, Mr. Grifferty. I know what you must think of me."

"A pair I will personally relieve you of if I see you within spitting distance of my daughter."

"I didn't mean to hurt her, sir. I apologize."

"Do you really mean that? Then feck off to whatever Whitechapel gutter you came from, Jew boy."

David got himself out of the street and onto the park side of the road, glancing over his shoulder to make sure Mr. Grifferty wasn't coming after him. He wasn't; he was standing in his garden like a gargoyle, glaring at David.

And Kate was long gone.

Stung, David stormed across the park, almost forgetting to grab his books off the bench. What did she want from him anyway? She'd always gone on about never wanting to get married. What did she expect him to do, show up with a ring? He had just offered her everything that mattered: his love, his heart.

Then it hit him: she didn't want anything from him. Not anymore.

Kate would not look back for David. As the cab turned into Victoria Park Road, she clenched her jaw, holding her neck rigid. The warm smell of him lingered in the cab.

Why had David come to her again, just to ask for more of the same? More sneaking around, more apologies. Kate didn't have time for it. She was a ticking clock.

She knew she could stop the driver and get out of the cab

and just tell David she was pregnant. He would keep her and the baby safe. They would cope with it together.

She also knew that if she told David, he'd try to fix everything and she'd resent him for controlling her. His family would make her the villain. He'd be ashamed of her. Her life would grow even smaller.

Still, Kate looked back, half hoping David would be running after the cab.

Of course, the frozen street was empty save for a few parked cars and a horse-drawn bread cart.

Kate wasn't even out of Hackney and it was already as if she didn't exist.

She felt hurt and stupid, but she also felt free. And free, she now understood, was the best she could hope for. She clasped her hands together, her body waking to the shambles of her life, every spark of awareness like a prickle in a waking limb. This was reality: Kate was utterly alone in the world.

And yet, somehow, her soul thrummed with anticipation. She was on her way to a new life. A song fragment from a Marx Brothers film rose up inside her: *alone, alone with a heart meant for you alone* . . . "You" wasn't David anymore; "you" was her baby.

Part II

Brighton

Chapter 19

1st July, 1940

Kate walked down to Brighton Beach alone, hoping for one last swim before the Ministry of Defense shut it down. Early that morning, a flyer had been delivered through the mail slot at the boardinghouse, warning of imminent attacks by sea. *DO NOT GIVE ANY GERMAN ANYTHING,* it read. *DO NOT TELL HIM ANYTHING! HIDE YOUR FOOD AND YOUR BICYCLES! HIDE YOUR MAPS!*

But today, thankfully, it wasn't German troops but day-trippers from London that swarmed the blustery beach: men with rolled-up trousers and women in smart bathing costumes and round-framed white sunglasses. An anchored sailboat flying a Union Jack bobbed near the shore. On the promenade, photographers paced with their clunky mahogany cameras, ready to make portraits on the spot for holiday mementos.

A group of Royal Air Force men had taken over Kate's favorite spot—equidistant between the two piers—their blue uniforms heaped on the shingle. The Channel was choppy and green and the wind whipped Kate's long hair into her mouth. It was a struggle not to fuss with it as she walked past the half-naked airmen and settled into an empty deck chair. A few of the soldiers swiveled to watch her, but they seemed unimpressed. RAF men were the celebrities of wartime and used to being gawked at—conspicuously handsome, tanned, and thick-wristed. Half of them had cleft chins.

A bee took refuge in the rocks around her feet and Kate wished it would just sting her. It would be nice to feel something other than desire, an ache which had never left her. She dreamed of David still, but in the morning she would put him away, a doll she was too old to be playing with. Somehow, the war had only made it worse.

She unfastened her leather sandals and stretched her feet on the sunbaked stones, closing her eyes and focusing on the shifting sounds of the water. The noise came close and receded, creating a landscape in her mind, empty space and then fullness. She opened her eyes and took out her magazine—a creased copy of the *Picture Post* someone had left under a bed at the boardinghouse—and tried to read. The issue bore the headline, *A PLAN AGAINST INVASION,* under a snapshot of three adorable British Expeditionary Forces, grinning and giving the thumbs-up signal. Kate laid the magazine in her lap, wincing at the nostalgia it stirred in her. There was a time she might have had her work in the *Picture Post.*

She watched as a group of school-aged girls attempted to place a flapping picnic blanket on the rocks. Kate envied their stylish head scarves and floral dresses and carefree laughter. The skin on their foreheads and legs were smooth, their beauty effortless. Even the plain one was lovely. They had no idea how gorgeous they were or how men would eventually drain it from them, how they would suck it all up for themselves. She felt overcome with tenderness for the girls; she almost loved them. One day, Margaret would sit on the beach like that and Kate would chase away any man who looked at her.

She remembered the first time she took Margaret down to the sea to put her toes in the water. The toddler—courting death since she took her first steps into the grate of a smoldering fireplace—had charged fearlessly into the waves, shouting with joy. Without her mother holding her back, she would have drowned.

Sighing, Kate looked out over the sea. France was that fuzzy line of gray resting on the horizon. The raw, fishy smell of the water and the gulls squawking and diving overhead made her miss the Thames.

One of the sunbathing airmen was staring at her. She knew him—an officer newly billeted at her elder sister's boarding-house, Puffin's Perch. He was stretched out on a deck chair, about twenty feet from Kate. His eyes were hidden by sun-glasses, but he was definitely tracking her. Flight Lieutenant Clifton Prouty was his name. He had checked in a few days earlier. Most of the hotels in town had been commandeered by the War Department, to house soldiers and staff. Even though many annual guests had cancelled after Dunkirk, Puffin's Perch was full to bursting with evacuees and defense workers.

Since Betsy the housekeeper had left them to become a land girl, it fell on Kate to do the rooms every morning. She had found that male guests were generally tidier than women, whose blocked-up sinks, dirty knickers, and overflowing wastebaskets seemed almost vengeful. The fellows usually left a scattering of beard shavings and a few balled-up tis-sues. Lieutenant Prouty kept his room spotless and he made his own bed. The only trace of him was the scent of carbolic soap. It made Kate feel as if she knew something about him: he was disciplined, considerate, self-denying.

Out of the corner of her eye, she now considered the sun-bathing lieutenant. He was built like a wall, not tall but very broad in the chest and arms, with a short military haircut and ears that stuck out like jug handles. Every part of him was deeply tanned. He was a bit rough looking, like his nose had been broken once or twice, and gray at his temples. He was at least ten years older than her.

When Lieutenant Prouty noticed her noticing him, he smiled. Kate looked over the water toward France, pretending to not recognize him.

For three years, she had been as guarded as a nun, devoted to her daughter's welfare, and the RAF men made her feel exposed. They were tossing a rugby ball around now, shouting at each other in deep, throaty voices. She took a deep breath and reopened her magazine.

The feeling would pass; it always did. "Stove, touch, ouch," she murmured to herself as she tried to find her place on the page. "Stove, touch, ouch."

Until she met David, Kate had not understood what a liability her body was. That autumn—nearly four years ago now—her body had betrayed her and she ended up a cleaning woman in a boardinghouse. Now not only a woman but an unwed mother, Kate's journalism career was over. In its place, she had a nocturnal toddler with David's reproving green eyes.

Later, while the guests had their dinners in the dining room, Kate, her sister Orla, and newly three-year-old Margaret ate in the kitchen downstairs. To the side of the table, Orla had hung a poster from the Southern Railway Company. *FAME! FASHION! BRIGHTON!* it proclaimed—ironically, as far as Kate was concerned. Margaret sat on the floor playing with two tin cars, her chin sunk into the baby fat around her neck. A halo of blond curls hovered at the crown of her head. She growled as she made one of the cars drive a track only she could see in the brown linoleum.

"Park your cars," Kate said. "It's time for your food."

Margaret gurgled a laugh and crashed her car into Kate's heel. Orla put a saucepan on the gas range to fry some mysterious gray meat. The long metal handle hung over the edge of the stove. Kate turned the handle toward the wall, where

Margaret could not reach it and pull scalding oil onto her head.

Kate arranged her daughter's plate with a sliced pickled beet and four toast points. The child had an old man's taste buds and loved sour things. In some ways, the war suited Margaret—with blackout curtains she finally slept through the night and she had always preferred root vegetables above all other foods. Bread was one of the only foods not rationed and it had always settled her tummy.

"Mammy used to do a roast every Sunday," Orla mused, poking at the sizzling meat rectangle with a wooden spoon. Twenty-five years after their mother's death, Kate still felt a stab of jealousy that Orla could use that word: *Mammy*.

The sisters did not look alike. Orla was short and curvaceous. Her complexion, like Kate's, was creamy and dappled with freckles, but she had their father's pale blond hair and ice-blue eyes.

"I *do* wish you'd not eaten the bacon ration, Kate," Orla went on, frowning. "Next time, feed it to Margaret at least."

"She doesn't like bacon."

"Everyone likes bacon. You should be careful, love. We hold on to our weight in this family." Orla held up her own plump wrist as evidence. "Even you will. I can tell. Mammy's mother was tall, too, like an egg on toothpicks."

If Orla didn't help so much with Margaret—and she did, she adored the child—Kate would have moved out of the boardinghouse and away from her sister's nagging. It wasn't that the place wasn't nice. It was a white stucco town house on the seafront, past its prime but comfortable. Orla and Kate worked the front desk in the lounge, an aggressively ugly room, with orange-striped wallpaper, a hulking mahogany desk, and a pink velveteen couch with crocheted antimacassars. The only boardinghouse residents who predated Kate were Orla and an Australian budgie named Robird who spent his days scuttering around a wicker birdcage that hung on a stand in the kitchen. His birdseed was kept in an urn over the stove and he constantly chattered and fussed with his little bell-framed mirror. Only Orla claimed to understand anything he said.

All of it was lovely. All of it was fine. Kate was safe in her sister's kitchen, even in the middle of a war. Safe as she rested her forehead against her daughter's. Yet she felt as trapped and vulnerable as Robird in his cage.

When her father appeared a few days later at Puffin's Perch, Kate's first impulse was to slam the door in his face. Brighton was just an hour's train journey from London, but this was his first visit since she had moved there. He had let three years pass without meeting Margaret. Being turned away would serve him right. But a weak part of Kate wondered if maybe, when Frank Grifferty laid eyes on his beautiful granddaughter, something would finally click in his heart and he would love her as he hadn't been able to love his daughter.

So, Kate laid out tea for him in the drawing room, where guests enjoyed their after-dinner coffees and listened to the news on the molasses-colored Bakelite wireless. Orla's girlfriends used the big card table in the corner for their monthly reversi tournaments. It was the nicest room in the house: austere, light blue, with a tan leather chesterfield sofa and two birch rocking chairs, a coal hearth, and cream lace curtains over cream scalloped blinds. The scuffed, matchstick oak floors were bare and the walls were hung with schoolboy watercolors of the South Downs by Orla's late husband, Edward.

Today, Mr. and Mrs. Villo were having tea in front of the window. They had tuned into BBC coverage of a dogfight between RAF Spitfires and German Messerschmitts in the skies above Dover. The middle-aged couple were on the edges of their seats, bickering about what the pilots should do.

Kate wished they would switch it off. The glee in the broad-caster's voice was disturbing. It was somebody's fiery death, not a football match. The boys in those planes were probably younger than her.

Her father settled into the chesterfield and smacked his lips. "I need a proper cup of tea," he said. "A big Irish cup of tea." He started to put his feet on the coffee table but Kate stopped him.

"You can't do that," she said. "This is a place of business. Did you bring your tea ration?"

"I thought this was a guesthouse. I'm a guest."

The fabric of his suit was almost translucent at the knees. War restrictions on manufacturing had made it extremely difficult to get new clothes, with each person allotted only twenty-four coupons every six months, but Kate was sur-prised her father hadn't enlisted a tailor to make his wardrobe over. It was strange seeing him threadbare; he had always been vain as a debutante.

"Yoo hoo, Mrs. Grifferty?" Mrs. Villo called, the name making Kate's father jump in his seat, though he'd barely reg-istered the gunfire blasts on the wireless. "Would you mind opening the windows for us? It's a lovely day and if we can't go to the beach . . ."

"Certainly," Kate said, and went to hoist open the win-dows, double-hung and sticky with old paint. A brackish breeze funneled into the room and the lace curtains billowed up, casting weblike shadows onto the walls.

"Where is your sister?" her father asked, shifting in his seat and lighting a cigarette from his jacket pocket, waiting for Kate to come back and put a fresh scone on a plate for him. "I've not seen her for ages."

He looked like a craggy old sea captain in that fresh blue-and-white room. He pointed at the milk until she poured some into his tea, brewed with her own tea ration.

"Orla is at the shops. Your granddaughter, Margaret, is napping upstairs. She'll be delighted to meet you."

"Ah, well. It's you I want to speak to. How are you getting on?"

"I'm fine," she said, cautiously. "Margaret is doing well. She's gorgeous, you'll see."

Her father grimaced. "Do you not have any biscuits?"

"Ah, no, anything sweet we tend to set aside for the guests. It's their holiday, after all."

"On holiday? With the whole continent in a war?" Begrudgingly, he took a bite of the scone. "Honest to God, it's a disgrace." A floury crumb flew from his mouth and landed on the coffee table. "No wonder Hitler has the Brits on the run."

The drawing room creaked open and Margaret tiptoed in wearing her short nightgown and bloomers, a shy smile on her lips. Her eyes were sleepy and her blond curls stood up three inches from the top of her head. She was carrying her baby doll, Bob.

Margaret had heard stories about her grandfather—the few nice ones Kate remembered—but had never met him.

"This is your grandfather," Kate said, pulling her in for a cuddle. Margaret looked up at him, eyes wide with surprise.

"Good afternoon, young lady," Kate's father said, in the tone of a shopkeeper turning away a customer after business hours. "I am speaking to your Mammy."

Margaret giggled, expecting to be fussed over by him, as she was by everyone else she met. "Grandfather," she cooed. "I want to tell you something."

"What is it, child?"

Margaret looked around the room, momentarily distracted. "Grandfather?"

"Christ on the cross," he said. "What is it, girl? Out with it."

"Grandfather?"

With a feeling of déjà vu, Kate watched him strain to keep

his patience. She decided not to help him by silencing Margaret.

"This is my time, young lady," he said, his face getting redder. "You can speak to me after I am done with your mother."

Margaret, in a small singsong voice: "My mammy, my mam." Her starfish hands explored Kate's cheeks and pinched the mole near her mouth. "Dot," she said. "Dot, dot, dot."

"Christ, she has your number," he said. "Do you always let her climb all over you?"

Kate sighed out her last hope for her father. He wanted something from her—that's why he was there. Not to meet his grandchild.

"Why are you here, Frank?"

"Don't call me Frank. I'm your pa. My foreman enlisted. He could've got an exemption, but he did it anyway."

"Well done him."

"It's left me in the lurch. I won't manage without him, Kathleen. I've lost six men in the last week. They're all joining up. All the young lads are leaving. I train them up and there they go." He made a bird-flying motion with his hands. "I resorted to hiring a girl in the office but didn't she just up and join the ATS? They're in and out like bleeding yo-yos."

"Well, there is a war on," Kate said. Margaret rubbed her eyes, turned her face into Kate's shoulder. "It's not meant to be convenient. Able-bodied men should do their bit."

"Aye. That's why I reckon you should come back to London and work for me. Do the bookkeeping, that sort of thing, until this holy show blows over and I can hire someone proper."

Margaret slid off Kate's lap and began to play with the smoke streaming up from Mr. Villo's cigarette stub in the brass ashtray, running her fingers through the swirls.

"I don't want to go back to London," Kate said. "Not yet. It's safer for Margaret here."

"Leave her with Orla."

"A child should have a mother."

"You didn't have one. You turned out . . . well, you turned out."

Kate felt the breath go out of her body. "You brought me up like I was a ward of the Church," she said. "That's not good enough for Margaret."

The marionette lines below her father's mouth grew deeper. "I thought you might like the chance to stand on your own. I'm offering you your freedom."

"I don't want freedom from my own daughter."

Margaret had set her eyes on her grandfather, narrowed them. Kate could see her mind working: she was puzzling out her next approach to him.

"When are you going to stop *talking?*" She whined, stomping her foot. "Don't you want to see me and Mammy's room, Grandfather?"

"Perhaps next time, child. I've a train to catch shortly."

"What a shame you must go so soon," Kate said, seizing the chance to get him out. She wanted him gone. She wasn't Frank's daughter anyway; she was Margaret's mother.

He sputtered. "I didn't mean I was leaving now. I thought I might have a sandwich."

Kate smiled, placed her cup on its saucer. "It is such hard work, running a hotel. So much to do. We shall wave you goodbye from the window, won't we, Margaret?"

Margaret howled: "Noooo! I want to show him my room! Can I just show him my room now?"

"No, darling," Kate said. "He needs to go."

"What a palaver," Frank tutted, nodding toward Margaret. "If you had asked me what to do, I would have told you to let St. Pelagia's sort this out."

"I did ask you. I asked you for help."

The Villos weren't listening to the wireless anymore; they were staring straight down at the card table, frozen, their ears cocked toward Kate and her father.

"And, if I recall correctly," she said, lowering her voice so only he could hear, "you told me to feck off. I fecked off. I made it easy for you."

Her father sighed to let Kate know that it had not, in fact, been easy for him when she got herself up the pole.

"You should have gone to the laundries," he said loudly, cranking up his Dublin twang. "There wouldn't have been any confusion. No deciding to keep it. You've got to credit those nuns. They tell their inmates what to do and they do it. They've saved scores of girls like you."

This was no sudden welling up of Catholic fealty; humiliation in front of the Villos was Kate's punishment for refusing him. A blast of rage rose up in her and she stood: she would tell her father exactly what she thought of him. He was a brute. She wouldn't stand for it anymore. She would slap him, just like she'd slapped Scargill.

She stopped herself.

Margaret could not see her mother like that—bawling out her grandfather. A child wouldn't forget that. That was not the person Kate was. No, she was not the cruel one. He was. Frank Grifferty: the Misery. Kate would not give him the satisfaction.

She looked at her shoes, smoothed the front of her skirt, took a deep breath through her nose, and smiled.

"Time to go," she said. "It really was lovely to see you, *Pa*."

"Well, never mind all that," her father said, perhaps a little defeated. "God bless you." He patted Margaret on the head, then rifled in his jacket and flicked a few letters on to the coffee table. "I went through the trouble of bringing you your mail, even though *you're* not inclined to help *me* . . ."

Kate waited until he was gone to pick up the letters. Only one was handwritten, with a London postmark dated 19 October 1939—almost nine months earlier—from St. Mary's Hospital. Her name and address were scrawled on the envelope in jagged, forward-leaning cursive. She held the letter to her chest and pulled in a breath.

David.

She would not open it. It was a message in a bottle that would make her want even more things she could not have.

Kate and Margaret shared the larger of the two bedrooms on the first floor, where there was a lockable wardrobe for baby things and a large brass bed with a lace counterpane. As the gas lamp Kate lit burst into light, their room appeared: Margaret's dolls and stuffed animals and blankets, framed snapshots of Margaret on the beach shingle and in a sandbox and hugging a dog she met at Queen's Park, a folding rack draped with Margaret's small clothing, a heap of last night's urine-soaked linens under the broken gas wall heater, an overturned glass beaker in a ring of milk on the carpet, a bedside table with a drawer that held a thermometer and a jar of honey and a spoon in case Margaret woke with a sore throat.

The room was filthy because Kate was too busy cleaning the guests' rooms to keep up with the whirlwind of rubbish Margaret created wherever she went. Slipping into her nightgown in the cold, cluttered semi-darkness, Kate was devastatingly certain of her own maternal ineptitude. The shameful part was, it wasn't for lack of effort. She had given up everything that once made her feel alive: freedom, sex, her career. She had more or less erased herself in service of Margaret; she couldn't even see herself in her own bedroom. Still, it wasn't enough. Motherhood, the way Kate experienced it, hijacked one's body, mind, and soul, then asked for a cuddle. It was the most annihilating, wonderful thing in the world.

Now, Kate's camera was only for outsmarting the quickness with which Margaret changed shapes. It was for capturing the sweet minutiae of each age before it disappeared, the prized possession of one day lost or discarded or passed on the next. A photo of Margaret with an old dummy made Kate want to weep with regret that she hadn't saved the stupid thing. Not for the first time, it struck her that all she photographed now was Margaret. Everything was about Margaret and maybe that was appropriate and right, but it wasn't necessarily truthful. It left Kate out of the story.

The letter from David remained unopened, stashed under the bed with Kate's portfolios and negatives and other artifacts from her former life.

In the morning, when the sun snuck through the edges of the thick black curtains, the coal fire had gone out and it was chilly. Margaret snored softly in Kate's arms and she kissed her head. In the garden, Orla was having a loud conversation about finger-training budgies with one of the boarders—a bird fancier who had taken an intense liking to Robird's "terribly rare" violet coloring.

Orla never seemed to reflect on life except in the most superficial ways. She nattered on about Robird, the weather, the state of the floorboards. Nothing vaguely interesting. If Kate was honest, she found her sister boring. She had no idea about Orla's inner life, or if she even had one. It sometimes struck her that Orla might be rather dull. But she'd generously welcomed Kate and then Margaret into her home with open arms and few questions. The sisters got on fine. Still, Kate always got the sense that Orla didn't want to really know her, or be known herself.

Kate left Margaret sleeping and washed her face at the bowl and combed her hair in the dark. It was long now and grazed her shoulder blades. As she once had when developing film, she worked by touch, twisting her hair into neat rolls along the hairline, and deftly pinned the ends at the nape of her neck. Then she went downstairs for a cup of tea.

While she put out the food in the dining room, Kate made small talk with Miss Fairchild, a retired schoolteacher who had recently evacuated from Stoke Newington with her companion Miss Skaggs. Mr. and Mrs. Villo were discussing the incompetency of the War Department. If Mr. Villo were in charge, the disposition of forces would be conducted in rather a different manner. The man seemed almost hungry for London to be bombed. Certain that the capital would be attacked imminently, he had dragged his wife down from London in June after Dunkirk. Mrs. Villo speculated on when Hitler would justify all the money they were spending on their room at Puffin's Perch. Apparently, they'd a perfectly good house in Wandsworth.

When Lieutenant Prouty, an imposing figure in his blue RAF uniform, entered the dining room, the Villos clammed up and Miss Fairchild blushed into her savory oatmeal.

Kate tried not to look at the lieutenant. But everywhere her eyes went, he was there. When he glanced at her and rubbed his neck—his tanned, freshly shaven neck—Kate felt herself grin. It was involuntary, she didn't know why she had to flirt like that. But it did please her to make a man who flew planes fidget.

"Good morning, Miss Grifferty."

"Mrs. Grifferty," Kate said, and when the lieutenant's eyes darted to the white-gold ring on her finger: "My sister and I are both widows."

That ring was the one thing Orla had demanded of Kate when she moved in, three months pregnant; she didn't want people thinking Puffin's Perch was the wrong kind of boardinghouse.

Lieutenant Prouty bowed his head respectfully. "I'm sorry for the loss of your husband, Mrs. Grifferty."

He smelled of fresh air and soap.

"Thank you. Going flying today?" Kate nodded to another guest entering the dining room, and did not look at the Cupid's bow of Lieutenant Prouty's lips.

"Unfortunately, not," he said. "Too old, I'm afraid. I'm just an instructor now. Desk job."

He nodded when he spoke, each dip of his chin a comma.

His accent seemed too refined for such a formidable, weather-beaten frame.

"That's a pity," she said. "It must be glorious."

"Best feeling in the world. After the war, I plan to get my own plane."

"Why, that's sensational!"

"Just imagine . . ." Lieutenant Prouty stood up straighter and his voice rose an octave, as if he was trying to cast it into the future: "Flying into Paris for oysters and champagne."

"If there is still a Paris, after the war."

Kate noticed Miss Fairchild watching them. She stepped back from Lieutenant Prouty and asked: "How long do you expect to be billeted with us, Lieutenant? My sister never said."

"I dunno," he said. "Six weeks or more. I'm organizing a new signaling course for recruits. As long as they keep coming, I'll be here. . . ."

While Margaret napped upstairs, Kate lay in the sun in the garden, stretched out facedown on an old tablecloth. The heat of the earth was soothing; she felt her body loosen as it reached her bones.

She had spent the morning in the Villos' room, trying to magic water into their pipes. It was impossible, the job needed a plumber, but there were no plumbers to be found anymore. They had joined up, along with the paper hangers and chimney sweeps and window cleaners. All those jobs were now under the purview of Kate and Orla.

When Kate's attempt at fixing the pipes failed, the Villos had threatened to move out. Kate convinced them to stay by lugging a copper tub into their room with pots of warm water from the kitchen so that Mrs. Villo could have a bath. Mr. Villo hadn't lifted a finger throughout the entire process. It was irritating and tiring and disgusting and Kate never wanted to see either of them again.

Finally alone, she examined the grass under her nose, taking in the insect's view. She rested her head on her folded arms and imagined David, his bare chest and his hands on her, and soon fell into a shallow dream. In her waking life, she mostly thought of him in relation to Margaret because they looked so much alike, but she dreamed of him constantly, in a different way: the feel of him against her, the full-body love she'd felt for him, and, if the dream went on long enough, the sharp sting of him turning away.

When Kate woke, a figure was standing over her: a man in silhouette. Heart racing, she pushed herself up to sitting and wrapped the tablecloth around her bare legs. Then she realized it was Lieutenant Prouty, standing at attention like he was holding a lemon in each armpit.

"Sorry, I hadn't intended to startle you, Mrs. Grifferty," he said. "Only I need a tool for my Ford and wondered if you could tell me where the nearest hardware store is."

She used her hand as a visor so she could see his face. "Of course, Lieutenant Prouty."

"Clifton."

"If you like. And you must call me Kate."

He smiled. "Very well."

"Actually, I need to nip to Cowley's for bread," she said, yawning, shaking off sleep. "The hardware store is on the way. If you give me a moment, I'll show you myself."

Sensing her mother enjoying herself, Margaret cried out from the window above their heads: "Mammy! I'm thirsty! Bring me my milk!"

"That's my daughter, Margaret," Kate said, feeling her face warm. "She'll have to join us. I hope you don't mind."

"Of course not. Love kids. My nephew, Charlie, is my favorite chap in the world. He's seven."

From the window: "Mammy! Milk! Now!"

"Sorry about that," Kate said. "Margaret is quite headstrong."

Clifton smiled good-naturedly. "The best girls usually are," he said.

When Kate brought Margaret down, Clifton knelt and put his hand out to her. His shoulders had gone soft, all the tension that animated him vanished. Margaret looked from him to Kate, a question in her eyes, asking if he was a friend. Kate smiled to her daughter and nodded.

"It's all right, darling. This is Lieutenant Prouty. He's our guest."

She and Margaret led Clifton along the seafront on the way to the hardware store. It had already changed beyond recognition since the beach closed. The army had intentionally blown up the center of the Palace Pier, leaving its arcades dark and spun-sugar archways ghostly. When Kate had first arrived in Brighton in 1937, pregnant and self-consciously thumbing the counterfeit wedding ring on her finger, the pier was a raucous meeting place, the heart of the town. Now it was desolate, disorienting, with barbed wire in weblike coils around its railings and in tangled spools along the waterline. Cement blocks obstructed the steps leading up from the beach. Somewhere under the waves, mines lurked, ready to explode when German U-boats made their inevitable land attack on England. For the first time in a while, Kate's hands itched for her camera, to help her make sense of it all.

Oblivious to the ugliness, Margaret ran ahead of her and Clifton, chasing seagulls and pigeons. Kate did not feel like scolding her. It never seemed to work anyway. She glanced at Clifton to see if he was horrified, but he grinned and shook his head knowingly.

"She keeps you busy, eh?"

"Yes," Kate said. "If I'm honest, I've no idea how to manage her."

"Children need discipline. They need to know the rules. What's allowed and what's not. They enjoy it, it makes them happy."

"That's just it. I'm a rubbish disciplinarian. My father barked at me constantly and I hated him for it."

Clifton nodded. "My sister, Daisy, went through this with my nephew, Charlie. She's a lovely mum, just like you. She never shouts. I have to set him straight. When he turned six, he started calling me Cliff. 'Oi, Cliff, bring me my cricket bat!' I told him, 'You call me Uncle Clifton.' " Clifton narrowed his eyes to show how stern he was and then burst out laughing. "I told my sister, it's disrespectful when children call adults by their Christian names. Sometimes you must tell Charlie no."

"I never have the heart to tell Margaret no. She hugs and kisses me and says I love you." Kate realized she was indirectly saying those three words to Clifton and got a little thrill from it. She thought maybe she saw something in his eyes, too, when she said it. "She melts me into a pool of butter."

He cleared his throat. "Well, girls *are* different," he said. "You feel this need to protect them. My sister is desperate for a little girl. It's all she talks about. She always dreamt of a big family, but she and Gerald keep being unlucky. I tell her not to get her hopes up, but . . ."

Kate turned this over in her mind: a child tried for, dreamed of. Poor Margaret had fallen out of the sky.

"I'm very sorry for your sister," she said.

"She's all right. She gives all the love to Charlie." Clifton grinned. "Spoils him ruddy rotten."

"Well, there are worse things than spoiling. My father never cared for me at all."

She was happy for Clifton to think her father dead, because he might as well have been to her.

Clifton nodded sympathetically. "My father was terrifying, too," he said. "Victorians, eh?"

They walked for a while in comfortable silence, both keeping an eye that Margaret didn't run into the road.

"Do you ever get scared?" Kate asked.

"Of my father? Not anymore. He died when I was sixteen. He was just thirty-eight years old. I'll be thirty-eight next birthday."

"No, not your father. I mean the war. Of flying. Of fighting."

"Scared?" Clifton considered this. "No. I'm scared of letting my students down. I'm scared of letting my nephew down. But not fighting, no. I'm too old now, but if I ever get another chance to fly the old kite, to *feel* it under my hands, boy, I'm running toward that plane."

Chapter 20

13th July, 1940

"I was going to send my children to Canada but it's too dangerous now," Doris's mother said to Kate. "I wouldn't trust the journey."

They stood side by side, watching their daughters chase each other around the Queen's Park swings. It was a nice park with horse chestnut trees and beautiful old elms and a lake with loads of ducks. Kate knew the other little girl's name—Doris—but not her mother's, even though they had been meeting in the park for months. It seemed too late to introduce themselves now.

That morning, Kate had received a packet of acceptance into the latest evacuation program: two tags to be worn by Margaret, a blank postcard to be sent by her foster parents to Kate with their address, a packing list, and a Southern Railways special ticket to Clapham Junction. Doris's mother had received the same packet for each of her children.

"According to an RAF officer I know," Kate offered, "the war will be over before long. Once the fighting really starts, it will be over in a few weeks. We'll make bonfires of our gas masks."

Doris's mother looked skeptical. "One never knows," she said and Kate felt foolish.

"So, you will send Doris on Tuesday?"

When war was declared the previous autumn, thousands of children had come from London to host families in Brighton. But the new threat of land invasion meant Brighton was no longer safe, either. A voluntary children's evacuation was scheduled for the coming week.

"Yes," Doris's mother said. "My husband insists it's the only sensible option." She sighed. "It helps that all five of ours will be together. Will you send Margaret?"

Though she was ambivalent, Kate nodded because she knew it was the right response. "Yes. I would go with her," she said, "but my sister can't run the boardinghouse without my help. She'd have to close her doors."

"If it weren't for my husband, I'd not have the stomach for it. If only the government would tell us where they're sending the children."

"I suppose they can't. Perhaps Doris and Margaret will be together?"

"Not likely," Doris's mother said with an air of wisdom. "There will be thousands of kiddies at the station on Tuesday. It will be absolute bedlam. You'll see."

The little girls caught each other in a running hug and Kate's heart went to her throat. Doris wouldn't be alone; her brothers and sisters would be with her. Strangers would look after Margaret.

"I used to never be afraid of anything, before I had Margaret," Kate said. "Now I find I'm always frightened."

Doris's mother frowned and Kate understood that she had said too much. It wasn't on to air one's petty anxieties in public. People were making much bigger sacrifices, and she hardly knew Doris's mother. But the sweltering heat was disorienting, it made her feel she'd run miles just standing there. And she hadn't had a friend since Gordy.

Kate sluiced perspiration from her forehead and steered the conversation back to impersonal speculation—*how will the Germans come, when and where will they come?* These were more acceptable pleasantries between mothers.

Kate took Margaret's hand and scanned the crowd for Doris's family. Her plan was to attach Margaret to them and make sure they were sent to the same village.

"I'm hot," Margaret cried, tugging at her hand. "I'm thirsty."

"You'll have your tea on the train with the other girls and boys," Kate said, striding forward. She was proud that her voice did not quaver.

Inside Brighton Station, the concourse was flooded with hundreds of children, labels pinned to their coats and gas masks on their backs. They smacked gum and jostled one another toward the trains with suitcases, bundles of clothes, younger siblings, puppies, even newts. The mood was celebratory. They seemed to think they were going on holiday. Government officials led them willingly onto the trains, while their parents lined the platforms, biting their lips, waving.

A nurse with an official badge spotted Kate and Margaret lingering near the turnstile. She ushered them over to a registration table. Margaret froze, pinned her heels to the ground, looked to Kate for a sign. Kate looked at the clock. Fifteen minutes until two, when the trains were set to leave.

To fortify herself, Kate thought of burning gasses and bullets raining from the skies. She imagined German commandos crawling up Brighton Beach with daggers in their boots. She thought of Freya, the little girl she met that day in 1936, at Miss Singer's school. How clearly Freya had been loved, with her hand-crocheted blanket and dainty blouse. Her mother had sent her away in order to save her life. And Kate must do the same for Margaret now.

The other mothers began to recede from the platform. Their children merrily waved, but Margaret gripped Kate's hand.

With a nauseating feeling of dread, she swept up her daughter and the case, and went to the registration table. It was all Kate could do to not cry. A young soldier with kind eyes tried to take Margaret, but she winched onto Kate's neck.

"Madam," the woman at the table said. "Your registration papers, quickly please? The train is leaving in a few minutes."

If Brighton was bombed and Kate died, Margaret would be an orphan. Would that be worse than them dying together?

"Look, all the other children are waiting for you," the soldier said to Margaret. "Come on, love."

"No!" she shouted into Kate's shoulder. "I don't wanna go-ho-ho. I want to go home."

Margaret's blond ringlets smelled of buttermilk. She was Kate's heart, all her emotions. The only person who had ever truly loved her.

Kate stepped back from the table and smoothed Margaret's hair back so she could whisper in her ear. "You know what, button?"

"What?"

"I don't think this is for us. I think we two are meant to be together, no matter what. What do you think?"

Margaret sniffled, looked incredulously at Kate. "Yeah!"

"And I just remembered, Aunt Orla needs your help, doesn't she? These other children probably don't have aunts who run hotels, do they?"

"I can help!"

"Yes, good point. Now that I think about it, you must stay here in Brighton with us. Is that all right with you?"

Margaret nodded. "Yes! I want to stay with you, Mammy."

"Good girl. I'm sorry about all this. Mammy's made a mistake. Let's go home."

So, with Margaret still in her arms, before anyone could tell her what a stupid woman she was, Kate turned and fled from the train station.

*   *   *

It was snug in the Puffin's Perch kitchen on rainy nights, so after doing the washing up, Kate stayed and sat and read the newspaper. Robird was blessedly silent, sleeping with a sheet draped over his cage.

While Kate read, she held a mug of tea between her hands to warm them. The entire front page of the *Argus* was about the children's evacuation—the brave parents, the delighted boys and girls. Kate folded the newspaper in half. Then she tore it, folded it again, and dropped it in the bin on her way upstairs.

On the darkened landing, she bumped into elderly Mr. and Mrs. Fisher making their way to bed after coffee in the drawing room. Kate fetched them fresh towels and then tiptoed into her own darkened room, where Margaret was sleeping. She leaned over the bed and laid her hand softly on her daughter's back to reassure herself she was breathing. She thought of Doris's mother, unable to check on her own children tonight, and fought off a feeling of guilt.

Kate had always known she was selfish; she had even liked that about herself. Her selfishness protected her. If she did not look out for herself, who would? But yesterday it had stopped her from protecting Margaret. It seemed that all the other parents were able to do it: stiff upper lip, hug the children goodbye, leave the station alone. Kate just could not shake the sense that Margaret was safest with her. But what if she was wrong?

Kate lit the tapered candle on the nightstand and reached under their bed, her fingers searching for the Woolworth's hatbox. She opened it and rifled through Christmas cards from school friends she hardly remembered anymore, dried flowers, ticket stubs, the crushed pinhole camera she'd made when she was twelve. She got to the bottom of the box, where she had stuck David's unopened letter with the photograph of him in Victoria Park, smiling crookedly at her. She had had dozens of photographs of him, but this was her favorite. *Bonfire*

Night, 1936, was written on the back. The dark framing his face was speckled with white dots. Kate did not remember if they were sparks or ashes. She slipped the photograph under her blouse and held it to her heart for a moment, letting herself feel him again.

Then she ran her fingers over the seal of his letter and smelled it. Had David's tongue sealed this envelope, had his lips grazed it? Kate inserted her thumb into the small opening at the fold of the envelope and gingerly broke the seal he'd made. Her hands trembling, her body stupidly greedy for the longing and pain his words were sure to inflict upon her, she read:

St. Mary's Hospital
Paddington, London, W.2.
18th October 1939

Dear Kate,
I often think of you and wonder how you are getting
on. I'm certain you are a great success and nothing
would please me better. I feel terrible about the way
things ended between us and you can never know how
sorry I am. The regret I felt when you left is something
I'm not sure I will ever get over, but it was entirely my
fault and you were right to go. I misled you. I see that
now and I'm certain that I never deserved you.
*   My father just died. It hurts to write the words*
but I felt I had to tell you. There's no reason you
should care. I wanted you to know for my own
selfish reasons. You understood me and I wanted to
somehow have that feeling again.
*   I don't know if this letter will reach you. I rang the*
Irish Times, but the secretary said she didn't know
you. Perhaps you're long gone. Perhaps you're back in
London, just a few miles from where I sit now, in my

surgery at St. Mary's, and yet you might as well be a thousand miles away.

I qualified in '37 and currently have a post at St. Mary's. If you ever feel that you would like to write and tell me how you are, I should be very glad, but for my aforementioned faults I won't expect it. Thank you for our time together because I have something wonderful to think of now when all is bleak.

Yours sincerely,
David

When Kate looked up, she was sitting on the floor. David missed her. He might still love her. She could write him back. It had only been nine months since he mailed this letter; even if he'd already left St. Mary's, they would surely have a forwarding address.

Dear David, she thought to herself, staring at the ceiling, recrossing her legs on the rug. *Thank you for your letter. Are you in the forces now?*

Idiotic.

I remember your face and marvel that I ever looked away.

Alarming. Desperate. He'd run screaming.

There's something you have to know. There's something I never told you.

Worst. NO. He would hate Kate forever. He would try to take Margaret from her.

Telephone Paddington 1149 was stamped in the left corner of the stationery header. Tomorrow morning, Kate could pick up the phone and probably hear David's voice on the other end of the line. A staggering thought.

She closed her eyes and played out this scenario in her head. It would be thrilling at first—the heart-stopping sound of his hello, a meeting arranged as soon as possible at the coffee shop in Victoria Station—but before their tea cooled, her selfishness and his guilt would rear their ugly heads. She would ignore it, they both would—whatever it took to go to bed together one more time. How satisfying that would be, and how alive they would both feel. *What fools we've been,* David would whisper, and Kate would press the tip of her nail into the vermillion border of his lower lip.

But then, inevitably, the feature film would roll: the revelation of her deceit, of the daughter she had stolen from him. His child, three years old, who she could have told him about but chose not to. Family was everything to David; he would never forgive Kate for such a betrayal.

It would only break both their hearts again and disrupt Margaret's life. All for one tawdry reunion in a train station hotel.

She dropped the letter in the box and kicked it under the bed and covered her face with her hands. Then Margaret rolled over in bed and said in a sleepy voice: "Mammy, Mammy, are you missing me?"

Chapter 21

18th July, 1940

In the center of Piccadilly Circus, the monument steps were crowded with prostitutes. The statue of Eros had been removed and replaced by adverts for war bonds: *Take up the challenge!*, they shouted, *BUY!*

Hotels in Piccadilly rented by the hour, if you asked. This one had been Sarah Jane's suggestion. David wondered if she wanted to feel cheap, or if this was the kind of place she imagined affairs took place. At the clinic, there were loads of patients like her—bored, hypochondriacal, posh women. They came in with imagined maladies because they wanted to be told there was nothing wrong with them. David examined and reassured them, and they thanked him profusely, only to return six weeks later complaining of bodily imperfections they could not recognize for what they were—the quotidian indignities of age.

David paid the man at the desk and waited for Sarah Jane at the lifts. He stifled a laugh when she came through the door in a tan mackintosh and dark sunglasses, as if anyone she knew would patronize such a seedy hotel. It was funny, he thought, for a married woman with three children and a lover to be so nervous about sex.

The woman who clicked past him in shiny, high-heeled

pumps into the lift was Mrs. Pomeroy. She would not be Sarah Jane until the hotel room door locked behind them. She primly adjusted her diamond bracelet and filled the lift with expensive-smelling lilac perfume. This phosphorescent lady bore no resemblance to the mothers he had grown up around. By her age, thirty-five, most East End women were as tired and ill-used as cart horses. When David thought of his mother, he thought of her rough hands peeling apples over the sink for a pie, or scouring the inside of the cooker with bicarbonate of soda. Sarah Jane, who lived in a Chelsea town house, was all soft skin swathed in cashmere. There was scarcely a crease on her. Her hands felt like silk gloves. It would surprise him if she had ever held a mop. Women like her did not have calluses. If David didn't know better—that she was just as miserable as everybody else—he would have been insecure in her presence. She was so palpably rich.

Once safely inside the room, Sarah Jane switched the light on and asked him to draw the curtains closed. She began to unbutton her blouse.

"You may begin the exam now, Doctor," she said.

"Not this game again."

With an edge to her voice: "David."

He sighed. Sarah Jane did this sometimes. It made him feel a bit queasy, but he had not been touched for weeks, so he played along.

"Lay down on the bed, please, madam."

She reached around her back and unfastened her brassiere.

"Find a tumor," she whispered, stepping out of her skirt. Then she lay on the bed with her arms pressed to her sides.

David rubbed his hands together and began palpating her breasts. He frowned.

"What is this here? I don't like it. I'm referring you to the oncology consultant."

Sarah Jane looked frightened. "Really?"

"No."

"What will happen next? What are my options?"

"I dunno. Mastectomy?"

Sarah Jane moaned in anguish. "Must we inform my husband, Dr. Rabatkin?"

"That would be advisable."

"David!"

"No. This is something we can sort ourselves."

He switched off the light, embarrassed that he was responding physically.

She purred. "Only *you* can cure me?"

"Yes," he said. "And it must be our secret."

Sarah Jane reached up and grabbed David and began wildly kissing him, but she did not have the magnetic pull on him that Kate had. Physics had no part in their affair. Sarah Jane's body was a means of escape for him. When he was with her, he didn't have to feel guilty about his father's death or worry that Simon would get killed in the war. As always, just before the crucial moment, he thought of Kate, and was filled with the most powerful euphoria, followed by a commensurate flood of grief that he would never be with her again.

Afterward, David and Sarah Jane lay next to each other for a while, not embracing but touching from shoulder to ankle. He folded his arms behind his head and closed his eyes to the loneliness he felt. *This is better than nothing,* he told himself, though he wasn't sure that whatever he had with Sarah Jane was. He waited for the melancholia to dissolve, as it usually did. His love for Kate seemed to be a chronic disease, but not fatal. He'd gotten on with his life.

Sarah Jane yawned and shifted her head onto his chest.

"Are you getting any more sleep?" he asked, nestling his fingers into her hair and massaging her scalp.

"No."

"Still just a few hours a night?"

"I'm afraid so."

"Your husband still snores like a bear?"

"Hard to tell. He sleeps in his office in Westminster most nights."

David tried to hide his curiosity about Sarah Jane and the way she lived with her MP husband. She was the only upper-class person he had ever known in a personal way. She never asked him about himself—convenient because he did not want her to know where he came from or who he really was.

The radiator kicked on and David threw the damp sheet and polyester counterpane off the bed. He looked over the length of Sarah Jane's body. Sweat pooled in her navel and she crossed her pink legs at the ankles and smiled at him.

"Wretched hotel," she said. "It stinks of onions."

"You chose it."

"I wasn't sure what you could afford."

David laughed as if he wasn't stung. He wondered what had given him away. They had taught him how to speak at school, but his Cockney twang had not entirely disappeared. Something humble and true obviously clung to him.

"Considerate of you," he said, and got out of bed and walked to the window. When he pulled the drapes back, sunlight shot into the room. Across the alleyway, a triptych billboard advertised wartime necessities: portable water containers, passport photos, and a remedy for something called "blackout eyestrain." David felt depressed again.

"I assumed this was where you brought all your men," he said, wanting to hurt her a little bit.

"Good Lord. What *men*?"

"You said you and your husband sleep in separate beds. And you're obviously quite experienced."

"You make me sound like Madame Pompadour. John and I didn't always sleep separately. When we first married, it was quite passionate. I suspect he had many women before me." She paused. "And after me, I'm afraid."

"Why did you marry him?"

"We grew up together. It wasn't really my choice. Our fathers are business partners. They always expected us to end up together."

"Do you love him?"

Sarah Jane was watching David as he stood naked in front of the window. He imagined that he looked like a shadow to her. A man with no face, no identity, no real significance.

"Yes," she said finally, and held out her hand to him. "I love him. Now come here. I only have fifteen minutes more."

"We were all given pistols," Simon said. It was a savagely hot Friday, the ninth of August, and they were having one last *Shabbos* dinner together before he left for training. He had just been to the RAF station for his kit and was regaling David and their mother with stories. "There was another Jewish bloke in the queue behind me and do you know what he said when I turned around? *Ir ken shatn zikh mit eyner fun di.*"

Their mother chuckled. "'You could hurt yourself with one of those'?"

It was a relief hearing her laugh. Since David's father died, the lines around her eyes had spread into an ancient flood-plain across her cheeks and she'd grown painfully thin. It was clear she saved most of her rations for her sons, though she would never admit to it. David hadn't seen her eat more than a few bites in months.

Simon's damp laundry was laid out to dry on every surface. They were just finishing a kosher sausage plait, his favorite for his last night in town. Their mother had even managed two bottles of beer, so the boys wouldn't leave her for the pub, but the kitchen was sweltering.

"You don't speak Yiddish, Simon," David said, wiping sweat from his brow.

"Yeah, I do. Mum's been teaching me."

"And he's taken to it like a duck to water," she said proudly. Lately, she and Simon had been in their own little club. She was still annoyed that David had moved out, not for a wife or the army, but for a wasteful pound-a-week bedsit near St. Mary's.

David tried, unsuccessfully, to catch Simon's eye as he switched on the radio. The opening drums on Benny Goodman's "Sing, Sing, Sing" shot through David's veins like a slug of coffee, but their mother winced.

"I've not been able to enjoy music since your father passed on," she mused.

"You'll like this," David said, sitting back down at the kitchen table. "It's Benny. He's an American Jew. A complete genius."

"Oh?" She leaned in to listen.

David had an acetate disk of Goodman's legendary show at Carnegie Hall and played it over and over again in his Paddington flat. To him, the music sounded like America—that glorious month he'd spent in New York back in the summer of '37. In America, no one cared what you were or where you came from as long as you were ambitious. It was a mindset that agreed with him.

"Talking of geniuses," Simon said, "I went up to Cambridge the other day, to be assessed by the Air Force Board. They asked about maths, what Pythagorean's theory is . . ."

"Pythagoras's theorem," David corrected.

"Right. That one. The right triangle thingy. So, I guess I got through that all right, and I was accepted into training as an actual pilot."

Their mother cried out, terror in her eyes. Simon chuckled and patted her shoulder.

"You're sure the air force didn't mean radio-telephone operator?" David asked. "That's what most people get. As long as they can read and write."

"No," Simon said. "I'm going to be a pilot. The real thing. I start my training straightaway. Mum, I'll be all right . . ."

Their mother had covered her eyes with her palm and was shaking her head into it.

"But how did you remember Pythagoras's theorem?" David asked. "You've not had maths since you were fourteen."

"I've a mind like a steel trap," Simon said, tapping his forehead. "Never forget a thing."

"You will be careful," their mother insisted.

"It's much safer in the sky than in the trenches, Mum. That's why I didn't fancy the army. It's far too dangerous."

David could have said that in the last war, pilots were cannon fodder. He could have cited a report he'd read about their life expectancy being about three weeks. But he didn't, for their mother's sake.

"My pretty little boy." She seized Simon's face in her hands. "My *shayna punim*. How proud your father would be. Oh dear, oh dear . . ." She closed her eyes and began shaking her head again. "Thank God doctors aren't liable for the call-up, Davy. We can only have one soldier in this family. I can't take more of this . . ."

Later, with their mother distracted by the size constraints of Simon's duffel, David hauled his brother to the roof with their mother's babka—a tangle of tender bread and cinnamon.

"After the war, I'll just sit on my arse," Simon said, pulling a huge hunk from the loaf. "All day, every day, eating babka. That'll do me."

"That would be one way of using your life," David said through a mouthful of bread.

They demolished the loaf in a few minutes and Simon lit a cigarette under his hand. The glow from the match was as bright as a torch on his angular jaw. He lit another cigarette off his own and gave it to David, cupped under his palm. They smoked, neither of them saying anything for some time. It was peaceful standing side by side, breathing the dry air and thinking, probably some of the same thoughts. The night was very black and the chimneys of the surrounding buildings stood out like giant chess pieces against the leaden sky.

Simon broke the silence: "Mum has got it in her head again that she needs to find a wife for you."

David ground the ember of his cigarette under his foot. "I don't do that anymore."

"Be a sport," Simon pushed. "It'll give her something to do with her nerves."

"No. I refuse to talk to her about my love life. She always brings up the Kate thing like *aren't we lucky that didn't go through* and how clueless I am and how sensible she is."

"I know that," Simon said. "Why do you think I've been set up with every bird from here to Coventry? I'm trying to keep her off your back."

"I never asked you to do that."

"Well, now I'm leaving, she's your cross to bear. You've got to let her introduce you to some girls. There's a whole new batch here for war work, they've been yakking about it down the synagogue. It gives Mum hope for the future."

"I'd rather join up with you."

"Nah, you'll be more use here, saving lives. At the hospital."

Simon was being kind and they both knew it. As a doctor David was officially exempt from conscription, but he was ashamed he had not volunteered yet. A lot of paramedical staff at St. Mary's had joined the Royal Army Medical Corps. The medical staff had so far mostly stayed put, though some of his colleagues were being transferred to other hospitals to shore up resources in places where the government thought bombing likely. Places like Bethnal Green.

Simon lit another cigarette off his first one. "No use both of us dying," he said.

"Sod off. You're not going to die. Like you said, safer in the air, isn't it?"

Simon didn't respond.

"I can't believe you're going to learn how to fly," David went on. "I have to admit, I'm jealous." He kicked at the peeling tar paper that covered the roof. "I'm proud of you, mate."

Simon grinned. "Well. That makes it all worth it."

After seeing Simon off at Liverpool Street in the morning, David maneuvered his old Raleigh bicycle past the ration line that wrapped around Spitalfields. The cardboard carton holding his government-issued gas mask thunked on his back as he traversed the torn-up paving stones.

When he rode past an old school friend and her mother, the women smiled wanly. Their eyes seemed to say: *It could be worse, couldn't it?* David understood. They had all lived in a perpetual state of fear since Germany annexed Czechoslovakia in 1938. They knew what was coming. Britain declaring war on Germany meant that at least someone was attempting to stop it.

He rode over the curb by Levenberg's pharmacy, where he had once stood gobsmacked, watching Kate stare down Oswald Mosley. Beneath those serene gold eyes, had she been even a little afraid? David could not remember why he had not asked her when he could. Now, Kate was a stranger to him. If he passed her on the street—and he often imagined he did, for a few breathless moments—he would not blame her if she kept walking.

This mile, this half-city, half-*shtetl* between Liverpool Street Station and the house in Spelman Street, was David's youth and it was thick with ghosts.

He saw a younger version of himself in Petticoat Market, a claustrophobic street of tin awnings, where the world was for sale. He remembered his mother's back, poring over tables of children's books for him and Simon, the clatter of wood hangers on miles of clothing racks, the smell of second-hand leather boots. The shops were still there—the draper, the tailor, the public house—all barricaded behind sandbags yet bustling as ever. Over in Brick Lane was Bloom's restaurant, his father's favorite. Then David's primary school, next to the picture house where he and Simon spent countless Sunday afternoons. Farther along, on the High Street, London Hospital, which had broken David down and built him into the sort of man who didn't want to live in East London anymore.

He had qualified as a doctor in 1937 and was given an unpaid house post at London Hospital. Then the next stage up, a registrarship, was followed by a locum in general internal medicine at St. Mary's Paddington. When war was declared in September of 1939, a few senior consultants went over to the Queen Alexandria Army Hospital and David was given charge of one of the medical wards at St. Mary's.

Everything had fallen into place, just as he and his parents had planned, and everyone was happy. Then David's mother rang him in his surgery, two weeks after war broke out.

"Apparently your father has nits," she'd said, her voice low with shame. "The doctor was not very nice about it at all. Couldn't stand far enough away from us."

"Nits?" David frowned. "That doesn't sound like Dad. He's so clean."

"Well, the doctor seemed quite certain. He sent us home with a script for a special soap and told me to boil all the sheets. My hands are raw from scrubbing. The doctor said most homes in the East End have them. He looked down his nose at us even though we had on our nicest clothes."

"I'll come see Dad myself next week. In the meantime, use the special soap and see how you do."

By the time David visited his parents, his father's skin and eyeballs were yellow. He was itching his back with a ruler.

"Why didn't anyone tell me you were jaundiced?" David asked, his heart racing.

"You've been so busy lately," his father said. "No one can tell you anything."

"Have you any pain in your belly?"

His father had rubbed his right upper abdomen, looking worried. "Why do you ask?"

David took his father directly to the Jewish hospital in Stepney Green, but his liver failed a month later, on the day Poland fell. It was a cancer that had spread. The death, the burial, and the *shiva* all seemed to fold into the war itself. It was just a time when terrible things happened.

The seventh of September started out as a quiet day. David had spent the morning helping out in Casualty. There was some heatstroke, a case of shingles, a few siren stomachs brought on by the daily false alarms over the past week. One poor sod thought he was having a massive coronary, but it was neurotic anxiety. Since the mid-August bombs, they'd been flooded with nervous afflictions like these, including several attempted suicides. The hospital had been warned to be ready for mass bomb casualties, but so far the first-aid tents in the road were empty, their canvas doors flapping in the wind.

David had a clear view of the road from the window in his surgery. A group of soldiers and pretty women in sundresses walked by, howling with laughter, passing ice creams and cigarettes between them. David watched after them wistfully, realizing that he did not have the instinct for fun without Simon; he would never fit in such a carefree crowd.

In the weeks after his brother left for training, David had spent most of his free time with Sarah Jane. He would phone her as he left the hospital and she would be waiting outside his flat when he came round the corner. He got used to her musky lilac scent in his room, her tortoiseshell hairpins on his bedside table, and in her strange way, Sarah Jane had begun to feel like his. When her politician husband abruptly shuffled her off to their country home on the first of September, David had understood two unrelated, ineluctable truths at the same time: Sarah Jane was not his girlfriend and

London would soon be bombed. And not just a few scouting blasts; this would be the big show.

Still, when the air raid sirens started up at half past four on the seventh, David didn't think much of it. They'd been going off at regular intervals for the last year. *Another dress rehearsal,* he thought.

But then he felt the planes, the low-frequency, metallic throb in his intestines, before the sound of them reached his ears. His surgery door rattled on its hinges and the floor shook. Then a whistle, louder and louder like a train bearing down, and a blast. An incendiary bomb, due east, then another and another. The ceiling lamp swung back and forth over his head.

David raced back down the stairs to Casualty. Between blasts it was eerily quiet. Even the drunks dried up; one grabbed David's arm and offered to scrub up and lend a hand. David told him to go down to the basement shelter with all the other patients who could walk.

"Any minute now, any minute," Sister Eugene, one of the senior nurses, barked as she walked past David. "Don't dally. Man your posts."

And then the doors flew open and casualties came in waves, first on foot and then on stretchers. The severely injured lay in the outpatient area, where there was room to fit beds side by side. Mouths gaping and covered with brown-gray dust, Egyptian mummies come to life. Faints, mauve-colored, half-dead by asphyxiation. David had never seen most of these injuries: spontaneous amputations, crushed faces, third-degree burns. The amount of blood alone . . . And dozens more minor injuries, mostly caused by flying glass.

A medical student came up to David as he was trying in vain to clean a woman's dust-choked calf wound and asked: "What the hell is going on out there, Doctor?"

"I don't know," David said, wiping dust out of his eyes. The smell of burning flesh was thick in his nose and throat. "I can't believe how much blood these people are losing."

"When you're done, could you see to this chap they just brought into reception? I don't know what to do with him. The occipital bone is shattered, blood's pouring down his neck."

"Guess what? That's your patient now, mate."

"But he keeps trying to leave. He won't stop running toward the door."

"He's *running*?"

"Yeah."

"Then let him go. There's more people here than we can treat and they can't run away."

It went on like this all night. David cut people out of their clothing with scissors: straight up trouser legs, through knickers and shirts. He wrapped wounds that could not be cleaned, administered morphine, transfused small amounts of blood and gave saline infusions, but the badly injured people just died. That's what happened; there was not much anyone could do for catastrophic trauma. It was a horrible, wrenching feeling, knowing he could not save someone. But before David could feel more than the edge of one casualty, he had to move on to the next.

There were crackles of artillery, the boom of mortar rounds in the distance. David registered the blasts to the east and remembered his mother in Bethnal Green. Another thing he could not think about. There were two Anderson shelters in the yard behind her building; surely, she would be there by now. And Simon was safe at training school in Shoreham-by-Sea, they had spoken that morning.

David looked at the clock above the swinging doors. It was five past seven o'clock in the evening. He looked again and it was eleven o'clock. After a few hours, the sound of German bombs had stopped terrifying him. He felt angry, and wildly alert. By the time he heard bombs land, they had probably already detonated. Fear would have squandered his focus. The only thing to do was try to clean up the human mess the bombs wouldn't stop making. He didn't think too much about the people themselves, he couldn't, only what they needed to stay alive.

At some point, he put his hand out and was given a cup of hot soup. He sipped it, thinking how good it tasted. A thought broke through: *A child just died before my eyes and I'm drinking chicken soup . . .*

But David knew he had to stay in the shallows. He had to stay there so he could work. So, he gulped down the soup and worked hard for the three hours before dawn.

His mother did not have a telephone line in her flat, so he could not check on her. As soon as he could, he would go to her. The Tube was probably closed, but he would walk if he had to.

After the long, single note of the all-clear sounded in the morning, David jogged through reception, under the St. Mary's Arch, and into Praed Street. Overnight, he had personally pronounced thirteen human beings dead and called for janitors to take their bodies to the morgue.

The buildings immediately surrounding the hospital were standing, but ash fell like snowflakes. A pearlescent barrage balloon flashed high up in the smoke. David walked. Up the road was a crater three meters wide and very deep—a pit of cool, wet earth that exhaled and made the hair on his arms stand up. He had not heard a blast that close and wondered if there was an undetonated bomb at the bottom of it.

He tried to quiet his increasing worry for his mother, so he could focus on listening for calls for help. None came. The eerie silence made it seem as if everyone in London was dead.

The Bore War, the Phoney War, was over. A year and four days after it was declared, the real war had begun.

Chapter 22

14th September, 1940

Kate's first feeling was that she had been burned. She couldn't think, she couldn't move. Everything was red. She was on a carpeted floor. Instinctively, she reached out for Margaret. In the dim light she saw the strawberry pattern of the dress she had pulled over her daughter's head that morning.

She said to herself: *Don't die.* She said to herself: *Margaret.*

On her hands and knees, Kate lurched forward, trying to cry out for help, but her mouth was full of something grainy. Gravel dug into her knees. Then she thought she was screaming, but it was the sound of a whistle, being blown over and over.

"Margaret," she coughed, tapping her daughter's cheeks, afraid to shake her in case her neck was broken.

Kate put her ear to Margaret's chest and felt it lift, like a visitation from God. She hauled herself to her feet, spitting and retching out the grit that filled her throat.

They were at the Odeon in Brighton. They had been watching a children's film.

The theatre doors opened and a man with a torch appeared. Emergency workers ran in and one of them scooped Margaret up.

"That's my daughter," Kate said, chasing after them. "She's three years old."

Margaret cried out for her. She was alive and Kate was going to keep her alive. She steeled herself against the panic mounting in her chest. It would not serve her mission; she shoved it away.

A bomb had ripped open the ceiling of the theatre. The afternoon sky was visible through a tangled fringe of rebar. Margaret and Kate had been in the eleventh row, third and fourth from the right.

With a hundred other children and parents, they had come for a matinee show of *The Ghost Comes Home*. All the way to the theatre, Margaret had pleaded for boiled sweets from the concession and Kate refused even though she had 20p in her purse.

Those sweets flashed in Kate's mind as paramedics loaded Margaret's limp body into the back of the ambulance. They haunted her as she climbed in after the stretcher, softly massaging the fingers of her daughter's one uninjured hand, whispering in her ear to blink, blink, blink the gray dust out of her eyes.

It was only when they closed the ambulance doors that Kate registered the sound of a woman keening and remembered that there were other people in the theatre. Other children were hurt. Had she trampled over them to get Margaret to the first ambulance that arrived? Kate did not remember. She remembered sitting in the cool, dark theatre, admiring Ann Rutherford's bolero jacket. A flash from the girders in the ceiling. A hand reaching for a milk bottle on screen and then for Kate's legs. The sound of hail and somebody shouting: "You've gotta get out! You've gotta get out!"

Then she was climbing into the back of an ambulance.

The streets were teeming with people, their faces tense with fear, but it only took a minute to reach the hospital up the road. As they approached, Kate remembered shoulders and a neck without a head in front of the screen and . . . No, there was only Margaret. Only Margaret, who was conscious and breathing. But there was something wrong with her arm. It was swollen and limp and bowed at the wrist. And her face was chalky white. Kate counted her own breaths so she would not hyperventilate and faint. Margaret whimpered and Kate put her hand to her cheek.

The ambulance circled the building and the paramedic calmly narrated what he was doing to Margaret—stabilizing her neck, monitoring her pulse. Kate heard herself telling the driver to drive faster, for Christ's sake. She heard herself panting. Finally, they parked and carried Margaret out on a stretcher. The hospital doors swung open and they were inside.

The waiting room ceiling was vaulted and there were rows and rows of long wooden benches, like a railway terminal. Patients lined up according to their categories. They carried Margaret to the front of the queue, through a door that read *Female New Cases*, and would not let Kate follow.

A nurse told Kate to take a seat on one of the benches, but it hurt to sit down, so she stood. On one side, her bottom felt like there was a grapefruit swelling under the skin. The waiting room filled with people in various states of dust-covered, glassy-eyed undress. Everything about the space was artificially cheerful, with sickly yellow walls and lights. Mothers with children scanned the room and sized up the other cases. Everyone wanted to be seen first. A nurse in a white winged cap walked up and down the rows, taking names and addresses.

Next to Kate, a woman was stripping off her son's clothing. He was covered in something thick and black, like tar. The boy peeked around his mother's rump to get a look at Kate's feet and she realized then that they were bleeding and she wasn't wearing shoes. Other pieces of her clothing were gone, too: her handbag, her hat. She put a hand to her throat—the Rosicrucian, her mother's ruby necklace, was gone, too. She had not taken it off since she gave birth. It didn't matter.

She kept her eyes on the door they had taken Margaret through. Her legs shook. Why were they keeping her from Margaret? Where was she?

The nurse station was a glass conservatory in the middle of the room. Kate went to it and rapped on the window. A nurse looked up at her, wrote something down on a slip of paper, and handed it to the nurse next to her.

"Please," Kate said, knocking again. "I need to know where my daughter is."

"What was her name again?"

"Margaret Rachel Grifferty."

"I'll check for you. It might be a moment, if you would just be calm. We're still processing casualties."

Casualties.

The nurse went back to her paperwork. Kate stood there dumbly, her teeth chattering, sweat bursting from every pore on her body. She felt very, very cold and nauseous.

"I saw the plane," a man behind her was saying. "Just one, a Dornier Do 17. I heard at least ten blasts."

"No, it was twenty," someone else said. "I counted. Round Whitehawk Road."

". . . dropping artillery before returning to Germany. Twenty hundred-pound bombs, along Edward Street. They were counting the dead when I left."

Kate banged on the nurses' window again. "What about my little girl? Margaret Grifferty?"

"Someone will come speak to you shortly, Mrs. Grifferty."

The waiting room was a parade of human misery. Kate didn't want to be one of them. She wondered if David worked in a terrifying place like this. How did he stand it? Her eyes lit on the telephone box on the opposite wall.

Paddington 1149.

She could phone David. Confess everything and beg his forgiveness. Then, she would be free from this long lie. Then, she might deserve Margaret's life.

But what if David did not forgive her? What if he hated Kate and blamed her for what had happened to their daughter? Kate could not bear it; she would actually keel over dead.

At the nurses' station, there was a bouquet of white silk flowers in a vase. Funereal flowers. Kate averted her eyes and tried to follow a pattern in the green-checked linoleum. Her thoughts were jagged and punctuated by flashes of light. It felt like someone was banging on the side of her head with a hammer.

After some time, she heard her own name and looked up. A nurse stood in front of her, a pitiful frown on her moon face.

My baby is dead. Kate knew it. Terror invaded her, filling her mouth with the taste of dirty coins.

"Slow breaths, Mrs. Grifferty," the woman said, placing a hand on Kate's arm. "You're quite pale. In and out, that's it."

"Where is my daughter? Is she dead?"

"No, love, she's wonderfully alive. Actually, that's her hollering for you from the back. She has a fractured arm and a concussion and quite a bit of bruising. We're splinting the arm now. Then you can take her home."

At five o'clock the next morning, the damp, tangled bed-clothes had taken on Margaret's smell and her warmth. Her long, dark eyelashes shifted and twitched with her eyelids. Kate held Margaret's free hand, studying her perfect fingers.

The room was too hot. Perspiration pooled between Kate's breasts and toes and thighs. She inched away from Margaret, rolled out of bed, and cracked the window. Sea air blew in, briny and cold and wet. Kate peeled off her damp nightdress, wrapped herself in a clean cotton dressing gown, and placed pillows at Margaret's sides so she wouldn't roll off the bed.

When Kate returned from the lavatory, the room was chilly. She laid her hand on the back of Margaret's neck—it was still scalding. Her forehead, too. Carefully, Kate pulled back the covers and removed Margaret's socks, remembering her father telling her once that heat escapes through the feet. Then Kate went to make herself a cup of tea and, though she felt like she was going to be sick, choked down a boiled egg while she reread Margaret's care instructions from the hospital: *Elevate and immobilize the arm until swelling goes down so a plaster cast can be snugly administered. At least two days of rest for the concussion. Clear liquids in case of vomiting.* Nothing about a fever.

Kate refilled the large teapot with water, thinly sliced two loaves of bread, and portioned out seven sets of butter and tea rations for the guests. At six, the new maid-of-all-work, Christina, arrived and together they finished preparing breakfast. Orla padded into the kitchen with her hair in paper rollers. She gave Kate a quick squeeze, told her she looked dreadful, and ordered her back to bed. But Kate was too full of nervous energy to sit down, let alone sleep. She went to wash and dress and pin her hair back. Margaret slept on.

While the guests chatted in the dining room upstairs, Kate mopped the kitchen floor. She was brittle with fear and it felt virtuous to be busy, like she was earning points with God. If she could get the kitchen clean enough, luck might turn her way. If it did not and Margaret never woke, the state of the house would be one less thing Kate did wrong.

At eight, she checked on Margaret again. She should have been awake by then. Kate could feel her daughter's fever before she touched her, heat radiated off her little body. Terror constricted Kate's throat. Perhaps Margaret had contracted a sudden cold, nothing to do with her injuries. Kate ran her fingertip under her daughter's nostrils, hoping for mucus, but the skin was dry. She moved one of the pillows and lay down next to Margaret, her side along the edge of the bed.

Kate hugged herself, trying to make herself small. She was not resting, she was observing. Margaret twitched but did not wake.

By noon, they were back at Sussex County Hospital.

"Go home," the matron said upon finding Kate lurking outside the children's ward after Margaret was admitted. "If your daughter wakes and sees you, it will only upset her when you leave. Come back tomorrow for visitor hours, between eight and nine in the morning. We should know where we are by then."

"I can't leave her."

"You're no use to her here," the matron snapped. Then, gentler: "Your daughter has a very high temperature and is being transferred to the infectious diseases ward. It's an intensive care unit with an infectious disease specialist."

"Will they put a hard cast on her arm?"

"No. We have to focus on controlling the fever for now."

Kate's stomach dropped. "It is so serious that you're not doing anything about her broken arm?"

"Potentially, yes."

"Does she have an infection?"

"We think so. But if the fever subsides in the next twenty-four hours, then probably not. Sometimes head injuries can cause febrile symptoms in children. All we can do now is wait for something to declare itself."

Kate should have let Margaret go to the country with the children's evacuation. She was a disgrace. David would not have let this happen to their daughter. How disgusted he would be with Kate now.

Hanging her head in shame, she walked out into the street and to the bus shelter. She waited for the fear to sputter out. It didn't. It never, ever would.

She prayed: *Just let me keep Margaret, God. Forgive me*

*wishing for more. I don't want anything more. I shun any-
thing more.*

The shelter was papered with government notifications:
*STAY AT HOME, LET NO LIGHT ESCAPE FROM
YOUR HOUSE, DON'T LET THE ENEMY SEE YOU,
KEEP CLOSE TO BUILDINGS AND AWAY FROM
CURB, WALK CAREFULLY, DON'T RUN.*
She thought about what that matron had said: *Something
to declare itself . . .* A euphemism for disease. For death.

The candle burning on Kate's bedside table had melted
overnight and the wood was covered with wax. The wick
had burned down to a nub, but it was still lit. She leaned over
to blow out the flame, dressed in the darkness, and pulled the
Leica kit from under her bed. It felt steadying to hold it in her
hands. She chose severe clothing—her work trousers, a white
blouse, brogues, and her father's old watch—to face whatever
came. Armor was called for. Her body felt alarmingly weak,
but emotionally she felt nothing at all. She was numb, except
for the skin over her ribs which itched like it was crawling
with ants. A few fragmented, frightening dreams were the
only evidence she had gotten any rest. There were still two
hours to fill before she could see Margaret.

None of what had happened seemed real. It did not feel
like she was in her own body; it felt like she was working its
controls from a second location.

She didn't remember a bomb falling on the theatre. If she
could see where it fell, and accept it, it would bring her back
to herself. Then she could be strong for Margaret. And she
had to find her mother's necklace. It was too precious, too
essential, to think of going through life without it.

The streets of Kemptown were eerily quiet. She passed a
church with its doors blown off. It looked as if a bomb had
dropped directly into it, gutting and catapulting the pews

through the front door. A double-decker bus trundling along St. George's Road had to swerve onto the pavement to avoid a splintered pipe organ. The sun was up, but there was so much smoke in the air that Kate cast no shadow on the paving bricks. As she walked, the lacerations on her feet opened and oozed inside her wool socks. But the pain was useful. It helped her feel where she was, each and every step.

A voice in her head said: *Nothing less than you deserve.*

"Shut up," she murmured, and opened up her camera bag.

The Odeon was very near the hospital. Around the theatre, emergency workers climbed over the still-smoldering rubble. The homes, shops, and public houses immediately surrounding it were wrecked, too.

The face of the theatre was somehow intact, even the swinging glass doors she and Margaret had walked through, naive as insects about to be stepped on. Kate went around to the back of the building, behind where the screen had been. It had been blown open. She slipped past a police barrier into the theatre stalls. The ones in front were in pieces, piles of seared lumber. The back of the theatre was almost unchanged. It was like a shoebox diorama, kicked in by a sadistic child. It smelled of wet charcoal and sulfur and cordite.

Kate took photographs of everything she saw. She didn't really know why she had come back there, only that there was nowhere else to be.

After a while, she found where she and Margaret had been sitting. Scanning the floor for her mother's necklace, she saw a flash of gold. It took a moment to understand what it was: a simple wedding ring on a woman's hand, unattached to a body, as lifeless and pale as molded clay. Kate snapped a photo of it and walked outside to tell one of the emergency workers, but she could not find any words. Her mouth was sealed shut and had a queer, metallic taste. She tried to sit on the ground, but her hip hurt too much. She kept walking, toward an AFS first aid station, where a paramedic was treating a volunteer who had fainted. The young man, a civilian, had spent the night searching for survivors in a collapsed basement. He appeared to have suffered gas inhalation, but refused to be taken to hospital.

"I'm not a real casualty," he insisted as they tried to put him on a stretcher.

Kate took a picture of him and the paramedic helping him. She noticed that her skin no longer prickled. Her heart was beating in her eardrums but the skin on her ribs wasn't crawling anymore.

She was halfway through her third roll when an official-looking woman in a tin hat appeared in her viewfinder.

"You're in my shot," Kate said.

"I am aware of that," the woman said. She was middle-aged, with a long face and small, black eyes like a bull terrier's. "Credentials, please."

This was not good. Kate smoothed her blouse. "Press," she said. "I work for the Central Press."

"Fine. Then you'll have a press pass. If you do not, I shall be forced to confiscate your camera and any film . . ."

"I left the pass at home," Kate said quickly.

"Likely story."

"Please. My daughter and I were watching a film when it was bombed. She's in hospital, I'm waiting until I can see her."

The woman's eyes narrowed. "What are you doing back here?"

"They wouldn't let me stay with her. I'm here to cover the story, all right? If you would just get out of my way . . ."

Kate tried to shoulder past her but the woman grabbed her arm. She was surprisingly strong.

"Right," she said. "We have these little things called Defense Laws. Carrying a camera round a bomb site is prohibited by law. You have to be able to prove you're a pressman. You can't just wander Brighton photographing burning buildings. Let me see your camera."

Kate clutched the Leica to her. "No."

"That's a German camera. Who gave it to you? Have you been in contact with any German nationals?"

"Of course not. I earned this camera."

"How did you acquire that film?"

"It's mine. Now please get out of my way."

"Absolutely not," the woman said. "Give me your camera and any film on you, or I shall have you arrested."

She raised a hand to wave over a police officer who was chewing on his chin strap and surveying the ruined theatre.

Kate's legs wobbled. She was desperate to sit down and catch her breath, if only this woman would leave her alone. The policeman came trotting over.

"This is an *active bomb site*," the woman was saying to her. "A prohibited zone. Unless you prefer to wait for your daughter in jail, you will immediately surrender all unlicensed surveillance equipment. PC Murray, please confiscate this woman's camera and any film on her person. Take her information as well. If she won't give it willingly, arrest her."

"There's bodies stuck in there, miss," the police officer said to Kate, a look of disgust on his face. "Have some respect."

The bull terrier woman shushed him. "Don't tell her anything, Murray, for God's sake."

"Right." He nodded. "Sorry, ma'am. Hand over the camera, miss. That's a good girl."

Chapter 23

17th September, 1940

The First Aid post at St. Mary's London was under the benevolent dictatorship of Sister Eugene. David was one of the doctors who rotated in and out based on need, along with several auxiliary nurses. It was in the hospital basement, frigid and candlelit when gas and electricity went out, but Sister Eugene kept it immaculately clean and the shelves were always stocked with neat rows of supplies.

Most casualties with functioning legs were sent down to First Aid. Several days a week, David set and wrapped bones, treated shock, and examined abdomens for internal bleeding. Late Tuesday afternoon, he was stitching up a subdermal laceration on the paper-thin skin of an elderly woman's arm. It would have looked prettier if a surgeon had done it, but their skills were currently reserved for catastrophic injuries.

At a quarter to five, an extremely tall woman in dungarees strolled in with a paint bucket over her shoulder and a wooden easel. She and Sister Eugene greeted one another, and the painter set up in the corner. She took a thick pencil out of a tin case and began to drag it across a stretched canvas. The scratches she made blended in with the other hospital sounds: rapid, leather-soled footsteps; trolley wheels on linoleum; the suction clasp of heavy doors closing. The way she pressed her lips together while she worked stirred a fond feeling in David. It made him smile. He could have watched the woman sketch all evening, but soon he had to return to his ward.

Upstairs, the corridors had been freshly washed and smelled of floor polish and antiseptic. David walked quickly, feeling energized. He went to check on a patient named Mr. Honeycutt, who had come in with a shattered leg that morning. Fortunately, there were still no signs of infection, but the nurse reported that his blood pressure had been slowly dropping all day. David ordered a bolus of saline and sat by the man's bed while they waited for it.

Geriatric patients were London's most loyal holdouts and David's favorites. They only wanted someone to look them in the eye and acknowledge that they were still people in this world. He loved listening to their stories, the memories they seemed compelled to hand off. The prospect of German occupation did not seem to frighten these *altacockers* as much as British plumbing, of which they complained bitterly and constantly. Neither poverty nor disease nor war had kept them from living to a ripe old age and they laughed off the idea of being evacuated.

A young auxiliary nurse walked past the bed and Mr. Honeycutt called her back.

"Nurse, have you met Dr. Rabatkin? He's *my* doctor." He sounded so proud, as if he were saying: *He's* my *son.* "Have you two met?"

"Afraid not," the nurse said, unimpressed, and went on her way.

"You're just like my dad," David said. "When I was a kid, he was always using me to talk to pretty girls."

"Aha!" Mr. Honeycutt chuckled. "You're onto me, Doc. I still think of myself as your age. What are you, thirty, thirty-five?"

"Twenty-six."

"Hmm. You look old for twenty-six." He placed a clammy hand on David's wrist. "Mustn't work too hard, son. You'll miss it."

"Miss what?"

"Life. Do you know I once saw Queen Victoria, getting out of a carriage?" Mr. Honeycutt widened his eyes and the years fell away from his face. "Ugliest woman I ever saw. Like a toad in a christening gown."

David laughed. "I have heard that. Do you mind if I check your blood pressure again?"

"Be my guest."

Mr. Honeycutt's blood pressure had dropped again while David was sitting there. Considering the severity of his injury, his lucidity also concerned David. Since the seventh of September, he'd become an expert on the forerunners of death. Critical shock patients occasionally presented with an elevated state of awareness, right before they died. It wasn't fully understood why, but David's guess was adrenaline. The body knew it was in mortal danger, even if the conscious mind did not.

"You should get some rest, Doc," the old man mused cheerfully. "You remind me of my son. People say your generation don't know the meaning of work, but it couldn't be farther from the truth. You work too hard . . ."

"Nurse," David called, "could you bring that saline, please?"

Mr. Honeycutt was still watching him, his eyes clear and bright.

"When is your shift over?" he asked. "Will you see to me before you go?"

"Does your son live nearby?" David asked, his eyes on the sphygmomanometer. *Seventy over forty.*

"No, he's in the forces."

"You must be proud of him. Which branch?"

"Army. He's a good boy." Mr. Honeycutt closed his eyes. "Always has been, even when he was little."

The saline never came and he died fifteen minutes later.

When David's shift was over, he went to First Aid to see Sister Eugene. She was measuring caffeine into syringes and lining them up on a tray by the sink. Sister Eugene had been a battlefield nurse in the 1914 War and David found her stoicism steadying. When he asked how she was holding up, she grunted, raised one wiry gray eyebrow, and continued with the syringes.

"These injuries are like nothing I've ever seen before," he said, trying to engage her.

"No. They wouldn't be."

"I was wondering, who is that lady who works in here?" he asked. "The painter."

"That'll be Mrs. Emma Percy. She's a medical artist. The board granted her use of one of the old operating theatres upstairs." Sister Eugene studied David's eyes, which burned with exhaustion. "You were meant to go home hours ago," she said, frowning.

"An obstetrics case took a turn for the worse and I got called up there. Poor old girl got bombed out of her house in Maida Vale and went into labor at thirty-four weeks. The husband is in Ethiopia."

"Oh dear. Did mother and baby pull through?"

"Looks like it. She's stable now. And the baby was bawling his head off when I left. Spitting image of Lord Beaverbrook. Uncanny."

"Perfect. Shall I make you a cuppa, Dr. Rabatkin?"

"No, I'm all right," David said. "Actually, I love pitching in when another doctor's patient takes a turn. I get all the excitement without my name being on it."

Sister Eugene finally cracked a smile. "And when it's over

and the room looks like a junta has taken place, *you* get to go home."

"Precisely. No paperwork." He rubbed his eyes. "Ack, there's just so much dust. I can't tell if I'm getting it out of the wounds."

"You're probably not," she said. "Don't fool yourself that you'll be able to keep up the standards you're used to. With bomb casualties, more often than not, they just die."

Emma Percy's studio was at the top of the hospital in a defunct Victorian operating theatre. When David visited the following day, she was standing at a large wooden easel, leaning back on one heel, brush paused, considering her next stroke. Large featured and about six feet tall, she was what David's mother would call statuesque. Her dark hair was pinned into coils at the crown of her head and she wore a paint-splattered doctor's coat, cinched at the waist with a leather belt.

David knocked on the open door. Mrs. Percy turned to him, her face impatient.

"Sorry to interrupt," he said. "I'm David Rabatkin. I was the attending doctor, when you were painting in the first aid station yesterday."

"Yes, I remember you," she said, revealing a faint Scottish burr, and waved him in. "Here, take a look at this. What do you think?"

She stepped back to reveal her canvas, a red-brown wash of paint engraved with a dozen vague figures.

"It's just a sketch," Mrs. Percy said. "A guide for when I start laying on the color."

With the handle side of her brush, she pointed to a figure in the middle of the canvas—a shaded face with large eyes and a shock of hair standing straight up.

"Recognize that fellow?" she asked. "I think I'm going to give you a mustache. I hope you don't mind. But Sister Eugene is the star of the painting. Are you the sort of doctor who will take umbrage to that?"

"Of course not. She's a legend."

"Rather. So, why have you come to see me?"

"Sister Eugene told me about your studio. I thought you might let me have a look at your paintings."

"I'd be delighted. Make yourself at home."

They could hear the twin antiaircraft guns blasting away in Hyde Park. Mrs. Percy twitched at each bang.

"I think the sound of those guns is meant to cheer people up," David said.

"Cold comfort," Mrs. Percy said. "We're sitting ducks. But talking of cheering up, do you find that sketch depressing? Please, say no. The War Artists Advisory Committee send back the melancholic ones."

"Why do they do that?"

"Bad for morale."

"It's serious, but not at all melancholy." David folded his arms. "If you ask me."

He glanced around at Mrs. Percy, trying to gauge her reaction.

"Good," she said, nodding. "There are some drawings I hate over in the corner there, if you'd like to shuffle through them. Take one, if you like."

Chapter 24

20th September, 1940

The morning after Margaret came home again, Kate woke up feeling like her own limbs were filled with concrete. She opened her eyes reluctantly, stared at the gas lamp on the wall, willed herself to get up. Margaret was already out of bed, bustling around their bedroom, examining her toys for evidence someone else had played with them while she was gone. Kate wasn't awake enough to speak yet; she stood and kissed Margaret's head and went to the kitchen for tea.

Just as Orla poured her a cup, Margaret sauntered into the kitchen in her muslin nightgown with her swollen, broken wrist hanging limp. "I took off my splint!" she announced, smiling widely. Her mouth was ringed with chocolate; she'd gotten into the Fry's Chocolate Sandwich Bar Clifton had brought home for her from the RAF station.

Kate screamed. Needing to get away from Margaret, she left the kitchen and limped up the stairs to her room. Orla would have to fix it. If Margaret reinjured herself, Kate could not cope. It was too much. Orla would have to see to the arm. Kate's mind felt broken—it kept looping from fear to despair, fear to despair.

She locked her bedroom door behind her and laid face-down on the bed. In seconds, Orla came shouting after her.

"Let me in, Kate," she said, rapping at the door. "You have to let me in. Margaret is scared now. She needs you."

Reluctantly, Kate unlocked the door. Margaret staggered toward her, whimpering now, bandages hanging in loose loops around her little arm. She had attempted to rewrap it herself. A blanket of shame fell over Kate.

"She's really worried about her arm now," Orla said, scooping Margaret up. The look she gave Kate was more concerned than reproachful. "Tell her it's all right."

"You're safe, love," Kate cooed, mustering her brightest smile. "You just gave me a shock."

Margaret turned away from her, into Orla's shoulder, soaking her aunt's dressing gown with tears and snot.

"You're all right, button," Kate said. "We'll just pop back to the hospital and they'll fix your arm up again, tickety-boo. We'll get a hard cast instead of this messy old splint. All right? Give her to me, Orla."

"No," Orla said firmly, stroking Margaret's hair. "I'm coming with you this time. You can't do this alone."

"What about the lodgers' breakfasts?"

"They'll have last night's rice pudding. Christina will sort it. You're not going back to that hospital without me."

Later Kate stood in the garden, drinking weak tea from a reused bag, watching Margaret play. It was impossible to sit comfortably. The bruise on her bottom, spanning from her spine to her hip, was pitch-black and so swollen she could not fit into her trousers. The ecstatic shock of Margaret's survival had worn off and dropped Kate lower than she ever remembered feeling.

A savage dusk, pink and orange, had fallen on Brighton. To the north, the dark gray clouds were dusted with the hazy golden light. Even with a broken arm and a concussed head, Margaret was running circles around her. Kate's cotton frock was creased and her angora cardigan bagged out at the elbows, making the sleeves graze her knuckles. She smoothed her hair, in case any of the guests were watching. She knew she looked like a slattern, but Margaret only wanted to play outdoors and Kate did not have the energy to tidy herself or argue with her daughter.

Other than her plaster cast, Margaret was good as new, but when a plane flew overhead she froze and stared at the sky and put her hand over her mouth.

"The bombs doesn't come here anymore," she said through her fingers, eyes wide.

"No, darling, the bombs don't come here," Kate lied.

"That's a fib!"

Margaret bolted past her, back into the house. By the time Kate made it up the stairs after her, Margaret was pacing on the first-floor landing, her hand still on her face and her eyes welling with tears.

"I don't want to be outdoors anymore," she cried.

Kate knelt down and hugged her. Margaret curled into her chest, her breaths short and fast.

"You're safe, darling, you're safe," Kate murmured, rocking her back and forth.

"Are the bombs going to hit our house?" Margaret squeaked.

"No, darling."

"Why not?" Her arms were locked around Kate's neck.

"Because . . ." Kate hesitated. "You can't get bombed twice. It's like lightning."

It was a stupid lie and she instantly regretted it, but she didn't know how to hold Margaret's terror with her own.

"But WHY?" Margaret pressed, clinging tighter.

"Because of our planes, darling," Kate said. "Lieutenant Prouty's friends. They're up there now, protecting us."

Margaret looked up at her, a portrait of skepticism. Kate couldn't even tell a decent lie to help her daughter.

"I think you had better run my bath now," she said, turning away and Kate felt banished.

*   *   *

That night, Kate soaked in Margaret's used bathwater—only five inches deep, per government regulation. Her arms wrapped her legs, her tailbone twisted to protect the tenderness of her bruised bottom. The bath was in a tacked-on room at the back of the ground floor and every time the front door opened, a blast of cold air blew through the two inches of open space under the door. Kate did not know how long she had been sitting like that, but the down on her arms was dry.

The memory of Margaret's birth had blurred to watercolor, the black pain compressed into a spot she could see but no longer feel. Kate clearly remembered when she first glimpsed her baby, a miraculous girl she was determined to do right by. Eight pounds and two ounces. She whispered her name to her: Margaret Rachel, after her mother and David's sister. A princess's name.

She remembered that small, red face. The nurse put Margaret in her arms and Kate was hit with the most audacious love, a love that deluded her into thinking she could raise her baby alone. She'd shooed the kind woman from the adoption society away. After that, her life became small, focused. Nothing but Margaret mattered; that had been the only way Kate knew how to approach the mammoth task of raising her alone.

A knock on the door broke her reverie. "Kate!" It was Orla.

"I'm in the bath!" Kate shouted.

"You've already been in there over an hour."

"No, I haven't."

"You have."

Kate stood up in the tub, her legs sharp with pins and needles, and wrapped herself in a towel. She flung the door open. Orla was standing there in her dressing gown and a bathing cap the same color as her pale-yellow hair.

"You didn't drain the tub, either," Orla said.

Kate yanked out the plug and handed it to her.

"And your knickers." Orla set the plug beside the goo-filled soap dish. "Under the gas, there."

She snatched up her knickers and stormed past Orla.

"Your temper, Kate, my goodness . . ."

"Perhaps we should get our own place," Kate said. "It's clear you don't want me here. I'm nothing but a headache for you."

Orla looked wounded. "What are you on about? You're no trouble. I was just teasing you."

Kate's lip started trembling, which felt odd because she was angry, not sad. "You've always resented me, Orla."

"No, I haven't. Shh. You're not yourself, darling. You thought you were going to lose your daughter."

"Don't patronize me. You resent me because it's my fault she died."

"Who? It's your fault who died? Margaret is going to be fine."

"Not Margaret. Our mother." Kate burst into tears. "Orla, I'm so very sorry."

"What are you apologizing for? I've never blamed you for Mammy's death."

"Then why did you abandon me with Pa? You never visited, never wrote."

"I didn't blame you! I don't." Orla hesitated. "But, maybe, you reminded me of this terrible thing that had happened . . ."

"I knew it."

"I should have overcome it. I should have loved you like you deserved, but I was just a child myself." She sighed. "Mammy and I were very close. We shared a bed together for most of my life. She'd almost died having me and the doctor warned Pa, no more. She wasn't meant to have another baby. It was his fault, if anyone's, that she died."

"And you're always lording it over me that you knew her

and I didn't," Kate wept messily. "You're always Mammy this and Mammy that."

"I talk about Mammy because you remind me so much of her. Since you've come . . ." Orla clutched her own throat. "I feel like I have a bit of her back. She had such beautiful red hair. When you were in her tummy, I'd lie next to her and plait it while she napped. She made up for all the love he couldn't give. After she was gone, all the good things just fell away . . ." Orla shook her head.

"I'm so sorry, Orla."

"It's all right." Orla enveloped her in a tight hug and Kate rested her chin on her petite older sister's head. "She'd be so proud of you. You're a brilliant mother."

"I am not," Kate said. "I'm useless. I'm frightened."

"I know, darling."

"I can't lose Margaret."

"You've not lost her. You won't. Get some sleep and tomorrow we'll have a new start, all right?"

Chapter 25

1st October, 1940

Margaret slept with her plaster cast propped up on a pillow. Her stuffed animals—the Siamese cat puppet, the dog with its face patched up so it looked like a burn victim, the candy floss–pink bear—were tucked around her to keep her from falling off the bed. Kate sat on its end, listening to her daughter's soft, rhythmic breathing. Margaret half opened her eyes, looked at her, and then closed them with a look of complete peace. A sob caught in Kate's throat.

Margaret was a new combination of joy and mischief and beauty every day. She was a howling streak of pink, slipping from Kate's hands after the bath and bolting naked into the kitchen. She was clenched fists, projectile tears, utter calamity when Doris once befriended another child on the playground. She was a fluffy head in front of the window, asking if the stars moved.

When Margaret drifted off, Kate rooted around under the bed, pulled out film and her Ikonta. She didn't need the Leica; that lady air raid warden could have it. The Ikonta had once been Kate's soul, freed from its packaging. It was what she saw as opposed to what people saw of her. And, best of all, it had never belonged to Scargill.

Kate had not been in a darkroom since he trapped her that night.

And what had it all been for? Why had it been so important to prove she could make it in a man's world? She thought working in a newsroom would impress her father, but he hadn't cared enough to be impressed. Meanwhile, Scargill had worn her down and leeched the joy out of the thing she loved most.

Margaret stirred, turned her face toward the candlelight. Kate loaded the Ikonta in the half-dark and set the shutter speed to 30 and the aperture at f/5.6. She set it up on the bedside table, framed Margaret's face, and clicked the shutter button. The light was faint and the picture might not come out, but Kate felt an old curiosity flash inside her.

Kate had not worked slowly since she was ten years old, poking around Hackney in the summertime with Orla's Kodak Brownie. It surprised her how much pleasure came from taking photographs for their own sake. Not just of Margaret, but of life outside. It felt illicit, like stolen time. She wasn't shooting to prove she had deserved to be hired by the illustrious Lindsay Scargill, or that she could work faster than Gordon, or to impress her father. There was time to experiment with focus and lens apertures other than a flash and f/16. She could mull over scenes. She didn't have to shoot blind and fly back to the darkroom.

After taking a couple of rolls, Kate went to have prints made at the camera store in the Lanes. Like many shops in Brighton, the place was going out of business. She walked away with a thirdhand enlarger with a lens and 120mm negative carrier inside it; three ceramic trays; two funnels; a thermometer; a tank; a safelight; chemicals; and the few rolls of film and paper they had left. Orla's cellar was equipped with the other essentials: gas, water, a big sink, and darkness.

Returning home, she watched Orla and Margaret under

the elm tree in the garden, hanging clothes to dry. Rather than rush out to cuddle Margaret, she let them be. Something about the careful way her daughter handed each sock and blouse to Orla seemed sacred. Margaret clearly felt special helping her aunt. Orla noticed Kate in the kitchen window and the sisters smiled to each other, each knowing they were feeling the same thing: how precious Margaret was, how lovely. She was both of theirs. For the first time, it struck Kate how lucky she was to have a sister. To have a sister was to be known. After all those years of distance, Orla was like an emerald found in the lining of an old jacket.

It had never been like this with their father. He'd taught Kate that being a family meant coexistence, a shared bathtub and kitchen. He was wrong. Orla, Kate, and Margaret were a real family. They gave each other strength.

Smiling to herself, she unplugged the small kitchen wireless and carried it down to the cellar. When she switched it on, Sandy McPherson's mild Canadian voice crackled and then flowed out of the speaker: "A little tune that you've probably heard before, 'Begin the Beguine' . . ."

She pulled open the yellowed paper shades, cleared the dust off the high windows with a rag, and propped one open. Humming along with the organ music, she laid out her supplies. Cleaning them felt like scrubbing her own mind. She happily arranged the shelves just as she liked them.

There were tiny cracks in the floorboard planks above her. With a roll of duct tape, she climbed onto a table and patched each hole. If the darkroom was done properly, she wouldn't be able to see her hand in front of her face. There was still a bit of light entering between the window frame and ledge. She covered that, too.

The sink was under the window, so that would be the wet side of the darkroom. Under the stairs would be the dry side. She decided three clotheslines were enough to start and tapped six nails into the wall with a hammer. When the lines were hung, she rigged up a metal fan to bring in fresh air through the window when it didn't have to be dark.

Kate closed herself into the pitch-black broom cupboard, cracked open an unprocessed roll of film, and wound it around the reel, relishing the dry, soft swish of the celluloid under her thumbs. She could still do it. When the tank was loaded and ready for developer, she stepped back into the darkroom and switched on her new red light.

While the film dried, she made prints from old negatives, to hang in her and Margaret's room: Parliament, blurred, taken out of a taxi window; tuberculosis patients from St. Thomas's resting in open air beds by the river; a cleaner dusting off dinosaur bones in the Natural History Museum.

That morning, Kate had taken some pictures of a skinny teenage girl working in an allotment garden. The girl wore knee-high rubber work boots under her plaid skirt. Her dark hair was plaited in two long pigtails. An old man, perhaps her grandfather, dug in the ground to her right. They looked hungry and determined. In one photo, a column of sunlight fell on the girl just as she looked at the lens.

Watching the image appear, it struck Kate that artists sometimes made their names in wartime.

Meanwhile, Kate could not help but note Lieutenant Clifton Prouty's ongoing interest in her. He brought Margaret chocolate when she returned home from the hospital. He gave them a lift to Hanningtons department store once, and glanced in Kate's direction whenever he told a joke at the breakfast table. But mostly, he seemed as distracted as she felt.

Then, about a month after Margaret came home, Clifton seemed to be everywhere. He would bring his tea into the garden while Kate was hanging the wash; she saw him two days in a row at Cowley's Bakery; he would be passing on the landing just as she came out of her room. And, when they did meet, he always said her name: "Hullo, Kate," "Kate, could you and your sister make use of a few extra bars of soap from the RAF station?," "Kate, I thought that was you . . ." It was awkward in the dining room when Clifton was there. Not because she minded his attention, but because it was clear that the other guests noticed it, too. Even worse, Orla saw and started to push Kate to make some sort of romantic overture.

"I just feel sorry for the poor man," Orla said, as they folded bedsheets in the larger third floor bedroom. Robird, squandering his daily quarter hour of flight, chortled on the curtain rail.

"I feel sorry for that bloody bird," Kate said. "One of these days I'm going to set him free. He should be flying around, looking at the world. Not trapped in here."

"Don't you dare. He'd never survive on his own." Orla whistled to Robird and he sailed down to land on her index finger. "You won't even look at him, Kate."

"Robird's brain is probably the size of a poppy seed. He's an idiot. He doesn't mind whether I look at him or not."

"Not Pretty Bird! Everyone looks at him, they can't help themselves. He's just too, too lovely." Orla made a kissy face at Robird and he cranked his neck weirdly. "I meant Lieutenant Prouty."

"I don't have time for lieutenants," Kate said. "You and Margaret run me off my feet every day. Can't you see that?"

"I do. I see several things."

"Like what?"

Orla glanced at Margaret, who was flirting with a tower of already folded sheets.

"I don't feel at liberty," Orla said.

"It's fine," Kate said, annoyed by Orla's knowing tone. "Spit it out."

"All right. That officer fancies you like mad. And you fancy him back."

"No. I don't."

"Yes," Orla said, stroking Robird's violet fluff. "You do. Don't make that face, sourpuss. Enjoy it. He perks you up. It's obvious. I would love a proper flirtation, not that that will ever happen again. I'm too old."

Kate laughed. "You're not too old. Clifton is your age, thirty-seven."

"It's not the same for women. You're too young to realize. He doesn't look twice at me. I'm lucky if an old pensioner gives me a second glance." She sighed. "It's just so boring." Robird was creeping up her arm toward her shoulder. "When Eddie died, I didn't want another fellow. Truth be told, I regretted tying myself down in the first place. I thought I'd all the time in the world. Not anymore. I wish someone had warned me when I still had a lovely figure and bonny, smooth skin like you do. It's no fun growing old alone."

"I'm twenty-five. I think I have a bit of time."

Orla looked skeptical. "Don't miss your chance. You might not have another as nice as this one."

Kate caught the stack of sheets just before Margaret pushed them over. She went to put them in the linen cupboard. "I'm better off on my own."

"Is that so? Well, if you want to be alone, make sure it's a decision you make, not something that just happens to you."

Chapter 26

The medical painter from St. Mary's, Emma Percy, began to invite David to the town house she shared with her husband, Charlo, and their seven-year-old daughter, Julia. It was in a leafy square in Kensington and strewn with moth-gnawed carpets and broken pottery and toys. Antique books tumbled off shelves onto the floor. Charlo did not appear to do any work other than his nightly air warden duties. Julia was always barefoot and carrying a cat or guinea pig, tangled hair streaming behind her. Emma's sister, Louisa, and a rotating cast of artist friends seemed to come and go freely. One of them was always in the kitchen cooking a wild bird or a hare, but there was never anything to eat. The best wines of the previous century flowed freely.

No one asked David what he did or why he wasn't married; perhaps they assumed that he, like several of the Percys' friends, was an unemployed homosexual. More likely, they found him too boring to care. They talked about famous painters they knew personally and plays and museum exhibitions they'd seen, and read out letters from writer friends in Europe. Sarah Jane would have fit in better than David; she was comparably eccentric and patrician.

"I'm not as interesting as your other friends," he observed

one afternoon over a glass of flavorless red wine in Julia's rock garden. He wished she would contradict him.

"That's all right, we needed a physician in our set," Emma said. "What if a doodlebug lands on the house?"

"Emma likes having a fit young man about," her husband, Charlo, said. "You're in short supply at the moment."

Emma plucked a tarnished silver spoon out of the pea gravel and pegged it at Charlo's leg.

"Owww!" Charlo howled, rubbing his shin. "I meant for Louisa's benefit. Gosh."

"David is *not* for my sister," Emma said. "She doesn't fancy him anyway. He's my friend." She turned to David. "Looking at my paintings, you seem to come to life. It pleases me so much, I can't tell you."

"She takes pity on me," David said.

"She took pity on me, too," Charlo said. As usual, he looked like he'd been sleeping rough, but his posh accent was so brittle, David's jaw ached listening to him. Charlo was sandy blond with a short white beard and a small, bulbous nose. He was friendly looking, of the Swedish ilk, and usually drunk. He was clearly proud to be associated with Emma, to set the stage for her pithy little stories. "It's worked out rather well for me," he said. "When Emma found me, I was as poor as a church mouse, forty, divorced, a sculptor . . ."

"In my father's eyes, I could not have made a less agreeable match," Emma said, a twinkle of glee in her eyes. "The Percys are notorious spendthrifts. I was quite rich, did you know that, David?"

It was obvious that she and Charlo were aristocrats, not just because of the size of the house and their cultivated speech. Only the congenitally rich could live in such shameless disarray. David's mother would have been scandalized by the filth.

"Pater cut me off," she went on. "But Louisa and I were already in the house and we simply refused to leave. I sold furniture. Charlo sold a few sculptures. And we rub along all right, don't we, darling?"

"I would have preferred the money," Charlo pouted. "I thought I was getting an heiress."

David was not overly fond of Charlo. Only someone born into privilege would have the nerve to claim poverty in the garden of his wife's Kensington mansion.

My father bankrupted us and died, David considered saying, *after losing the one-bedroom flat I grew up in. The doctors didn't treat his cancer properly; they assumed that because he was poor, he was simply infested with bugs.*

But that would sound like he felt sorry for himself. The last thing he wanted was the Percys' pity. It pleased him that they did not seem to perceive that beneath his degree and middle-class job, he was a poor boy, educated on charity from people like them. So, he parroted something he'd heard Sarah Jane say once:

"Well, there's a war on. All nice people are poor."

David turned over in his sheets on the morning of the first of November, and reached for his blanket. The clock on his bedside table showed six fifty-three. Seven minutes until his alarm went and he'd have to spring from bed, wash his face, and return to the hospital to eat and start work. He had his meals there now, in exchange for administering a weekly blood drive and helping resident students with local air raid casualties.

He did not have to cross his long, narrow room and open the blinds to know what the sky looked like that morning. Bombs fell every night, submerging London in a cloud of ash and dust. Fire was the weather of this war, smoke the clouds, and soot the dew. Ash collected on spiderwebs in corners and left veils on trees. The eastern horizon was a wall of red. Because of its proximity to the port, East London had become a pyre. David's mother still refused to evacuate her home and he was always expecting bad news.

At David's bedsit in Central London, a dusky orange glow filtered through the blackout curtains—autumnal sun and the atmospheric aftermath of last night's bombs. They had pounded the capital for hours: crackles and walloping bangs to the east and south of him. David had crumpled up some toilet tissue and plugged it in his ears until, eventually, he fell asleep.

In a weird way, being under siege suited him. It had sopped up some of his grief for his father—the sense of unease, the depression. Since the bombs started falling, he felt purposeful. His grief had something to do with its hands.

He turned over again and studied the large sketch pinned to the wall above his bed. It was one of Emma's, in coal and chalk: storm clouds coming to a head above a forbidding Scottish cliff. When David was a child and frightened of thunder, his mother had assured him that it was just angels playing snooker. He had thought of her the night before—frightened and stubborn in her own bed, vigilant, waiting.

David would never have guessed how much waiting war would require. It was not courage that was called for, when fire filled the sky above your head. It was the ability to dull your senses and wait for the days, months, or even years to pass. There were heartbreaking stories from the last war of notably brave men suddenly running headlong into enemy fire before a battle began. Perhaps they hadn't been able to sit with the fear. It seemed to David that that was his task, now. To stay alive in order to keep others alive. To wait until life began again.

Early Monday afternoon, David crossed Bayswater Road with his stomach in a hard knot and his chin tucked into the collar of his overcoat. Sarah Jane had just returned from the country and sent him a letter, asking him to meet her in Hyde Park as a matter of great urgency. He wished she had asked for an assignation in his flat or even the hotel in Piccadilly.

A public meeting meant she was going to end their affair, he was certain of it.

It surprised David how desperately he wanted to be wrong. Not because he loved Sarah Jane. He didn't. Nor had he asked for or been given any guarantee of seeing her again. But he was lonely and increasingly envious of her husband. What kind of man had so much that he would neglect such a beautiful, sensual wife? Sarah Jane's husband obviously did not know what to do with her, and David had begun to fantasize that he did.

Because of rain, last night was the first in fifty-seven consecutive nights that London had not been bombed. There was still a wet, metallic edge to the wind and smoke lingered between the buildings. Even in the open air of the park, David could smell and taste ruin on his tongue.

He spotted Sarah Jane on a bench by the Serpentine. She was watching a barrage balloon launching from the football pitch. Her hair, normally pinned and dark at the back of her head, was curled in loose, coppery waves. On the ground at her feet was a basket with a small bottle of Macallan-Glenlivet, a Schweppes soda water, and two cut-crystal tumblers.

"Funny old time for a drink," David said, reluctant to sit down next to her. "November in the park."

"Oh!" Her laugh was jittery. "Just delivering you a cocktail. It's a service I offer."

"You look stunning."

"It's kohl eye shadow," she said, framing her face with a flourish of her hands. "I'm channeling Cleopatra, to give me strength."

David did not like the sound of that. He watched Sarah Jane carefully prepare a drink for each of them with a silver cocktail stirrer. They sat in silence for a moment—her fussing over his collar and his hair, him watching the silver barrage balloon hover above the lake. Its mirror image quivered on the surface of the water.

"I wanted to meet you here," Sarah Jane said finally, "because I believe our time together has run its course."

David sunk into the bench. "Hence the cocktail," he said.

"I'm afraid so, darling."

"You don't want me anymore."

"I do. But I love Johnny."

"I've never heard you call him *Johnny* before," David said, struggling not to betray his jealousy. "If it's to do with him, I'm happy to remain a secret. I'll see you whenever it suits you." He moved his knee next to hers. Sarah Jane did not shift away.

"We don't *have* to stop," he said. "It is up to you, you know."

She shook her head, her brow furrowed. "I thought you might have someone else as well?" she said, the words lilting into questions. "A nice girl? The sort you see outside hotel rooms?"

"No," David said and her soft brown eyes moved over his face, assessing, pitying. He could see she was struggling for words. He looked straight at her to show he didn't need sympathy.

"I'm choosy," he said curtly, and drank his whisky.

"You should be spoilt for choice," Sarah Jane said. "There haven't been so many lonely women in the history of the British Empire. What is it you want?"

"Someone with direction. A good person. Jewish because I can't be bothered. Not too posh, so she doesn't look down on my family . . ." Realizing he sounded exactly like his mother, David trailed off. He sighed. "Sarah Jane, I've no idea what I want." If he did, he wouldn't be there with her. "I had someone wonderful once. Years ago."

"What happened?"

David hesitated. *Why should I tell her anything more about myself?* Sarah Jane had just proclaimed she never wished to see him again.

"She wasn't Jewish," he said. "My parents wouldn't even meet her."

"Ah." Sarah Jane nodded. "And you prefer to keep yourself to yourself."

"No, I don't prefer it at all. It was complicated. You wouldn't understand."

She balked. "Wouldn't I? My husband isn't Jewish."

"Neither are you."

"My maiden name is Rosenberg." Sarah Jane's eyes lit up with delight. "I can see from your face I've shocked you. Bless your heart! Why did you assume I'm Gentile?"

She was correct, she had shocked him.

"For starters, Jews don't say *bless your heart*," David said.

"Ha! You're just like the rest of them. I disapprove of people who arrogantly assume they know who and what other people—"

"Your son is called Christopher. He plays polo, for God's sake."

"Is that all?"

"He's nine years old. It's a catastrophic brain injury waiting to happen. No self-respecting Jewish mama would stand for it."

"I love my children," she said. "I have to let Christopher play polo. He would never be accepted if I didn't."

"If you love them so much, why have you been *shtupping* me and not their father?"

Sarah Jane's face snapped shut. "People make their bargains," she said. "At least I know what mine is. John has never been faithful and I have to protect myself."

It was clear that David had gone too far, he'd hurt her, and he instantly felt sorry. She did not owe him anything. The only decent thing was to let Sarah Jane go gently, as loosely held as an injured bird.

She began to stroke the skin of her neck. It reminded David of Kate, a mannerism she had when she was pretending not to be upset. He'd never realized how alike the two women looked: reddish hair, large eyes, tall. And a little odd.

"I apologize." David moved his foot away from hers. "That was cruel of me. I shouldn't have said it."

"No, it's all right. I have a good life. My children have the best of everything." Sarah Jane swirled whisky around her glass, and stared into it as if divining her future.

"The woman I loved. Kate . . ." David paused, enjoying the sound of her name out loud. "It feels like she lives inside me, even now. And you're right, I probably did keep her at an arm's length. It wasn't going to go anywhere and I was trying to protect her."

"And yourself." Sarah Jane smiled sadly and patted his hand. It was a friendly gesture, maternal, and with it she broke the spell of lust between them. David looked at her, her primly crossed ankles and her posh suit and her smoldering eyes. She was a mum. She was a wife, and not his. Of course this must end.

"I am sorry, Sarah Jane."

"Don't be," she said. "We've had a marvelous time. Now go and find someone you don't have to keep at a distance. Learn from my little tragedy. A good Jewish girl, if you think that will be simpler." She grinned. "Just not me."

There were no bonfires allowed on Bonfire Night in 1940, but the Percys threw a party anyway. David arrived on time and in a bitter mood. Until she ended things yesterday, he'd harbored a scheme of Sarah Jane accompanying him to this party—and of impressing Emma and Charlo with his posh lover and bohemian morals.

The scent of roasted meat lingered in the air in front of the house. David let himself in and went immediately down to the kitchen, where Charlo was hacking at a large, roasted bird. He wore a frilly white maid's pinafore over his dinner jacket.

"Good news, old man," Charlo said with a cheeky grin. "I've been cooking this devil for hours and it's perfect, even though the ruddy gas keeps switching off."

Emma swept into the kitchen in red lipstick and a long black slip that looked like it was meant to go under a more substantial dress. "Would you like a drink, David? Champagne?"

"My pheasant is perfect, Emma," Charlo boasted and David resisted the urge to roll his eyes. "Cook be damned. All this time, we didn't need her."

"I'd love a gin," David said. "If you have it."

Emma thought for a moment and said that they might and that David should go look in the cellar. He did and found the bottle of inexpensive gin he'd brought the Percys as a gift the first time he visited. They must not have liked it. Even then, he'd known it wasn't good enough. Embarrassed, he tucked it behind a crate of Burgundy, grabbed a bottle of champagne, and brought it back to the kitchen.

"Where do you keep the glasses?"

"*Coupes,* darling," Emma said with a wink. "Cupboard."

"Wait! Try this first," Charlo said, and handed David a fork speared with meat.

"It's delicious," David said, and meant it. It was sweet and smoky with the perfect amount of spice. *Not so spiced that you can't taste the bird,* his father would have said. Charlo made another special bite for Emma, who declared it marvelous. David filled his *coupe* with champagne. Charlo snapped a tea towel at Emma and she shook her head.

"You really are after me tonight," she said.

Charlo giggled maniacally. "I'm *after you* tonight . . ."

"Oh dear," Emma said, skirting away from her husband.

"I think it's time for me to join the party now," David said, trying to sound like he was in on the joke and not jealous of the Percys' closeness. Leaving them flirting in the kitchen, he trudged upstairs to join the party.

Later, two of Charlo's sculptor friends kissed loudly on the sofa next to David, the man holding the woman's hair back from her heart-shaped face. Feeling out of place, David politely averted his eyes as she tilted her head and licked the man's cheek.

Emma had lit dozens of candles around the crowded drawing room and shadows flickered on the ivy-frescoed walls. People were chatting about last night's bombing in the West End and the American presidential election, which was happening that day. Everyone was hoping that President Franklin Roosevelt would be reelected and have a mandate for the United States to officially come to Britain's defense. Roosevelt was favored to win by a slight majority, but Willkie was showing better than expected in early exit polls. The challenger had promised the women of America that he would never send their sons to European battlefields.

"The New York vote is balancing to a hairsbreadth," a gloomy, tweedy man was saying. "Roosevelt won't take the presidency without it. If Willkie does well, even if he doesn't *win*, his party will gain fifty seats and Roosevelt won't be able to do diddly for us . . ."

David sunk deeper into his gloom. He was drunk. Emma and Charlo were still in their own little world, talking close by a bar cart, drinks curled to their chests. She was making him laugh and everything seemed terrible. David reminded himself that Emma wasn't his girlfriend. He did not even fancy her, he'd just been sucked into her orbit. This wasn't his ruin of a mansion. The guests were the Percys' typical menagerie: her family's former butler, a few waiters from the Savoy, the former head of the London Zoo, middle-aged lecturers from the London School of Economics and Slade, and the trust-fund ceramicists and feeble-bodied poets of Charlo's clique. David supposed he was one of Emma's specimens, too. He wondered if she filed him under doctor or Jew.

Just as he was about to finish off the bottle of champagne and go home and sleep, Emma called him over to her. She curled her finger and summoned him like the patrician she was. She couldn't hide where she came from any more than David could.

"I have someone for you," she whispered conspiratorially, linking her arm in his. "Julia's adorable teacher, over there. Miss Ross. Now that all the children have gone, we've adopted her."

She gestured toward a woman David had not noticed before. Miss Ross was chatting with a professor from the LSE. With dark blond hair, pink cheeks, and full lips, she was what David pictured when people talked about an English Rose.

"Miss Ross is our Little Bo Peep who's lost her sheep," Charlo said, eyeing up his daughter's teacher. "Emma should paint her."

David wondered if the Percys planned to paint and sculpt them all. "Actually, I was just leaving," he said.

"Come on!" Emma dragged him toward Miss Ross. "I'll introduce you. You're a perfect match."

Miss Ross and the professor were discussing who should fund the educations of child evacuees. ". . . but Keynesian analysis does justify policies that redistribute wealth," she was saying.

The professor raised an eyebrow. "I know Professor Keynes very well," he said. "He panders to the egos of liberal policy makers. No one wants to admit that we may spend all the money we like, but poverty will never be solved."

"Does it not strike you as morally repugnant . . . ," Miss Ross said, not noticing David and Emma standing beside her, "that we have children starving to death in poorhouses, while others inherit more than they could ever dream of needing? Redistributing that sort of wealth seems like a good place to make a start."

Emma cut in: "Miss Ross, this is Dr. David Rabatkin. We work together at St. Mary's. And, David, you've met Professor Mayfield, I think."

"Hello," David said and Miss Ross turned to look at him.

Suddenly he was dead sober. Her eyes were large and intelligent and emerald green. "I could not agree more with what you were saying, Miss Ross . . ."

"Helena," she said.

"Helena. At the hospital where I did my training, most of the children we treated came in with malnourishment-related diseases. Even if one cannot see the merit of providing sustenance to hungry children for their own sake, wouldn't it be better for factory owners if their future workforce was not hobbled by hunger?"

"But that's always been true," Professor Mayfield sputtered. "What Miss Ross is suggesting is repackaged Marxism."

David shrugged. "Perhaps some people are more invested than others in maintaining the status quo. If you'd ever witnessed a postmortem on a thirteen-year-old London chimney sweep—which, by the way, I have—you might be less troubled by how welfare is packaged. The poor child had the lungs of a Derbyshire pit mule and weighed just three stone . . ."

As the conversation continued, Helena's body seemed to lift to get closer to David's. Soon, it felt like the professor and Emma were their chaperones.

They left the professor scowling into his glass of port and walked through the French doors into the dark garden. Searchlights combed through the black night, looking for German planes for the antiaircraft guns to blast out of the sky. Smoke floated in the moonlit air like fog, ghosts of buildings destroyed in the nightly bombings of the last two months. It smelled of gunpowder but was less stifling than the Penhaligon's and turpentine fug inside.

Helena tapped the toe of her Mary Jane on the toe of David's polished black wingtip. "A doctor *and* a philanthropist," she said. "Impressive."

"I'm not a philanthropist. Just stating the facts as I've observed them. I'm not one of the Percys' upper-class set. I grew up near Spitalfields."

Helena clasped her hands together. "Oh! My *bubbe* came from Shoreditch."

David understood this coded statement and question. She meant: *I'm Jewish. Are you?*

He smiled. "Mine, too," he said.

There was this shorthand that made it easy to talk to Helena. They'd had a lot of the same experiences, and they both implicitly recognized that. She was pretty and clever and came from a close-knit family she talked about frequently. For their first date, David took her to a chop suey in the Strand. It was the most fun David had had since Simon left. They ordered a dozen of the glossy steamed buns and split them, guessing at what the fillings might be.

Like David, Helena was raised in a kosher home, but had not kept one since she moved out on her own. None of her family were immigrants—she didn't even know when they got to England or where they had come from—and he had the sense that she was somewhat well-off. She seemed to wear her Jewishness more lightly than the people he knew. It was something she could take on and off to suit her audience. David tried not to think about why that appealed to him.

Helena had grown up in Putney, but now shared a small flat near the Percys with two other women. They were all schoolteachers, transitioning to war jobs. Helena brought David there one Saturday afternoon. They were meant to be going for a walk, but she forgot her pocketbook and wanted to go back for it.

"Sorry, Hel, I'm just on my way out," her roommate said, running into them on the stairs.

David stepped out of the girl's way and glanced at Helena, but she would not look at him. Her face had gone red. Inside the flat, she made a show of rifling through drawers and cupboards, only confirming David's suspicion that he had been brought there intentionally. Feeling triumphant, he settled on the settee and ran his fingers through his hair.

"I'm so sorry," she said. "I've no idea where my pocket-book is."

"That's all right," David said. "You don't really need it. We don't even have to walk, if you don't fancy it."

"I'm hopeless," she said with a little laugh, flopping down beside him. "I lose everything."

David thought of a retort to that, but Helena was obviously well brought up and might not appreciate a rude joke, so he kept his mouth shut.

"Would you like a cup of tea?" she asked. Her face was so close to his that he could smell her licorice toothpaste. "We've used all our sugar ration, but . . ."

He kissed her and there was that old feeling in his chest. A kind of completeness. With Sarah Jane, it had been more transactional: *You can use my body if I can use yours.* Now, with Helena, it was like a new friendship, but better. David was actually having a good time and, for once, he wasn't going to think of Kate.

Helena's lips were soft and pillowy, a pleasant sensation, and her body melted instantly into his. She touched him, massaged his thighs and his upper arms. David brushed his lips along her neck. Reflexively, he thought of Kate, shoved her away, and then he was with Helena again and it was nice. Not wave-knocking-him-off-his-feet-and-dragging-him-out-to-sea nice, but nice. And he thought, why not Helena? It would be so much easier this way. He pictured going to Friday dinners with her, to the cinema, sharing a newspaper together in bed. Their families meeting and being mutually delighted. Maybe she even had a sister for Simon.

For the first time, David could picture life after the war: an ordinary, lovely life.

Chapter 27

Kate and Clifton sat on the rusted white wrought-iron deck chairs in the garden. It was cold and windy, but dry, and the smell of burnt leaves made her feel cozy. Silence was possible in Brighton, of a sort she had never experienced in London.

Clifton leaned back in his chair and squinted at the low, bright white sky. Then he smiled at Kate, considered his own hand wrapped around the arm of the chair, and stretched his legs out on the russet elm leaves that covered the grass. It looked like he had shaved hastily. His skin was raw and he had missed a few spots of light hair on his jaw. Kate had seen him that morning walking from the bath to his room, a towel around his waist. She could smell him now—his carbolic soap, his hair grease. Clifton was past the first flush of male glory, he had gray hairs and there were little wrinkles where his ears connected with his face, but he grew more handsome the more she knew him.

In the middle of the garden, a clothes-drying rack stood up out of the grass. As an additional service, the lodgers could have their laundry done and men's shirts flapped in the wind like big, rain-soaked white birds. Margaret—her arm completely healed, dressed in shorts, a wool jumper, rubber boots, and Clifton's tin air raid hat—came charging outside and boomeranged around the clothes rack pole. A patina of snot glistened on her chubby red cheeks. When Kate grabbed her and scrubbed it off with the sleeve of her cardigan, Margaret reached around and pinched her mother's bottom.

"My favorite thing about Mammy is her big bum," she said to Clifton, with a mischievous wrinkle of her nose.

"Margaret!"

"What? I like the way your skirt swishes around it! Do you like it, Clifton?"

In spite of the childrearing advice he'd offered his sister, he had never been Lieutenant Prouty to Margaret. Just Clifton.

"I'm not telling you," he said, mock serious. "You're not to be trusted."

Margaret screwed up her face at him—the exact expression David made when he thought someone was a bit stupid. Her soft curls were darkening, which made their resemblance even more uncanny. She never let Kate forget David.

Clifton stood, swept Margaret up with one arm, and placed her on his shoulder. Margaret, with the fifty-yard stare of a queen on a sedan chair, allowed him to convey her around the border of the garden. Watching them together, Kate felt a sharp pang of affection for the lieutenant.

"Kate," he exclaimed suddenly. "Would you ever consider marrying me?"

Thinking he was joking, she laughed. "You wouldn't want to marry me. You hardly know me."

"Why not? I think we would get on well."

"Clifton. You're not serious."

"Try me."

As strong as he was, he looked vulnerable standing there in the middle of the garden, his eyes as guileless as a Labrador's. Margaret yanked hard on his ear, but he did not flinch, just gently moved her hand away. Kate could not discern exactly what she felt for him—if there was anything other than friendship and attraction—but when he reached out for her hand, she gave it to him.

"I like you, Kate," Clifton said, pressing her hand. A pleasant, warm sensation spread up her arm. "And I think you like me. We've not known each other long, but I could be transferred to another station at any time. And I'm not getting any younger, am I? I want to be married. I have to follow my gut, steer into the wind, if that's going to happen. What do you say?"

Kate looked at Margaret, who had slid down Clifton's side and was untying his shoelaces. He never scolded or ignored or placated her. He talked to Margaret like she was a person, laughing out loud at her attempted jokes. He would be an excellent father. He was kind and Kate truly liked him. She liked him too much to lie to him for the rest of her life.

"It's not so simple for me," she said cautiously. "I have a child. I have responsibilities. It wouldn't be fair on you."

"But I would look after you both! This war won't last long. I have a house in Buckinghamshire that belonged to my parents. Margaret will love it. There's plenty of space for a darkroom if you want to keep taking pictures. We'll get you a governess. Margaret could have a proper home. I don't believe you want your daughter growing up with strangers from the four winds."

"Orla is not a stranger."

He frowned. "But you're a mother and a widow. You should be looked after. Both of you."

After everything she'd been through, this struck Kate as funny and she started to laugh. Clifton was the one who needed protecting—from her. If he knew who she really was, the things she'd done and still wanted to do, he wouldn't want to marry her. He would be as disgusted with her as her father was.

"I'm not a saint, Clifton," Kate said, recovering herself.

She wiped a tear from the corner of her eye. "You should know that. I don't need looking after. Orla made me tell people that my husband died when I was . . ." She tilted her head toward Margaret. "But it's not true. The truth is, I was with a man and he left me. I was never married."

It was a relief to finally say it. Clifton went completely still. He looked at Kate, aghast. "He abandoned you?"

"Shh! I never told him about the, ah, b-a-b-y. My father threw me out and I came here."

"How could anyone . . ." Clifton shook his head. "Where is the scoundrel now?"

"I don't know. London, probably."

He frowned. She was a fallen woman and a liar and he was going to bolt.

"I don't mind about any of that," he said finally. "I know you're a good person. I see it in you. I'm not really bothered about what you did in the past."

Kate was speechless. It deeply touched her that he was still so eager to marry her. This was a man who would make excuses for her, even at the cost of his own dignity. A selfless man.

"Well?" He squeezed her hand, a trace of anxiety in the way he chewed the inside of his lip. "What do you say? Will you have me?"

She looked at Margaret, who was beaming up at Clifton, twirling a sawtooth leaf between her fingers and presenting it to him.

"I say you're wonderful," Kate said. "And I say yes." There was no other intelligent answer. She was tired of being a scandal, of her daughter being a secret. And in her heart, she knew she was losing her grip on her self-imposed celibacy. A husband would solve all of that.

Clifton's laugh was loud and confident, as if he'd known all along Kate would accept him.

"Darling," he said, picking Margaret up again and swinging her into the air between them. "I will make you girls very happy."

Mrs. Kathleen Grifferty
77 Marine Parade
Brighton

12 November, '40
Dear Mrs. Grifferty,
I understand that my brother has mentioned that I am extremely anxious to meet you. My husband, Gerald, and I are delighted at your news and we both look forward to welcoming you to our family. My brother tells me you will marry soon in a registry office in Brighton which sounds perfectly sensible. Have you given any thought to what you shall wear? There are no decent frocks to be found. I could send you my wedding dress if you would like it. It's good French silk, ivory, and I won't mind if you prefer to chop it up and make it over. I am full of ideas. Would you be good enough to write as soon as convenient if you would like me to post it?

I hope you will find a way to visit soon, as I long to meet you and your little daughter. The war has not really come to us and you may find you enjoy the tranquility and not wish to return to Brighton. This is my private hope. Well, it was my private hope but I suppose I've told you now. When you do come, there's our darling evacuee, Judith, she's fourteen years old and from London. She looks after my Charlie and would be happy to look after your Margaret as well. Charlie adores his uncle Cliff and scarcely sleeps with excitement over your news.

Mrs. Grifferty, I should like to help you in any way I can. I hope we shall be friends. Please accept my

*heartfelt condolences at the loss of your husband. You
must be a very strong woman indeed to have managed
on your own this long. I can't tell you how much I
admire you already.*

   Yours sincerely,
   Mrs. Gerald Winters-Gough (Daisy)

It was a charming letter and breathtakingly kind, but Kate
could not help thinking that if Daisy Winters-Gough knew the
truth of Margaret's origins, she would not be so welcoming.

"Your sister wrote me a very nice letter," she told Clifton
over tea in the drawing room.

"She told me she was going to. Daisy is a good sort."

"She offered me her wedding dress." Kate hesitated. "How
did you explain to her about Margaret's . . . well, how she
came to be?"

Clifton shrugged and went back to the file he was reading.
"I told her your husband died," he said.

"I suppose that means we'll always have to lie to Marga-
ret," she said sullenly. "Exactly what I had hoped to avoid.
I had planned to tell her, one day. I don't like all this lying.
That widow myth is for Orla's benefit, not mine."

"All this *lying*?" Clifton put his cup down and looked hard
at her. "I'll tell my sister whatever you wish. I only said you
were widowed because that is how you introduce yourself."

"It's understandable if you're a trifle afraid of what she'll
think."

"Certainly not! You can tell her it was a single performance in a doss-house with a French sailor for all I care. I'm
not bothered about what my sister or anybody else thinks of
you. I know you better than she does."

"Hardly."

"Nonsense! Time is not a measure of how well people
know one another. I'm a brilliant judge of character. And
from the first time we spoke, I knew I had to marry you."

* * *

Kate set aside bones and carrot tops and other scraps to make rich broth for soups. There was a trick to feeding people on rations, a sort of chemistry, and she enjoyed puzzling it out. She wondered what it would be like to have her own home with just three people to cook for and not twelve. When she became Clifton's wife, she might even have her own cook.

While Kate chopped the rotten bits off old vegetables, Orla sat across from her at the kitchen table, shelling peas.

"You keep sighing," Orla said, not looking up from the ceramic bowl she was dropping peas into. Her perfume was called Mary's Garden and smelled of roses entombed in talcum powder. It was the last dregs of a gift from her husband, and she normally only wore it on Christmas and Easter. But their burly neighbor, Nick Abbott, had visited Puffin's Perch that afternoon and Mary's Garden was on the air. Nick had come for lunch and brought three eggs from his garden chickens.

"For your little girl," he'd said shyly, handing them to Kate, but his dark eyes were on Orla.

Hours later, Orla was still glowing. Kate understood that she had made herself lovely especially for Nick, who was probably in his early forties and far from a pensioner. Batting her eyelashes at him, Orla had looked like a teenager again and it struck Kate that her sister's story was not yet written. Her life wasn't over and neither was Kate's.

So, as they prepared dinner, she decided to finally tell Orla about Clifton's proposal. To make it real.

Orla exhaled sharply; her hands froze over the bowl of peas. "What do you mean?" she asked.

"He said he wants to marry me and take me and Margaret to live near his sister in Buckinghamshire. He has a house there."

"My goodness. How do you feel?"

Kate still did not feel ready to tell her sister that she'd accepted. "I said I would consider it."

"Well, he has that nice sandy hair and the officer's uniform is *so* attractive." Orla raised her eyebrows knowingly. "Lucky girl. If he were a priest, I'd take vows as a nun."

Kate, relief and delight filling her up, laughed out loud. "Orla!"

"I quite fancy the idea of being in service to a broad, strong chap like that." Orla teasingly shimmied her shoulders. "Don't you?"

"I don't fancy the idea of being in service to anyone. But apparently the women in our family are all man crazy."

Orla shrugged, kept on with the peas. "It would explain why Mammy put up with our miserable father. He was ever so handsome in his day."

If Orla—not to mention their mother—was as lustful as Kate, it couldn't be such a dreadful character flaw. Orla was far from a tart; she wore dressing gowns buttoned up to her chin and kept budgies. Kate walked around the kitchen table and hugged her sister in her chair. Robird squawked peevishly from his cage.

"Anyhoo," Orla said, sighing dreamily. "You'll make the right the decision."

"Why did you marry Edward? Did you love him?"

"Not at first, but I was desperate to get away from Pa. I wanted a life of my own." There was a tinge of sadness in her voice. "Love comes with time."

"So, you think I should go through with it?"

"I think you can't expect another offer from a fellow as nice as that one." Orla straightened in her chair so Kate was forced to let her go. "But I'll miss you awfully."

People still said the war wouldn't last long, but a progression was underway. Things were getting worse. They all felt it. There was only bad news. When Kate was being nice to herself, she did not listen to the wireless, but that never lasted long. Everyone crowded around it in the evenings, hungry for clues to survival or some bit of news that would confirm the war was almost over, for better or for worse. The boarding-house guests shook their heads at each other, tsking the tragedy of it all, sighing with fed-up-ness. Everyone understood each other. That was the only good thing.

Three evacuees from London, a pregnant woman and two little girls, checked in to the boardinghouse the morning of the fourteenth of November. When the woman came through the door, Kate smiled at her and she collapsed into her arms, sobbing. All Kate could do was stroke the woman's back and lie repeatedly that everything would be all right.

"I didn't check on our neighbors," the woman wept. "I'm a terrible person. I grabbed my children and ran. I didn't even look back . . ."

Her younger daughter, about six years old, danced around her legs.

"We can get a new house, Mummy," she sang hysterically. "We can get new neighbors. Don't worry."

Kate understood the woman's guilt. She understood feeling useless. If only she could go out into the world and *do something*, not just stand guard over one child, always with the knowledge that she had failed at it. She hadn't kept Margaret safe.

The *Luftwassen* hit Coventry overnight and there were a thousand reported casualties. Everyone in the boardinghouse was on edge. London was no longer Germany's primary target, and with a large RAF station nearby, Brighton was acutely vulnerable. She wondered what the true scope of the destruction in Coventry was. There had been almost no press coverage of the Odeon bombing two months ago.

Orla was having a private party that evening in the drawing room. Her girlfriends were embarrassed to be seen in a pub, but they loved to drink together. Booze was hard to come by and they had not gathered for some time. At a quarter to seven, Antonia, a grocer's wife, arrived at Puffin's Perch with her sister, Susan. Minutes later, Josephine arrived with the reversi set and half a jug of Drambuie. Orla was still upstairs, finishing reading Margaret her bedtime story.

Kate joined the ladies in the drawing room and they wanted to gossip. About her.

"Orla tells us you've had an offer of marriage from one of her lodgers," Josephine said, wriggling with vicarious pleasure.

"Have you seen him, Jo?" Antonia asked. "Cor, my blouse popped open when he let me in the door."

"Tell us everything, Kate."

"Not much to tell," she said quietly. Clifton's room was next door to the drawing room and she didn't want him to overhear. "We've been spending time together and he just said, do you want to?"

"Makes good sense," Josephine said. "Margaret should have a father, though Orla's heart will break missing her."

Kate would miss all this, too—the bustle of the boardinghouse, her sister, the seaside. She cut herself a piece of Stilton off the tray and ate it on a cracker. Upstairs, she could hear Margaret fleeing sleep. Kate slipped off her shoes and nestled her feet under her on the sofa, pleased that it was Orla putting Margaret to bed.

While they waited for Orla, Josephine taught Kate how to play reversi. It was lovely being in a group of women who weren't paying guests and, before long, the Drambuie revealed that her life would be a series of wonderful surprises. A coveted man wanted to marry her. Margaret would have a father. In the room next door, she thought she could hear Clifton's razor swishing and clicking in the sink.

After an hour or so with Orla and her friends, Kate was in a full swoon of drunken optimism. She excused herself to go to bed, but tiptoed in stockinged feet toward Clifton's room. She wanted him to see her like this: housedress, no lipstick, as close to naked as possible. Just herself. Light shone under his door into the dark corridor. Giddy, Kate knocked and Clifton answered in white-and-blue-striped pajamas. Their eyes met and they both grinned, stood up a little straighter.

"I was just wondering . . . ," she said, crossing one ankle over the other. He did the same. ". . . if you could remind me what time the banquet is tomorrow? I forgot."

"Noon sharp. It's going to be a hell of a do. I'll get to show you off." Clifton went to put his hands in his pockets and, finding none, pressed his arms to his sides. "Here, would you like to come in? There's not much for hospitality, but I might have a bottle of something . . ."

He stood aside for Kate to walk in. When he folded his arms over his chest, she wondered if they were meant as a shield, to keep her at a distance. She wondered if he didn't crave touch the way she did, or if he was not attracted to her after all.

There was a doorstop of a novel open on the bed—*A Tale of Two Cities.*

"I've always wanted to read this," Kate said, picking it up.

"That is my favorite book, ever. 'I see the lives for which I lay down my life, peaceful, useful, prosperous and happy, in that England which I shall see no more,'" he quoted. He had one hand over his heart, like he was pledging loyalty to Dickens. "That line changed my life. I read it all the time. My happiest memory from childhood is reading in the alcove under our stairs. I remember it every time I crack that book."

She did not know if it was the thought of him as a boy or that he wanted to tell her about his life, but contentment glowed inside her, comforting as a fireplace in winter.

Clifton was grinning sheepishly, adorably, and Kate moved closer to him and clasped her hands around his neck. He had such a nice, warm neck and he leaned in to kiss her and there was magic there, just as she'd hoped.

"You've been having a bit of fun with the girls," he said. "I can taste the whisky on your lips."

Kate imagined the shapes their bodies would make, the freedom they would give each other. She had never thought of him like that before.

Heart racing, she ran her hands down his muscular torso, admiring the feel of him. This fine man would be hers. Everything would be all right. She would have a husband, and he would be her sanctuary. There would be no more shame, no more disaster.

Clifton was backing her onto his bed.

"No," she said. "I don't want to do that. I just want to kiss you."

"Okay," he said amiably, and pulled her toward him. He was a good man.

Then Kate thought: *Why shouldn't we have a go?* They were going to be married after all.

"Actually," she said. "I would like to . . . if you would."

Clifton sprung up and rummaged through a drawer until he found his wallet, and took a little square packet out of it. Kate had never actually seen a French letter before and it made her queasy. She looked away. David had never used those. He would just pull himself out of her in time.

And a lot of good that did.

When she turned back to Clifton, she was shocked to see him stepping out of his pajamas. She had never seen an aroused naked man in stark relief before. David had always been beside her, part of her, in bed. Clifton looked like Johnny Weissmuller in *Tarzan*. Kate focused on his face as he leaned down to kiss her and then gently leaned his weight against her until she lay back on the bed. She reached down and pulled off the simple pair of knickers she was wearing and he pushed inside her, once.

There was the sensation of parts moving, a mechanical act, nothing more. She didn't want that. He was halfway inside her a second time and Kate put her hands on his chest to stop him.

"I've changed my mind," she said.

"What?"

"I've changed my mind. I don't want to do this."

Clifton was up and off her in less than a second. "Righto," he said, already across the room. He took a loose cigarette out of the pocket of his pajama bottoms, which were neatly folded on the chair. "Just a minute." He found a lighter, lit the cigarette, and stood there, still naked, in the frame of the closed door. He ran his hand over the bristled top of his head and sighed.

"I'm sorry . . ."

"I'll be right with you," he said, not looking at her. Embarrassed, Kate wondered if he wanted her to leave. She eyed the window, imagined climbing out of it and shimmying down the drainpipe. Everything suddenly seemed ruined.

She smoothed her dress down, then propped herself up on her elbows and watched him smoke. The thick muscles that flanked his torso contracted as he exhaled. It was a curious thing—she could feel desire building again at the sight of him standing on the other side of the room, but when he had been inside her, it felt wrong.

"I didn't know you smoked," she said finally.

He chuckled and she was relieved. "Only in emergencies," he said.

Kate smiled. "It was nothing to do with you," she said. "You're lovely."

Clifton waved her off. "Not a problem. Probably for the best anyway." He stubbed out the cigarette in the sink and ran it under water. Then he crumpled it and the French letter in a sheet of paper and tossed it in the bin.

She searched for what she wanted to say while he buttoned his pajama shirt.

"I think I'd like to do things properly this time," she said. "After we're married. Give myself a fresh start, you know?"

Clifton came to sit beside her, kissed her sweetly on the lips.

"Then a fresh start you shall have," he said. "We'll wait until after the wedding, like the thoroughly decent sorts we are. Shan't be long now."

"Clifton . . ." Kate dropped her head onto his shoulder. "Thank you."

He was so eager to demonstrate his respect for her. An expression appeared in her mind, something a school friend had said when describing a new beau: *He treats me like the fuzz on a peach.*

Clifton reached up and patted her head. "You deserve to have whatever you want, my darling," he said. "I'll never stand in your way."

When Kate came out of Clifton's room, Orla was standing in the hall, waiting for her. Her face was rigid and blotchy pink and Kate knew she'd been caught.

"What are you *doing*, Orla?" she scolded. "You gave me a such fright, you're lucky I didn't scream and wake the entire house. I was just saying good night to him. He is my fiancé after all. You shouldn't *lurk* like that, it's unsettling . . ."

"Stop it," Orla said. "I don't care what you've got up to. Listen to me. I've just received a call from London. I'm afraid it's bad news. The house in Hackney was bombed. It's gone."

"Gone?"

"Yes."

"Good Lord," Kate said, the breath going out of her. "Part of me always thought I'd live there again. Frank had better not come here. I really can't be bothered . . ."

"Frank is dead."

"What?"

"Our father. He's dead, my love. It was a Luftwaffe parachute mine, dropped in front of the house. His foreman just rang, he's been trying to track us down. Apparently, it happened two weeks ago."

Kate's head felt funny. She leaned against the wall, away

from Orla's candle, needing darkness. She heard the words her sister was saying, and understood them at the top of her head, but her body seemed to have suspended all operations. Kate didn't want to feel this overwhelming sadness for her father. It was like teetering on the edge of a black pit, and Orla was there, but she couldn't reach her.

"Is our house still standing?" Kate asked, through chattering teeth.

"No, my love, I've told you, it's gone."

"Pa dying alone like that . . . I wasn't very nice, last time I saw him. I packed him off . . ." Kate's voice failed her.

"He wanted to be alone," Orla said softly. "It's not your fault. He was just a greedy, tormenting Irishman."

Frank's threadbare trousers that day in July. His round, watery, blue eyes. His request for help.

Had Kate been unfair to him? He had raised her, after all. She'd had almost every comfort.

Every comfort except the one that mattered most.

Why not love a daughter, if you had one? It was such a serendipitous thing. Frank Grifferty had never loved Kate. It was unfair, outrageous, really, that she should have to grieve him now. It made her furious. That her father, so unfeeling himself, should impose the burden of grief upon her now was intolerable.

"Goddamn that man," Kate said as tears her father did not deserve began to prick at her eyes. "There will be a funeral to arrange. As if we haven't enough to manage."

Orla did not say anything. She sighed heavily and rubbed at her forehead.

"Orla, won't there be a funeral?"

"He's already been buried, my love. They put what was left of him in an emergency burial ground, in Camden. The wharf was destroyed, too, apparently. The night before. But one of us needs to go up to London to see Pa's business manager and submit a claim for war damage payments."

*   *   *

A week later, Margaret sat on the bed, sliding photographs around on the quilt like playing cards. With shrewd eyes, she watched Kate putting on makeup in the mirror in the wardrobe. Margaret was clearly determined to delay her mother's departure for as long as possible and her first approach was diplomatic:

"Mammy, who is this?" she asked, holding up an eight-by-ten glossy photograph.

Kate looked at it. "It's me. When I was at art college."

"Who made this picture?"

"I did. With a tripod, and a cord with a little button that goes *click*."

"You look like Snow White."

Kate leaned down and buried her face in Margaret's curls. "Thank you," she murmured, breathing in the scent of her daughter's skin. "Let's put these photos back in their special box now."

Margaret swatted her mother away. "But you said I could look!" She began to huff and puff like a tiny dragon and eyed the Woolworth's hatbox, which was full of old drawings and photos and papers. "You SAID!"

Before she could hurl the box off the bed in protest, Kate took it away and placed it on top of the wardrobe.

"Hush. We'll look more when I return from London," Kate said, pinning her black, saucer-shaped hat into her hair. There wouldn't be a funeral, but black felt important for this journey. "I'll be home by bedtime. You're going to have a nice time with Aunt Orla and Clifton."

Without being asked, Clifton had offered to help look after Margaret while Kate was gone. He continued to surprise her. Kate had never particularly trusted men. All the men she'd even attempted to get close to had disappointed her—they'd lied or withheld, patronized or menaced. Kate wanted them, but would have preferred not to. Clifton wasn't like that. He was so thoroughly decent and straightforward and generous. The kind of man who saw the best in people, especially Kate.

The night before, Kate had dreamed she was in Hackney and chunks of flesh fell from the sky. She would not go back to the house in Gore Road. She didn't want to see where her father died. She barely had her feet under her as it was. The last express train from Victoria left London at six o'clock in the evening. Kate would sign the papers in an office near Trafalgar Square, stretch her legs, snap a few pictures, then come home to Brighton.

Ninety minutes later, she was in Central London. It had been hit badly the night before, with bombs falling straight through till dawn. In Leicester Square, men in tin hats and coveralls and work gloves wrapped cords around wreckage that had been blown off buildings. Other men dragged the debris away. Kate's neck stiffened at the too-familiar smell of wet charred wood and she was grateful Margaret was not with her.

Charing Cross Road resembled an ashtray. On one side of the street, the shops were unharmed; the other side was a smoking black heap of rubble. Everywhere she looked, the underworkings of the city—tunnels, wires, beams—were laid bare like the bowels of a dead seal.

On the ground in front of a bookstore, a body was half covered with bricks. Someone had put a blanket over the legs, but one pink-slippered foot peeked out. The slipper looked like something Orla would wear; it made Kate's heart ache.

She watched soldiers carry a huge, broken arched window out of another building, what had once been a small bank. They hoisted it over a mound of broken glass and mangled steel. It seemed too great a task for human arms, but they were doing it. What remained of the building shuddered in the wind. Firemen wrestled hoses, shooting the smoldering rubble with thick streams of water.

There were still leaves on the plane trees in front of St. Martin-in-the-Fields, which somehow stood unharmed. Soldiers helped a man push his car out of St. Martin's Place. His windshield had been blasted out and he grinned at Kate through a frame of broken glass. She took pictures of it all, filling two rolls in minutes, wishing she had a movie camera.

Kate had read the papers on the train up, but she knew that the worst of the Blitz was being censored to keep up morale. The papers downplayed the devastation. An article heralding WAR WORK FOR 500,000 WOMEN took up half the front page of the *Mail*. Yet, THOUSANDS OF BOMBS ON BIRMINGHAM got a mere square inch in the lower-right corner. The *Eastbourne Gazette*'s cheery lead story was RESIDENTS' ADVENTURES WHILE BOMBS FELL.

Hitler already had all of Europe in his palm and England was small and outgunned. Nazi soldiers could be in the streets before long. Seeing Central London blown up, a sense of doom settled into Kate's bones. *England was losing.* She no longer had any doubt.

In Trafalgar Square, the lions and Nelson's Column were miraculously intact but everything was boarded up. The museums were closed. From the top of his column, Nelson stoically overlooked what was up until a month ago Trafalgar Square Station. Now, it was a quarry overflowing with rubble. People paused behind the barricades and gawped at the wreckage. They wore smart office clothing, trench coats and hats and dresses, and carried briefcases. They smoked and stared and tried to take it in. Somebody offered Kate a cigarette and although she had never smoked one in her life, she accepted it.

Her eyes went to the closed National Portrait Gallery, where four nurses stood, three young and one old. The old nurse wore a black cape and glasses. They were talking to each other and laughing. A green T-type bus, converted into a first aid vehicle, was idling next to them. Kate darted through traffic to take a last photograph of the nurses under the museum sign before finding her father's business manager's office.

There was a profile in the window of the bus: a man looking down, writing something.

David. Instinctively, Kate knew it was him.

She dropped the cigarette, walked toward him, tapped on the window. David turned to her and she watched his eyes adjust, squinting, as if she'd shined a torch in his face. From behind the glass, he mouthed her name, then held up a finger: *Wait one sec.*

He loped around the front of the bus in his shirtsleeves, holding a clipboard.

"Oh my God," he said. "Kate."

She laughed a little. "David."

He smiled. They stood there for a moment, stunned. Kate looked up into his face, marveling at his still-perfect lips, his black hair. She could feel it; the thickness of it between her fingers. How could an ordinary human face physically *pull* on her like that? She reached out to touch David's arm and he wrapped her in a hug. Her hands registered the seams of his shirt, and the weight of all the years she'd been in love with him hit her at once. When had she first felt it? At the Royal? In her bedroom? No, it was that day on Hampstead Heath—that queer feeling in her chest. An old feeling. Older than Kate. Old as there had been people.

She touched David's cheek and his eyes crinkled at the sides. Then he pulled away from her, gently but unmistakably.

"It's incredible to see you," he said. "What are you doing here? Are you back living in London?"

"No. I live in Brighton now. My father died. I had to come up to sort out a few things."

"I'm so sorry. Is there a funeral?"

"No, my sister and I said goodbye to him a long time ago

and we don't want to do it again. It's all right. We weren't close, as you know."

"Hmm." David frowned. He gestured to her camera. "Still taking pictures? That's good."

"Of course."

He gestured at the bus behind him. "They need people who know how to drive, so sometimes I go out with the misery buses to service the shelters. I work at St. Mary's Hospital."

"I know. I got your letter. I'm sorry about your father, too."

David nodded. "Thank you. When do you return to Brighton?"

"A few hours. I only came up for the day."

"Kate, I . . ." He hesitated and his eyes clouded over. Then, he seemed to decide something. "Have you eaten? Can I give you lunch?"

Thinking of Clifton, Kate was going to say no, but she said: "I eat lunch."

They both laughed, and leaned closer together, remembering how well they knew each other. There was a perfect second that felt to Kate like a flash of bright white light, a shared heartbeat of understanding. It wasn't about lunch, or Brighton, or even their shared past; it was feeling the same thing at the same time. It felt so good to have that with David again.

"I just have to sign some papers first." She looked at the slip of paper in her bag. "It's, ah . . . 8 Duncannon Street. Just that way."

"Brilliant," David said, his face lighting up. "That'll give me time to get this rig back to the hospital. I'm just about to meet a friend at my favorite chop suey. It's in Buckingham Street. You'll join us."

The chop suey was divided into a Japanese section and a Chinese section. The ground floor was the Japanese section and each rectangular table had a little gas ring and a pot of oil in the middle. Kate sat on one side of the rectangular table;

David's *friend*, Helena Ross, sat across from her. Helena was absurdly pretty and taught children and wore an expensive-looking aubergine coat. Kate wondered if she was Jewish, but could not ask. Not only because it would be awkward. If Helena wasn't Jewish, it would mean David simply had not loved Kate. And her day had already been sufficiently devastating.

Before David picked a chair, Kate saw him hesitate. He pulled out the chair next to Kate, and she relaxed a little. But Helena was obviously his girlfriend. He sat there, grinning like they both belonged to him. Helena looked at him like a flower tilted toward the sun and Kate wished she had never returned to London.

That love feeling Kate had had when David hugged her was gone. She told herself that it was only a reaction to the shock of seeing London in ruins. David was a buoy Kate had needed to cling to for a few seconds whilst catching her breath. She felt better now. She didn't need anyone but herself.

Kate glanced at David and tucked her hair behind her ear, and saw Helena notice her do it. There was a recognition in Helena's eyes then: *You want to look pretty for him, do you?* Kate cringed inwardly.

"Sorry to have barged in on your lunch," Kate said, her face hot.

"Don't be silly! It's marvelous to meet an old chum of David's. He only speaks of Simon, who I'm just longing to meet . . ." Helena's voice was high and squidgy, like a baby that wants you to keep playing with it.

"Soon, I hope," David said.

A waitress brought three sets of wooden chopsticks wrapped in paper and a plate of fresh, raw ingredients. She said hello to David and Helena—apparently, they were regular customers—and disappeared.

"We're meant to cook our own food," Helena said to Kate, turning up the flame under the pot on the gas ring. "It's quite good fun. Look, the oil is already hot!"

David chuckled at Helena's delight and Kate felt angry at him for inviting her and also incredibly stupid. She sent her thoughts toward Puffin's Perch, which held comfort, because it held Margaret and Orla and Clifton. She imagined Clifton puttering around under the bonnet of his Ford, Margaret at his heels asking questions faster than he could answer them. Kate glanced at her watch—with any luck, she would be back with them in a few hours.

"Put some rice in your bowl," David said to Kate. He loaded a metal skewer with pieces of white fish and quartered onions and dipped it into the sizzling oil. As it fried, he spun it around and chatted with Helena about one of her flatmates, who was apparently a scandalous drunk and causing poor little Helena distress.

"One of Daisy's soldier beaus brought a bottle of absinthe home from France," Helena explained to Kate in her dainty voice. "On Saturday night they were in an absolute state, I mean blotto, and he poured the entire bottle into a metal mixing bowl and set it on fire. She burned her hand horribly. I had to take her to hospital."

"What happened to her fellow?" Kate asked.

"Hel threw him out, quite rightly," David said.

"Were you there, too?"

"No. But I've heard the story. She rang me the next morning."

Orla should have made the journey instead of Kate. Trafalgar Square had been mind-bending, but it was even more surreal to find herself eating chop suey with the father of her child and his baby-voiced girlfriend.

"What about you, Kate?" David asked warmly. He seemed to be having a grand time. "How is life treating you? What news outfit did you say you're with down in Brighton?"

"I'm not with a news outfit . . ."

Kate could not tell David too much about her life. He'd

bombard her with questions and next thing she knew, she'd blurt out the truth about Margaret.

"Actually, I'm a cleaning woman," Kate said briskly. She had a sense that David wanted her to be impressive for Helena, and she wasn't going to do that. "I work for my sister. She manages a boardinghouse."

"Oh!" Helena said brightly. "That must be interesting."

"Not really."

David looked confused. "But you said you still take pictures . . ."

"I do. For myself. When I'm not scrubbing toilets."

"And you're satisfied with that work?"

"Of course. Why shouldn't I be?"

"It's just not like you. You were always so ambitious."

"Don't tell me you've become a snob, David. It wouldn't suit you."

"I think it's *wonderful* you're helping your sister," Helena said. "Family is the most important thing."

"I agree," Kate said. "Wholeheartedly."

"Well," David said, analyzing her with eerily familiar eyes. "That's new."

Just then, an Asian couple walked into the restaurant with a little girl about Margaret's age. Kate's hand trembled as she lifted her glass of water to her mouth. She put the water down, slid her hand under her leg to hold it still.

And David kept staring at Kate. He was really annoying her. Her skin felt prickly. She surreptitiously scratched at her arms.

"Do you have a sweetheart, Kate?" Helena asked, lifting her bowl of rice to her lips and dropping rice into her mouth with the chopsticks. "I'll bet you do. You're so pretty."

"No, I don't have a *sweetheart,*" Kate snapped. The thought of Clifton as her sweetheart bothered her. What they had was more grown-up than that. "What a silly word."

Helena looked hurt and Kate was sorry.

"The truth is, Helena, my life is rather boring," Kate said, smiling apologetically. "It's nothing like it was in London." She could feel David's eyes on her as he slid fried chunks of fish onto her bowl of rice. "Actually, I'd prefer to hear more about your flatmates. I do love a juicy story."

"So, you've not completely changed," David said, leaning back in his chair and resting one hand on his thigh. He smiled a private little smile and Kate's heart rose up into her throat.

David ordered a bottle of baijiu and they talked about Helena's flatmates' sundry boyfriends and their irritating habits. Kate ate more than her share of chop suey to ensure her mouth was always full. She drank too much of the baijiu, which tasted of whisky and flowers. She asked Helena about her work as a teacher, her favorite former pupils, her opinion of President Franklin Delano Roosevelt, and by the time the meal was over David had grown taciturn. His eyes clouded over and Kate felt she had somehow bested him. An onlooker would have thought that she and Helena were the old chums.

"Shall we go for a drink after at the Savoy?" David asked, a tinge of desperation in his voice. "The bar is always crawling with American journalists. I've often thought . . ." He trailed off. "It's only two o'clock. We'll be done in plenty of time for you to catch your train."

Kate glanced at Helena, whose face had gone blank.

"I think I have too much on," Kate said. "I should go see my father's wharf. What's left of it, at least."

David's shoulders slumped and Helena smiled, obviously relieved.

"Drinks at the Savoy . . . ," Kate mused, putting on her coat. "You are rather grand these days, David."

Helena and David laughed. As they all left the restaurant, he tripped over the doorstop and almost fell on the pavement.

"David!" Helena squeaked. "Are you all right?"

"I'm fine," he said, collecting his long limbs. Kate could see he was embarrassed. She was grateful to catch a final glimpse of the lanky, insecure boy she remembered. Perhaps that was what this lunch was for: to say goodbye. She would always love David, but the woman she had become did not want him. Not enough to give him any kind of control over her life.

They said farewell with no plans of meeting again, but with a hug between the women and a vague promise to look Kate up if ever "they" found themselves seaside. David just raised a hand in the air and gave her a fake, toothy grin and she knew he wished he had not seen her. Neither of them had ever known what to do with the thing between them.

Kate did not go to the wharf. She went straight to Victoria Station and caught an earlier train, needing Margaret's chubby arms around her neck.

"This train will terminate at Brighton Station in approximately one hour," bellowed the Cockney announcer and Kate shifted in her seat. The train was stuffed with people. Beneath her, she felt the residual body heat of the last commuter; it stirred a queer feeling of fellowship in her. She was still a Londoner, in her heart. Pushing her sleeves up, Kate saw that the pale undersides of her arms were covered with tiny red pinprick spots. Hives, and they itched. She had gotten herself too worked up, sitting too close to David, endeavoring not to see Margaret in him.

But she would not allow herself to get sentimental. She set her teeth to it. The past was the past. David was a different person now, as was Kate. He had found Helena. She was settled with Clifton. Margaret was happy. The only humane thing was to let everybody be.

What she'd seen in Trafalgar Square had made it clear that there were much bigger problems to face. It was time to prepare for the worst, set up the most stable life possible for herself and her daughter. Unlike David, Clifton could be counted on. He knew his own mind. Not to mention that a Jewish father would make Margaret blood-chillingly vulnerable if Hitler seized England. It wasn't David's fault, but it was true. Plus, he didn't want Kate anyway. If he cared for her at all, he wouldn't have paraded her in front of Helena like that.

So she shoved him out of her soul and, for the first time, really felt him go.

By the time the train pulled into Brighton, the red spots were gone and Kate felt approximately one hundred and seventy pounds lighter.

The following evening, there was a white box waiting for Kate on the letter table in the hall. She did not have to open the card to know who had sent a white chrysanthemum corsage, wrapped in wax paper. It was a wet, blustery night, and the sender had tucked cab fare into the envelope with his engraved calling card: Christopher Clifton Andrew Prouty.

Kate studied her reflection in the mirror over the hall table and pinned the flower to the collar of her dress—the chocolate satin frock she'd worn on her first date with David. She was relieved it still fit. It had been a while since she had really looked at herself. Her figure was fuller than before her pregnancy and her wavy hair had darkened—it was more brown than red now. And sometime between giving birth and weaning Margaret, a smattering of dusky freckles had sprung up on her cheekbones. She shrugged into the warm, camel-hair coat she'd had since convent school, snug now at the shoulders, and phoned for a cab to take her to the Regent Ballroom.

It was a domed structure on top of the Regent Cinema, near the clock tower. Clifton was waiting outside for Kate under a large umbrella. When she saw him standing there in his blue RAF uniform with its starched collar and tie, her heart skipped.

The ballroom was a whirl of colored lanterns, with walls painted in red, blue, and yellow, and packed with people Kate's age and younger. The room smelled of anticipation— sweat and nail varnish and cigarettes and perfume. There was something so optimistic about French perfume at that moment, at the dark end of 1940. Somebody had decided that this dance was worth whatever precious little they had left. People would fall in love tonight. Others would row and leave alone. Kate was going to dance and drink and feel free. Someone told her that the floor was on springs. She hadn't been anywhere near so jolly since Margaret was born.

When Clifton went to the bar, a boy of no more than nineteen politely asked Kate to dance and she accepted. For a while, Clifton chatted with the bartender; his back to the dance floor. Then he turned around, saw Kate dancing with the boy, leaned on a column next to the bar, and watched them. She felt his eyes on her. Another soldier asked her to dance, and she accepted, but every move was for Clifton and they both knew it.

Finally, Clifton crossed the ballroom and asked Kate for a dance. "We'll Meet Again" by Vera Lynn was playing and everyone in the place kept bursting out singing at the chorus. Exhilarated by movement, she draped herself on his shoulder, whispered in his ear. She could feel how proud he was to be with her. He did not even mind when she laughed at his clumsy steps.

Later, Clifton introduced her to his signaling students as his fiancée, Mrs. Kate Grifferty. Kate said hello to the men and tried on being an officer's wife.

Then her eyes rested on a familiar face and she realized with alarm that it was Simon Rabatkin's. She saw that Simon recognized her, too, and she found herself taking a step away from Clifton.

"Flight Lieutenant Prouty," Simon said, with a friendly grin. "Mrs. Grifferty and I are old pals. Might she consider a dance with me?"

Kate's stomach flipped over. She couldn't tell Simon she was *pretending to be a widow* without telling the truth about Margaret. He would think she was insane.

Simon pressed: "What do you say, Mrs. Grifferty? I'd love a catch-up."

He was handsome as ever and Clifton looked almost as panicked as Kate felt. She needed to get Simon away from Clifton before he mentioned Margaret.

"A dance would be fine," she said quickly.

"Old friends?" Clifton asked, studying Simon's countenance. The men were the same height and face-to-face. "Is that so?"

"Yes, indeed. I was hopelessly in love with a girlfriend of hers." Simon frowned mournfully. "I never quite got over it, I'm afraid. Don't reckon I've even looked at another woman for years . . ."

Relief visibly loosened Clifton's shoulders. "In that case," he said jovially, "knock yourself out." He pecked Kate's cheek, and pulled out a chair for himself next to another officer.

Simon offered Kate his arm and led her to the floor. He made no comment, just pursed his lips at her like she was being very naughty indeed.

"I go by Mrs. Grifferty at the boardinghouse my sister owns," she explained, her heart racing. "I live there and it makes things simpler with the male guests if they think I'm married."

"Not *all* the male guests, apparently."

"Clifton is a gentleman."

"Clifton! Rather." Simon pronounced "rather" in the posh way Clifton did.

"Thank you for not making a scene," Kate said. "We're engaged to be married."

"Yeah." Simon hesitated. "I just heard the happy news. I'm pleased for you."

His face was still a version of David's—and of Margaret's. As he spun her around the floor, Kate felt like she was gazing into a trick mirror. Nostalgia overtook her and she had the urge to tell Simon everything that had happened to her.

Instead she produced a contented sigh and said: "I'm very happy. We're very happy."

"Are you? Pleased to hear it."

They swayed to the music. Questions bandied about in Kate's mind: *Had David said anything about seeing her? Did he miss her? How serious was he about Helena?*

"How is your brother?" she asked, in the most indifferent tone she could manage.

Simon's eyes twinkled. "Our boyo is lucky as ever. He's got a big job now. He's been given charge of his own ward at St. Mary's Hospital. You should look him up sometime . . ."

A lump was forming in Kate's throat.

"You must be proud," she said, swallowing hard and looking away. "Well done him."

"Kate? Are you all right, love?"

"Of course. Just a bit tired," she said briskly. The song had not changed yet, but she could not look at Simon anymore. The poignant familiarity of his face was too much. She glanced over her shoulder. "I'd better, um . . . Clifton will be looking for me."

She turned and walked as fast as she could without running, down the stairs and into the wet night.

Kate lay awake in bed that night, thinking over all she felt. She lay like a nun's corpse, flat on her back with her hands pressed into her chest. The gas fire was lit and Margaret was tucked up next to her, but there was a chill deep in her bones.

The flicker of Margaret in Simon's eyes was the family that

might have been. His face, his expressions, his humor—all shades of David's.

She had been so desperate to leave David behind. She had to. Now someone else loved her. Not just someone—a lieutenant in the Royal Air Force. She should feel vindicated.

But what Kate felt was a scribble of shame and sadness and confusion.

Chapter 28

25th November, 1940

"You won't believe this," Simon said, his voice crackling over the telephone line. "I just saw your old dream girl. Small world, ain't it?"

The hair stood up on the back of David's neck. "Who did you see?" he asked.

"Kate."

Hearing someone else speak her name was like being struck. David looked at the drop ceiling running the length of the hospital corridor, pulled in a deep breath to compose himself. Kate was still in every cell of his body. All forty trillion of them had risen up and said *YES*, the moment he saw her in Trafalgar Square last week.

David really could not have this again, this all-consuming obsession. He hadn't even wanted to see her again, just as he had nearly excised her from his soul. The woman made him feel like a lunatic—not a man, just an urge.

But seeing her had made him so high that he thought it was a good idea to bring her to lunch with Helena. Now both women probably hated him.

"Fucking hell," David said under his breath.

"Speak up!" Simon shouted. "I can't hear you, mate. Connection's rotten."

"I didn't say anything. Where did you see Kate?"

"At an RAF dance, in Brighton. She lives here now," Simon said. "We even had a dance together. She's engaged to my C.O. Not the brightest bulb, but not a bad bloke. He looks like a rugby player. They live at the same boardinghouse."

David's heart burned. "Why are you telling me this?" he asked. "I don't wanna know."

"Because she asked about you. I told her what a blinding success you are and she welled up and ran out of the ballroom. She's pining for you."

"She isn't," David said stoically. "I ran into her myself, in London last week. I'm not going to charge down there and make a mug of myself."

"Nobody's watching you, Dave. Nobody cares."

"I care."

"But I've got an address," Simon insisted.

David said nothing. He searched for Kate, found her under his ribs. He felt her smooth arms entwined in his. This was what he'd dreamed of for years. This was also where he could make a mistake. He didn't want to hurt her again, or himself.

"My instructor, the geezer she's marrying, billets at her sister's boardinghouse," Simon said. "It's called the Poof's Porch or something. On the seafront in Kemptown."

He covered the receiver and David heard one muffled half of a conversation. "Oi, that's my comb, Segal! Give it here!"

"Simon!" David shouted. "This is my life, mate."

"Sorry, I'm back now. So, when are you coming down?"

David considered his brother's question: Why shouldn't he go get the woman he loved?

Because Kate belonged to someone else now.

Because she was never his.

Because, even in the unlikely case she still loved him, their life together would be difficult.

Because of his mother, who had loved and looked after him his whole life.

Can I see Mum? David would ask, standing in a different hospital corridor in 1963. *Sorry,* Simon would say, softly shutting their mother's door behind him. *She doesn't want to see you.*

Because of his ancestors, who so loved Judaism that they carried it on their backs for thousands of years.

Because of Helena, and that disastrous lunch. As soon as Kate disappeared around the corner, Helena had turned darkly toward David.

"What are you playing at?" she'd asked. "Why did you make me sit through that?"

"Sit through what? We had a nice time."

"I'm not an idiot, David. You never stopped staring at her. You looked like you wanted to eat her."

David loved the flush of Helena's skin, her quick mind, their easy rapport. She was perfect, would fit into his family perfectly.

But the only person he felt in his own chest was Kate.

The Bancroft Road Jewish cemetery was a secret garden bordered with dormant lilac bushes and lime trees. Like most Jewish cemeteries, it was behind lock and key and you had to make an appointment to visit. Otherwise antisemitic vandals would destroy it.

On Tuesday afternoon, David picked up two smooth, flat stones—one for him and one for Simon—and warmed them in his hands before balancing them on top of his father's rounded headstone.

Life was fleeting but stones were permanent. He remembered going to the London Jewish Hospital with Uncle Sol and Reg Zolowitz and a few other men from synagogue to retrieve his father's body. By that point, his dad was like an empty house. The animating force had gone. There was no reason David would find him now, in this patch of earth, over a year later.

When David was a child, they were always sitting *shiva* for friends and family. Spanish flu, tuberculosis, polio: infectious disease burned through East London, taking thousands of lives each year. Typhoid had taken his own baby sister, Rachel. It was a big part of why David studied medicine; the naive dream of stopping the people he loved from dying had never completely left him.

"I'm here, Dad," he said. When he knelt down and laid his hands on the ground, hot tears stung his eyes. He hated the idea of his dad being underground. *It's not him,* he told himself. *Remember.*

"Mum's good. I'm going round for dinner tonight. Simon is training to be a pilot, he's doing really well. Apparently, it's quite safe. Nothing like the last war, so you mustn't worry."

Why am I placating a corpse? He sat down on the ground next to the headstone.

"I'm not here for your blessing," he said, picking at the grass, "if that's what you're thinking. I know I wouldn't receive it."

Again, David closed his eyes, searching in the dark for his dad. For a moment, he thought he felt him.

I love you, Dad, he thought. *I miss you.*

In the end, that was all there was to say.

Later, in her flat in Bethnal Green, David's mother asked him: "Did you eat already? I know you spend a lot on café food . . ."

It occurred to David that now he was the only one left in his mother's life who would recognize her smile for what it was: a mask for her pain.

"Are you all right, Mum?"

She swatted at him. "Of course I am. I'm always all right."

He followed her into the kitchen, where she switched the wireless on to some silly old vaudeville music. From the icebox, she produced a small feast: a roll of Bloom's garlic salami, half a loaf of brown bread, a plate of salted sliced tomatoes, one boiled egg. David worried she hadn't been eating, but if he asked she would deny it.

"It's nice to see you listening to music again," he said, drumming his fingers on the table.

"Your father always liked that about me, how musical I am, so I don't think he'd mind."

"He wouldn't mind. He'd want you to be happy."

"Al Jolson was a favorite of his," she said, "so I think I'm all right."

"Mum, do you reckon the twenty-six-year-old you would like the fifty-five-year-old you?"

"Philosophical today, eh?"

"I'm just thinking . . . ," he said. "People younger than me make all these decisions for their lives and then have to live with them for the next forty, fifty years."

"My mother died at fifty-three," she said, slicing a hunk off the salami roll and folding it into a piece of bread for David. "I get such a fright whenever I think of it."

"Simon rang me," David said, as evenly as he could.

"Is he hurt?"

"No, he's in rude good health. Still training. But you'll never guess who he saw in Brighton. Kate."

"Who?"

"Mum. You know who I mean."

"That *goyishe* girl? Honestly, David, it took me a moment to remember. I don't keep track of your love life anymore. It's too bleak."

"Simon reckons I still might have a chance with her."

Silence.

"I've never stopped thinking of her," David went on. It was excruciating to speak about romantic feelings this way in front of his mother, who was staring at the table grain. "If I'm honest, I've never stopped loving her."

His mother just looked up at him over her new reading glasses, which he had bought for her.

"There is a war on." David could hear his voice getting louder. "And I love this woman. I want to enjoy my life before it's too late."

"A war shouldn't change your morals," she said primly. "It makes life harder, but I don't think many of us would entertain *that* sort of behavior. You won't have a friend in the world if you do this. Neither will I."

"I'm not here for your blessing."

Her eyes flashed. "Then why are you here?"

"I'm here to tell the truth. I think you deserve that, after all the lies Dad told you." As soon as he said it, David knew he had passed the point of no return.

"Your dad," she said, her voice hard, "was the best man I ever knew."

"He wasn't! He lied all the time. He ruined us ten times over. But you loved him anyway. I loved him anyway. He wasn't perfect, he didn't always behave the way we would have liked him to. He made life harder than it needed to be. But you blindly supported every damn thing he did. Why can't you do the same for me?"

"Because you're my son! A wife is charged with loving her husband in spite of who he is. A mother is charged with making her son into someone a good woman could love. I believe I have done that. You are everything your father might have been . . ." His mother put the crook of her elbow to her face, shook her head. "I know he wasn't perfect. If it weren't for his horrible, maudlin mother. Your grandmother. I blame her. Your father had to live in a fantasy world to survive her."

This surprised David. "I've never heard you speak that way about Bubbe."

She dropped her arm. "That's because she died before you

were born," she said. "Your dad had two bad parents. His father wasn't a bad person, just very unstable. He was always asking us for money, for his next business, his next big idea. Your dad would always say, 'Don't you give my father one penny because we'll never see it again.'"

She smiled, remembering, and reached over the table to take David's hand. They had matching thumbs. David felt like crying. He wondered if his mother knew she had married the same sort of man as her late father-in-law. The wounded look in her eyes made him suspect she did.

"I've been a good mother," she said. "Have I not?"

David nodded. "The best."

"And you have been the best son." She rubbed his hand. "All I ask in return is that you don't go to that girl. Don't turn your back on your family. Don't turn your back on me."

"I'm not turning my back on you. I love you, Mum. I'll always look after you."

She inhaled sharply, her hand to her chest. "*Oy.* You gave me a fright, Davy. You won't go to her, you promise?"

"No, Mum. I am going."

Chapter 29

29th November, 1940

A parachute mine caused a blast of boiling water and gas to pour into a Liverpool underground shelter. 166 civilians were cooked alive. As the report came through the wireless in the drawing room, Kate retched silently, but the feeling soon subsided. Every day brought another horror down the wires. She redoubled her efforts dusting the furniture with a pony-hair brush. Then she polished the gilt mirror frame with onion water, one of her governess Mrs. O'Malley's Victorian methods.

She was still cleaning when the lodgers from the smaller second-floor room—a frumpy middle-aged couple from North London named Mr. and Mrs. McKay—came down in spats and hiking boots.

"You're dressed for the outdoors," Kate said, attempting cheerfulness. "Where are you off to?"

"The South Downs," Mrs. McKay said. "We've always wanted to go and now we're here anyway . . ."

"How nice. I've not been."

"But you must! It will clear your head, in times like these. Your little girl would love it."

Times like these. How bored Kate was of that phrase. Better just to say it outright: *At the end of the world.*

Mrs. McKay gave her a bus schedule and directions and by ten o'clock, Kate and Margaret were at the top of the 54, on their way to the Downs. Margaret was snug in her seat, bundled in her red coat, navy stockings, and sturdy shoes. In a string shopping bag, Kate carried two apples, a thermos of tea, their gas masks, and a little money in her pocketbook for them to have a nice luncheon at a pub. Her camera sat on her lap; she was going to attempt a Julia Margaret Cameron–inspired portrait of Margaret among the sheep or goats or whatever animals grazed the Downs. *Margaret in the Wilderness,* she'd call it. She was going to pretend the war wasn't happening, just for a day.

And the McKays were right. The Sussex Downs were glorious: rolling, electric-green hills as far as the eye could see, dotted with the ruins of several ancient, stone cottages. The valleys were just deep enough to get one's blood pumping but not too steep for Margaret. Well-tread paths wound around the hills. They passed other ramblers, old men alone and couples like the McKays. Kate felt young and strong as she and Margaret scampered up and down the undulating mounds of earth.

At the top of one of the hills, there was a small pub. Kate and Margaret shared a Yorkshire pudding with only mushy peas and potatoes. There wasn't any meat to be had. Margaret drank sheep's milk and Kate sipped half a pint of cider and felt pastoral. They sat by a large window that overlooked the Downs and talked about the Shetland pony mare and foal they had followed across a meadow.

Perhaps, when Margaret was older and the war was over, pleasant days like this would become more frequent. The toddler sitting opposite her would become a young woman. Kate wondered if they would need Clifton then. Even if they didn't, Kate hoped she would want him.

She had once believed art came out of chaos, but had learned that it did not. An artist, especially an artist who was also a mother, needed a tether fastened to her ankle so she could float into the ether and still find her way back. Clifton was strong enough to hold her steady. He would want what she wanted and help her get it.

Margaret began to rub her eyes and they walked slowly back to the bus stop. The late-afternoon sun lay in golden shards on the hills, stark against shadowed valleys, and Kate took a few photographs. It was, she and Margaret agreed, a perfect day.

When their bus crossed back into the city, Margaret declared loudly and repeatedly that she did not want to sit anymore. Kate had to hold her back from running up the bus aisle.

"Let me go!" Margaret shrieked, and then promptly wet herself, soaking her black tights and filling her leather shoes with urine that spilled onto the bus floor.

"You'll be cleaning that up, love," the bus driver said.

"Sorry."

He clucked his tongue. "That little girl should be in the country. It ain't safe in Brighton no more."

Fuming, Kate used a cotton handkerchief to soak as much as she could from the slatted floor and grabbed Margaret to hop off at the next stop. They were still over a mile from the boardinghouse and Kate was carrying the child, the string bag, her camera, the two gas masks.

Margaret kept doing a somersault maneuver to escape Kate's arms, throwing her head forward and straightening her legs so it was impossible to hold her upright. She pinched the side of Kate's neck, twisted the tender skin between her fingers. Kate yelped in pain and gripped Margaret's chubby thighs tighter to stop them kicking.

"If you do that again, Margaret, I'll . . ." She grasped for an effective threat. "There will be no pickled beets for your tea."

"NOOOOOO!" Margaret howled.

"None tomorrow, either. Stop wiggling."

It took them half an hour to hobble back to the boarding-house. By the time it came into view, they were both in tears. Clifton was in the drive in front of the house, climbing out of his shiny black Ford, and Kate was overwhelmed with grati-tude the moment she saw him. He was holding a thick manila envelope and spinning it between his hands.

"Burning off some energy?" he asked, beaming at Kate, ruffling Margaret's hair.

"This child does not tire," Kate panted, trying to retie one of Margaret's boots. "We walked for hours today."

"Energy that makes more energy. Is that one of Newton's laws?"

"Margaret's law."

"You shouldn't carry her so much. Let her walk."

Clifton thought he knew everything, even though he was not a father himself. Kate did not mind it, most of the time.

"What'd you girls get up to today?" he asked.

"Walked the South Downs. We needed a bit of fresh air. I was rattled by the news."

"You took the bus? I've told you, I prefer to give you a lift. Can I help you with your handbag? It's spilling out."

He grabbed the tangle of straps and string off Kate's shoul-der. She remembered too late that there was a wee-soaked handkerchief in her net bag. Meanwhile, Margaret had run around the side of Clifton's car and flung open the door.

Kate apologized, trying to prise Margaret off Clifton's steering wheel. "I'm afraid she's wet."

"No bother," Clifton said. "Why don't you both get cleaned up and we'll take her for a spin?"

"That's a lovely offer, but she needs her nap now."

He nodded. "Understood. I'll make you a cuppa while you're getting her down."

A man sat on the stoop in front of Kate's boardinghouse, polishing what looked like a pair of children's shoes. He stood up, ran his free hand over the top of his military haircut, and glared over the Channel like he was daring the Germans to come and get him. Middle-aged, clean-cut, with a torso like a gorilla's: Kate's rugger-mugger RAF hero, no doubt. The man tucked the little shoes under one ham-hock arm and went inside the house.

David waited a moment before crossing the road and going to the door, so the guy wouldn't be lurking in the vestibule. A brass plaque on the boardinghouse door read: *PUFFIN'S PERCH, Est. 1911, Mrs. Orla Sherwood, Proprietress.* David cringed, wondering what Kate's sister must think of him. But he'd come this far. Engaged or not, Kate had loved him once. This was his last shot.

He knocked twice on the door. The window in it was stained glass, so he would not be able to see the person who opened the door in advance. He needed something to say:

Hullo, I believe an old friend of mine lives here . . .

Is there a Miss Grifferty in the house? She's an old friend . . .

Inside, a child was screaming its head off. Suddenly the door opened: Kate, her hair loose and long and wild, her face stricken.

"David?" She quickly closed the door behind her, pulled a bobby pin from somewhere in her hair, and started twisting a handful of it away from her face. "What are you doing here?"

"Simon told me he ran into you. He said you lived here, and I wanted to see you again."

She pinned the hair into place and eyed him suspiciously. "Why?"

"Because . . ."

As always, Kate's beauty stirred a melancholy feeling in David. It felt like something essential slipping through his fingers.

"Because I missed you," he said. "I miss you."

"Right. But when I saw you last week, you introduced me to your girlfriend, Helena."

"She's not my girlfriend. We're friends."

"If you're going to lie to my face, I'm going back inside."

"All right, we *were* something, but now we're not. You can't fault me for trying to get on with my life. I thought I'd lost you forever."

"You did lose me forever," Kate said grimly, folding her arms over her chest. She looked up at the first-floor windows. "And you've had plenty of time to get used to the idea."

She was obviously afraid of jeopardizing her engagement. Fair enough. But David wouldn't just let her go. Before, she had wanted him to fight and he gave up on her. He wasn't going to make that mistake again.

"I tried to live without you," David said urgently, "but even when I had what I thought I wanted, or should want, I felt empty. Because my heart isn't mine. It's yours, you claimed it a long time ago."

The child had stopped screeching, but Kate didn't seem to be listening to David. Again, her eyes darted nervously back to that window, like she'd left something burning on the hob. When she turned her head, he saw that she had some grass in her hair.

"Why do you keep looking back there?" he asked.

"I'm not," she said. He then noticed that her shoes were caked with mud.

"Have you taken up farmwork or something?"

"No. If you must know, I've been on a country ramble."

"A country ramble! With who? Your fiancé?"

Kate blanched. "Simon told you."

"I've seen the man myself," David said. "And I don't like the look of him."

"He's an RAF instructor. He's a good person."

"I don't care. He's not the one for you. As soon as I heard you were getting married, I knew I had to get down here . . ."

Kate's eyes narrowed into a glare and David knew he was in for a walloping, but he didn't mind because she had not gone inside yet.

"Ah, now I get it," she said. "You're jealous. Pathetic. You've no right to show up here and demand things of me, just to soothe your pride."

"Then demand things of me! Tell me how to make it right between us."

"Leave," Kate said. "Go away from here. That's what you can do." She was very close to him now, her lips inches from his.

"If you don't want that bloke to see me," David said, desperation rising in his chest, "let's go someplace else. I just want to talk to you. We couldn't really *talk* with Helena there."

Kate shook her head. She didn't say anything.

"Please, Kate."

"All right," she said. "Later though. There's something I have to do first."

David felt like punching the air. This was the first battle won. Victory was in sight. If he didn't have confidence in his own charm, he did in the magnetism between the two of them. The more time they spent together, the less Kate would be able to resist it.

"Name the time and place," he said.

Two hours later, David waited in the rising moonlight at the gate to Queen's Park. At ten past seven, Kate appeared. She walked toward David, a dimmed torch in her hand. He recognized her shape before he could see her face. When she came closer, he could see that her hair was damp. Apparently, she had bathed and changed clothes for their meeting, which he considered to be signs in his favor.

The low moon came out from behind the clouds and put

Kate's pale face and neck into sharp focus. They just looked at each other. David wished he could make her laugh. He'd always loved her laugh; it made him feel like he'd won something.

Instead he blurted out: "I still love you, Kate."

She shook her head. "You don't even know me. Not anymore."

"I do. I've memorized you. The shape of your body. Your laugh. Your gold eyes. Your courage. The way you look at me. The way time stops when I'm beside you. All of it. If my family don't like it, they will have to cope."

"Your family . . ." Kate stepped back from him, blinking.

"They haven't changed. Nothing has changed, except me."

"Having a family to love and support you is important," she said quietly. "I understand that."

Kate herself had changed. He hadn't noticed it as much at the chop suey, but there used to be a current of anger in her that was easy to trip. Now she seemed a bit meek. Her eyes were softer. They'd both lived through the deaths of their fathers. David wondered what else she had lived through.

"You won't want to face life without your family," she went on. "I wouldn't, without my sister." Kate took David's hand and led him to a bench next to a pond. He could not believe she was touching him again. She was trembling faintly.

She's nervous, he thought. *She wouldn't be nervous if she didn't care.*

"With your father gone and Simon in the forces," she said, "your mother will need you more than ever."

"You're different, Kate," he said. "You're softer."

"I know. I hate it." Then: "I need something from you, David."

"Name it."

"I need you to forgive me . . . for something I've done. But when I tell you, you may not be able to."

"Oh." He thought he understood. "I don't care if you've been, ah, physical with that bloke," he said, clearing his throat. "If that's what you're worried about."

"It's not him." She hesitated. "But . . . there is another person involved."

"Bloody hell, Kate. I guess you'll have to chuck him, too."

Her laughter was a relief. "It's not another man," she said. "Before I tell you, you must swear you'll do exactly as I say."

"I'll do anything you want."

"I have a little girl," she said. "I have a daughter. She's my whole life, she's everything to me and I won't let anyone ever hurt her, or disappoint her, in any way."

"I see," David said carefully, his thoughts racing. He wasn't sure what he felt. "Is the RAF bloke the father?"

"No."

He closed his eyes. Every obscenity he had ever said or heard ran through his mind. He understood that Kate's answer to his next question would set the course for the remainder of his life.

"How old is she, your daughter?"

"She was three this August."

David could not speak. His mind was darting back and forth in time, every memory adding up to him being a fool.

"Say something," Kate said, her voice authoritative. She was not pleading anymore.

David took a deep breath.

"The child is mine," he said.

"Yes. You are her father. But, she's not yours, she's mine."

"You were pregnant? Why didn't you tell me? What the devil were you thinking?"

"You had already chosen your family over me. I could see it in your eyes, that day you came to my father's house. I wasn't going to trap you."

David flinched. "You knew *then*? Did you even go to Dublin?"

"No. There was no newspaper job. There probably never will be again."

He shook his head. He felt disoriented, like he'd walked into a mirror he thought was another room.

"Sorry . . . have I . . . have I got this right? You bore my child without telling me. You lied to me. You didn't give me the chance to do the right thing," he said, standing up. "I would have helped you. I would have married you."

"I didn't want to be another of your obligations," she said softly. "I wanted you . . . I wanted you to love me."

"I did love you. I do."

"I'd never trusted anyone before," she said. "I trusted you. I thought you knew how to not get me pregnant. When I found out about the baby, I was so angry with you. But I couldn't give her up." Kate wiped her nose on her sleeve and shook her head. "Once I knew she was coming, that was it. It was her and me."

"You already loved her."

"Yes." Kate smiled, the dimple in her cheek appearing for the first time since he'd seen her again. But it disappeared quickly. "Then, something really terrible happened, the worst thing that's ever happened to me . . ." She paused.

"What?" David asked. "You must tell me everything now. What is it?"

"There was a bombing here, at the cinema. Margaret and I were there and . . . Don't look like that, we're all right now! But we were injured. She was hurt very badly, she broke her arm and hit her head very hard and there was a lot of blood and people died and I didn't know for a while if she would come through . . ."

"Oh my God." He reached back and found himself on the bench again.

"But she did!" Kate grabbed David's wrist and shook it as if trying to wake him. "And I thought of you, I thought of you so much, I wanted to ring you, but I felt so guilty because maybe I should have let her be evacuated . . . I was paralyzed by fear . . ."

From outside his body, David listened to Kate talk about their daughter and struggled to metabolize the truth of his life. He had a child he had never met and she'd almost died before he could hold her. Kate had deceived him. She didn't even trust him to help her when their daughter was in mortal danger.

"She came through after all," Kate was saying. "She's strong as a little ox. And I'm glad you're here, because you should know her, you'll be mad about her, everyone is."

Everyone. The cast of strangers she had allowed to share his daughter's life. David felt bitter and angry and unworthy thinking about them.

"I need to meet her," he said. "When can I meet her?"

"I don't know. Not yet. Do you forgive me?"

"No. Tell me her name."

"Margaret. Margaret Rachel."

"Rachel was my sister's name."

"I know."

He let her hold his hand. They sat in silence for a while.

"I'm sorry," she said. "I didn't know what to do."

I could have told you what to do, he thought, but he knew she would hate that. Kate was pathologically independent. Even more than he had ever imagined.

"Has she had a good life?" he asked.

"I think so. I've given her everything I could."

"Everything except me."

"I never had you to give."

"I'm her dad, Kate. That wasn't yours to take away."

"You broke my heart!" she cried. "I was lost. It was innocent, the way I felt about you and then you left. I'm sorry. I thought we were . . . I don't know what I thought. I thought we were very different and special and strange and . . . But I was an ignorant child . . . My father threw me out . . ."

She kept apologizing and explaining, and he listened, all

the while knowing he would forgive her. Life without Kate, without the dream of her, was hollow.

A premonition of their future came to his mind: the changing evening sky, after the war, Regent's Canal. The two of them on a picnic boat, surrounded by their children. Just the thought gave David deep satisfaction.

"It's all right," he said finally. "I think I understand why you did it."

She sniffed, looked at him incredulously. "Really?"

"Yeah. You didn't have anyone. You didn't understand family. You did your best."

David was still angry, but Kate looked so distraught, he wanted to comfort her. He needed to. He hugged her to him and pecked her drily on the lips, like one might kiss a baby cousin or an elderly aunt. But it didn't feel like kissing his aunt. It felt like touching his lips to a metallic surface after skidding across a rug in wool socks.

"Yeah," he repeated, surer now, and kissed her again. And again.

For Kate, the sex was as good as it had ever been. Better, because this time David had pulled her down on top of him. This was new. They did not speak but a conversation was had, forgivenesses were asked for and granted, a reunion was celebrated. Slowly, their bodies came back together and everything made sense.

But then, the moment it was over, nothing made sense.

Now Kate slumped on David's chest, her heart pounding against his and her arms around his neck, and remembered Clifton's existence. She remembered his goodness and the plans they'd made together for a decent life. As soon as she'd absolved herself of one deceit, she'd yoked herself under another.

If only she hadn't followed David into the night, if only she was still at home in bed with her little girl.

The moon was behind the clouds. They were under a tree and it was very dark and cold. She could only hear David's breathing and the faint buzzing of planes, high in the sky. She slid off him and felt around for her shoe that had come off. There were shells on the ground, walnuts fallen from the tree.

"When are you going to tell him about me?" David asked suddenly.

"Tell who?" Kate asked, though she knew very well who David meant.

"Your fiancé."

"He already knows where Margaret came from," she said obstinately. She didn't want to talk about Clifton with him.

David sat up and looked at her. His trousers were still undone. She had undone them. "I meant," he said, "when are you going to tell him you're not marrying him?"

The moon appeared from behind a cloud and David's face was so open and pleading that Kate had to turn away. "I'm not telling him that," she said to the tree.

"You're not . . . How can you say you're *not*? Kate, I said goodbye to my mother yesterday, probably forever. I told her I'm going to marry you."

"Why? I never said I'd marry you."

"You asked me to forgive you," he said sharply. "I forgave you for keeping my child from me. I *forgave* you, Kate."

"Did you? It doesn't sound like it."

"I will! Eventually. Because I love you. And I think you love me. Don't you?"

Kate searched herself, sighed, told the truth: "Yes. I love you. I always will, I suppose."

"Then it's settled."

"No." Kate stood. She brushed off her knees and shins, which were damp and stamped with grass. "It is not settled," she said, slipping her shoe on. "I've no idea what I want. I need to decide what's best for me and my girl."

David shook his head. "But this is our chance to be a family. It's our chance to do things properly."

"It's too late to do things properly and I don't care anyway. Stop bloody *pushing* me. I'm sorry I deceived you. You deserve to know Margaret. But you're not in charge of her, I am. Clifton is a good man and she adores him. I'll not cast him off just because you appear out of thin air and seduce me."

"Seduce you! I was just trying to get my head around all this and you pinned me to the ground and *shtupped* my bollocks off."

"For God's sake, David! Shut up. Someone will hear you."

"Shut up?" he said incredulously. "You want me to shut up? Right." He stood up and buckled his trousers. Kate remembered watching him dress in his parents' flat that day after the ballet. "You weren't thinking about anyone hearing us a minute ago."

"I wasn't thinking about anything at all a minute ago. We shouldn't have done that."

"Why not? We have history. We have a kid together." He grabbed her wrist and put it to his lips, and a spark went down her arm, so bright and hot that she trembled. "We have *this*."

"We do," she said carefully. "But I'm not sure what *this* is worth."

"It's worth everything! This is a good thing, Kate. A miraculous thing. Marry me. We'll have a half dozen more kids, Margaret will have a proper family. I'll fix everything for you both, I'll make up for all the lost time—"

"You have nothing to make up for." Kate pulled her hand away. She was starting to panic and needed to get away from David. "I don't want to be fixed. I don't want . . ." She stopped herself, afraid of hurting him.

But he pushed, a raw edge to his voice now: "You don't

want what? You don't want me? You don't want our daughter to have a father?"

"No, I think you know that I *do* want you, but . . ."

"But what?"

"I don't want to make any rash decisions. This is all happening too fast. I need to go home now, David. I need to think. I've already stayed too late." Kate was so confused that she worried she might cry. "Please, please let me go now."

"All right." David's face softened. "Let me walk you home though."

"No, don't." She kissed him on the cheek and he frowned. "Please. Go catch your train. It's better for me if I go alone."

"Damn you, damn you, damn you . . . ," Kate whispered to herself as she walked home to the boardinghouse. On shaky fingers, she counted the days from her last period on her hands: *twenty-three, twenty-four, twenty-five . . .* She exhaled a sigh of relief. The next would arrive in two days or so. Surely, she was all right there. But this was still a disaster.

Half dozen more? What had David been on about? She had one perfect daughter. That was enough. That was more than enough.

She remembered the day Clifton proposed—the day of her confession—and how understanding he had been. *I know you're a good person. It doesn't matter what you did in the past.* Why did he want her? What a nasty piece of work of a wife she would be to a nice man like him.

She remembered the blind trust she had once given David. He'd let her down. Kate couldn't rely on him. If she agreed to marry him, her and Margaret's lives would be even more unstable. Sex—the clear-eyed aftermath of it—threw Kate's vulnerability into sharp relief. She could not have another baby. She could not. With or without a husband.

The worst part was, before David reappeared on her doorstep that afternoon, Kate had known what she wanted. She and Clifton cared for each other. Margaret loved him. After just a few months, Margaret and Clifton's bond was stronger than Kate and her own father's had ever been.

David was a stranger to Margaret. He worked in a Central London hospital where it rained *Sprengbomben* every night. His family, other than Simon, hated Kate.

Turning into Marine Gardens, she felt the back of her wool skirt. It was shamefully wet. She rubbed her hands together to warm them. She was freezing. Why hadn't she worn gloves? Why was she so irresponsible?

Kate was not worried about the sin of what she'd just done in full view of the stars and God and all the chaste saints. She was worried she would never be able to stop doing these things. It wasn't about being good or Clifton or David. It was about Kate sabotaging Margaret's peace. Because of everything Kate craved for herself she might not be capable of giving her daughter a nice childhood.

She prayed that Clifton had already gone to bed, but it was only eight thirty, and he was waiting up for her.

"Hullo, darling," he called as she darted past the door of the drawing room, where he was drinking a coffee with Mr. McKay. "That was a jolly long walk. McKay and I were about to mount a search party."

"Yes, sorry," she said, poking just her head in. "I've over-done it today, I'm afraid. Going straight to bed."

"Take a hot water bottle," Clifton said, starting to stand. "Here, I'll make you one."

"No! Stay there. I'm a bit warm actually. I just want to go to sleep. G'night!"

"Good night, darling. Wait, a cable came for you, about a half hour ago. It's on the table in the foyer."

But Kate went straight up the stairs. She could smell David and their lust on her clothes and needed to hide her shame under a pillow for a while. She could not face Orla. Questions ran through her mind as if on ticker tape: What if she was pregnant again? How had she done this to Clifton? What did she owe David? What would become of Margaret in all this?

Two hours later, Kate was still awake, turning the same questions over in her mind. She had found no answers. Margaret's soft, innocent breaths were making her feel even worse.

Kate switched on the gas lamp and looked in the round porthole mirror above the dresser. There were shadowed craters under her eyes and deep lines in her pink, emotion-swollen face. She was twenty-five. Time was passing and life had not been gentle. She wasn't going to get any younger or prettier. A sobering thought. She knew what Orla would say to these thoughts: it was time to lock down a man, before it was too late. Too late, indeed. Kate laughed bitterly, thinking of how her big sister would react to what Kate had just done and, worse, the possibility of another baby. Orla would say, probably rightly, that Kate had no choice but to throw herself at David's feet.

But it hadn't come to that yet. Kate might be all right. She might still have a choice. The thought of being pregnant again made her shudder. She felt very afraid.

Then she remembered the photos she had taken of herself when she first realized she was pregnant with Margaret. She had been waiting until she had access to a darkroom again. How had she forgotten? Her body, before the war. She had to see it; she wasn't going to sleep anyway.

With trepidation, Kate crept down to her darkroom and there it was in one of her London negative boxes: a canister of film with a red bow.

She developed the negs and squeegeed them and hung them above the radiator. Then she made herself a cup of tea and looked in on Margaret again while they dried. She put on a nightgown and a robe and brushed her teeth. The house was silent except for a windstorm outside that rattled the windows. Kate felt calmer. Clifton and David seemed far away, almost irrelevant. She wasn't going to have another baby; her period was coming soon.

When she made the first contact print around midnight, Kate saw that she'd damaged the negs a little in her haste; at some point in the developing process, they were bent, leaving a scattering of white dashes on some of the prints. And the tone was rather flat. Other than that, they looked intriguing.

She was already pregnant with Margaret in these photos. Everything had changed, but she was not afraid yet—not of her body or anything else. Why? When had she changed? When had she become a fearful creature? Was it when Margaret was born and Kate fell head over heels in love? Yes. But it was the fear of *losing* Margaret, not loving her, that caused the anxiety. She did not think she could survive loving, and worrying over, a second child that much.

Kate pulled a contrast filter from her old kit and printed the image that looked strongest to her. Then, with excitement fizzing in her chest, she watched it appear in the developing tray. Taken over her shoulder, only half of her bare back was in the frame, the deep angle of her waist leading up to the sharpness of her shoulder and the wedge of dark hair cut close to the nape of her neck. On the right side of the image, a lone chandelier crystal hung from the washcloth bar and a mound of white towels on the door hook. The horizontal expanse of the mirror took up the center of the image and a clutter of jars and tubs ran along the rim of the sink: face powders and creams, a box of laundry soap, a prayer candle. It made for an interesting, balanced, weird photograph.

Kate felt herself smiling. She knew she'd taken a good picture when it made her smile. No matter the subject, it felt like an itch in the dead center of her back being scratched. It was not happiness or vanity or pride in her own skill; she smiled because she loved certitude, not in the world or in herself, but in the composition of the photograph. That's what she was looking for when she set out to take pictures: a visual rightness that could be felt in her body. She studied the print again, and again it tickled the corners of her mouth.

Encouraged, Kate printed from another neg, a front view of herself this time. Her pert nose, her eyebrows arched curiously. Her still flat, concave belly. Her breasts, their pregnancy-engorged roundness outlined 360 degrees, and her upturned nipples, like large eyes gawking at the ceiling. The dirty, frosted transverse windowpanes behind her head. And her mother's lost necklace was there and the black freckle on the inner ledge of her right breast and the soft gray vein traversing her dusky left nipple.

Another pleasantly surreal image: a tight shot of St. Francis on the prayer candle, with Kate's out-of-focus breasts looming in the background.

In the photographs, Kate saw a flicker of her old spirit, independent of the external conditions of her life, then and now. For the past few years, she had been sure that being Margaret's mother was the most important, essential thing about her. Perhaps it wasn't. Motherhood was actually an applied thing; it was an image layered on top of the original. So would being a wife, if that's what she decided to do.

—⁓—

29 NOVEMBER 1940
KATHLEEN GRIFFERTY 77 MARINE PARADE
BRIGHTON
PLEASE REPORT GRAND HOTEL 13:00 TOMORROW,
30 NOV, RE PHOTOGRAPHS.
W. TWISSELMAN.
MINISTRY OF INFORMATION.

The Grand was the finest hotel in Brighton, a stately dame that had presided over the seafront for eighty years. Back in

May, it was requisitioned by the Ministry of Defense and closed its doors to the public. It was full of soldiers and military police.

Who the hell is W. Twisselman? Kate thought as she reread the telegram at the hall table. It was the morning after David's return and her night in the darkroom, and she was nursing an emotional hangover. Absentmindedly, she munched on a piece of toast she'd nicked from the lodgers' breakfast spread. Then she remembered her Leica being confiscated at the Odeon, the rough policeman, and the female official's threats of prosecution. What if she was going to be arrested for the photos she took at the bomb site? She couldn't just refuse to go to the meeting; they already knew where she lived. Panic rising in her throat, she called for her sister and showed her the telegram.

Orla had the idea that they'd be less likely to give Kate trouble if she looked like a dotty housewife, a person no one would take seriously. She gave Kate a frowsy old frock to wear—butter-colored with a white floral pattern, two sizes too big. She set out after lunch feeling like a fugitive in disguise.

The hotel entry was guarded by soldiers, but at the mention of W. Twisselman, Kate was allowed in and told they were waiting for her in Room 718. As she rode the lift to the seventh floor and walked along the corridor, her heart pounded in her ears. She was delivering herself into a potentially dangerous situation. She thought of going back to the lobby and asking one of the soldiers to accompany her, but W. Twisselman might be a soldier, too.

In a few seconds, Kate was meant to enter a hotel room with a stranger. Like hell, she would. She wouldn't cross the threshold. She would stand in the hall, well back so he couldn't grab her, and find out what he wanted.

She knocked on 718 and took a step back. The door swung open to reveal a woman—the bull terrier bitch from the

Odeon, wearing a smart gray suit with mother o'pearl buttons. Kate relaxed at the realization that at least she wasn't going to be manhandled.

She managed a professional tone: "Are you W. Twisselman?"

"Yes," the woman said.

"Well, I'm Kate Grifferty. You sent me a telegram."

"Come in, Miss Grifferty."

It was an ordinary hotel room, with a bed that did not look slept in. Kate's Leica sat on a desk by the window, next to a stack of five-by-seven photographs.

"Have a look," Miss Twisselman said, keenly watching Kate.

Kate shuffled through the pictures she'd taken of the theatre where she and Margaret had nearly died. They made her feel sick, but she couldn't stop looking.

"You're lucky you weren't arrested that day, Miss Grifferty." Miss Twisselman had an extraordinary voice, gravelly and rich with a slight lisp that obscured the edges of her Rs. "I know you lied to us. You aren't press. You haven't been for four years."

The room seemed to dip under Kate's feet. She wanted to run but the woman was between her and the door. "Are you arresting me now?"

"No. You can take your camera back. Not the photos."

"I don't understand." Kate shook her head, bewildered. "What is this about? Why do you want these pictures?"

"Lest they should cause disaffection to His Majesty," Miss Twisselman said in a formal voice, "or interfere with the success of his forces by land or sea."

"The pictures are yours. But you can't have gone through all this trouble just to give me my camera."

"Indeed. I've gone through all this trouble to offer you a job. We've got a vacancy at the Ministry of Information Photography Division and I'd like to put your name forward. I can't tell you anything about it except that you would find it very interesting. You would work long hours, six days a week, sometimes seven. The salary is four pounds and ten shillings a week. Would that appeal to you?"

Kate looked around the room. She suspected she was being tricked into admitting something and the policeman was about to jump out from behind the drapes. "Why do you want *me*?"

"You have a remarkable eye and can shoot incredibly well in low light. Most importantly, you and your child were injured in that bombing, yet still you were able to document the damage. You have the temperament for this kind of work." She paused to light a cigarette, priming the lighter until it caught. "And Gordon Davies at the *Times* provided an excellent reference . . ."

"Gordon! He's at the *Times* now?"

"Yes, among other places. How is Margaret, by the way?"

"Very well, thank you. She's expected to make a full recovery." Kate paused. "You know my daughter's name."

"Of course. Do you think I would bring you here if we didn't know for certain you aren't a threat? And Gordon Davies's word means a lot."

Gordy, you beauty, Kate thought. Gordon had made it to the *Times* and, evidently, some kind of government role. He hadn't let Scargill or anyone else stop him. And now he was giving Kate a leg up. He remembered how good she once was. Her mind raced.

"Can I just . . . What would I have to do?"

"It will change all the time. You'll be based at Senate House in London and go where you're sent, often into dangerous situations. The main thrust is convincing our allies that even with our backs to the wall, Britain is still fighting-fit. Are you familiar with the Mass-Observation project?"

"No."

"Hundreds of volunteer diarists and artists around the country documenting British life. The M of I have contracted with them on occasion. The idea is to set up a similar project, but under full control of the War Office."

"What will the pictures be used for?"

"Historic record. Propaganda. Bin liners." Miss Twisselman smiled cryptically. "The point is, they're ours to use or destroy as needed."

Kate flipped through her photos again. She had made Brighton look like it had been razed to the ground. "Propaganda for whom? The Germans?"

"Leave that to the Ministry. Do you want the job?"

"Yes, but I have a daughter. I can't bring her to London. It's not safe."

"Miss Grifferty, no city in England is safe. Look out the window." She gestured at the open window with her cigarette. "See the barbed wire on the beach? This room we're standing in will be at the front of a land invasion. I'd have thought you'd send her to a quiet place in the country after what you've been through . . . I can put her on a list for evacuation straightaway, if that's any help?"

"I'm already looking into my own accommodations for her," Kate lied. "But she's very young. I won't send her to strangers, I don't care how far from danger they are."

"Well." Miss Twisselman blinked her little black eyes at Kate as if she had just said something very foolish. "I'm sure Mother knows best. If you want the position, come round to Senate House in Bloomsbury next week. Someone will interview you. Bring your CV. If you're approved, you'll start Tuesday after the New Year."

On her way out, Kate went to the washroom in the hotel lobby. Her period had arrived. She didn't have to marry anyone.

*   *   *

Arriving home, Kate yelled for Orla to come into the drawing room. "Hurry! I've got a job! The M of I have offered me a job."

"The what?"

"The Ministry of Information," Kate said importantly, closing the door behind them and locking it. She told her sister everything that had happened with Miss Twisselman.

"Jesus, Mary, and Joseph," Orla said, pulling her into a hug. "You've done it. Four pounds a week is an enormous sum . . ."

Orla shook her head in disbelief. Pride glowed in her eyes. Kate knew what she was thinking: *My sister has done something amazing.*

In the time since she'd left the Grand Hotel, a sense of destiny had come over Kate. She was going to help Britain win the war. She *was* a photojournalist. People were going to know her name. From that moment, people would see her differently. She would see herself differently. Orla was right: she had done it. She had broken through that opaque wall that divides subjects from objects. Kate had a sense of finally taking her place in the world.

Orla broke her reverie: "What about Margaret?"

"Yes, I was going to ask you . . . couldn't you look after her? Just until I get settled . . ."

"Darling, I'd love to, but with you gone, Christina and I would have twice the work keeping up this place . . ."

In a devastating rush, Kate remembered who she was, remembered her life, and collapsed on the sofa.

"What should I do, Orla? Please, tell me what to do so I can take this job. I want it, I want it so badly. I need to do this. But I can't leave Margaret with someone I don't know. What if they're like Pa or those dreadful Villos or worse?"

"Right . . ." Orla thought for a while. "Well, if you're asking me, send her to Buckinghamshire, to Clifton's sister. She said she has room for Margaret and you need to get Margaret out of Brighton. We're too near the seafront. I don't know how long I'll be able to hold out myself. I didn't say anything before, and . . . well, it's better that she doesn't go to a stranger. They're going to be family, aren't they, after you're married?"

Kate went and stood at the window so Orla couldn't see her face.

"Aren't they, Kate?"

Kate was reading aloud from Margaret's current favorite book, *Orlando the Marmalade Cat*: " 'As it was getting late, Orlando decided to stay the night . . .' "

Margaret was rapt but Kate paid no attention to the brightly colored drawings of a cat on holiday in France, nor to the words as she spoke them. She had read this book aloud dozens, if not hundreds, of times and could recite it by memory. Glancing down occasionally to check her place, Kate was free to think over her life.

In the days following her job offer, she had made herself very busy, doing everything she could for the house and for Orla and Margaret. There was no question in her mind that she would accept, it was just a matter of how.

And it had finally come to her what was bothering her about David: he wanted to claim her and she could not stand that. As much as she still desired him, his demand to marry and impregnate her again was invasive. With Clifton, she felt freer, though she wasn't sure why.

After Margaret was snugly asleep, Kate picked up the photograph of David on Bonfire Night from her bedside table and stared at it, trying to exhume something within herself. She could print that negative a thousand times, but it would not bring back the certainty she'd felt then. A photograph was a flimsy souvenir of love. But then Kate noticed the indentation below David's lip and for one breath she could smell the bonfire and London and her heart soared.

Sighing, she laid the picture of him on the table, next to a framed photograph of Margaret unwrapping a present in their bedroom last Christmas Eve. She was holding the half-opened box—a die-cut barn and farm animal set—up to her shoulder, grimacing with delight. Behind her, the small, scraggly tree and messy room. Margaret wore a vest and bloomers and her hair was tied with white ribbons into uneven bunches. It was Kate's favorite photograph, because Margaret looked as fierce as a tiger cub. She had her father's eyes, his mouth, the way he held his neck. But she had her mother's tenacity.

Chapter 30

7th December, 1940

*M*argaret. David focused on Margaret. He longed to hug her and check her over and memorize everything about her. She had arched eyebrows, like Simon's, and a cowlick. David guessed that was from him. She had a sturdy little peasant's body and strutted around the playground like she owned it, fists clenched, elbows out. David wasn't sure she looked like him, but she was familiar. Like his mother's people, the Bakers. Kind of swarthy, but fair. David liked her straightaway. He could see that his child was a force: laughing, barreling from swing to slide to a rocking horse on a rusty spring and back again.

The playground where they had arranged to meet was in Queen's Park. Kate had made David promise not to speak to Margaret or approach them, and he wouldn't. There were no other children playing and the park was mostly empty. It was a wet, blustery day and the army was running a drill driving a tank in and out of the pond. The corporal's swearing traveled clearly over the water. Kate had wrapped her and Margaret's heads with babushka kerchiefs and they looked charming and windswept. Every few seconds, David glanced at them over a P.G. Wodehouse someone left on the ward that morning.

Unfortunately, Prouty was at the playground, too, stiff at

Kate's side. David suffered his jolly laugh and despised his desperation and ignorance about Kate. Prouty barely cast a glance at David; he was not even aware he had a rival. If he looked over his shoulder, David could see the tree under which he and Kate had made love, just over a week ago.

Watching Margaret, David had a sense of déjà vu, a vision of a future memory. This moment: the gunmetal sky, the sweary corporal, a particular marine dampness. All of his anguish and longing would be gone and he would just remember Margaret's bright face. She'd light up his mind and regret would drape his heart like wet flannel.

Prouty began to push Margaret on the swing, and David could not help but notice the adoring way the little girl gazed at him. And he heard how Prouty spoke to her, with the gentle confidence of a father of ten. It made David feel like his head was going to rocket off his body.

Kate obviously did not care what David felt. She *wanted* him to see all this.

What if—*oh God,* his head fell into his palm—Kate loved Prouty and simply *remembered* David? What if it was as simple as that?

David didn't need to see any more of the family tableau she had created for herself. Her nerve was, as usual, breathtaking. To dangle his daughter in front of him while installing a new father entirely. It was a mean, selfish thing to do and just like Kate. She deserved that old git. If he was what she wanted, David wasn't going to stand around and watch.

He closed the paperback and dusted off his trousers. He thought: *I'll leave her and all of this. I'm under no obligation to stay.* He took a long look at Margaret, stood up, and let himself out of the rusty gate that bordered the playground. Brighton Station was just a mile walk; he could be back there in time for the ten-fifty train.

David was halfway up the hill above the playground when Kate caught him.

"Where are you going?" she asked, panting. "Don't go off in a strop."

"I'm leaving."

"I thought you wanted to see Margaret."

"What is *he* doing here?"

"I tried to stop him. He insisted on giving us a lift because it looks like rain. Don't worry, he doesn't know about you and me. I'm not going to tell him, it will just hurt him."

"I don't give a damn what he knows. What is he doing with our daughter?"

"Are you having a laugh? She's my daughter. He's my fiancé."

David's stomach turned over painfully. He couldn't speak.

". . . I'm sorry but this is a bit hypocritical," Kate was saying, "after forcing me to have lunch with your Helena. I didn't invite Clifton here. He just came. You *invited* your girlfriend. You wanted to show her off to me."

"I just wanted to keep speaking to you! I already had plans with her and she was waiting for me. I wasn't going to leave her sitting alone at the restaurant, worrying I was bombed. And I didn't know we had a child together, for Chrissake!"

"David." Kate said both syllables of his name deliberately, like he was an idiot. "Clifton isn't her father. He knows that. That's the important thing."

"You wish he was."

"My life would certainly be easier. But no, I learned a long time ago that you can't wish people into anything other than what they are. Myself included."

"You're still going to marry him."

Kate paused. "Yes," she said. "I believe I will. I think it's the right thing."

"Why? How can you even consider it?"

"Because he wants what I want. He's a good man. Do you know he went back into the air force when the war broke out, even though he's nearly forty?"

"I've seen more casualties in three months than a paper

pusher like Prouty has seen in a lifetime. You know what, maybe marrying him is a good thing. At least you won't be alone. He's too old to be deployed."

Kate's eyes narrowed. "I've been alone every day of my life. I'm not afraid of it."

"If you weren't afraid, you would have sent Margaret to a safe place in the country, like all the other children. She wouldn't have been in the theatre that day and nearly been killed."

"How dare you?"

"You wouldn't be angry if you didn't know it was true. Margaret should be somewhere safe."

"She is safe. With *me*."

"Not in Brighton, she ain't. This is bomb alley, sweetheart. Last chance for Hitler to offload. I've actually made a few inquiries. Some friends of mine sent their daughter to her grandparents' pile in Scotland. There's plenty of room for Margaret there."

"I *knew* you'd try to take her from me."

"I'm not taking her from you," David said. "I've only her safety in mind. But she's my child, I'm not going to just go away and forget about her. Or you."

"Kate!" Prouty shouted from the playground fence. He was frowning, holding Margaret on his hip like a nursemaid. "Who is that person?"

Kate startled. They'd both forgotten anyone else was there. She called back: "The green grocer! I forgot to pay our tab last month."

Prouty's brow knit. "What? Do you need money?" Margaret plucked his hat off his head and put it on her own, but he didn't take his eyes off Kate.

"No, darling! I'm all right!" She dug through her bag, pulled out a shilling, and pressed it into David's hand.

"What am I meant to do with this?"

"Play along, please," she said, her eyes desperate.

He gripped her hand. "Come back to London with me."

"No." Kate's face fell. "I'm sorry, David. I have other things to think of now. I don't want more children. I don't want to marry—"

"But you don't have to marry him!"

Her eyes flashed. "I don't want to marry you. We don't want the same things, you know that. You can meet Margaret another day. I'll ring you at the hospital tomorrow, all right?"

Then she walked away with everything David cared about and left him standing there like a ghost.

Chapter 31

12th December, 1940

The stairs were wet and narrow, too narrow for the hundred or so people streaming down them with no handle. David didn't like the look of it, but it was too late to find another shelter. Airplanes thrummed overhead and they could already hear bombs hitting down by the docks. His mother clung to his arm as they maneuvered their way down into the shelter, borne eighty feet into the earth on a river of anxiety and sharp elbows.

It was incredibly cold but relatively clean in the new, half-completed Bethnal Green Underground station. Tracks hadn't been laid yet so there was a cavernous space below and a watery echo from an underground river somewhere nearby.

Hundreds of East Londoners lived here full-time; they'd set up their own subterranean village. Row upon row of metal triple bunks had been bolted into the walls. During the day, people used them as settees. David spotted a small library being assembled in an alcove on the first platform.

Today, the Tube shelter café was serving tea and delicious-smelling bacon sandwiches. He bought one for a shilling and ate it in front of his mother. She looked at him like he'd gone crazy.

"It's food," David said. "It's dinnertime and I'm starving."

"I'm not saying anything," she said, raising an eyebrow. "I make a point of not saying anything."

He laughed. "Sure you do."

That afternoon at lunch, when he told his mother about his rejection by Kate, she'd made no effort to hide her relief. David did not tell her about Margaret. Eating *treyf* was one thing; fathering a child out of wedlock with Kate was another. His mother didn't need to know. He didn't need the headache of her knowing.

In the Underground shelter, everyone was restless, some singing in rounds to pass the time: "*. . . knees up, knees up, never let the breeze up, ohhhhh KNEES UP Mother Brown.*" A bomb landed somewhere above. Kids played kiss chase on the unfinished tracks. People staked out encampments for their families. Their cigarettes and candles and gas lamps made David more nervous than the thuds of bombs; all that bedding could catch fire in a flash.

He and his mother found a place on a bench near an elderly couple she knew, the Manns. They were equipped with bedrolls and blankets and a little side table with a gas lamp.

"We're down here every night," Mr. Mann explained loudly, to be heard over the din. He was knitting a long yellow scarf and already wearing his pajamas, although it was barely past five. "We just sleep better down here, ain't it?"

Mrs. Mann nodded enthusiastically. "Our three sons are in the forces," she said, "but the girls are down here with us. There they are, Zuz and Elena." She pointed to two teenage girls sitting on the edge of the platform.

"Your grandchildren?" David's mother asked.

Mrs. Mann shook her head. "My cousin's daughters. They came to us from Warsaw in '38, before you couldn't get out."

"What a blessing that you got them in time," David's mother said.

"Yes. We're optimistic that my cousins are all right, too. They're stuck in Rumania. Which we reckon is safe as anywhere at the moment."

"It is," David said, along with other words to that effect,

although Mrs. Mann's cousins were not all right and Rumania was not safe and they all knew it.

"Oh dear, oh dear, oh dear," his mother mused. "Terrible times."

"Funny thing is," Mr. Mann said, "those lovely girls have brightened our lives up so much. We haven't been so happy since our boys was little."

It struck David as remarkable this Mr. and Mrs. Mann could feel anything approximate to happiness in the middle of this tragedy.

His eyes followed an old woman in an ARP uniform as she strode along the platform booming out instructions, stopping to scold a little boy for bringing a dog without a muzzle into the shelter. The boy cowered and hugged the mutt close, holding its jaws closed in an effort to satisfy the woman. With his scrawny arms, he looked achingly vulnerable. He could not have been more than ten.

David thought of Margaret. He couldn't stop himself worrying about her. Was Kate or Prouty or whoever the hell it was keeping her safe? David didn't know and Kate had made it clear that he had no right to intervene in any way.

It wasn't fair. Worse, it was foolish. David *could* make Margaret's life easier, he had the intelligence and resources and character to significantly improve his daughter's circumstances. But Kate didn't want that.

David's mother was still deep in conversation with the Manns. To pass time, he picked up the rolled-up sixth of December *Jewish Chronicle* from the foot of Mr. Mann's bedroll and read:

Two thousand Jews are to leave Radom for resettlement elsewhere in Poland, says a Nazi news broadcast from Cracow. This follows a recent announcement that numbers of Germans are to be settled in Radom. Evidently the expulsion of the Jews is intended to make room for them. The

Jews remaining in the town, it is stated, are to be herded in a new ghetto in the centre of the town. . . . In Lodz, where 80,000 Jews are being gradually starved to death in a similar ghetto, an order has been issued forbidding them to use gas or electricity from 8 p.m. until dawn. . . . A new Nazi order completely deprives Lodz Jewish children of milk. . . . Speaking at Cracow the Nazi Labour Minister Ley declared: "The superior the race the greater its demands. The Germans in Cracow must therefore have better housing and more luxurious dwellings than Poles or Jews. The Germans aim to dominate the world because they think they deserve it. . . ."

The world was such a terrible, brutal place; it seemed to David that nothing good could ever happen again.

Another bomb landed, closer this time, followed by a quake. The lights flickered and then everything was quiet. People looked at the ceiling for a moment, then continued their activities. The cacophony of conversation and songs started up again.

A family of six had set up camp next to the Manns. The wife poured out a beaker of milk for each child. The husband seemed dazed, slumped on her shoulder, his cigarette dangling dangerously close to their shared flannel blanket. The wife gently moved his hand away from the blanket and mouthed the words: *"Chin up, love. The kiddies."* The husband sat up, pecked his wife on the cheek. Then he pulled a storybook from a duffel bag and began to read aloud to the children. It was a startling, almost instant transformation from broken scarecrow to steady patriarch.

Meanwhile, the woman resumed her tasks. David was awestruck by her. She was heroic. The children chattered happily and the oldest, a girl, stroked her baby brother's hair as he lolled in her lap. Somehow, this family scaffolded one another. The husband had needed help, his wife wanted to help him, and *he let her help him*.

Was it so much to ask, to be allowed to look after the woman he loved? How else were people meant to make it through?

David was seized by the sensation of missing Kate, but what had he really lost in her? The dream of a woman who did not need or want him. Maybe someday the wrenching love he felt for her would dissipate, maybe it wouldn't. Either way, it only hurt him. He'd just have to accept it.

Margaret was another story.

As clever and stubborn and relentless as Kate was, David was those things, too. He had to—*he would*—find a way to be part of his daughter's life.

Kate was never going to marry that daft lieutenant and she didn't want David, either. Not enough to give up a jot of her precious, bloody-minded autonomy. She didn't understand family; if she did, she wouldn't have hidden Margaret from him in the first place.

Observing the families on the platform, David thought of the generations to come. A life he could build in defiance of those who wished him and everyone like him dead.

In Lodz, eighty thousand Jews are being gradually starved to death. . . .

David thought of Margaret and what was owed her. She deserved to know where she came from, she deserved a father.

Margaret could be his chance to look outward, to walk with the living, to create a future. To build a bright, small fire to help light the vast darkness.

"Mum," he said, steeling himself, imagining that brave woman next to the Manns putting her hand on his shoulder. *Chin up, love. Margaret.* "There's something I want to tell you."

*   *   *

For a long time, David's mother was quiet. The all-clear sounded and some people started to stand up and make their way aboveground. Others slept on, as if the siren was a neighbor's alarm clock.

"Mum, say something please."

"You've given me a shock," she said. She shook her head. "A real shock."

David had expected this. Next, she would tell him what a terrible son he was.

"A girl," she said. "A three-year-old girl? You met her? Does she take after us?"

"Yes. She does. And after her mum. She has these dark blond ringlets . . . She's beautiful."

"I can't help but think . . ." She trailed off, her eyes filled with tears. "I can't help but think of Rachel. She had blond ringlets, too."

David flinched. "I'm sorry, Mum."

His mother stopped him. "No." She closed her eyes and thought for a moment, then shook her head. "The time for apologies is past. This is a child, Davy. We will never apologize for her existence. It wouldn't be right. How she got here, well . . . But she's our blood. She's family." She stubbornly jutted out her chin. "How can I help?"

Kate and Margaret met David at the café in Brighton Station, as arranged, at nine in the morning on Friday, the twentieth of December. First, Kate's heart soared at the sight of the two of them together, then it sank. She had made such a mess of everything. David, her beautiful David, whom she'd wanted forever. Kate had dreamt of him for years, but Margaret averted her eyes like he was a stray dog with no hind legs.

Over Margaret's head, David mouthed to Kate: *"What*

should I do?" and Kate felt a flash of fury toward him. No one had given *her* any instructions. But David looked so worried that Kate threw him a lifeline.

"Margaret," she said, "David is a doctor, like Dr. Lazare." Dr. Lazare was the only thing Margaret remembered from the hospital, the nice old man who removed her cast after her arm healed.

Margaret's eyebrows rose. "Does he know how to fix bones?"

"Ask him yourself."

"No," Margaret said. She slid her teacup toward the edge of the table until Kate blocked it with her hand. "I don't want to."

Kate sighed and explained to David that yesterday she'd been officially offered a job with the Ministry of Information, a good one, and had accepted.

"God, congratulations. Will your sister look after Margaret?"

"She can't. Margaret is going to Buckinghamshire to stay with Clifton's sister." Kate touched Margaret's small shoulder and she tensed. How frightening it was to be a child, to have no control over one's own life. "I want her out of the city. You were right about that. And she's going to have a lovely time, aren't you, button? Clifton says there's a farm nearby. Margaret loves animals."

"When does she go?"

"Right after Christmas."

"So soon." He held Kate's gaze. "Can I see you in London?"

"No." She looked down. "It wouldn't be fair to Clifton. I need to sort things out with him. He makes me happy, he makes Margaret . . ."

David flinched and Kate trailed off. She thought he must hate her for making him a stranger to his own daughter.

But then he seemed to gather himself. "I understand," he said. His brow smoothed and he smiled at Margaret, who was still scowling, and took a stuffed zebra out of the bag at his feet.

"I *do* know how to fix bones," he said. "In fact, I think I'll check the arms and legs of this zebra I brought with me today. I think I'll call him, hmm, does he look like a Mr. Stripe?"

At the sight of the toy, Margaret's face softened a little. She propped her double chin on her palm, sighed wearily. Kate sipped her tea.

"No," Margaret said. "He looks like a Cathy. He's a girl."

"Yes, I see that now," David said, bending back the zebra's leg. "Goodness me, I don't think poor Cathy's got any bones . . ."

Margaret was not having it. Again, she turned away from David, and father and daughter had matching frowns.

Everything had been easily arranged with Daisy. Clifton wrote her and she immediately rang Kate to inquire about Margaret's favorite foods to see what she could arrange to have on hand. She said she was delighted to have a little girl come to stay. Kate liked her warm voice and her humor and found herself telling Daisy all about the Odeon bombing and what Margaret had been through. Daisy listened and understood and promised not to take Margaret to the cinema, in case it upset her.

On the day Margaret was meant to go to Buckinghamshire, Clifton put his hand on Kate's shoulder and she made herself not pull away. It was not that she did not care for him, but her mind was somewhere else. She needed to be alone, in full battledress. Otherwise, she would never be able to let Margaret go.

"Thank you for taking her to Daisy's, Clifton . . ."

"That's all right."

His face looked funny and Kate knew he was thinking worried thoughts about her. She could see it in his shoulders, the way he hung his head as he walked around to the driver side of the car. She called after him. "I will miss you!"

Then she ran to him and kissed him and he brightened a bit. He wanted to believe her. She wanted to believe herself.

"Soon as I'm settled in London," she said, smoothing her hand over his neck, "we can sort things out. Make some plans. I'm just not ready to get married, not yet."

Clifton clouded over again. "Yeah, you said." He turned his face away like he couldn't bear to hear anymore.

"You'll thank your sister for me, won't you?"

"No need. Daisy's already got an evacuee and plenty of space for another. She'd much rather have Margaret than some strange Cockney child."

"You'll give her my letter? And the portrait of you I framed?"

Clifton patted the flat brown paper package under his arm. "I've told you, I will."

Kate knelt down to Margaret, who was kicking at her little green cardboard suitcase. She held her daughter and kissed her nose, her ears, her lips. The sweet smell of Margaret, the plump softness of her cheek, made Kate ache to call the whole thing off. But she didn't. She swallowed a sob and dropped a veil over her senses.

"I will see you in a week, button," Kate said. "Then I'll leave again, but I'll come back. It won't be forever, just until it's all safe for us to be together again. You'll have a lovely long holiday with your new friend Charlie. His Mammy wrote to tell me their little cocker spaniel just had five puppies."

"Puppies?" Margaret's eyes brightened. She thought for a second and held up four fingers. "This many?"

Kate unfolded Margaret's thumb. "This many . . ."

"Can one be mine?"

"They will all be yours to cuddle, until you come back to me."

Margaret ran to the car and flung open the door. "Let's go, Clifton!"

Please, Kate prayed, cold panic washing over her as Clifton's car pulled away from the boardinghouse with her daughter. *Please let me be doing the right thing.*

Chapter 32

15th January, 1941

Kate went to work. She loved being back in London again, even with the noise and the danger and the dirt. At Senate House, the women outnumbered the men and there was a great feeling of camaraderie Kate had never experienced before. Everyone talked of America a great deal; in the photography department, there was a big push for images that made it look as if Britain was nearly winning, if only she could get a teeny, tiny bit of help. This, of course, was not true. There were strict parameters for the photos Kate took: no bodies, no blood, no stricken faces, no overt struggle. Twice a week, she would send photographs via airmail to press attachés at the British embassies in America and Canada.

The M of I put Kate up in a temporary lodging house in Bloomsbury which was blacked out and gloomy. She was allowed to stay there for a month for free. Every Friday she picked up her salary, a little brown envelope with four pounds ten shillings. Then she sent a pound to Orla and a pound to Daisy, and set everything else aside for a place for her and Margaret.

Kate wrote Clifton every day, just as she'd promised. The problem was, after the first few days, she did not miss him. He was just another person who wanted things from her. He took up space that belonged to her work and Margaret.

Alone in bed at night, Kate thought of how far her baby was from her and it was like looking over a very high, very steep cliff. Her stomach turned over and everything was wrong and frightening. The feeling would linger for hours and Kate had to carry it with her into the mornings, a vertigo that threatened each step. But she never stumbled, and she never seriously considered giving up.

A paper warehouse in Wapping was hit and Kate went down to shoot it. East London was both familiar and disorienting, like a dream. Emerging from Shadwell Station, she felt a tug toward Limehouse and her father's old wharf. It was an ache too deep for her to name, but it hurt. She smelled her father in the fog, saw him in the blackened London brick. Kate considered the life he had lived there, mostly alone. He'd always made it seem full to bursting, without room for her, but he must have been lonely sometimes. She wondered if her father had ever felt the guilt and worry she felt now, away from Margaret. Kate did not think so. She hoped that made her different from Frank.

At the docks, flaming spools of paper the size of automobiles spilled from the bowels of an eighteenth-century warehouse. The fire services were there already, but they only had two hoses and the Thames was at low tide. Neighborhood women ran to and fro from the riverbank with buckets of water, which turned to steam in midair.

Taking the pictures, excitement percolated inside Kate until she felt nothing else: no regret or confusion or even the sense of time passing. And it was perfect shooting for the M of I: the light of the fire and the dark of the warehouse, chipper AFS lads and brave housewives working together, drama with no human victims. A scene that would make people believe England could win.

At an Emergency Food Office in Richmond, about half an hour by train from London, Kate was photographing

Women's Voluntary Service workers answering questions about ration books and handing out clothing to a crowd of bombed-out Londoners. After she finished, Kate walked through the streets of Richmond, which was the nicest little town she'd ever seen. There was no broken glass, no houses ripped open, no stink of cordite. The streets were tidy and lined with trees. There were still birds, unlike in London; they had not fled. Richmond hadn't been bombed, at least not yet, and it was almost as if the war had never come.

Near the train station, she saw a painted *TO LET* sign in the upstairs window of a tall, narrow, redbrick Georgian house. On a whim, Kate knocked on the door and when the landlady let her in, it was like air filling her lungs. The vacant flat was spotless and freshly distempered white. In Richmond were sounds Kate had not heard in London since before the Blitz: the strong flow of water through pipes, children kicking a football in the street, a robin's tweedling song.

The best bit, though, was the private stairway from the flat's galley kitchen to the back garden. It was chockablock with onion and beetroot and the fallen yellow leaves of a regal English oak.

A little girl could grow there, too.

F/Lt. Prouty,
Officers Mess,
RAF Station,
Shoreham,
West Sussex
2nd February 1941

Dear Clifton,
I apologise for my silence over the last week. I did not mean to worry you, as it appears I have from your letter, and I'm sorry. I did not write because an awareness has come over me and I wanted to make sure it was not a

whim but, as I expected, an epiphany about who I am and what I can be to you. I am so sorry to tell you that I cannot marry you. This past month in London has reminded me that I am fine on my own and in fact I prefer it. All the love and devotion and domesticity I have in me must go to my daughter. There is no other man. In fact, I've never been so sure that Margaret is the one and only great love of my life. Without her, I would be quite content to spend the rest of my days as a "bachelorette" in the Metropolis, chasing down one adventure after another with my camera.

The reasons I have for being alone might not be clear to you. It's not that I don't care deeply for you, because <u>I do</u>, but I don't want a life for you where the woman you love is always pushing you away. It would break my heart if Margaret married a man whose overriding reflex was to turn away from her. That is precisely what you will have with me. You and I are both motherless children, so please allow me to give you the advice that I'm sure any loving mother would: I am not good enough for you. I won't make you happy. I'm selfish and ambitious and independent and find that I have no desire or ability to change. I won't be able to love you the way you deserve.

It may hurt you further to read this, which is not my intention, but I need you to know that I write from a place of experience. I know what it is to be in love. I was horrifyingly in love with Margaret's father, I dove in headfirst and struck the bottom of the pool. It damaged me, certainly, but I can't put the blame of what I'm doing to you upon him. That disaster only confirmed what I've known since I was little, which is that that kind of love makes a girl intolerably vulnerable. It's nothing <u>at all</u> to do with you. I know how trustworthy you are. Your kindness and good sense will make you

*the perfect husband to someone who deserves you. I can
say with perfect clarity that I do not. And, forgive me if
I'm wrong, but are you <u>really</u> in love with me, Clifton?
Search in your heart, is any sadness you may be feeling
upon receipt of this letter for me, or because you know
how much you will miss Margaret? I've never been
praised for my insight, but my guess is that what you
<u>really</u> want is a family. Find someone who wants to have
children with you. You've been so accepting of my desire
to have no more babies. Don't be! You are meant to be
a father and the world desperately needs kind children
raised by kind men like you. I did not have that, my
father's heart was quite closed to me, and as I write this
I realise it may have contributed to the predicament I
find myself in now. My intractable independence was
forged by neglect. I did not choose it, but I must live
with it, and this time in London has reminded me that,
wicked as it may be, I enjoy it.*

*Hang on, I'm writing this from the office and sirens
are going . . .*

*Back now. False alarm. I won't bore you any more
with explanations for my poor behaviour. I only want
you to know that you've been only good and my desire
to break our engagement is due to my own limitations.*

*Please do me the favor of not worrying about me.
It's not fair on you and I'm fine. I've let a flat in a quiet
street in Richmond which has a garden for Margaret
and enough room for Orla, when I can convince her to
close up the boardinghouse. It's as safe a place as I can
imagine where I can still work in London.*

*I'll make arrangements with Daisy to retrieve
Margaret soon, as I do not wish to impose upon your
family's generosity any more that I already have.*

*I hope that when the shock of this letter subsides, as
I know it will before long, you will be able to forgive*

me. For my part and Margaret's, we will always consider you a cherished friend.

I eagerly await any response you can find in your heart to write.

Sincerely,
Kate

To Miss Margaret Rachel Grifferty
Tees Cottage, Aylesbury, Buckinghamshire
7th February 1941

Dearest Margaret,
How are you and how is Cozy? Daisy wrote me and said he sleeps at the foot of your bed and that you are a very big girl looking after him.

Every night I go out and see the first star in the sky and make a wish to see you. Have you been looking, like we talked about last time?

I found a flat for us and I cannot wait for you to see it. I like it best of any place I've ever lived. It's in a quiet place called Richmond and our two bedrooms are connected by a funny little door just your size. A very nice lady named Mrs. Pratt owns the house and lives in the garden flat below us. She loves doggies and says Cozy will be very welcome.

I will pick you up the morning of the 1st of March (just a few weeks!) and bring you to our new home. Be very good with Daisy in the meantime and we will have tea and cake on the train.

Love to Daisy and Charlie and everybody at Tees.
From Mammy

P.S., Daisy, could you please have Margaret ready for me to collect her on the 1st? Clifton has not responded to my last letter. I imagine you know why. But please write and let me know he is all right, and

*tell him he would be wasted on me. I am so sorry
about all of this. Thank you for looking after my girl
so well.*

—⚡—

Three weeks later, Kate carried her camera and a sponge
cake wrapped in newspaper through St. Pancras station. She
bought a cup of bitter black tea at the station's canteen and
surveyed the indigo dawn above the train tracks.

Under the glass-and-iron roof of the darkened station, soldiers gathered in a circle of dim light around the timetable.
As Kate waited for her train, she flipped through magazines
at W. H. Smith. That's when she saw it on the cover of *Life*:
a photo she took of a group of grinning auxiliary firemen in
front of the extinguished paper warehouse. The photo was
cropped too far in at the top right; it would have been better
for the river to be in the frame. But never mind. Kate grabbed
it off the stand and pored through it, looking for more of her
pictures. The M of I had never told her about this. Of course
they hadn't. As far as they were concerned, it was a photograph
taken by nobody. But really it was Kate's. She felt like stamp-
ing her feet, shouting for the soldiers at the timetable to come
look. The Ministry had dozens of photographers throughout
the country taking photos, but they'd chosen Kate's to send to
the Americans, to convince them Britain was still in the fight.

She was not bothered that the picture didn't have her
name on it. Well, she was, but she cared more about what it
meant—that she could make her way and leave her mark on
the world, doing this work. As impossible as it seemed, Kate
had never stopped wanting it.

Her eyes filled with tears and she closed them and David
appeared in her mind. She thought how they were alike, born
wanting more than they were meant to have. Margaret would
be that way, too—she wouldn't be able to help it—and Kate
was glad.

Epilogue

Richmond

After the War

5th November, 1945

For the first time in six years, fireworks were allowed. It was to be a proper, old-fashioned Bonfire Night and Kate was preparing a party in the back garden, putting the final touches on a pyramid of logs, old newspapers, and dry leaves. Every garden, park, and vacant lot in town had a similar pyre built up. Orla had found some gunpowder crackers and squibs, leftover from VJ-Day, and was in the kitchen with her husband, Nick, brewing mulled wine for the adults and hot chocolate for the children. Margaret, too young to remember a real peacetime Bonfire Night, was in the garden carving a jack-o-lantern of her dog's face. She had been at it all afternoon, hellbent on perfection.

Kate, still in her green tweed work suit, brushed leaf dust off her hands and went inside to put on a bit of lipstick. She paused at the drawing room window to check the traffic in Sheen Road. It was only sunset but people had been setting off fireworks in Richmond Park for hours. Poor Cozy the dog was a shivering ball of black-and-white fur between the sofa and the radiator.

Theirs was a full household and Kate was the head of it. Orla had closed Puffin's Perch in '43, after a devasting daytime raid blew the windows in and tragically killed one of the lodgers. By then, she and Nick Abbott, their next-door neighbor, were engaged to be married and they moved in with Kate and Margaret after the wedding.

Pulling the pins from her hair and shaking it out, Kate watched David's Vauxhall pull in front of the house. Even from a distance, she could see he had the weight of the ruined world upon his shoulders. So much had been lost. Kate didn't know how anyone could go on, only that she had to. They all did, for the next generation more than themselves.

While most men grew babyish tummies in their thirties, after two years on the North African front David had only grown rangier. The Hellenic beauty of his face still touched her, but it was a knot she didn't need to untie anymore. After years of practice, she could turn away and find inspiration in other faces, other bodies.

Most recently, that body belonged to Arthur Keyes, a fledging writer at the *Times,* where Kate had just been promoted to features editor.

Making her way to the front door, she wished David would allude to the Bonfire Night they'd spent together in 1936. Margaret was born nine months later. Inviting him and his family over on the fifth of November was probably intentional, but Kate didn't suffer from introspection anymore. Nonetheless, she could recognize a perverse urge to provoke David. She didn't want to make him angry; she just wanted him to *remember,* for one second.

But Margaret's father, always correct, coming into the house with his wife and two small boys, of course said nothing about the significance of the date. A friendly hello kiss on the cheek for Kate, same way he greeted Orla, followed by a hearty handshake for Nick.

Emmanuelle, David's Moroccan-Jewish wife, was pregnant and blooming in a navy slack suit with horn buttons. Her glossy, onyx-black hair was pinned in a knot at the nape of her neck and her gold wedding band stood out against her olive complexion. David had met her in Egypt just after El Alamein, where he was serving as a major in the Royal Army Medical Corps and she was a nurse in a requisitioned children's hospital.

Max and Simon, eighteen-month-old twins, tumbled in behind their parents.

To Emmanuelle's credit, she had never turned down an invitation from Kate and Margaret. Any other woman would have disappeared them both. Orla speculated that David's wife's liberality came down to her being a French speaker and therefore more or less French. Kate did not care about Emmanuelle's relaxed French morals; she cared that Margaret felt loved by her father.

Over the last two years, the two families had gathered half a dozen times, and Margaret was always welcome in Emmanuelle's home.

"Let's put on a bit of music," Orla chirped. Before Kate could suggest something to suit her own mood, Orla offered: "Emmanuelle, would you like to pick one of our records?"

Emmanuelle smiled lazily. "Let Daveed choose," she yawned. "He's the musical one."

David rubbed his hands together. "Happy to oblige. First things first though, where can Manu put her feet up?"

Kate resisted the impulse to roll her eyes. David led Emmanuelle to the oversized armchair by the window and slid a pillow under her back. Then he walked over to the record player and thumbed through a box of Kate's records while the ladies exchanged anecdotes about Margaret, Max, and Simon. Nick returned to the kitchen, and David placed Glenn Miller's "Moonlight Serenade" on the turntable. It was exactly what Kate would have selected.

"*Mon Dieu,* this shall put me under," Emmanuelle sighed, snuggling into the chair. "Kate, I have never been so tired. I cannot hold my eyes open. It was never so bad with the boys. Did you have this fatigue with Marguerite?"

Kate did not look at David, and she knew he wasn't looking at her. She wanted to say that she had hated being pregnant and therefore tried not to remember it, but Emmanuelle
was smiling at her hopefully. "Umm," Kate said, rubbing her
chin, remembering she had forgotten about the lipstick. "Yes,
come to think of it. It was so long ago, though, I can scarcely
recall . . ."

Emmanuelle raised a playful eyebrow at David. "Perhaps
this means we're having a girl this time, Daveed."

"Those boys are running you off your feet," Kate said,
privately hoping all future Rabatkin children would be boys;
Margaret deserved whatever specialness she could hold in her
father's life. "I've no idea how you manage them both. Of
course you're shattered."

"But she is still so charmingly *slender*," Orla fibbed, patting Emmanuelle's hand, her pale eyes crinkling kindly. She
and Nick had clearly been fine-tuning the mulled wine recipe.
"I'd never even have guessed you were in the family way."

The kitchen was Nick's domain, but Kate needed something to do. "Make yourself at home, everyone," she said,
more sharply than she'd intended. "I'll fetch Emmanuelle
some water and give Nick a hand."

"Cheers, Kate," David said, barely glancing her way. He
was compiling a small stack of records now, obviously planning the music for the entire evening. Kate took them from
his hands and shuffled through—one was her Billie Holiday.

"Too slow," she said, setting it aside. "Your wife is right.
You'll put us all into a drone state. This isn't 'Music While
You Work,' David." He chuckled and she was happy. The
closest she could get to David now was by making him laugh.
"Anyhow, we won't be able to hear these tunes over the fire-
works."

Kate went into the kitchen. Two candles stuck in milk
bottles burned on the table and the drapes were wide open,
filling the kitchen with lavender winter light. Nick, swigging

at a bottle of cider by the stove, plucked the skin from a frying pan of hot milk and whisked in cocoa powder and caster sugar. He was an unassuming soul, but in the kitchen he buzzed with expertise.

Kate filled five teacups with mulled wine and lined them up on a tin tray with a glass of water. She smiled, listening to Margaret lead her half brothers in a game of orphanage outside.

"Come, let's go through to the garden," Kate called, lifting the tray and opening the kitchen door to the exterior stairs. "Margaret and I have built a gorgeous bonfire for everyone."

In the garden, Margaret leapt into David's arms and he held her there for a while, her long, coltlike legs swinging against his. The sky had darkened to indigo now. Kate struck a match and tossed it onto the stack of wood. It flared and burned out.

"Hey, I was going to light it!" Margaret cried, and scrambled to her side. "Mammy, can't I try?"

"All right, button." Kate handed her the matches.

Meanwhile, Emmanuelle was fishing something out of her cup of wine.

"Is it an insect?" David asked, peering over her shoulder.

"It's a clove," Emmanuelle said.

"Leave it," he said. "Cloves are good for your dyspepsia."

"*Merci*, Daveed," she cooed, grazing a hand down David's cheek, and his eyes softened into an expression Kate remembered and, for a second, it stung.

He loves her, Kate thought, looking away, *as tenderly as a parent loves a child*. It was not jealousy she felt; she would never want to take David from Emmanuelle. It was plain sadness that their time had passed.

What if Kate had accepted David's proposal, four years ago? She certainly wouldn't be at the *Times*. Sex, the one thing that had always worked between them, might have gone stale by now. Kate's life would be a hailstorm of distractions:

a hostile mother-in-law, a husband who spent most nights at the hospital, numerous children. There'd be at least one more baby by now, probably two or three, and Kate would have been wrangling them alone, especially back when David was in Africa. She never wanted a baby again. Margaret was eight now and went to school all day. It was manageable. Actually, it was marvelous. Kate was free, her body felt like it really belonged to her. As long as Margaret had everything she needed—and she did—Kate could do as she pleased. She could not imagine a situation that better suited her, no matter how solid and climbable David looked in his gray collared jumper.

Kate reminded herself of all this as she stalked to the bottom of the garden, where the bonfire was starting to burn. She put her arm around Margaret and pulled her close. For a moment, her girl nuzzled into her, then pulled away and went back to poking at the logs with a fire iron. Above their heads, sparks floated on the air like glowworms.

"Margaret, come away from those flames, love," David called. "You'll injure yourself."

"It's all right, Dad!" Margaret grinned conspiratorially at Kate and tucked her hair behind one ear. "I'm with Mammy."

Author's Note

Kate and David's love story is not my own, but I know what it's like to bridge two cultures for love. While I was not raised Catholic, I come from a long line of ardent Irish Catholic women and I converted to Judaism before marrying my now husband. Kate does not convert to Judaism—that wasn't really an option for her and, even if it was, she wouldn't be inclined to do so. However, like me, falling in love with a Jewish person made Kate even more aware of the insidious nature of antisemitism.

I lived in England in my early twenties and wrote a master's dissertation on British women artists and writers during World War II, but never once came upon the British Union of Fascists (BUF) in my research. The wartime art and literature I studied—often officially sanctioned—did not touch on the fact that, just prior to the war, there were strong antisemitic and fascist sympathies across the United Kingdom. It wasn't until I pushed past the mythology and listened to testimonies of ordinary people that I realized that World War II, and the Allies' stance on it, could easily have gone the other way.

It's a commonly held belief that Brits and Americans were always anti-Hitler. To the contrary, because of the horrors they had lived through in World War I, appeasement of Hitler was an attractive option to many. Understandably, people wanted to live in peace, not lose their sons and brothers and husbands to another global war. But there were also strong fascist sympathies in England and the United States, where political fearmongering, antisemitism, racism, and toxic nationalism drove people of both the upper and working classes toward fascism. Men like Sir Oswald Mosley and his counterparts in the United States exploited fears about war and immigrants to seize power and build their own platforms—a strategy that will likely feel unsettlingly familiar to today's readers.

I became aware of the BUF and the Battle of Cable Street exactly eighty years after it took place in London on October 4, 1936. Just before the start of World War II, two of the country's largest immigrant communities—Jewish and Irish, along with various labor unions and political groups—banded together in the streets to block the BUF from parading through East London's Jewish neighborhoods.

On October 5, 2016, I happened to be listening to a Public Radio International story about Cable Street's anniversary, including an interview with an elderly man who had been in the East End that day, Bill Fishman. "And you could hear in this conglomeration of people, the chants, 'One-two-three-four-five, we want Mosley, dead or alive,' " Fishman remembered. "And all across there were these banners flying, and I remember them as though it was yesterday. I pushed my way through these banners. People were there, I can see them now, young and old, but mainly local people, consisting of Irish and Jewish working class. They'd come there to stop the fascist invasion of our patch."

Perhaps because of my own history, I thought: *There's a Romeo and Juliet story here!* That is how Irish photographer Kate Grifferty and Jewish medical student David Rabatkin came to life in my imagination.

Kate is a combination of many people, but one stands out. When I was in graduate school in Brighton, writing about women's narratives of the Blitz, Lee Miller's images kept coming up. Miller was an American Surrealist, photojournalist, and model who made her home in England. She is credited with persuading *Vogue* to publish graphic photographs of the liberations of Buchenwald and Dachau, driven by the conviction that if people did not *see* what had happened in the concentration camps, they would minimize it. Her article and photo essay were published under the title: "Believe it!"

I had the opportunity to meet Miller's son, Tony Penrose, in 2005 and he took me through her personal archive at Farleys House in Sussex. Her letters and Surrealist-inspired photographs from London during the Blitz changed my understanding of trauma and how artists help us process it.

Kate's artistic journey was further colored in by Suzanne Bardgett's *Wartime London in Paintings*, Christopher Bonanos's *Flash: The Making of Weegee the Famous*, Vicki Goldberg's *Margaret Bourke-White: A Biography*, Judith Mackrell's *The Correspondents: Six Women Writers on the Front Lines of World War II*, Antony Penrose's *The Lives of Lee Miller*, and Julia Van Haaften's *Berenice Abbot: A Life in Photography*. The prewar and wartime photography of Bill Brandt and George Rodger were also essential in setting many of the scenes in *Bonfire Night*.

The details of David's life in Jewish East London came from interviews with people who lived there at the time. I am particularly indebted to Sylvie Roberts (1922–2019), whose bright spirit infuses every page of this book. We met by phone in 2017 and she enthusiastically shared her memories with me whenever I had a question about where my characters would hang out, what young people got up to in the 1930s, or how religiously observant David would have been. Sylvie and I met in person in 2018 and she, along with her nephew and niece, Harry and Shirley Hart (both in their eighties), generously toured me around Hackney, Bethnal Green, and Limehouse.

I also made great use of the Imperial War Museum archive in London, which includes thousands of recorded interviews with British survivors of World War II. Getting things like the cadence of David's speech right—as a 1940s Londoner and physician—would not have been possible without listening to those voices. I particularly drew from the testimonies of Betty Anne Mitchell, Ben Cecil, Arthur John Tindall, Frederick Wackett, Stanley Gladstone, Sir John Crofton, Basil Reeve, Louis Kenton, Joan Atherton Harrison, and Francis Desmond O'Neill.

Several other museums helped me make the details in this book true to history, especially: the Metropolitan Museum of Art's 2021 exhibition *The New Woman Behind the Camera,* the American Swedish Institute's 2021 exhibition *Kindertransport—Rescuing Children on the Brink of War,* the Museum of London, the London Transport Museum, and the National Portrait Gallery in London.

Other firsthand accounts came from the *Jewish Chronicle* archive, the British Newspaper Archive, the *Times* (London) archive, Mollie Panter-Downes's *London War Notes,* Harriet Salisbury's *The War on Our Doorstep,* Erik Larson's *The Splendid and the Vile,* Louise London's *Whitehall and the Jews,* and Simon Szreter and Kate Fisher's *Sex Before the Sexual Revolution.* "My Brighton and Hove" (mybrightonandhove.org.uk) was also helpful, especially regarding the Kemp Town Theatre Bombing on September 14, 1940, which killed four children and two adults, as well as forty-eight people in surrounding neighborhoods.

The BUF was funded in large part by Mussolini's Rome, and the Battle of Cable Street was one of the reasons that money dried up. Sir Oswald Mosley's embarrassment by East Londoners was viewed as weakness by Mussolini, who in turn lost faith in him. All the more reason for Mosley to cozy up to Adolf Hitler and further embrace antisemitism as the BUF's pet cause. (Mosley and his wife, Diana Mitford, were married at the home of Joseph Goebbels, Hitler's propaganda minister, two days after Cable Street.)

Because of the riots that Mosley's paramilitary march caused, Parliament enacted the Public Order Act of 1936 to limit the activity of extremist groups in the UK. In spite of this, BUF membership immediately increased, as did violent antisemitic attacks.

Although Mosley and the BUF ultimately failed at the ballot box, antisemitism remains a blight on both rationality and compassion. Authoritarian leaders still seek to turn our universal human need for connection and safety into fear and hatred and, like Kate and David, we must actively search for light to hold up to that darkness. And vote.

Anna Bliss
March 2023

Acknowledgments

Thank you to my loving family, all of whom have supported me in writing *Bonfire Night*. I would especially like to thank: my mother, Kathryn Engelhardt-Cronk, for being a great reader and passing her passion for literature to me; my husband, Michael Bliss, for his love and encouragement; my sons for cheering me on; and Tom Cronk, Jane Cronk, and Stefon Taylor for providing on-demand edits and story counsel over the last six years. I am grateful to my grandmother, Claire Engelhardt, who generously shared her memories of coastal boardinghouse life in the 1930s and '40s. Thank you also to the Bliss, Fine, and Mallin families for sharing their family photographs and stories from the period.

My agent, Heather Jackson, is a human lighthouse and I'm grateful every day to have her as my partner in publishing. A very heartfelt thank-you to my editor, John Scognamiglio, whose insight brought everything essential about this story into focus. He and the wonderful team at Kensington Books—especially Kristine Mills, who designed the cover, and Vida Engstrom, who leads the publicity department—have made me feel understood and supported from the beginning.

I will be forever grateful to Heather Lazare for her brilliant edits as well as her Northern California Writers' Retreat, which first made me believe I could write fiction.

I am fortunate to have lifelong friends who are gifted writers and editors, most notably Dorothy Guerrero, Margaret Williams, and Stephen Harrigan. Their wisdom and feedback at every stage of writing *Bonfire Night* was invaluable. Thank you also to my friends Dr. Jonas Aharoni, Dr. Alisha Laborico, Dr. Damon Francis, and Erick Ordin, RN, for sharing their knowledge regarding disease, injury, and David's medical life. For patiently checking my dialogue for Americanisms, thank you to Liz Smith, Ceri Miller, and Ainslie Peters. I am also grateful for the creative insight and support of Charles Nickila, Kelly O'Rear, Louis-Philippe Charette, Grace Davies, Laine Carlsness, Ryan Radis, Kirk Hawkins, Desiree Nzara, Richard Hart, Reggie Bliss, Richard Bliss, Marsha Bliss, Marty Thall, Phillip Daman, Jennifer Bliss, Jeremy Bliss, Pamela Plaza, Margie Quina, Marisa Currie-Rose, Francine Warner, Shirley Hart, Harry Hart, and Sylvie Roberts.

I am also thankful for the guidance of my creative writing teachers Elissa Bassist, Lindsey Lee Johnson, Danya Kukafka, Taylor Larsen, and Sharlene Teo.

Finally, thank you to historians Stephen Burstin of Jewish London Walking Tours, Tony Kushner at the University of Southampton, Keir Waddington at the University of Cardiff, and Mathew Thomson at the University of Warwick for answering my questions in the early stages of this book.

BONFIRE NIGHT

ABOUT THIS GUIDE

The suggested questions are included to enhance your
group's reading of Anna Bliss's *Bonfire Night*!

DISCUSSION QUESTIONS

(Spoiler Alert! Don't read these if
you have not yet finished the book.)

1. "Mr. Scargill studied the Zeiss Camera Company calendar on the wall next to the desk. He seemed to be trying to remember something. He uncrossed his legs, moved something around in his trouser pocket, and then crossed them again. Kate felt like she was looking down on them both from the ceiling. This was the routine and there would be no escape. If she wanted to keep her job, she would have to stand there and pretend, mostly to herself, not to notice." Other than the need to keep her job, why do you think Kate initially tolerates Scargill's behavior? How do her reasons differ from Gordon's? *Bonfire Night* is set eighty years before the #MeToo movement. In what ways have things changed? How have they stayed the same?

2. "Kate had expected to see lonely children. That was the point of her visit: to not close her eyes to them, to help tell their stories. Yet she hadn't realized how afraid it would make her feel for David, and for the world. She remembered Mosley's Blackshirts that day in Whitechapel—the cool, self-assured hatred in their eyes. Why had she assumed that there were so many miles between that hatred and murder?" Kate is aware of antisemitism, she knows that newspapers will exploit a chance to malign Jewish people, but is shocked when she hears about antisemitic violence. How do you explain her naiveté? What lessons can we take from her awakening?

3. There were many taboos and risks around premarital sex in the 1930s, but Kate and David's relationship quickly

becomes sexual. Does it surprise you to learn then that many British (and American) people in the 1930s engaged in some sort of sexual activity before marriage? How might have insufficient access to birth control have changed your own early decisions about sex?

4. "David did not have the heart to tell [Kate] that his parents had not asked anything about her. She was invisible— in a category that had no relevance to them whatsoever. Kate would not understand, and think badly of his parents, which David couldn't bear any more than them thinking badly of her." How did you feel about David's parents' attitude toward Kate? Did it make you dislike them? Have you or anyone in your family held similar views about religion, ethnicity, or class and marriage? If it wasn't for a difference in religion, do you think David and Kate would have gotten married? Are they well suited to each other?

5. "David took his father directly to the Jewish hospital in Stepney Green, but his liver failed a month later, on the day Poland fell. It was a cancer that had spread. The death, the burial, and the *shiva* all seemed to fold into the war itself. It was just a time when terrible things happened." Discuss this. How does the backdrop of global events shape personal experiences?

6. "*. . . but are you really in love with me, Clifton? Search in your heart, is any sadness you may be feeling upon receipt of this letter for me, or because you know how much you will miss Margaret?*" In her last letter to Clifton, Kate claims that Clifton is not in love with her anyway. Do you think she believes this or is she making excuses in order to free herself from guilt? What do you

think about Clifton? Would you have chosen him over David, or neither?

7. "Kate picked up the photograph of David on Bonfire Night from her bedside table and stared at it, trying to exhume something within herself. She could print that negative a thousand times, but it would not bring back the certainty she'd felt then. A photograph was a flimsy souvenir of love. But then Kate noticed the indentation below David's lip and for one breath she could smell the bonfire and London and her heart soared." What do you make of this? Is Kate still in love with David at this point or is it just a memory? Did she make a mistake in rejecting him and setting out on her own?

8. "She smelled her father in the fog, saw him in the blackened London brick. Kate considered the life he had lived there, mostly alone. He'd always made it seem full to bursting, without room for her, but he must have been lonely sometimes. She wondered if her father ever felt the guilt and worry she felt now, away from Margaret. Kate did not think so. She hoped that made her different from Frank." Kate's father is a difficult man but they have things in common. What bonds them? What makes their relationship untenable? How does the life Kate ultimately creates for her daughter reflect on the way she herself was raised? Is she a good mother?

9. "Now it was desolate, disorienting, with barbed wire in weblike coils around its railings and in tangled spools along the waterline. Cement blocks obstructed the steps leading up from the beach. Somewhere under the waves, mines lurked, ready to explode when German U-boats made their inevitable land attack on England. For the

first time in a while, Kate's hands itched for her camera, to help her make sense of it all." How does photography help Kate process trauma? Why do you think she returns to take pictures of the bombed theatre while Margaret is still in the hospital?

10. Bonfire Night is celebrated every November fifth in England, normally with fireworks and bonfires, parades and costumes. From an American perspective, it has similarities with the Fourth of July and Halloween. At the end of the book, the war and the blackout are over and Kate and David and their families are finally able to celebrate Bonfire Night with fireworks again. What does that signify to them? What did it mean to you to celebrate holidays with friends and family after the global COVID-19 pandemic? What role, if any, did grief play in those celebrations?

Visit our website at
KensingtonBooks.com
to sign up for our newsletters, read
more from your favorite authors, see
books by series, view reading group
guides, and more!

BOOK **CLUB**
BETWEEN THE **CHAPTERS**

Become a Part of Our
Between the Chapters Book Club
Community and Join the Conversation

Betweenthechapters.net